PRAISE FOR THE NOVELS
OF DAVID BELL

The Forgotten Girl

"David Bell is a natural storyteller and a superb writer. *The Forgotten Girl* is a mystery lover's mystery—a quick-paced and intriguing tale of what happens when the past catches up with the present. Mr. Bell understands the hearts and minds of ordinary and not-so-ordinary people, and his keen insights add a powerful dimension to his crisp writing."   —#1 *New York Times* bestselling author Nelson DeMille

"David Bell's *The Forgotten Girl* is both a tightly woven mystery and a frightening look at addiction, the mistrust it creates, the power of secrets, and the hurt created by the little lies we tell ourselves. I never felt like I had my feet under me. Bell has crafted an unforgettable story full of surprises. Don't miss it."

—J. T. Ellison, *New York Times* bestselling author
of *When Shadows Fall*

"David Bell writes spellbinding and gripping thrillers that get under your skin and refuse to let go. This is his best so far."

—Linwood Barclay, *New York Times* and #1 international
bestselling author of *No Safe House*

Never Come Back

"David Bell [has] established himself as one of the brightest and best crime fiction writers of our time . . . a definite page-turner. . . . Bell, once again, has written an incredible, unique thriller that will have you hooked!"   —*Suspense Magazine*

"[A] page-turner. . . . Bell does a good job exposing the seaminess underlying seemingly placid small-town life."   —*Publishers Weekly*

"David Bell should be a household name for crime fiction lovers. . . . The twisted threads of this complex novel come together for the most explosive of revelations and family secrets."   —SheKnows Book Lounge

continued . . .

"An intriguing, layered psychological thriller." —*Kirkus Reviews*

The Hiding Place

"An artfully constructed tale . . . a powerful, provocative novel."
—*Publishers Weekly*

"David Bell does a masterful job of crafting a crime story . . . a riveting book with surprising but believable twists on every page."
—*Suspense Magazine*

"A truly fascinating novel . . . an intriguing and complex plot that will keep the reader guessing up to the last chapter." —I Love a Mystery

"An incredibly engaging, emotionally investing read. What David Bell does exceptionally well is maintain a heightened level of suspense from beginning to end." —S. Krishna's Books

"Bell has written another winning thriller that is certain to entertain, frighten, and swiftly climb bestseller lists."
—*Bowling Green Daily News*

"Highly recommend[ed]. . . . I cannot wait for [Bell's] next masterpiece." —Caffeinated Book Reviewer

"[Bell's] book has lessons that will reverberate with the reader and remain after the conclusion is savored." —*The Louisville Courier-Journal*

"[An] amazing book going on my 2012 favorites list. It's a haunting story of a terrible crime, and the family secrets and lies surrounding it that finally surface over two decades later." —Book of Secrets

Cemetery Girl

"*Cemetery Girl* is more than just an utterly compelling thriller—and it certainly is that. David Bell's stellar novel is also a haunting meditation on the ties that bind parent to child, husband to wife, brother to brother—and what survives even under the most shattering possible circumstance. An absolutely riveting, absorbing read not to be missed."
—Lisa Unger, *New York Times* bestselling author of *Heartbroken*

"*Cemetery Girl* is my favorite kind of story because it takes the familiar and darkens it. This story is essentially about a missing little girl, but trust me: you have never read a missing-persons story like this one. . . . A fast, mean head trip of a thriller that reads like a collaboration between Michael Connelly and the gothic fiction of Joyce Carol Oates, *Cemetery Girl* is one of those novels that you cannot shake after it's over. A winner on every level."
—Will Lavender, *New York Times* bestselling author of *Dominance*

"*Cemetery Girl* is a smasher. It twists and turns and never lets go, and . . . it could happen just this way."
—Jacquelyn Mitchard, *New York Times* bestselling author of *The Deep End of the Ocean*

"*Cemetery Girl* grabbed me by the throat on page one and never let up. An intense, unrelenting powerhouse of a book, and the work of a master."
—John Lescroart, *New York Times* bestselling author of *The Ophelia Cut*

"Smart, stark, and haunting. This is perfect reading for a spooky autumn night, but be forewarned you might have to later sleep with the light on."
—*Tucson Citizen*

"A tense and terrifying journey that brims with emotional authenticity. Bell manages not only to build suspense effectively but also tell a story that goes way beyond simple thrills."
—*Booklist*

"The story is engaging and tugs at the reader's heartstrings immediately . . . fast-paced and compelling."
—Fiction Addict

"Compelling . . . please don't miss reading this book. You'll do yourself a huge disservice if you do."
—Fresh Fiction

"An intense ride, twisting through some creepy psychological terrain."
—*Houston Chronicle*

"A nail-biting page-turner. . . . David Bell has delivered a first-rate thriller that provides the reader with enough sketchy characters to engage and challenge even the most seasoned reader. Followers of the genre can celebrate the addition of another gifted storyteller."
—LitStack

"Disturbing, brilliantly engaging, and a must read for thriller fans."
—*Suspense Magazine*

ALSO BY DAVID BELL

Cemetery Girl

The Hiding Place

Never Come Back

THE FORGOTTEN GIRL

David Bell

 NEW AMERICAN LIBRARY

New American Library
Published by the Penguin Group
Penguin Group (USA) LLC, 375 Hudson Street,
New York, New York 10014

USA | Canada | UK | Ireland | Australia | New Zealand | India | South Africa | China
penguin.com
A Penguin Random House Company

First published by New American Library,
a division of Penguin Group (USA) LLC

First Printing, October 2014

REGISTERED TRADEMARK—MARCA REGISTRADA

LIBRARY OF CONGRESS CATALOGING-IN-PUBLICATION DATA:

Bell, David.
The forgotten girl/David Bell.
p. cm.
ISBN 978-0-451-41752-7 (paperback)
1. Brothers and sisters—Fiction.   2. Missing persons—Fiction.
3. Family secrets—Fiction.   I. Title.
PS3602.E64544F67 2014
813'.6—dc23   2014015517

Printed in the United States of America
10 9 8 7 6 5 4 3 2 1

Set in Apollo MT STD
Designed by Alissa Theodor

PUBLISHER'S NOTE
This is a work of fiction. Names, characters, places, and incidents either are the product of the
author's imagination or are used fictitiously, and any resemblance to actual persons, living or dead,
business establishments, events, or locales is entirely coincidental.

For Molly

Prologue

The detective came into the room. He wore a sport coat and tie, the collar of his shirt open. He didn't look at Jason. He tossed a small notebook onto the table, pulled a chair out, and sat down. He flipped the notebook open and scanned one of the pages.

"Can I go yet?" Jason asked. "You said this wouldn't take long."

"Easy," the detective said.

"You said this would be a friendly chat, that I didn't need a lawyer or my parents."

The detective looked up. "Haven't I been friendly?" He pointed to the empty Coke can on the table. "I got you a soda." He flipped the notebook closed and smiled, but it looked forced. "We're almost finished here. I just want to go over some things we talked about before. Now, you said you and your friend, Logan Shaw, fought pretty hard the other night. You told me you landed a couple of good ones against the side of his head."

"One," Jason said. "One good one."

"One good one," the detective said. "Sometimes that's all it takes. And you were fighting over a girl?"

"Yes. Regan."

"Regan Maines." The detective nodded. "So you two guys fight over a girl. Okay, no big deal, right? Boys will be boys and all

1

that. And you end up clocking your friend pretty good. Again, no big deal. Who hasn't gotten into a little dustup with one of their friends? Happens all the time, right?"

"I've never been in a fight before."

"Never?"

"Never."

The detective made a disapproving face. "Okay. Not all guys fight with their friends. Okay. So you fight with your friend, and you deck him, and then he goes off into the woods because he's pissed at you. In fact, you said he was crying a little, right?"

"Yes."

"Were you crying too?" the detective asked, the corner of his mouth rising into a little sneer.

"I might have been. Yes."

"And you're eighteen?"

"I'd like to call my dad," Jason said.

"Easy. We're almost finished here. I know your old man. He's a good guy." The detective scratched his head. "Okay, all of this stuff you've done seems pretty normal to me, except maybe for the crying. But after that, after your friend goes off into the woods and you don't see him anymore, that's where it gets tricky for me. You see, here's what I don't understand. Your friend disappears after you have a fight with him, and you know everyone's looking for him. By the way, his father, Mr. Shaw, he's very upset about his son being missing. Very upset."

"He didn't care much about Logan when he was here."

"Hey," the detective said. "Don't be smart. That man's a good father. He's a pillar of this community. He always does the right thing. And speaking of the right thing . . . you knew all these people were looking for Logan, the guy you punched upside the head, and yet, you didn't tell us about that fight you had. Did you? Not the first time we talked to you. You said everything seemed normal when you last saw him. But then a few hours later, after we'd talked to some other people and came back to you again, you decided to tell us about this fight. Do you see why that doesn't make sense to me?"

"I told you—I was angry with Logan."

"That's why you decked him. Because he wanted your girl—"

"No, that's why I didn't say anything about the fight the first time you came by the house. Logan can be . . ."

"What? Can be what?"

"Manipulative, I guess. He has moods. I figured he was just mad and wanted to take it out on all of us by going away for a while. He knew we'd worry eventually. I didn't want to give him the satisfaction of getting to me. When you came back to my house, and I found out people were really worried . . . his dad, for example . . . that's when I told you about the fight. It was only a few hours later. And nothing's changed since then. My story's the same now as it was three days ago."

"Are you sure?"

"Of course—"

Someone knocked. The detective stood up and opened the door, revealing a uniformed police officer. The two men whispered about something, and the detective nodded his head. "Tell them we'll be right out. We're finished here." He closed the door and came back to the table. "Your old man's here."

"Good."

"Before you go, I want to ask you one more thing. Where do you think Logan Shaw is?"

Jason sat back in his chair. He looked at the detective's face, the skin heavily lined, the eyes tired. He almost —*almost*—felt sorry for the guy.

"I don't know," Jason said. "He always talked about leaving."

"Would he really do it?" the detective asked. "His dad and mom are here. His friends. The family has a bunch of money. Would he run off and leave all of that?"

Jason thought about the question, then said, "Sometimes I think Logan is capable of just about anything."

Chapter One

Through the thick plate-glass window of the restaurant, and blinded slightly by the bright noon sun, Jason thought he saw his sister, Hayden.

A quick glimpse, something he couldn't really trust or believe. A flash of her face, her distinctive brisk walk. Brown hair, big eyes—and then she was gone from his view. But Jason continued to stare. He leaned his face closer to the restaurant window, trying to see through the passing flow of people—working people in their suits and skirts, families with children—and decide if it had really been his sister. He hadn't seen her since—

The voice of his companion brought him back to the restaurant.

"Are you still with me?" the man asked.

The man. Colton Rivers. A high school classmate and now a successful lawyer in Ednaville. They were finishing their meals, their business, and Jason wasn't sure what had been said to him. The sounds of the restaurant filled the space. Clashing silverware and murmured conversation. Someone laughed loudly at the next table.

"Excuse me?" he asked.

"Something catch your eye out there?" Colton asked. "Or someone?" Colton winked.

"Sorry," Jason said. "I was daydreaming, thinking about being a kid." Jason looked out the window again, squinting against the light. People continued to walk around, carrying out their business. He didn't see Hayden. He *hadn't* seen her, he decided. Just another person, a woman about the same age with the same hair color. Hayden had no reason to be in Ednaville. He didn't know where she was living, but it wasn't in their hometown. "My parents used to like to eat here at O'Malley's. We'd come as a family."

"Mine too." The waiter dropped the check on the table, and Colton reached for it. "I've got this. You're doing me the favor, remember? The summer festival is a big deal in Ednaville, and with you designing the posters for the committee, we know they're going to look good."

"I'm glad I can help out," Jason said. He tried not to sound as distracted as he felt. He forced himself not to look out the window again.

Hayden?

"How about a drink?" Colton asked. "Sometimes I have one before I go back to the office."

Jason thought about it for a second. There was no strict provision against it in the America's Best offices. Since he worked on the creative side of things, no one would really pay attention to what he did anyway.

"Sure," he said.

Colton signaled the waiter again. He ordered a scotch, and Jason asked for an Old Fashioned. The drinks came, and Jason said, "Okay, Colton, you've built up enough suspense. What do you want to ask me? Do you have more work for the festival? Do you want me to sit in the dunking booth?"

Colton lifted his glass. "That's good," he said. He smacked his lips after putting the glass down. "You know my dad started our firm. He still comes in and piddles around. Gets in the way mostly."

"I remember your dad." The drink helped Jason. It brought an ease and a lightness to his mind. He hoped it would help him stop thinking about Hayden.

"Sure. A good man. He's been handling wills and estates for a lot of families here in Ednaville for many, many years. Some of the biggest and richest families in town. He's passed some of them on to me now. They deal with me, of course, but a lot of them, I can see the way they look at me. They're thinking, 'He's not really as sharp as the old man, is he?'"

"I'm sure it's tough in a town like this," Jason said. He wanted to be sympathetic, but he couldn't see where Colton was going. Jason's drink was good, and he swallowed more of it, hoping it wouldn't cause him to doze off at his desk in the middle of the afternoon.

"My dad passed one family off to me, and they've proven to be a little thorny. The father's sick and old and getting ready to . . . well, you know. Move on."

"The big move on," Jason said.

"Exactly. He's divorced, never remarried, and he only has one child. Everything is supposed to go to that child, but there are some complications."

The liquor had loosened Jason up enough that he simply said, "Colton, what the heck does any of this have to do with me?"

Colton picked up his glass and rattled the ice, but he didn't drink. He put it back down, then leaned forward and spoke with his voice lowered. "You understand I really shouldn't be discussing this with you."

Jason looked around the restaurant. The lunch crowd was

starting to thin, and there was no one close by. Jason leaned in closer to Colton. "So don't tell me, then."

Colton smiled without showing his teeth. "You were always a little bit of a wiseass. Most creative people are." His face grew serious. "I figure if I can get this sorted out, my old man will get off my back, the other clients will see that I can do the job, and my life will hum along just a little more smoothly. And that's what we all want, right? A smoothly humming life?"

"Sure," Jason said. He thought of Nora and the progress they were making on their marriage. "Sure."

"My client, the old man who is sick and dying, is Peter Shaw. His son, the heir we can't locate, is of course—"

Jason finished the sentence for him. "Logan."

Colton was nodding. He finished the rest of his drink. "Logan Shaw. Your best friend from high school."

Jason felt his face flush. Not from the drink, but from the unexpected surprise of hearing Logan's name mentioned again. He hadn't expected the conversation to end up at that place, but he understood that Colton had wanted it to go there all along, that the summer festival was really just a pretense to get him out to lunch. Jason swallowed what remained in the glass.

First Hayden? And then Logan?

"You want another?" Colton asked. He waved to the waiter. "Two more here."

"No, I'm fine."

"You sure?"

"Yeah."

Colton dismissed the waiter, then turned back to Jason. "I'm sorry to spring this on you."

"No, you're not," Jason said, trying to give Colton a dirty look but also feeling the temptation to laugh at his brazenness.

Colton didn't blink. "Okay, I'm not sorry. I hoped the subject would naturally come up while we ate. We're talking about the summer festival and graduation and high school. I figured we'd get there, but when it didn't . . ." He shrugged. "I had to go for it."

"I don't know what you want me to do for you," Jason said. "You're trying to find Logan, right?"

"He's in line for a lot of money," Colton said. "A lot of money." Colton shook his head and licked his lips as though he could taste the paper currency and silver coins. "Well? Can you help me?"

"You want to know if I know where Logan is?"

"I know there was that unpleasantness between the two of you on our graduation night. I know you fought up there on the Bluff. It was over a girl, right? Regan . . . what was her name?"

"Regan Maines. Now she's Regan Kreider."

"Did she marry Tim Kreider?"

"Divorced."

"I know the cops got after you a little when they couldn't find Logan."

"A little?" Jason asked. "Have you ever been a murder suspect?"

"You probably weren't really a suspect," Colton said. "You were questioned. You were one of the last people to see him."

"A fine point, I guess. It wasn't pleasant."

"Anyway, I know you had that happen. But the two of you were best friends since grade school. Have you ever heard anything from him? Have you seen him? A letter? An e-mail? A Christmas card? I figure he's got to be in touch with somebody from his old high school crowd."

Jason leaned back in his seat and looked out the window again. The clouds shifted above, obscuring the sun and casting a portion of the square into shadow. Jason reached up and scratched the back of his neck, his movements causing the leather of the booth to creak.

"I haven't seen him since that night, Colton. As far as I know, he kept his promise. He told Regan he was leaving town, and he did. He and I said some things to each other when we fought, things we shouldn't have said. I can understand if he wanted to put that night in his rearview mirror. I wanted to."

Colton looked at Jason with sympathy. Jason almost believed Colton regretted bringing it all up.

Jason said, "He always wanted to go out west. He didn't really care about his dad's money. He used it in school, but he wasn't hung up on it."

"Really?" Colton said.

"Did you have a different impression?" Jason asked.

"I didn't know him very well."

"But?"

"You knew him better," Colton said.

Jason decided he'd never know exactly what Colton meant, so he asked something else. "Couldn't you just hire an investigator to track him down?"

"They've done that," Colton said. "There were always a lot of rumors about what happened to him. You heard some of them, right?"

"Some. I went off to college."

"People said the craziest stuff. That he joined a religious cult, for example. Others said he knocked a girl up, a poor girl in another county, and his father wouldn't let them get married, so Logan ran off with her." Colton shrugged. He lifted his glass and looked into the bottom wistfully as though he wished a drop of the scotch still remained. "Of course, some people just think he's dead. Maybe he walked out to the highway and got picked up hitchhiking and whoever picked him up did him in. Maybe he got robbed and killed. You know, a rich kid might be a target. Maybe he had amnesia and wandered off. Lots of nonsense."

"What happened when they hired an investigator?" Jason asked.

"The old man has done it a couple of times. Once, they got close. Must have been about fifteen years ago. Guy followed a trail to Arizona and then lost it across the border in Mexico. He found someone out there who swore she knew Logan, that some guy she dated told her the truth about leaving his hometown and his rich family and heading out west."

"Really?" He felt hope rising, although he couldn't have said why.

"The investigator could never pin anything down. He showed this girl a picture, and she couldn't be certain it was Logan. Of course, time had passed. A photo of Logan at eighteen may not be what he looks like at thirty-five or so. And you never know with some investigators. They see an old guy with money desperate to find his son, and they figure they can string him along. It's a gravy train. We'll do it again if we have to. I just thought you could save us some time."

"Sorry." Jason looked at his watch. He had a meeting in thirty minutes, and the drink seemed to have settled in the back of his neck, creating a tightness there. "I have to be getting back."

"Sure. Thanks for tolerating my questions."

But Jason didn't stand up. Thoughts of Hayden and Logan ran through his mind, two almost ghostly presences. He asked, "The family hasn't heard from him at all over the years?"

"The old man's gotten some cards and things from time to time. Nothing much. His parents split up when Logan was just a kid. I'm sure you remember that."

"That was before I met him."

"His mother doesn't have much to say about it. She's remarried and lives in Barker County. I've talked to her, but she says she hasn't heard from Logan or Logan's father, and she's moved on. I'm sure she got a nice piece of the old man's money when they split. So, other than those few cards in the mail, the family's heard nothing."

Jason slid to the end of the booth. "Well, if you do track him down, tell him I said . . ."

"Yeah?"

Jason paused, thinking it over. What would he say to Logan after all that time? Nothing came to mind. Nothing seemed adequate.

"I guess just tell him I said, 'Hey.'"

Jason walked to his car, the keys in his right hand digging into his flesh. The sun had reemerged, and Jason slipped his sunglasses on. He scanned the faces he passed on the sidewalk, looking for Hayden again. A grimy guy with a long beard played guitar outside a coffee shop, and across the street, in the square itself, two mothers jogged while pushing strollers. He unlocked the door and tugged the handle, taking one more quick glance around.

He saw the woman again. Over in the square, momentarily obscured by the two jogging women. Jason took a step in that direction, moving away from his car, but two vehicles passed, forcing him to stop and wait. When the cars were gone, so was the woman who looked so much like Hayden.

Jason watched Nora cook. Two pots gurgled on the stove top, and Nora wielded a large knife, chopping vegetables with machinelike efficiency. Jason knew his role in the preparation of dinner—stay out of Nora's way when she got going. He leaned back and absorbed the cooking aromas. The smell of onions . . . and maybe something tomato-based.

"How long have we lived here now?" Nora asked.

Jason knew she knew the answer. But she wanted him to say it. She was about to make a point, and again, Jason understood his role. He was the setup man, feeding her the lines she needed to complete her argument. He liked the ritual. It made him feel closer to his wife.

"Five and a half years," he said.

"Five and a half years, right?" she said, continuing to chop. "And I still can't get used to the people asking me if I have children. Today it was the woman in the bank. I'm forty-two, I'm married, but no, I don't have children. It's a choice some people make. Some people put their careers first, right? Is that so hard to understand? Why do people feel like they can ask such things?"

"You want me to explain the social customs of small-town Ohio?" Jason asked. "Again?"

"It's like the religion thing," Nora said, ignoring him. "Why do people still try to get us to go to church with them? We don't go to church, right? Big deal. Was the town like this when you were growing up?"

"Probably."

"Do people ask you these questions?" she asked.

"Not really."

"It's because I'm a woman, right? They think they can ask me these things because I'm a woman."

"You're an idealist," Jason said.

"What?"

"You're an idealist," he said again. "You think people will change for the better and act reasonable if you just talk to them enough."

"So? Is that wrong?"

"I like that about you," he said.

"Don't jerk my chain."

"I mean it. I like that quality."

She threw several things into one of the pots and wiped her hands on a towel. Jason continued to watch her. She still looked good, better than he did, in his opinion. Only a few rogue strands of gray had invaded her red hair, and those were only visible on close inspection. Her fair, freckled skin remained wrinkle-free. She kept in shape, ate well, worked at the public library. He wondered if she'd ever get used to the fact that they lived in Ednaville, Ohio, instead of New York City, where they'd met.

"What about you?" Nora asked. "Did anything interesting happen to you today?"

Jason swallowed his beer. He wasn't going to mention Hayden. He'd thought about it all afternoon, sifting through his memories of what he saw on the square. He decided it wasn't her, that his mind ran away from him when he saw a woman who happened to look like his sister. No need to stir things up.

Nora sat at the table and took his hand. "Hey? What's on your mind?"

"You did ask me about my day, didn't you?" He squeezed her hand back. Her skin felt cold, probably from handling produce.

"I did. It's what married couples do. They talk. Open lines of communication."

"You sound like that marriage counselor in New York."

"You wanted to see her as much as me."

"I know," Jason said. He squeezed her hand again. "No complaints from me." He swallowed more beer. "You asked about my day. Well, I got complimented. I went to that meeting with Colton, the guy from the festival committee, and he told me I'd hardly changed since high school. Looks-wise, that is."

"Well, that should make your day," Nora said, squeezing his hand back. "Is this Colton guy handsome?"

"No, he's fat and bald."

"Well, we take our compliments where we can find them. Are you doing the work for him?"

Jason nodded. "He's thrilled. He thinks he's getting a big-time New York advertising guy to make the poster for the summer festival."

"He is, isn't he?"

"Just like the Ednaville Public Library is getting a former supervisor from the New York Public Library system to work at their circulation desk?"

"It's your hometown. We could have moved anywhere."

"I know," Jason said.

"You regret coming back?"

"When I see all these people I knew growing up, I start to think Anchorage sounds nice."

"We all do what we have to do, don't we?" Nora laughed and let go of his hand. She went back to the stove and stirred both of the pots. "I was thinking maybe we should go away the weekend of the festival this year. Between that and high school graduation, the town gets so overrun. And Rick and Sheila have been begging us to come back to the city for a visit."

"I know."

"We haven't been back in three years."

Jason finished his beer. He started picking at the label.

"Rick says the economy is doing well there. People are really hiring again—"

"I've been out of that game a long time," Jason said. He knew he sounded short, and he regretted it.

"Not that long," Nora said.

"It's been almost seven years since I got laid off," Jason said. "Rick didn't say it, but I bet all the people they're hiring are twenty-two. I look young here in Ohio but not in New York."

"Well," Nora said. "It was just a thought. I know getting laid off still stings. You've done good work for America's Best, and we have a lot of friends in the city."

"People come and go," he said.

"Jason, listen, this was supposed to be a temporary move. Remember? Until we got our feet back on the ground financially. And we both thought if we came here, if we were away from the craziness of the city, we'd get closer too. Our marriage would get stronger. And it has, hasn't it?"

"It has," he said, softening his tone. "And you're right. If I promise to think about it . . . can we eat? I'm hungry. And everything smells so good."

Nora turned the burners off, her movements quick and confident. "Sure," she said. "We'll talk about it another time."

Chapter Two

Jason met his high school friend Regan Maines Kreider in Burroughs' Coffee Shop. He needed the midafternoon jolt of caffeine— and he needed to talk to her. He'd slept poorly, his dreams full of images of Logan. Logan on Thompson Bluff the night of their high school graduation. Logan drunk and emotional, lashing out, ready to fight. And the two of them coming to blows, wrestling each other to the ground and swinging their fists, both of them angry and verging on tears.

Jason could still feel the last blow, the one he delivered to the side of Logan's head, the one that put him on the ground and ended the fight. He flexed his hand under the table.

Regan settled in across from him a few minutes later. She sipped her coffee, her eyes watching Jason over the rim of the mug. Regan had had two children and worked full-time in the mortgage department of Farmers' Bank and Credit. They met this way, maybe once a month, and talked about their lives—job worries, movies they'd seen, the changing face of the town.

"Well," she said, "you've got me curious. Normally we just shoot the shit, but now, out of the blue, it sounds like you have something serious on your mind. I've spent the morning wondering what it could be."

"I didn't mean to be mysterious," Jason said.

"It's okay. I'm a divorced mom of two. My life could use some mystery. What's on your mind?"

"The past," Jason said.

"The past?" Regan said. She looked around the room. "Do they serve whiskey in this place?"

Jason laughed. "I don't think so," he said. "Do you remember Colton Rivers from school?"

"Colton Rivers." Her voice was a little mocking. "The guy who's been running for city council since the day he was born. Who could forget him? He does those awful TV commercials for his law practice."

"Exactly. I have his phone number memorized I've seen the commercials so many times. Well, I saw him in person yesterday. He invited me to lunch because he wants me to design posters for the summer festival."

"Okay," she said. "I'm guessing there's more to the story than that."

"Yes. The thing is," he said, "Colton didn't really want to talk to me about the poster very much. He was using me for something else. Get this—he's trying to find Logan."

Regan's expression didn't change, but something did leave her face. The animation that had been residing there, the energy and life that was so readily apparent in her eyes, faded.

"I'm sorry," Jason said. "I know we've never really talked about that night."

"You left for school early," Regan said. "You were gone as fast as you could go."

Her words stung a little. He suspected they were meant to. She was right—Jason couldn't wait to get away from Ednaville and start a new life in college. He found a summer program and started taking classes early. He hadn't looked back. He hadn't wanted to.

He almost apologized to Regan right there in Burroughs', but decided that would be too awkward. Instead he said, "Colton wanted to know if I had heard from Logan over the years. If I knew of an address or anything for him."

"Why?" Regan's voice sounded tight and clipped. "What could he possibly want with Logan now?"

"His dad is dying. Did you know that?"

Regan nodded. "I've heard. I know he's . . ." Using her index finger, she made a circular motion around her temple. "I think he sits in that big house with a team of nurses and watches the time tick away."

"Logan's the sole heir. Colton wants to find him and make sure he knows he's got a boatload of money coming to him."

"He knew that. He always knew that."

Jason noticed Regan's right hand, the one that was holding her drink. Her thumb swished back and forth across the mug, smearing a small drop of coffee around on the surface. Someone ordered an espresso, and the machine hissed while the drink was created.

"You haven't heard from him, have you?" Jason asked.

"Of course not," Regan said.

Jason waited for her to say more, but when she didn't, he said, "What exactly did he say before he left that night?"

Regan's thumb stopped moving. She let go of the mug and leaned back in her chair, folding her arms across her chest. "I thought I told you."

"You told me a little back then. That was twenty-seven years ago." Jason leaned forward. "Look, I'm not trying to upset you. It seems like me bringing this up is bothering you, and that's not what I wanted to do."

19

"I just haven't thought of it in a long time. I didn't really expect this to come up today. I thought we were just . . . having coffee. Old friends catching up like we usually do."

"I didn't expect it to come up with Colton. When he asked me about Logan . . . shit, it just came out of nowhere. But I've been back in Ednaville for five years. I can't help but think of it from time to time. He was my best friend. The three of us, we were the best of friends. It all changed that night. So much changed. . . ."

He left the thought unfinished, but they both understood. He and Regan had become closer the summer they were eighteen. Before that, they had spent a great deal of time together, doing all the things kids their ages did. Seeing movies, attending parties, sneaking cigarettes and liquor while trying not to cough. He and Regan had a ritual of walking home from school together on Fridays, slow, wandering walks during which they talked about . . . everything they could think of. School, parents, their hopes and dreams and fears. That summer after graduation, the two of them circled each other like the scared kids they were. Enjoying the flirtation, and both of them probably secretly terrified that it would come to fruition, that the whole friendship would be laid on the line with an infinite array of complications.

What Jason knew then, and Regan barely suspected before graduation night, was that Logan felt the same way about her. And when they all went to the Bluff to celebrate graduation, Logan decided to tell Regan how *he* felt, how much she meant to *him*. When Regan let Logan down, telling one friend that she only had feelings for the other, Logan sought Jason out, and Jason ended up in the only real fistfight of his life.

Regan took a drink. She said, "He just told me he was leaving Ednaville. He said he was done with all of it, done with all of us.

I don't know. . . . He said the town was too small, that his dad was an asshole. That was pretty much it."

"I wonder if he ever went to college."

"He didn't care about college. He didn't need to go. He had money."

"He *intended* to go. He was accepted to some good schools."

"That was all for show. Sure, he would have gone. But you know how he was in school. He got by on charm and his family name. And when that didn't work, he pressured people. Teachers and classmates. This is a small town. Everyone knew he had money. He got by on that. It wouldn't work in college."

"You seem angrier than I would have expected."

"We had to grind it out in life. He didn't."

"That's true." Jason waited, then said, "I thought you'd feel a little . . . sad. Or nostalgic thinking of him."

"Maybe I'm getting too old for that," she said.

"I know Logan could be difficult. Believe me, I know that."

"I'm glad you see him a little more clearly now than you did back then."

"I saw him clearly," Jason said. "I knew him better than anybody else."

"You hero-worshipped him," Regan said. "That's different from knowing somebody. Do you want a refill?"

Jason pushed his mug across the table, and while Regan went back to the counter, he stared at the tabletop, alone with his thoughts. Ice cubes tumbled into a glass somewhere, and Regan and the barista made murmured small talk. Regan was right—Jason had looked up to Logan more than he liked to admit. But Logan was one of those guys everyone looked up to. He was confident, outgoing, daring. And he came from money. The status of his family gave his

21

every action, his every gesture, a quality that seemed to a teenager's eyes almost superhuman. Logan seemed untouchable.

Jason wondered, on more than one occasion over the years, why Logan ever showed an interest in him. In grade school, Jason was a quiet kid, smaller than the other boys and more interested in studying than anything else. On a few occasions, he helped Logan with math problems, and after that, Logan started including Jason in things. Invitations to birthday and pool parties came Jason's way as well as a coveted seat at Logan's lunch table. It always felt to Jason like Logan saw something in him that others didn't, that there was an untapped potential inside Jason, something waiting to bloom that slowly did as the years went by. It was hard for Jason to not see Logan as playing a role in bringing Jason's real, more confident self out.

Regan came back and put the steaming mug before him. She didn't say anything and seemed to have closed something off from Jason, to have withdrawn from the conversation a few degrees. There was none of the lightness that usually existed between them, the comforting ease of old friends who shared a long history.

"I guess I feel like I should go and see his dad," Jason said.

"Why?"

"I hate the thought of the old man dying alone. He's divorced, no other kids. I knew him fairly well. As well as you could know the workaholic, emotionally distant father of your best friend."

"He probably won't remember who you are now."

"I understand that. But his son isn't showing up, I guess."

"You're right that Logan *should* be doing it."

"But he isn't. Would it hurt anything to go see the old man? I wasn't really here when my parents were slipping away. Maybe it's silly."

Regan leaned forward, smiling. Some of the warmth returned

to her face. "It's sweet that you want to do that. I didn't know his father at all really. When we used to go to Logan's house, his dad just used to grunt at me. I got the feeling he didn't have much use for girls. It's probably lucky Logan didn't have any sisters. His mother was always kind, but Mr. Shaw? Bleh."

"You remember his mother?"

"Sure. Don't you?"

"Barely. She never seemed to be around when we were kids."

"They were divorced." Regan smiled as she remembered something. "Mrs. Shaw was in some kind of women's club with my mom when we were growing up. She'd come to our house from time to time. She always asked about me and how I was doing. Was I planning to go to college? Was I thinking about a career? She talked to me like I was an adult, not the usual bullshit."

"Hmm. I guess I never really talked to her."

"You were a boy," Regan said. "But you should go see his dad if you want. It can't hurt anything—you're right." Regan looked at her watch. "I have to be getting back to the bank. Every fifteen minutes I'm gone, I get one hundred e-mails to respond to."

"I understand. Try working for a big company. We get e-mails telling us how much toilet paper to use in the bathroom."

"That's adulthood, I guess." She stood up and gathered her keys and her phone.

"What do you think he's doing now?" Jason asked. "Logan, I mean. Is he a beach bum? Is he a businessman? Did he get married and have kids?" Jason shook his head. "What on earth would he be doing?"

"It's probably best not to indulge ourselves with a lot of what-ifs," Regan said.

Jason got the feeling she was talking about more than just Logan.

Chapter Three

Jason and Nora were getting ready for bed when their front doorbell rang. They'd already done the dishes and turned out the lights on the first floor, leaving just a lone bulb burning on the front porch. It was past ten. Jason held his toothbrush, and Nora looked startled.

"Who the hell is that?" she asked.

Jason rinsed his mouth and, wearing just shorts and a T-shirt, started down the stairs to the front door. Halfway to the bottom, Nora called after him.

"Are you sure it's safe? Maybe you shouldn't answer."

"Safer than New York, I would hope," he said. He didn't know if she heard him. He slowed his pace as he approached the front door. No one ever just showed up at their house, especially late at night. He figured it was probably kids playing a prank, ringing the bell and running off. Jason leaned over and peered through the narrow window that ran parallel to the door. What he saw brought him up short.

The person on the porch who stood with her back to him looked familiar. So familiar that her posture, the shape of her body, struck a chord inside him, one that hadn't been struck in years.

"Who is it?" Nora called.

But Jason didn't say anything. His hands felt sweaty as he undid the two locks and the chain and pulled the door open. She turned around as the door came open, and there, in the sickly pale glow of the porch light, Jason came face-to-face with his sister, Hayden, for the first time in five years.

"Hey, big brother," she said through the screen.

Jason was surprised by what he saw. Hayden looked . . . clean. Her hair, her clothes, her hands. All clean. She wore black slacks and black shoes and a neatly pressed blue button-down shirt. One hand rested on the sleek leather purse she wore over her shoulder and the other held a smartphone. She had always been tiny, almost frail. In the years since high school, when her drinking was at its worst and she was likely consuming most of her calories in the form of alcohol, Hayden always appeared fragile, her skin nearly translucent. She looked like that the last time he saw her, the time that caused the five-year break. When Jason hugged her or touched her during her longest benders, it felt as though her bones might snap beneath his touch. Like she was a bird.

But the version of Hayden on the front porch looked healthy and trim. Her cheeks were full and carried a trace of color.

"I bet you wish this was the pizza guy, right?" she said.

Jason still hadn't spoken. "No," he said finally. "I don't."

He couldn't think of anything else. He stared at his sister through the screen as june bugs and moths dipped and dived in the space between them.

Hayden raised her eyebrows. "Am I allowed to come in?" she asked. "I understand if after last time . . ."

Jason undid the lock on the screen door and pushed it open. "Come in," he said, stepping back. "Of course you can come in. Jesus, Hayden, I'm sorry. I didn't mean to just stand here."

Hayden slipped past him and through the foyer, trailing the faint scent of cigarette smoke. Jason didn't know what to do. He flipped on the lights in the living room and let his sister go ahead of him.

Nora asked again from the top of the stairs, "Jason? Who was it?"

Jason looked at Hayden, who had taken a seat on the sofa. Then he said loudly, "It's my sister. It's Hayden."

"What?" Nora said. "Really?"

Before anyone could say anything else, Nora was coming down the stairs, her bare feet slapping against the hardwood. She wore a modest, knee-length nightgown and brushed past Jason as though he weren't there. Hayden rose from the couch when she saw her sister-in-law.

"Hey, girl," Hayden said.

"Oh, Hayden. Look at you."

The two women hugged in the living room. They held on to each other and swayed side to side. Then they stepped back, and Nora gave Hayden a long appraisal.

"You look great," Nora said.

"Thanks."

"You look . . ."

"Sober?" Hayden said.

Nora nodded. "Yes, you do. Healthy, I guess I was going to say. But sober works." The two women sat next to each other on the sofa and Nora asked, "What on earth are you doing here? Are you moving back to town?"

Hayden looked up at Jason. He remained standing, his hand resting on the back of a chair. A tension hovered between the two siblings, something unspoken. As always, Hayden was the one most ready, most eager to give it voice.

"I wasn't sure if I would be welcome back," she said.

"Of course you are," Nora said. "Right, Jason?"

"Sure," Jason said, but he still didn't take a seat. "I'm just kind of blown away. You're the last person I expected to see on the porch."

Hayden maneuvered the purse around to her lap and undid the clasp. "I wanted to give you something," she said. She dug inside and extracted a plain white envelope. She held it out toward Jason. "Here," she said.

"No," Jason said.

"It's five hundred dollars," Hayden said. "I know the car cost more—"

"Oh, no," Nora said. "Jason, tell her. We don't want it."

"I *want* to give it to you," Hayden said. "I'm working now. I've saved this money. I saved it to give to you. Please, Jason. Just take it. It will make me feel so much better knowing that you took it, that you let me off the hook just a little bit."

Jason came around the chair and sat down. He waved away the envelope that Hayden still held in the air between them. He crossed his legs and studied his sister. She looked good. She looked cleaned up and straightened out. But Jason also knew that meant nothing when it came to Hayden and her drinking. How many times had she been through rehab? How many times had she quit only to start again with greater intensity?

"Are you here alone?" Jason asked. "Where's Sierra?"

"That's what I want to talk to you about," Hayden said.

"What is it?" Jason asked. "What's wrong?"

Hayden brought the envelope back down to her lap. She stared at it for a moment, then looked back up at her brother.

"I do need something," she said. "A favor. And I know I don't have a leg to stand on with either one of you. But this is different. It really is."

Jason looked over at Nora. Her eyes widened, her head nodded ever so slightly. *Go on*, she was saying with the look. *Go on. She's your sister.*

Jason looked back at Hayden. An image from their childhood flashed into his mind. It was involuntary. Hayden . . . a little brown-haired girl in a sandbox, holding a plastic bucket with one hand, the index finger of the other stuck into her mouth. She tottered, lost her balance, and fell back on her butt, spilling the sand. Before she could cry, Jason, a year older and bigger, was there, helping her up. Receiving praise from their parents for his act of brotherly protection.

He had to help her. He *wanted* to help her.

"What is it, Hayden?" he asked. "Why don't you tell us all about it?"

Chapter Four

Hayden still held the envelope clutched between her fingers. She looked at both of them.

"The first thing I want to do, *need* to do really, is apologize to the two of you for my behavior the last time I was here."

Nora made a gesture with her hand like she was smoothing something across a flat surface. "There's no need to do that."

"Actually, yes, there is. I was a bad sister, and I took advantage of your trust and hospitality. I just want you both to know I'm sorry for that."

Shortly after Jason and Nora moved back to Ednaville, Hayden had come to visit. She was drinking then, heavily drinking. She showed up at their door with her hair matted and her clothes dirty. She smelled like she hadn't bathed in a week. Jason remembered similar times with Hayden when they were in high school, and the tough love their parents eventually began to practice. Jason was still in that mode, because he initially was reluctant to let Hayden stay, but Nora convinced him. She said family was family, and they were obligated to let her in.

For two days, all went well. Hayden didn't drink in front of them. She showered and washed her clothes. On the third morning, Jason and Nora woke up to a police officer on their doorstep.

Hayden had taken the keys to one of their cars during the night and, after drinking at Apollo's, a local bar, drove it into a tree. The police arrested her, and later that day Jason and Nora found four hundred dollars missing from a drawer in their house. They never saw Hayden after that. She never called or wrote or came by.

Everyone remained silent. Hayden looked at Jason as though she expected him to say something.

"Are you apologizing as part of some twelve-step program?" Jason asked.

"Jason," Nora said.

"That sounded harsh, Hayden, but I want to know," Jason said. "You've apologized to me before, so I really want the reason behind this one. Is a shrink making you do it? A minister? It's not Mom and Dad this time because they're dead."

"It's okay," Hayden said. "I know why you feel that way. Yes, this is part of a program. And I understand that you think I've done this before, and it's okay if you're suspicious. I'd be suspicious of me too. All I can say is that while I have apologized to you before, I never meant it before. I mean it this time. All of this is going to stick. The sobriety, everything. This is real. It's who I am now."

Nora jumped in. "I think it's fabulous. Really."

Jason wished he had kept his mouth shut, that he had let Hayden say her piece without interjecting his own comment into it. So much of his life had been spent accommodating his sister, so much time had been spent walking on eggshells and blithely encouraging her in every struggle—both real and imagined—she engaged in, that he no longer felt he could listen to her talk without challenging her assertions. But he had to admit Hayden looked different. And she did seem different. For the first time, the language she used about her recovery matched the reality she seemed to be existing in. And he couldn't ignore the feeling he had when he saw her silhouetted on the porch. The hope that sprang into his chest, the simple, deeply rooted desire to see his sister again.

"Okay," Jason said. "Apology accepted. It's long over anyway. Everybody's moved on."

Nora said, "And we're sorry we didn't help you more back then. Maybe we could have, I don't know, been more understanding of where you were."

"I understand," Hayden said. "*You* don't need to apologize." Hayden raised the envelope toward Jason again. "So," she said, "will you accept this as the beginning of restitution for the car and the money I took?"

Jason shook his head. "Just keep it," he said. "Please. You can use it to start a new life or whatever you need it for. You can use it for— Well, that brings me back to the question I asked you before. Where exactly is Sierra? Is she . . . ?" A multitude of scenarios sprang into his mind. Had something happened to his niece? Had Hayden lost custody or contact with her daughter?

Hayden must have sensed Jason's concern because she said, "She's fine. In fact, she's here, with me."

"Where?" Nora asked.

"She's in the car, waiting for me to give her the all clear."

"Bring her in," Nora said. "My God, we haven't seen her in so long."

"Just a minute," Hayden said. "You see, I wanted to talk to the two of you alone before I brought her in."

"You mentioned a favor," Jason said. "Is that what you wanted to talk about before Sierra came in?"

Hayden nodded. She took the envelope, which had become

wrinkled under the pressure of her grip, and stuffed it back into her purse. Her hand shook a little as she adjusted the clasp. When Hayden looked up again, Jason pretended not to have noticed the shaking.

Hayden said, "I have something I need to do here in town. I can't really tell you what it is, and I know that makes me look bad. I'm sure that's a huge red flag, and you may just tell me no. But I don't want you to. I really don't want you to."

"Is this thing you have to do part of your . . . recovery?" Jason asked, trying to be delicate.

"It is." Hayden ran her hands over the tops of her thighs, back and forth like that, the skin making a light swishing sound against the material. When she resumed speaking, Jason detected a thin edge of anxiety in her voice, the sense that she wasn't really in control of everything swirling around her. It was rare to hear that tone from Hayden. She was always cool, always assured. Even when she was at her worst and in the depths of her deepest struggles, she managed to sound as though she could handle whatever came her way. Jason knew Nora may not have noticed that edge in her voice, but Jason did. He'd heard it a few times in his life and understood what it meant. "I don't want to downplay the apology I owed to you guys because it was and is very important to me. But this is much more important in a way. It affects . . . Well, I don't want to say a lot more than what I've already said."

"So you're not going to tell us what this thing you're doing is," Jason said.

"I can't. Not because it's really a secret or anything, although I guess it is. But more because . . . I don't really know if it's going to work. I don't know what the end result is going to be, and some other people are involved." She shifted her concentration directly to Jason as she spoke, boring in on him in a way that seemed to signal something he couldn't quite understand. "A lot of people are involved. It's delicate."

"People we know?" Nora asked.

Hayden ignored the question. She kept her eyes on Jason, as though she was waiting for something.

Jason didn't know what she needed. "What's the favor, then?" he asked. "If we don't know what you're doing, how can we help you?"

Hayden shifted her attention back to both of them. "It's Sierra," she said. "I need the two of you to keep an eye on her while I'm taking care of this. It might be a day. It might be two. I'm not sure."

"We'd love to," Nora said. "Right, Jason?"

"Isn't she in school?" he asked.

"She is," Hayden said. "She has a week to go in her junior year. But I took her out. I told the school we had a family emergency. They gave her some assignments and things to do and let her go. It's fine. Sierra was born here, remember? She lived here when she was a kid. She knows Ednaville. She likes it here. And I know she'll be safe with the two of you."

"Safe?" Jason asked. "Are you doing something dangerous?"

"No, not like that. I just mean . . . I can trust you both. You're family."

"You know, some questions have been running through my head. Some basics. Where are you living now, Hayden?" Jason asked. "We don't know anything about what's going on in your life. We don't have an address or a phone number. What is happening with you?"

"Right. Of course. You deserve to know those things. That's totally cool. I'm living over in Smithfield. Redman County. It's just an hour away. That's where Sierra is going to school. Redman Consolidated. I'm working for a dentist's office over there. I guess I'm like the office manager. It was a stroke of luck to get the job. The dentist is in AA with me, and he needed someone to help. I've been working there for a year. I've got benefits and everything."

"The last time you were here, though, you didn't have Sierra with you," Jason said. "She was with Derrick, right?"

"She was. Mostly with Derrick's mom."

"And she still sees Derrick?" Jason asked.

"Sometimes."

Jason sensed the conversation was hitting a wall with Hayden. He said, "She can stay, but we're both working, you know? We won't be around all day."

"That's fine," Hayden said. "Sierra can take care of herself. She's not a baby. I just don't want her alone all the time."

"It's okay, Jason," Nora said. "We can work something out so we can see a lot of her. I have some flexibility."

"You really don't mind?" Hayden said. She patted her purse. "I could leave this money for Sierra. She's a teenager. She's seventeen. She eats a lot and uses a lot of water."

"No," Nora said. "Don't be silly. But for God's sake, bring her in. She's sitting out there in the car all alone."

"Okay," Hayden said. "I'll text her and tell her to come in." Her thumbs flew over the phone. "Done." Hayden stood up. "She's going to look so different to you guys. I guess you haven't seen her since when?"

"Six or seven years probably," Nora said, standing up. "I'll get the door."

Jason stood up as well, although he wasn't sure why. Nora slipped away to the foyer, and Jason found himself standing face-to-face with Hayden.

"I saw you on the square yesterday," he said. "Why didn't you talk to me then?"

"I was working up my courage. I used to get that out of a bottle. I'm still learning to do difficult things when I'm sober." Hayden shifted her weight from one foot to the other. "I guess you still see Regan, right?"

"Why are you bringing her up?" Jason asked, his voice lowered. It was classic Hayden. Somehow, some way, she knew how to change the subject and throw Jason off-balance.

"You always had a thing for her," Hayden said. "I just figured since you were back in town and all, you'd be seeing her. Obviously, I was right."

"I see her from time to time. We catch up," Jason said. "We're old friends. And just friends."

"I know," Hayden said. Her voice dropped even lower than Jason's. "I'm sure . . . Well, I'm glad the two of you are friends. I'm sure it's good for her. That's all I'll say."

"What does that even mean?" Jason asked. "Hayden, what are you up to?"

He didn't get an answer. Jason heard Nora squeal at the front door and knew that Sierra had arrived in their house. He took one quick glance at his sister, and Hayden met his gaze. But he wasn't sure what he saw there when they locked eyes. A plea? Fear?

Something he'd never understand?

Chapter Five

Nora led Sierra into the living room, where Jason and Hayden were waiting. Nora stood by the girl's side, her arm around her shoulders, presenting her as though she were the prize on a game show.

"Look who's here, Jason," she said.

Jason took in the sight of his niece and the difference between the little girl he had last seen and the young woman who stood before him. Sierra appeared to be several inches taller than Nora, and her long hair, a lighter shade of brown than her mother's, reached just past her shoulders. She carried a duffel bag in one hand and wore a backpack. She shrugged her shoulders as the scrutiny of the three adults continued, and when she arched her eyebrows and smiled, Jason saw the strong resemblance between his niece and his sister. Except for the height, he could easily have been looking at a replica of Hayden when she was in high school. Although Jason quickly realized, based on a moment's observation, that Sierra exuded a clear-eyed calm and maturity that his sister never possessed at that age.

"Hi, Uncle Jason," she said. She wore jeans and an Ohio State University hoodie.

"Hi, Sierra." He considered stepping forward and hugging

his niece, but thought better of it. Would she want to be hugged by an uncle she hadn't seen in years?

Sierra was looking at the floor near her feet. "Do you mind?" she asked, raising the duffel bag.

"Sure," Nora said, her arm still on the girl's shoulders. "You can put it down right there."

Sierra lowered the duffel bag to the floor with a soft thump and then slipped out of her backpack. "I'm sorry we're just barging in on you like this. I told Mom to call first, but she wouldn't. It's kind of rude, I know."

"It's fine," Nora said. "But it's a little chilly outside. Maybe I should put a robe on."

"You see, Mom," Sierra said. "We're catching people in their pajamas."

"It's fine, honey," Hayden said. "My brother is used to it from me. We're family."

Jason turned to Hayden. "Yeah, what's that they say? Home is the place that when you go there, they have to take you in?"

"That's Robert Frost," Sierra said. All the adults turned to look at her. "Sorry. I'm studying for the AP English exam. There's a lot of Robert Frost."

"We should all sit," Nora said. "But I'm going to run and get a robe. Jason, why don't you put water on for tea? Or would either of you prefer coffee, even though it's so late?"

Nora started for the stairs, but Hayden's voice stopped her. "Actually," she said, "I need to get going."

"Already?" Jason asked. "It's so late. I thought you'd be staying here tonight at least. We have the room."

"I know," Hayden said. "And I'd love to stay the night. But I have some things to get started on."

"You mean . . . the thing you were talking about?" Jason asked.

Hayden looked somewhat uncomfortable, and the two siblings turned their attention to Sierra, who looked at Nora and said, "I think this is the part of the conversation where I'm supposed to leave the room."

Nora said, "Why don't I show you up to the guest room? You've never been here before, have you?"

"I guess I haven't," Sierra said, bending down to pick up her bags.

"Wait," Hayden said. She walked the ten feet across the room to where her daughter stood. "I'm just going to go while you're upstairs with Nora. Okay?"

"Okay, Mom. I know you don't like good-byes."

"Just come up when you're ready, Sierra," Nora said, moving toward the stairs. She cleared her throat and jerked her head, a not so subtle way of telling Jason that he needed to leave the room as well and give the mother and daughter privacy. Jason nodded to indicate that he understood and announced that he would put the water on in the kitchen, even though no one had said they wanted it.

Hayden started talking before Jason left. She didn't seem to care if anyone heard what she was saying to her daughter, and Jason listened as he walked out of the room.

"I know I'm turning your life a little upside down again, kiddo," Hayden said. "But this is the last time. I promise."

"It's fine, Mom."

"It's not fine. Really." Hayden laughed a little. "Sometimes I wonder how you turned out so well."

Jason entered the kitchen. He stood at the island in the center of the room and filled the teakettle with water and turned the burner on. From his position, he could still see into the living room where his sister stood in front of her daughter. He couldn't

41

hear what they were saying to each other, but Hayden seemed to be doing most of the talking, looking up at Sierra, who listened intently and nodded from time to time. Hayden reached into her purse and took out the envelope again, the same one she had offered to Jason earlier. She handed it over to Sierra, who took it and stuffed it into the back pocket of her jeans.

Hayden then reached up and kissed Sierra on the cheek. She put her arms around the girl and pulled her into a tight hug. Sierra rested her chin on Hayden's shoulder and closed her eyes while the embrace lasted. They held each other that way, and Jason looked down, embarrassed that he had spied on such an intimate scene.

He listened to the soft whisper of the gas flame as it heated the kettle on the stove. He and Nora had chosen not to have children and put their careers first. As the years went on, Jason found himself watching the interactions between parents and their growing children with the fascination of someone observing a mystery he would never fully understand. The subtle affection, the nonverbal communication, the loving gestures.

Jason heard someone going up the stairs, and then Hayden called his name. He turned the burner off and walked out to where his sister waited in the foyer.

"I'm going to go now," she said.

"Okay," Jason said. He saw the emotion in his sister's eyes. Not quite tears but almost.

"Thanks for doing this. Really." Hayden reached up and used the back of her hand to wipe at her eye. She sniffed. "She's a good kid. She won't disrupt your life at all." She smiled. "I have no idea where she came from. I really don't. Sometimes I look at her and think she must be an alien baby someone left with me, and my real kid is out there somewhere partying and raising hell."

"You love her," Jason said. "That's all that matters."

Hayden looked up. "Thanks for saying that." She took a deep breath. "I wish Mom and Dad could see her now and know their granddaughter."

"Their only grandchild."

"Right. I hadn't really thought of that."

"And," Jason said, "you probably wish they could see you now. Right?"

Hayden laughed a little. "God. Yes. Mom would take all the credit, wouldn't she? She'd say something like, 'I'm glad you finally listened to what your father and I were telling you all those years.'"

"And Dad would probably say, 'You clean up awfully well when you want to.'"

"He would. He totally would. By the way, you look more and more like the old man every day. I thought you should know that."

"Is that an insult?" Jason asked.

"Just an observation. You haven't gone bald. That's the only difference." Hayden adjusted her purse and straightened her posture. "I'm going to go now. Okay?"

Despite the emotion she displayed with Sierra, Jason couldn't detect the frantic edge beneath Hayden's words anymore. Perhaps what he had thought was fear had simply been nervousness over coming into Jason's home after all those years and all the problems. But he couldn't be sure.

"Hayden," he said, "do you need me to . . . I don't know . . . come along with you on whatever you're doing? I feel like I should."

"No," Hayden said, her voice firm. "I have to do it myself."

"Can you at least tell me where you're going or what you're doing?" Jason asked.

"You'll know eventually. You will." She rose onto her tiptoes and kissed Jason on the cheek. "Thanks, big brother. Forty-eight hours at the most. Forty-eight. Then I'll be back for my girl."

Hayden turned away and went through the door quickly, disappearing into the night.

Chapter Six

At the top of the stairs, Jason turned right, away from the master bedroom and toward the guest room, where Sierra would be staying. Nora sat in a rocking chair, her robe belted across her middle, and Sierra sat cross-legged on the bed. Jason stopped in the doorway, feeling a little like he'd interrupted a private moment between the two women.

"Well, your mom left," he said.

"I know," Sierra said.

"Do you—"

Even though Sierra cut Jason off, she did it as politely as she could. "No, I'm sorry, Uncle Jason. I don't know where she's going or what she's doing. Believe me, I asked. If your mom pulls you out of school a week early and drags you off to your aunt and uncle's house, you ask questions. But she wouldn't answer any of them. She was just like, 'It's nothing to worry about.' "

"Hmm."

Sierra looked at Nora. "And what do you do when someone tells you not to worry?"

"You worry," Nora said.

"Exactly. But Mom won't let anything slip. She's a vault when she wants to be." Sierra mimed turning a key over her lips.

45

But Jason wasn't ready to move on. "She said it has something to do with her AA program. Does that tell you anything?"

"Not really," Sierra said. "She's been apologizing like crazy. She called some guy she worked with ten years ago and apologized for not sticking up for him when he got fired. She won't stop."

"Has she apologized to you for anything?" Jason asked.

"Like fifty times. I finally told her to stop. I could tell she was going to do it again downstairs when she left, but she stopped herself. Enough is enough, you know? I get it. She's sorry she was a crappy mom sometimes and a drunk. I almost went into foster care once, when she was in really bad shape."

"You did?" Nora asked.

"It was close. A social worker came a few times and asked a lot of questions. I knew what they were thinking." Sierra shrugged, but her casual attitude appeared to be a front. She didn't look either one of them in the eye. "I bounced around a lot . . . my grandma's house mostly. Then I was with Dad. I think that's when Mom was here the last time. I know all about the wrecked car and stuff. But it's okay. She's better now."

"And we're so glad for that," Nora said. "She looks great. Better than I've seen her looking in years."

Jason came all the way into the room and sat on an ancient, leather-covered ottoman that once belonged to his parents, the material creaking under his weight. What would his mom and dad *really* make of all of it? Would they believe in Hayden's transformation? Jason knew the answer—they wouldn't. They'd remain supremely cautious, just as he was. But how much time had to pass before one's behavior was accepted as a permanent change? Did he want to be as negative and doubtful as his parents?

"You probably want to go to bed soon," Jason said.

"I like to stay up late. I read when the house is quiet."

"It's always quiet here," Nora said. "No kids."

"That's cool," Sierra said. "I always thought I'd want to live in New York like you guys did. When Mom said she was bringing me to you, I hoped you had moved back to the big city. But then she said it was just Ednaville."

"Has your mom been in touch with your dad lately?" Jason asked.

Some of the sprightly energy left Sierra at the mention of her father. Her face turned a shade paler, her eyes just a bit flatter.

"I haven't seen Dad in two years," she said.

"You haven't?"

"He had to move to Indianapolis for a new job," she said. "I guess you didn't hear." She picked at a loose thread on her jeans. "He got laid off from his old job and couldn't find anything in Ohio. I'm supposed to go see him sometime soon, but I don't know when."

She gave up on trying to pull the loose thread free. She smoothed it into place with her thumb.

"So, he's not around here?" Jason asked.

"Wouldn't Mom have brought me to him if he lived close by instead of bothering you?" She looked back and forth between Jason and Nora as though the answer were obvious. She turned to Jason and said, "Look, I know you're fishing, and that's cool. I'd fish too if I were you. Your nutty sister shows up with her teenage kid, and you're all like, 'What the hell's going on here?' Right?"

"She's always been responsible when it comes to you," Nora said.

"Yeah, she has. Mostly." Sierra stared at a fixed point in the room, somewhere in between Jason and Nora.

No one spoke until Nora said, "But you're worried about her a little bit? Aren't you?"

Sierra shrugged. She started picking at the thread again. "She's like a cat, you know? I figure she has nine lives." She looked up at Jason. "But . . . can you maybe guess what I'm going to say next?"

Nora turned to look at him as well.

Jason said, "You're always worried that this time is the tenth?"

Sierra nodded. She looked wise beyond her years.

Back in their bedroom, after they had left Sierra alone to sleep or read, Nora scooted toward the middle of their king-sized bed and whispered, "Did Hayden have anything interesting to say to you when the two of you were alone?"

Jason put his book down, tented it on top of his chest. "Not really. No."

"What do you make of all this?" Nora asked. "What do you think Hayden's up to?"

"Up to?" Jason said. "When you say it that way, you make it sound as though we can't trust her."

"It's just an expression."

"I agree, of course. We can't entirely trust her," Jason said. "We really can't. But you're always defending her, and I'm trying really hard to give her the benefit of the doubt. It's not easy for me, so that's why I'm surprised to hear you put it that way."

"I don't *always* defend her," Nora said. "I just like her. And I try to balance the way you think about her from the past with new possibilities. The way you see her is screened through your parents."

"And our smashed car. And about a million other disasters of all sizes from when we were growing up. She got thrown in the drunk tank once in Chicago, about fifteen years ago. That will drive your parents to the brink, having a child in a big-city jail and no way to talk to her."

"I understand where you're coming from. We don't have to talk about it. . . ." Nora scooted back to her side of the bed.

Jason didn't pick up his book. He didn't want to turn into his parents, judging Hayden and never allowing her out of the box she was placed in at such an early age. Seeing Hayden again, even for such a short time, had brought a swirl of emotions. Anger. Regret. Joy and fear. He remembered their late-night talks as children, their secret and meaningless conspiracies against their parents, their shared adolescent angst over school drama and the mysteries of the opposite sex. She was his sister. His baby sister, even if she was just one year younger. He'd be lying if he didn't admit—at least to himself—that hearing Hayden call him "big brother" again melted much of the steel he'd erected in his heart against her.

"I don't know," Jason said.

"Don't know what?" Nora asked.

"Hayden. What she's here for." Nora turned her body toward him again, listening, the sheets rustling as she moved. "I'm trying not to be cold. Not to be a judgmental ass. I'm just curious. I'm sure it's this AA stuff like she said. Making amends, you know? I've been trying to think of who she might owe an apology to in Ednaville. Mom and Dad would be the obvious choice, but they're dead and gone. There's us, and she already dealt with that."

The toilet flushed down the hall, followed by the sound of running water. Nora lowered her voice even more. "Who else was she close to in town?"

"She had a lot of friends in high school," Jason said. "She mostly ran with a rough crowd. No surprise. The drinkers and the stoners and the guys who came to school in army jackets and never shaved. I'm sure a fair number of them still live here. People like that don't leave Ednaville. But I have no idea if she owes any of them anything."

"It doesn't have to be big," Nora said. "Remember my cousin Steve? He went through AA, and he went around apologizing for the smallest stuff. Like Sierra said, she seems to be sorry for everything."

"Yeah," Jason said.

He replayed Hayden's words in his mind. Not what she said, but how she said it. Her tone.

"What is it?" Nora asked.

"I just worry she's in trouble," he said. "That she's in over her head somehow. Even if she is recovering, she said it's only been a year or so. That's fragile. Someone could fall off the wagon so quickly, and the whole thing could slip away. I've seen her do it before. So many times she disappeared from our lives, despite all the promises."

"You're forgetting something." Nora pointed in the direction of the guest room where Sierra was staying. "She's going to come back for her. She'll stay on the straight and narrow for her."

"Why now?"

"Look at how well that kid is doing. You can see how proud Hayden is."

"Sierra was around when Hayden came the last time."

"It seems different—that's all I can say. She's not going to let that girl go or hurt her. Is she?"

As if on cue, the door to the guest room closed. Jason didn't answer the question. Sierra was seventeen. It had taken that long for Hayden to clean up, so would things really be different?

Nora said, "I think it's nice to have those sounds in the house, don't you? Just being here, Sierra brings energy and life, right?"

Nora reached out and rubbed her hand against Jason's upper arm. "I wonder about how quiet our life is sometimes."

"I thought we liked it quiet."

"We do," Nora said. "But you know you like seeing your niece." She poked him in the arm playfully. "Don't you?"

"I do. Of course I do. She seems like a good kid." Then he picked up his book. "We made that decision about not having kids a long time ago, Nora. A long time. If we play a role in Sierra's life, then that can be . . . a kind of substitute for that."

"Sure," Nora said, rolling back over. "Although I don't agree with you that it's the same. It might be close, but it's not the same."

Chapter Seven

Nora looked surprised when she saw Jason approaching the circulation desk of the Ednaville Public Library at four thirty. She had been bent over a stack of books, using a stubby pencil to make a note on a scrap of paper. Jason cleared his throat as he walked up, and Nora straightened, her eyebrows raised in greeting, expecting a library patron.

"Oh," she said. "It's you."

"It's me."

"Did you get out of work early?"

"A little. They probably won't even notice that I snuck away."

Nora folded the scrap of paper and laid it aside. "I'm glad you're here," she said. "I think Sierra could use a distraction. I mean, I'm assuming you're here to spend time with her. Right?"

Jason looked around the first floor. He didn't see his niece. "Why does she need a distraction?"

"She's worried about Hayden. She hasn't really said it. You know, she's chatty, but still a little guarded."

"Most teenagers are guarded, aren't they?" Jason asked.

"She's tried to text and call her mom, and Hayden hasn't responded since this morning."

Something cold passed through Jason when he heard that. "Was she supposed to hear from her?"

"I've got two people on the phone here," Nora said. "Sierra's upstairs reading or studying or something. Why don't you go up and talk to her?"

"Okay. I will."

"You're her uncle. She *wants* to talk to you."

"We'll see you at home, then."

"Oh, wait," Nora said. "There's something else I have to tell you." She stepped closer and lowered her voice. "There's a dead cat in our backyard."

"A dead cat?"

"Yeah. It's right on the patio. I thought it was sleeping there at first, but then . . . It's dead, Jason. I don't know what happened to it."

"Do you know who it belongs to?" he asked.

"It might be the neighbors'. I didn't have time to deal with it, and I didn't look closely. We went out to buy groceries. I cooked, and then I took the garbage out and the cat was there." She shuddered a little. "I thought maybe you could move it so I don't have to see it again."

"Why do I get all the shitty jobs?"

"Because you're a big, strong man."

Nora picked up the scrap of paper and bustled away. Jason walked across the thin carpeting and through the hushed, air-conditioned silence to the stairs. When he was a kid, the library looked very different. They had remodeled the place sometime after he went away to college, and he never quite felt comfortable in the new space, even though Nora worked there.

When he reached the top of the stairs, he looked around. He saw a scattering of what he considered typical library patrons.

Older men and women, browsing slowly. Mothers trailing small children. Disaffected teens slouching in corners. It took him a few moments to find Sierra. She sat alone at a table in the far right corner of the room, books and papers spread in front of her. She stared at a laptop screen, earbuds sticking from the sides of her head, the tinny chords of a band Jason knew he'd never heard of leaking out. She wore a black "Free Pussy Riot" T-shirt and had her hair pulled back in a ponytail. When she didn't notice Jason, he waved his hand in front of her face to get her attention.

She pulled the earbuds out, the music growing slightly louder. "Hey."

"I don't mean to interrupt you."

"It's cool." She shut the music off. "I'm just doing this work they assigned me."

"Have you been here a while?" Jason asked.

"Since one o'clock. I hung out at the house with Aunt Nora this morning. She made us lunch. She's a good cook, you know?"

"I know."

"Oh, right. Of course you do. It's a good thing I ate before I saw the dead cat."

"It happens. I'm hoping a hungry dog will pass through and save me the trouble."

"Gross." She made a face. "Anyway, I figured I'd spend the day here rather than sitting at home. I mean, your home. I like libraries. I don't know if I've ever been in this one."

"Maybe when you were little."

"Maybe." She started chewing on her thumbnail.

"How old were you when you moved away from Ednaville?" Jason asked.

"Which time?" Sierra asked. "We lived here more than once."

"I guess I was wondering when you last went to the Owl."

"The Owl?" Sierra's face brightened. "I haven't been there in forever."

"If you're hungry, we could go and get something to eat."

"Are you kidding?" She started packing up her things. "You don't have to ask me twice."

In the Midwest, people called a place like the Owl a creamy whip. It was a freestanding, low, concrete building that dished up soft-serve ice cream, shakes, hamburgers, and fries through a walk-up window. No one knew why it was called the Owl, except for the presence of a comical owl, one with large eyes and ruffled feathers, painted on the sign out by the road. People usually ate in their cars after ordering or else they sat at the sticky red picnic tables in the parking lot, shooing away flies and avoiding the sun. Jason and Sierra both ordered through the tiny window, the heat from the fryers and the grill brushing against their faces. They picked up their burgers and fries, then found a spot in the shade. It was just before five, and the flock of families who came by for after-dinner ice cream hadn't arrived yet.

During the short car ride over, they engaged in small talk. What was Sierra studying? What were her favorite subjects? The girl seemed a little distracted. She stared out the window of the car, observing the passing scenery and occasionally saying, "I remember that" or "They tore that down." Jason tried several times to bring up Hayden and hadn't found the right entry point. But as they ate, Sierra checked her phone over and over. The fifteenth time she did it, Jason spoke.

"Anything from your mom?" he asked.

"Not since this morning." Sierra shrugged. "She told me last night that she might not be responding to all of my texts. I think she just didn't want me to worry."

"Does she always answer right away?"

"No. She forgets sometimes. She turns the sound off on her phone at work and then she forgets to turn it back on. I'll text her a bunch of times and be like, 'Mom, turn your phone on.' Of course, she can't hear me when I say that."

"If she told you she might be out of touch . . ."

"I know. You're worried too." She tilted her cup into the air, swallowing milk shake. She smacked her lips. "Whole milk. Nice. Mom started buying skim." She wrinkled her nose. "Anyway, I'm used to things being a little adventurous with Mom. Sometimes I look at my friends, and I think, 'What would it be like to have normal parents?' I don't mean two parents in the house or money or any of that stuff. I just mean parents who are . . . I don't know."

"Predictable?"

"Exactly."

"But your dad's done okay, hasn't he?"

"Dad? Okay?"

"Lately he has."

"I guess you're right," she said. "And you don't have to sugarcoat anything for me. Mom told me all about his police record. I know he got arrested for assault once and did a little jail time for DUI and reckless driving. I get it."

"That was mostly before you were born."

"Mostly. But, yes, he's doing okay. I know he loves me and all of that. He's a nice guy when he's around." She picked at her fries. "Mom will call. She always does." She smiled as though at a private joke.

"What?"

"It's stupid. When I was a kid, my mom got me this video with all these stupid little-kid songs on it. One of them was called 'Mommy Always Comes Back.' It was supposed to teach kids that when your mom drops you off at day care or school or whatever that she'll eventually come back and pick you up. You know— she'll be predictable. Most kids don't really need that, I guess."

"Do you know why she brought you here?" Jason asked. "You're seventeen. You're obviously capable of taking care of yourself. She could have left you at your house and let you finish the school year."

"Good question. I asked, but I didn't get an answer. Mom can be evasive when she wants to be. She kept saying that family is important. That was all I got out of her."

Jason looked down at his food. He had reached the point in any meal he ate at the Owl at which he started to regret what he had eaten so far but still felt incapable of stopping his forward progress through whatever remained. The breeze picked up, and it pushed a greasy odor from the back of the restaurant ahead of it. The fetid smell should have killed his appetite but didn't.

"Maybe you can try again tonight," Jason said.

"You don't believe she's better, do you?" Sierra said.

"What's that?"

"Mom," she said. "You don't believe she's better."

Jason couldn't lie. "I'm not sure, Sierra. Recovery from a drinking problem is a long process. Lifelong. She's just at the beginning."

"Mom said you'd say something like that."

"Did she?"

"Yeah. She told me about the wrecked car and all the crazy stuff in high school. Did she really get suspended for mixing scotch with her chocolate milk in the cafeteria?"

Jason stopped eating. "Scotch and milk. I'd forgotten about that one. You'd think I'd remember. It sounds like the most disgusting drink ever made."

Sierra pushed her empty plate aside and used a napkin to wipe her hands. She threw the napkin on the plate and then seemed lost in her own head. Finally she said, "I know part of the reason I'm here is because she wanted to see you again. She didn't say that, but I could tell. She wanted you to see how she's doing. And she wanted me to get to know you and Aunt Nora. Mom's been all into family stuff since she got out of rehab. Showing me old pictures, talking about Grandma and Grandpa. And you."

Jason pushed his own plate away, across the cracked and blistered surface of the picnic table. His parents had brought him and Hayden to the Owl countless times every summer, and he remembered their smiling and sticky faces, laughing and joking while finishing every bite of ice cream like there was no tomorrow. He couldn't help but be moved by Sierra's words about Hayden. Jason hadn't been the best student growing up, but he'd always been a good kid, and he knew that part of Hayden's troubles came from being compared to him by every adult she encountered. Her rebellion made sense in hindsight. She ran in the opposite direction from him, with the opposite crowd. It was the only way to create her own identity.

"I know it could be tough on your mom, being my sibling."

"Why?"

"She was the youngest, so she was always compared to me. I was the good kid, and she was the bad kid. I played that up with our parents sometimes, took advantage of it. It made things tougher on your mom than they needed to be."

"Why didn't you and Aunt Nora have kids?" Sierra asked.

"Our careers came first a lot of the time," he said. "We talked about it a lot. And I mean *a lot*. We always thought we would, but we kept putting it off. And then one day it just seemed like we weren't going to do it. It happens."

"That's cool," Sierra said. "I don't know if I want kids or not."

"Your aunt Nora and I had some struggles with our marriage."

"You did?"

"Sure. We kind of fell into a rut, took each other for granted. There were money troubles when I lost my job. Pretty typical stuff for a couple at a certain point. Nobody cheated. Nobody did anything weird. We just . . . kind of lost our way. We've been doing better back here in Ednaville. Who'd have thought it . . . Ednaville is for lovers. I'm not sure if having a kid would have made our marriage troubles better or worse."

"I don't know," Sierra said. "Mom acts like you guys are the perfect couple."

"Hardly. But we figured it out. We're still kind of figuring it out, but it's good. We love each other. That's all that counts. And I think you have plenty of time to figure out if you want kids or not," Jason said. "But we're glad you're staying with us."

"Really?"

"Really."

"Because you didn't seem that cool with it last night. You looked at Mom like she was throwing a grenade into your lap."

"You're an only child, right?" Jason asked.

"Sure."

"Imagine if you did have a sibling, and you hadn't seen that sibling for five years, and then she just shows up on your porch. Out of the blue. Would that freak you out a little?"

"Point taken," Sierra said. She looked around. More families were arriving. Fathers carried multiple ice-cream cones and stacks of napkins. Mothers wiped at faces and shirts while the kids squirmed and fussed, their voices squeaky and thin. "I missed this whole scene when I was growing up. Dad was gone when I was five. Mom was . . . You know how Mom was." She started gathering up their wrappers. Before she could take them away, her phone dinged. She quickly put the trash down.

Jason waited, watching Sierra as she read the screen.

"It's from Mom," she said.

Sierra kept staring, as though it was a long message. She raised her index finger to her mouth and started nibbling on the nail. Jason tried to keep quiet, but finally he couldn't wait anymore.

"What does it say?" he asked.

Sierra turned the phone around so Jason could read the message.

Remember—I love you, baby! Always!

Chapter Eight

Jason drove with no destination in mind. He considered going home but decided that Nora was right and what Sierra needed more than anything else was distraction. She didn't speak as they drove away from the Owl and back toward downtown. She stopped commenting on passing sights. She didn't say anything. She pulled her feet up onto the seat and stared out the window, her fingernail in her mouth again.

"Do you want to see the house your mom and I grew up in?" Jason asked.

"Always," Sierra said.

"You've always wanted to see it?"

"Why did she say 'always'?" Her voice was hollow. She kept her head turned away from Jason. "It would be one thing if she just wrote and told me that she loved me. She does that kind of stuff all the time. But why did she say she'd *always* love me? Isn't that what you say to someone when you think you're never going to see them again?"

Jason couldn't dismiss Sierra's concerns. When he saw the text, he too thought it sounded like a farewell. If Hayden had ended up in some kind of danger, some situation she wasn't going to be able to get out of on her own, then why not ask for help in the text? Why not dial 911? And if she wasn't in danger, what did the message mean? Had she chosen some other path in her life, one that Sierra couldn't be a part of?

"I'm sure it's nothing to worry about," he said. "She probably just meant it like a regular 'I love you.'"

Sierra whipped her head around. "I think we should go to the police. I think she's in danger."

Danger? Jason thought. *Or trouble?* There was a huge difference between the two.

"Hold on now," Jason said. He had made two turns away from downtown, and they were now on Park Street, heading into the residential neighborhood where he had lived as a child. "We have no reason to get the authorities involved. I think you're just nervous and worried, and that's fine. But what would we tell the police if we called them?"

"Tell them about that text. Tell them we think Mom's in danger."

"That's not really enough to bother the police with." Jason turned east on Eighth Street and slowed the car to a stop in front of a brick house with a wide front porch. Sierra didn't look outside the car. She was still turned to Jason, her face intensely focused. "Your mom said she'd be back in forty-eight hours, right? And it hasn't even been twenty-four. I think we just need to give her that time."

Sierra turned away. She looked straight ahead, across the hood of the car. In profile, she resembled her father, Derrick, a little. They both had the same rounded tip of the nose, the same slightly raised upper lip.

"You were freaked out by the text too," Sierra said without turning her head. "I saw it on your face."

The kid was smart—he had to give her that. She didn't miss a damn thing.

"Forty-eight hours," Jason said. "Forty-eight hours." He pointed across Sierra toward the house. "See that?" he asked. "That one there?"

Sierra didn't look. "I've seen it. I've been inside."

"When you were little?"

She nodded. Jason understood why she had withdrawn, but he also felt compelled to try to draw her out. Did all parents feel that way when confronted with a moody or unhappy teenager? Did they strive for anything that might engage the child?

"Your mom and I had rooms on the top floor," Jason said. "Mine was on the left and hers was on the right. It was convenient for her." Jason pointed again. "See that tree over there? She used to go out the window and climb down when she wanted to sneak out of the house."

Sierra looked at the house, following the line indicated by Jason's finger. She pulled out a tube of lip balm, the cap making a little snapping noise as she opened it, filling the car with the scent of strawberries. Sierra asked, "Do you think about the past a lot?"

"Sometimes," he said. "I live in the town I grew up in. I'm middle-aged. That's a combination that leads to thinking about the past."

"I want to ask you something, then," Sierra said.

"Something about your mom?"

"Something about you," she said, turning back around to face him. "Maybe it has to do with Mom."

"Okay. We're kind of on memory lane anyway. Shoot."

"I want to know about this friend of yours who disappeared."

Jason sat back in his seat. If he'd been given one hundred guesses at what Sierra was going to say, the statement she uttered wouldn't have been one of them.

"What are you talking about?"

"Mom told me once that you had some friend, some guy, and on the night of your high school graduation he just up and left. He got pissed at everybody here, and he just walked away and never came back. I'm curious about it."

"He didn't disappear," Jason said. " 'Disappear' suggests something else, something sinister. Like he was kidnapped. He just left like you said."

"Can you tell me about it?" Sierra asked.

"Why are you so curious?"

"Mom brought it up one time. Years ago. I was a little kid. And then for a long time it never came up. To be honest, I guess I just forgot about it. But maybe six months or so ago I remembered that she had mentioned this guy who disappeared from her hometown, and that he was a close friend of yours. What was his name? I forget. Was it Larry or something?"

"Logan."

"Logan. That's it." Sierra appeared lost in thought.

Someone on the street started a leaf blower, its droning howl cutting through the otherwise pleasant evening.

"So you asked her about it six months ago?" Jason said, prompting her.

"Right," Sierra said. "She got a little pissy when I brought it up. She told me I shouldn't ask about things like that, that they were none of my business. That wasn't like Mom. She never minded if I asked her questions, even about the most personal stuff. I know a lot of things about her I don't want to know."

Jason remembered his sister's frankness, especially the disclosures from their family therapy sessions. "I hear you," he said.

"So why was Mom bent out of shape about me mentioning this guy?" Sierra asked. "Was she in love with him?"

"She wasn't in love with him," Jason said. "She was dating your dad in high school."

"Was she dating Dad all the time? Were they exclusive?"

"Your mom wasn't—" But Jason stopped himself before he said, *Your mom wasn't exclusive with anybody, even your dad*. He said, "Your mom knew a lot of people in high school. She was popular."

"I can guess what that means."

When Logan came to their house—the very house they sat before— he and Hayden engaged in a fair amount of flirty banter. Hayden acquired the habit of answering the door wearing just a towel or a pair of skimpy shorts, and she greeted Logan by saying his name with a kittenish purr. But Logan wasn't the only one of his friends Hayden acted that way around. It was just that Logan was Jason's best friend, and he spent the most time at their house. Did anything happen between them? Anything more than hormonal teenage verbal jousting? Jason would have known, wouldn't he? Somebody—either Logan or Hayden— would have told him. And Hayden did spend the majority of her time with Derrick, Sierra's father.

"Are you just curious about the story?" Jason asked. "Or do you think it has something to do with why your mom is here?"

"Mom came back here out of the blue, and she bawled me out when I asked her about the guy. Doesn't that seem odd?"

"Did your mom use the word 'disappear'?" Jason asked.

"I was trying to remember. The first time I heard the story . . . I guess I can't remember what words she used. Maybe I just inferred that she meant disappeared. When I asked her this last time, six months ago or whatever, I know *I* said 'disappeared,' and she didn't correct me."

"But she didn't say anything else about it, right?"

"No, she didn't. She told me to get lost. So, come on, who was this guy?"

A blur of images of Logan scrolled through Jason's mind. Swinging a golf club or a tennis racket. Throwing back a beer or a shot. He thought of his conversation with Regan and her claim that Jason "hero-worshipped" Logan and didn't see the real him. Was it possible to remember a complete picture of someone, to see a person with his flaws and his strengths? Did he think of Hayden as anything but the lost and wild child? Did he only see the other side of her—intelligent, loving, perceptive—when he was forced to? Was it the same with Logan? Jason knew that the people who left when they were young remained forever frozen in place, never touched by the ravages of time. Aging. Graying. Gaining weight. Losing options.

"He was my best friend," Jason said. "We were best friends since the sixth grade. Our families were very different. His was pretty well-off, but I guess we met each other before anyone really thought about all of that. I don't know—we were kids. We played sports together. We rode our bikes. In high school, we partied together. The usual stuff."

"And that's it?" Sierra said.

"Pretty much."

But Jason remembered the first time Logan took him to the Shaws' country club. He remembered the huge chandelier, the waiters in their sharply pressed white shirts, the way everyone called him "sir" as though he were already an adult, even though he must have been about twelve. Jason worried over which fork to use and whether to rest his elbows on the table. His hands almost shook as he reached for water or bread. It felt to Jason then—and it still felt that way to some extent—as though Logan opened the door to another world for Jason, one he would never have seen without their friendship.

"What about when he disappeared? Or left. Whatever you want to call it."

"It's not important," Jason said. "There's nothing to tell."

"Nothing?" Sierra asked.

Jason shifted around in his seat and put the car in gear. "We should be getting home. Nora's going to be getting off work, and it's kind of been a long day."

Chapter Nine

Nora wasn't home yet, and when they came into the house, Jason tried to get Sierra interested in something else. He offered to watch a movie with her, and when she said no to that, he told her that there was a baseball game on TV. Sierra said she was going to go read, and she trudged up the stairs, her footfalls sounding heavier than Jason thought possible. He suspected she'd be sitting up there, reaching out to her mother, sending texts or making phone calls.

Jason tried to distract himself by reading as well, but he couldn't concentrate fully on the book in his hands. He felt heavy and bloated from the Owl, and he kept thinking about the message Hayden had sent to Sierra. Like Sierra, Jason fixated on that one word. *Always.* Did it mean anything more than what it said on the surface? Twenty-four hours remained. If at the same time the next night Hayden hadn't reached out to them, he'd figure out what to do.

Then he remembered the job Nora had assigned him. The dead cat.

"Shit," he said.

He went out to the back door and undid the lock. Before he pulled the door open, he wished again that a predator had come along and removed the cat the natural way. And then he hoped that Nora had simply been wrong, that the cat had been sleeping or injured and had since risen to its feet and wandered off.

But he knew he was engaging in wishful thinking. He expected to find a dead cat on the patio, and he did. Not only did he see the dead cat, but he recognized it as well.

"Pogo," he said.

Pogo belonged to the family next door, the Nelsons. They had three children—two boys and a girl—and Pogo, their orange cat, used to wander through Jason and Nora's yard. He'd scratched the cat's ears on a few occasions, and once set out a bowl of water on a blazing summer day.

Jason stepped out and studied the body. What prompted Pogo to up and die on their back porch? Did cats drop dead of heart attacks like people? Was that what happened to Pogo?

But something about Pogo's posture didn't seem random. He was on his side, his legs straight out as though someone had placed him there, almost gently. He didn't look like the victim of a larger predator or even an accident. And then Jason noticed that some blood had trickled out of Pogo's mouth and dried around his head.

"Gross."

Jason jumped.

"Jesus," he said.

"Sorry."

He turned as Sierra stepped out onto the porch, her feet bare, the Ohio State hoodie zipped up to her chin.

"I didn't mean to scare you," she said.

"This dead cat just creeps me out," he said. "And now I have to go tell the neighbors their pet is dead. They have little kids. I see their daughter, Victoria, carrying this cat around all the time. She'll be devastated."

"What killed it?" Sierra asked.

"I don't know." Jason turned to go inside and get a bag, but then Sierra spoke.

"Wait," she said. She crouched down, studying the cat from a lower angle. "Did you see the blood?"

"I did."

"Isn't that weird?" she asked.

"No weirder than the dead cat being here in the first place."

"No, really." Sierra stood up and placed her hand on Jason's arm. "What if this is about Mom?"

"The cat?"

"What if someone killed the cat to scare Mom or something? Or to scare us? Did you think of that?"

"No, I didn't. Look, Sierra, the cat probably got hit by a car and limped back here. Or it fell or something. No one hurt the cat on purpose. It isn't even ours."

"But it lives next door."

Jason put his arm around the girl, the same way Nora had the night before. "I know you're freaked out about your mom. I understand. But don't let every little thing spook you."

"You jumped when I came out," she said. "You were spooked."

Jason pulled the girl a little closer, then let her go. "I have to go get a bag or something and go next door."

After making his unpleasant delivery to the neighbors' house, Jason returned home. He started to read, trying to distract himself from the image of Pogo's dead body and the look on poor Mr. Nelson's face when he saw what was in the grocery bag, and then his phone chimed. He assumed the text was from Nora, but when he looked, he saw it was Colton, asking to come by the house briefly. Jason couldn't imagine what business Colton would want to discuss in person at seven thirty, but he welcomed the distraction. He told Colton to come by. When the car pulled up, Jason stepped out onto the porch. The light was draining from the day, the air cooling. Jason took a deep breath and saw a few stars appearing in the rising purple darkness at the horizon. A few doors down, some kids threw a football, their high-pitched shouts the only noise. Colton drove a Cadillac, and he emerged from the driver's side wearing a polo shirt, white shorts, and some kind of woven leather sandals. His feet looked tiny, and he waved as he approached the porch.

"I'm sorry to barge in on you like this. But I was nearby and wanted to see if you were home."

"It's no problem. Do you want to come in? I have beer or coffee."

Colton used his thumb to point in the direction of the car, which Jason noticed was still idling, the headlights glowing. "I can't stay. My girls are in the back."

Colton had two daughters, Jason knew. Grade-schoolers. On more than one occasion, Jason had been forced to look at pictures of the girls. Awkward school portraits. Dance recitals. Soccer games. Jason always smiled at the photos and complimented Colton on how fine the kids looked despite his lack of interest.

Jason turned his head a little, back toward the house, where the guest room window was cracked open and a light glowed from behind its curtains.

"What's on your mind, then?" Jason asked. "Do you have more questions about Logan?"

"Logan?" Colton almost said the name as though he'd never heard it before. "No, not that. Did you think of something?"

"No," Jason said. "Nothing."

Colton laughed, but it was a low, unnatural sound. He stuffed his hands into the pockets of his shorts and shifted his weight from one foot to the other. "I guess it seems a little strange, me coming over like this. I feel like a gossipy old lady."

"What is it, Colton?" Jason asked. "Is something wrong?"

"Jason," he said, "is your sister living here in town again?"

Jason felt his head move ever so slightly to the left, as though the invisible hand of the universe had given him a slight tap on the cheek. "Did you see her?" he asked, trying to sound calm.

"I did," Colton said. "And here's why I wanted to tell you in person and not over the phone. You see, I took the kids down to Center Park tonight. There was a little children's concert down there, and to be honest, Gloria just wanted us out of the house for a little while. But when we were down there, getting ready to leave, I saw a car a few spaces down from ours. Kind of a junker, you know? But the passenger window was open, and I saw a familiar face in there. It was Hayden. I thought to myself, *Goddamn, I didn't know she was still around.* Confidentially, I used to have a huge crush on her when we were all in school."

Colton's cheeks flushed red. Jason looked back at the upstairs window again and said, "Can we move closer to the street to talk about this?"

They did, Colton's sandals making little slapping noises against the sidewalk. They stopped near the front of Colton's car, the low hum of the engine covering the other sounds of the night. Jason looked into the backseat and saw the two girls engaged in a conversation of their own, their heads bobbing, their gestures grand and exaggerated.

"Is Nora home?" Colton asked.

"No. Hayden's daughter is staying with us. I don't want her to hear."

"Oh," Colton said, lowering his voice even more. "I forgot she had a daughter with Derrick. How old is she now?"

"Seventeen."

"Wow. Time flies."

"So, what happened at the park?"

"Right. When I saw Hayden, I went over to say hello. You know how I am. But when I got close to the car, it looked a little like Hayden . . . Well, she hadn't been crying. That's not it. She wasn't crying. But her eyes looked kind of glazed. She seemed, I don't know, absent in a way. And then, here's the kicker, Jason. I bent down to say hello, since I was already there, and I looked past Hayden and saw who was driving the car."

"Who?"

"It was Jesse Dean Pratt."

Jason felt cold. The wind had shifted, raising the hairs on the back of Jason's neck and along his arms. He stared at the ground before him, and in the bright glare of Colton's headlights he saw oil stains in the street and tiny bits of broken glass.

"Are you sure, Colton? About both of them?"

"A guy like me wouldn't forget a face like Hayden's. No way. It was her. And Jesse Dean, I've seen him in the last few years. He doesn't look that different. He doesn't act much different either. He's been in the justice center a time or two. Some things don't change. Besides, when I waved, Jesse Dean waved back. He wore a big stupid grin, and then he dropped his car into gear and backed out. Left me just standing there in the lot. But it was him, Jason, and it was her."

"Did Hayden say anything to you?" Jason asked. "Did she ask for help or do anything?"

"She looked right at me and smiled a little finally. It seemed forced, but if she wanted help, she could have asked for it. She could have jumped right out of the car. Jesse Dean wasn't holding her or anything." Colton narrowed his eyes as he saw the scene in his mind again. "There was someone in the backseat as well, maybe more than one, but I couldn't see who they were. And they were having a good time, too. Jesse Dean handed a bottle wrapped in a paper bag over to whoever was in the back. Then they drove off. I thought about calling the law and reporting them for the open container, but then I thought of Hayden. I thought of what she was like in high school. You know, she was always nice to me, the squarest, nerdiest guy in the school. People remember that high school stuff and how people treat them. I figured it would be best just to tell you."

"Thanks."

"Are you okay, Jason?" Colton asked. "I don't want to freak you out. I know Hayden was kind of friends with Jesse Dean back in school, so maybe it's no big deal she's with him."

"I guess they could still be friends. I don't know who all she's hanging out with." Jason looked Colton square in the eyes. "Are you sure she didn't seem to be in danger or trouble?"

"I can't say anything for certain," he said. "But if she were in real trouble, would they come right to the park around crowds of people? There were police officers there. Anybody could have seen them. They looked more like they were partying with that bottle making the rounds."

"Maybe that's why her eyes were glazed," Jason said.

Colton shrugged. "Like I said, I don't know. I live in a house full of women, and I never can read them or understand what they're thinking. She could have been high or it could have been something else. Who knows?"

"Do me a favor, Colton," Jason said. "Can you keep this under your hat? Hayden's daughter is here, and I don't want people to talk."

"You've got it."

One of the rear windows of the car rolled down, and a little girl stuck her head out. "Daddy? Are you coming? Steffie has to go to the bathroom."

"Okay, hon," Colton said. He turned back to Jason. "Look, if there's anything I can do to help."

"It will be fine. I think Hayden is just . . . reconnecting with some old friends."

"Sure," Colton said. The two men shook hands. "If I see or hear anything else, I'll let you know."

Jason watched him climb into his car and drive off. When he turned around to the house again, he saw the curtain in the guest room fall back into place.

Chapter Ten

Jason stepped inside the house, and Sierra's voice greeted him from the top of the stairs.

"Who was that?" she asked.

Jason stood at the bottom of the steps, craning his head back a little so he could look up at his niece. Her hands rested on the banister on one side and the wall on the other, her body leaning forward until it looked like she might tip over and go headfirst down the stairs.

"Just a friend," he said. "Did you hear anything from your mom?"

"Nothing. *Silencio.*"

Jason lifted his foot and placed it on the bottom step. "You know how we were talking about my friend earlier? Logan?"

"Yes."

"Did your mom ever mention any of her other friends from back then? I mean, besides your dad."

Sierra rocked a little at the top of the stairs. She looked like a ski jumper at the beginning of a long run. Her hair was down, and it shook around her face, partially covering it so Jason couldn't see her expression.

"Any other names?" she said.

"Yes. Has your mom talked about anyone else lately? People she might be seeing here or talking to."

"Do you mean a name like . . . Jesse Dean Pratt?"

Jason jerked his head up. "Did your mom say that name?"

Sierra stopped rocking, but she didn't say anything.

"Sierra?"

"Is he someone special?" she asked.

"Where did you hear the name?" Jason asked. "It's important."

Sierra paused before answering. Finally, she said, "Do you work with Jesse Dean Pratt? Because I thought whoever came to the door had to do with work."

"I know Colton through work."

But Sierra had turned away from the top of the stairs. Jason went up and, when he reached the landing, saw that Sierra's door was closed, a thin strip of light glowing along the bottom. He knocked and received no response.

"Sierra?"

He expected to have to knock again, but the door came open, leaving him face-to-face with his niece. "What?"

Jason took a calming breath. "Just tell me if that's a name your mom mentioned recently. Did she say anything about Jesse Dean before she came to Ednaville? Did she say his name on the phone, or mention him to anyone else?"

"Who is he?"

"Okay. Jesse Dean was a scumbag. *Is* a scumbag. I didn't even know he was still alive. He was a couple of years older than us when we were in school. I don't know what all he was involved in, but I know he spent some time in jail, back then and again after I moved away. I suspect he dealt drugs and probably did some other things."

Sierra looked at Jason from the corner of her eye. "Is that it? Is that all you know about him?"

Jason rubbed his hand across his chin. "He was friends with your dad back in high school. And he was kind of friends with your mom. By default, I guess. Your mom and dad were dating, so your dad's friends became your mom's friends." Jason shifted his weight again. "I don't know what ever became of Jesse Dean. I moved away, and like a lot of people I knew back then, he just faded from the picture. Does that answer your question?"

"You're saying both Mom and Dad ran with a bad crowd?"

"Is that a surprise to you?" Jason asked. He looked around the guest room and saw very little clutter. Sierra had been keeping order in her space. No dirty clothes on the floor. No scattered shoes or towels. "People change, remember? That's what your mom told me last night."

"I hear you," she said. "Mom mentioned the name Jesse Dean to me."

"When? Recently?"

Sierra said, "I've been thinking about this a lot, ever since Mom up and decided I was going to come and stay with you. I promised myself I wouldn't mention any of it if Mom just came back okay, but first she sent that text, and now your friend shows up saying he saw Mom with this guy. I want to know what's going on."

"Fair enough. So what did you hear?"

"I overheard Mom talking to him on the phone one day, maybe a week ago. I didn't hear much, but it seemed like Mom was pissed. It was like this Jesse guy was trying to talk her out of something, you know? And Mom kept saying that she had made up her mind, that she was going to do it no matter what."

"But you don't know what she meant?" Jason asked.

Sierra gave Jason the kind of withering look only a teenager could muster. "If I knew that, I'd know everything, wouldn't I?"

"Did they mention your dad at all? Like I said, Jesse was friends with your dad."

"I didn't hear Dad come up. I think Mom knew I was eavesdropping. She has a sixth sense for that. She moved into another room and shut the door. I couldn't make out anything else, but it did sound like her voice was raised a couple of times."

"And that's it?" Jason asked.

"*It?* She has that conversation with that guy, saying she was going to do something, and then she comes here, where that guy used to live? And then she's with him? And she sends me that text?"

Jason considered it all. What could Hayden possibly have to do with Jesse Dean after so much time? Before Jason could say anything else, Sierra said, "I tried looking him up on the Internet, but there were about ten Jesse Dean Pratts. And none of them were listed in Ednaville."

"He could live anywhere."

"But there are a bunch of Pratts in Ednaville. Do you remember where he lived when you were in school? Maybe his parents are still in that house? We could go."

Jason stretched his brain. Jesse Dean. He knew he lived south of town, on what his parents called the wrong side of the tracks as though that were the given name of the neighborhood. He remembered the street, having driven by it during high school. Kids pointed it out to one another, awe in their voices. *That's where Jesse Dean lives.* It wasn't impressive. A little box of a house with a junk-filled yard. Jesse's father was never around, and his mother might very well be dead. The truth was simple— yes, the text and Colton's visit set off alarms in his mind.

"Your mom said she'd be back tomorrow night."

"You don't want to call the police and tell them about this? Some convict is with my mom. Just tell them that."

"Hanging out with an old friend is not against the law," Jason said. "Even if the guy is a convict."

"But what . . ." Sierra raised her hand to her eyes, as though she were shading them against a bright light. "What if she's . . ."

"Hurt?" Jason said. "She didn't say anything to Colton."

Sierra was shaking her head. Back and forth.

"And don't worry about the cat. That's nothing."

"It's not that."

It came to Jason then with the suddenness of revelation. Sierra wasn't really worried about Jesse Dean. She was worried about something else, something even more dangerous related to her mother.

"The bottle?" Jason said. "Are you worried because they were passing around a bottle?"

Sierra's shoulders started shaking. Jason took a step toward her, but she managed to say, "What if she starts again, Uncle Jason? What if she starts again?"

For a moment, Jason didn't know what to do. He moved closer to his niece, reaching out to her with one hand. But he couldn't just pat her on the shoulder, could he? He couldn't just tell her to buck up and hope for the best. So he took the girl in his arms, letting her rest her head on his shoulder while she cried over the fate of her mother.

"Twenty-four more hours, kiddo," he said as he held her. "Let's give her those twenty-four hours."

Chapter Eleven

Sierra stopped crying eventually and then told Jason she just wanted to read for a while to ease her mind. Jason asked her to come downstairs, to sit in the living room with him so they could read together until Nora came home, but Sierra declined. She said she just wanted to be alone.

Jason brought his book to the kitchen table and opened a beer. Once again, he couldn't concentrate on reading, and he found he couldn't enjoy the beer either. While he had never struggled with alcohol, he simply didn't have the taste for it that night as the quiet of the house settled around him. He kept thinking of Hayden in that car, the bottle being passed back and forth. Had she fallen again? He knew recovering alcoholics had to change the patterns of their lives. They couldn't run with the same crowd or go to the places where they used to drink. Had Hayden come back to Ednaville, fallen in with her old friends, and lapsed into the same behavior?

Nora came home around nine thirty, and she took off her jacket as she entered the kitchen.

"How's it going?" Jason asked.

She laid the jacket aside, came to the table, and sat down. "How's Sierra?"

"She's fine," Jason said. He pushed the beer bottle away. "Fine, but upset."

In a low voice, Jason told Nora everything that Colton had told him about seeing Hayden in town with Jesse Dean. While he related the details, Nora lifted her hand to her mouth and cupped it there as though stifling a cry. But she didn't say anything. She listened, and she kept listening in the same way as Jason added the part that Sierra told him, the part about Hayden apparently talking to or about Jesse Dean on the phone.

When he finished the story, Nora moved her hand and let out a deep breath. She didn't say anything.

"Do you want a drink?" Jason asked.

Nora shook her head.

"I don't have much taste for it either."

"And Sierra heard all that?" she asked. "What this Colton guy said."

"We moved away to the street, but I think she listened at the window. She might as well hear it all. She's seventeen. She's seen the best and worst of her mom."

"Would this Colton guy really know Hayden if he saw her?" Nora asked. "Can you trust him to be accurate?"

"He was in love with Hayden in high school. In lust, I should say. A lot of guys were. But he was just a few feet from that car. He's right. It was her and Jesse Dean. No doubt about it."

Nora folded her hands, her elbows resting on the tabletop. She almost looked prayerful. "I think you're wrong. I think we need to call the police. If this guy, this Jesse guy, is a criminal, and he's with Hayden, we need to let the police know. They could help her. Maybe she is in trouble."

"It's not a crime to fall off the wagon. And it's not a crime to hang out with a petty criminal and a thug."

"He didn't see her actually drinking anything, did he?" Nora asked.

"What are the chances she didn't?"

Nora pushed herself up and started across the kitchen. She grabbed the phone. "I don't care what you think. We need to tell someone—"

"Wait." Jason stood up as well. "Just wait."

"What?"

"There's something else. Something you haven't thought of."

Nora held the phone in her hand. She looked back at Jason and stopped, waiting.

"What? What haven't I thought of?"

Jason came over and took the phone from her. He set it back down in the charger. "I didn't think of this right away either, but I thought of it tonight after I talked to Sierra. We don't know where Derrick is, do we? Sierra says he's in Indiana, but who knows? She hasn't heard from him in two years. If Hayden has really fallen off the wagon, if she's out with these guys partying and drinking and driving or whatever else they're doing, and we call the police and report them, what's going to happen to Sierra? If Hayden ends up in jail for something, what about Sierra?"

"She can stay here. With us."

"Sure. *Maybe.* We're okay with that. But do you know that's how the system would work? You heard what she said last night. She almost had to go into foster care once. What happens if some social worker shows up? Even if she goes into the system for a few days, and we have to get her out . . . I don't want to think of that yet."

Nora leaned against the counter. She seemed to be in agreement.

"And her father," Jason said. "If he came back for her, or if she were sent to him . . . I think we're better off just having her here and waiting to see what happens. Hayden said she'd be back in another day. I'm willing to give Hayden that. I told Sierra the same thing."

"You didn't mention foster care to her, did you?"

"No, of course not. But she knows. I guess she's less worried about that than we are. She wanted to call the police too."

Nora folded her arms across her chest. "You have to go out looking for Hayden tonight. We can't just sit here."

"I've thought of that. Where would I look?"

"Start at the park where Colton saw her."

"They were leaving."

"Do you know where this Jesse guy lives?"

"I might be able to find the house he lived in almost thirty years ago. I might."

"Well?"

"And what would I do there?"

"If Hayden's there, you could bring her home."

Jason stepped away. He walked around the kitchen with no real purpose in mind. He felt caged up. Uncertain. He wished he had insisted on going with Hayden. He could have demanded to know where she was going. Or he could have followed her. But what would all that have done? Driven her away? Pushed her toward something else? Something worse?

"Okay, I'll go. I'm not sure what good it will do, but I'll go."

"Thank you."

"I'm doing it for you. And for Sierra."

"Just make a quick circuit of the town, then come home. If you don't see anything, come right back."

"I'll get my keys."

"I'm going to change and check on Sierra."

"Oh," Jason said. "The cat."

"Shit, I forgot all about it."

"It was the Nelsons'. Pogo. I took it over there. In a bag."

"Sorry. Damn, I bet their kids will be crushed."

Jason decided not to mention Sierra's suspicions. There was enough going on.

"I'm sure they are," he said. "That's another good reason not to have kids. You don't have to tell any children their favorite pets are dead."

He grabbed his keys and left the house.

Jason drove with the windows down, the cool night air filling the car. The sky was clear, the stars bright. He kept wiping his hand against his pants leg, the memory of handling the dead cat still fresh in his mind. He entertained the foolish hope that he'd see an abandoned kitten on the side of the road, one he could bring home to the Nelsons.

He stopped at Center Park first. The park and the parking lot were empty, the sodium-vapor lights casting their glow on nothing. Jason drove around the parking lot, but he didn't know what he was looking for. If Hayden had been there earlier—and he had no reason not to believe Colton—then why would she still be there long after everybody else had gone home? He made a circuit of the lot, then came back where he started and parked by the entrance. He stared at the small lake, which was still and barely rippling.

They had a family picnic at Center Park once. It was for their parents' anniversary. Jason couldn't be sure of the number, but it must have been twenty-five or so. Some of his aunts put it on, renting out a picnic shelter and cooking food. No one had mentioned it, but Jason could see the worry on his mother's face when Hayden wasn't there when she was supposed to be. They all were thinking it—even relatives who barely knew them but certainly knew of Hayden's wildness. *She's drunk again. Irresponsible. Undependable.*

Hayden showed up almost an hour late. Relatives were making speeches, toasting Jason's parents with cans of beer and sparkling wine. His parents drank in the attention, but the distracted looks remained on their faces. The party wasn't the same for them without their other child being there.

Jason gave his little toast. Something clichéd and embarrassing. He didn't remember many of the words, but he knew he said "I love you guys" about five times. His mother hugged him. His dad patted him on the back. He was the good boy, the reliable one. *At least we have Jason,* his parents probably thought.

Hayden showed up when the toasts were about finished. Jason saw her park her car and breeze through the parking lot, her hair loose in the hot wind, her purse oversized and dangling from her left arm. He moved to intercept her, just to make sure she wasn't going to embarrass herself and everyone else.

"Hey, big brother," she said.

"Hey, little sister."

The odor of alcohol came off her in waves. Jason wondered if she had been bathing in it.

"Is Mom mad I missed the toast?" she asked.

"They're just finishing," Jason said.

"That didn't answer my question."

"Mom and Dad are happy," Jason said. "They're fine."

"Ah, I see," Hayden said. "They're happy I'm not here."

"They're just happy."

"I've got my toast ready," she said.

"They're finished—"

"They have to hear from me," she said. "I'm their baby girl."

She made a deft step to the left, and then she was past Jason before he could stop her. She walked through the crowd to the chairs where their parents sat, and Jason heard the murmurings. Hayden ignored them.

Both of their parents looked up, their faces showing fear and surprise. Hayden leaned down and kissed each of them on the cheek, and Jason could see his mother offering Hayden a seat, asking her—telling her—to sit down.

But Hayden wouldn't hear of it. She spun to the crowd and held her arms out, asking for quiet.

"Oh, Jesus," Jason mumbled to himself. He took a step forward, but there was nothing he could do to stop what was about to come.

"Are you all awkward now?" Hayden asked, causing nervous laughter among the relatives and friends. "Are you all worried about what crazy Hayden is going to say?"

Jason was. He stuffed his hands in his pockets, digging them in deep. He looked at the ground. But then Hayden started talking. Her words weren't slurred. She didn't ramble. She didn't curse. She delivered a straight-ahead, heartfelt appreciation of their parents and family, making sure to emphasize the unflinching, unconditional love they provided.

"I can only tell you all," Hayden said that day, "that I was born into the best family in the world, with the best parents in the world."

Everyone applauded. Hayden hugged their parents, who were both wiping their eyes. The party resumed, only it had taken on a new energy, one provided by Hayden. She walked through the crowd until she reached Jason. She stood before him and shrugged.

"Well, big brother? Did I surprise you?"

Jason acted out of instinct. He reached out and did something he rarely did—he hugged his sister. He pulled her tight against his body, and as he did, she let out a little "whoop" of surprise.

"Wow, Jason," she said. "You surprised me with the affection."

Jason held her a moment longer, and before letting go, he said, "And you never fail to surprise me, Hayden. You never fail to surprise me."

Jason watched the dark water. He reached up and wiped a tear from his eye.

"Shit, Hayden," he said, even though no one could hear him. "What are you up to now?"

He shook his head and started the car, deciding that sitting in a darkened park wasn't going to get him any closer to answering the questions he had. He was about to put the car in reverse when someone—or something—knocked against the driver's-side window.

For the second time that evening Jason nearly jumped out of his own skin. He looked over, through the closed window, and saw a thin, ragged-looking woman standing there. Jason thought she was homeless. Her hair was cut short, almost in a buzz, and she wore an army jacket over a stained long-underwear shirt.

Jason thought about driving away, even going so far as to place his hand on the gear knob, but the woman made a gesture asking him to roll down the window. She made the gesture again, and then she said something that sounded like his name.

"What's that?" he asked.

"Roll it down, Jason," she said.

No doubt about it. She knew his name.

He lowered the window. "Do I—?"

"Well, well," the woman said. "Jason Danvers. Mr. Big Shot."

She spoke with a slight lisp, and Jason saw that she was missing two front teeth. "You actually rolled the window down for me."

Jason studied the face. He saw the deep lines, the sunken eyes. But there was something familiar there, something from the past that nagged at his mind.

"You don't remember me?" she asked. "Figures."

"Wait a minute," he said. "Rose? Rose Holland?"

"That's right, Fancy Boy. You remember me from high school, don't you?"

"Sure. It took a moment."

"I look different, don't I? Strung out, right?"

"I don't know."

"Right," she said. "You don't travel in my circles."

"I didn't in high school either," Jason said. "You were popular, more popular than me. Weren't you—"

"Yes, I was on the homecoming court. What's it to you?"

"Nothing," Jason said. "What are you doing out here?"

"I could ask you that," Rose said. "But I bet we're looking for the same thing. Do you know what that is?"

Jason wanted to say: *Drugs.* But he didn't think Rose would appreciate him making assumptions about her, so he didn't answer.

"Are you looking for your asshole sister?" Rose asked.

Jason's heart sped up. "Yes, I am. Have you seen her?"

"Where is she?" Rose asked.

"I don't know," Jason said. "That's why I'm looking for her. She was here earlier tonight. If you see her—"

"Can it." Rose stuck her face into the car, so that when she spoke, Jason felt her spittle hit his face.

"Hey." Jason leaned back.

"I came by your house earlier today looking for that bitch sister of yours."

"She's not at our house. I was just there."

"I know. I left a message, though."

"What message?"

"But I'll give the same one to you, and you can pass it on when you see her." Rose poked Jason in the chest, her eyes still angry. "Tell her to stay away from my man."

"Who's your man?" Jason asked.

Rose stepped back. She straightened up and tugged on her army jacket as though suddenly concerned about her own appearance. "You're so precious and stupid," she said. "You don't know who anybody is."

"Who is he?" Jason said, his own anger rising. "Who is Hayden with?"

Rose tilted her head to one side. "My man," she said. "Jesse Dean Pratt." She spit once on the ground, then turned and started off into the night.

Jason pushed his door open and stepped out. "Rose? Wait."

She kept walking.

"Rose? If you see Hayden, tell her I'm looking for her."

Rose slowed for a moment, turned toward Jason, and casually flipped him the bird. Then she kept walking away, and Jason decided it was best to let her go into the darkness.

Jason drove down his street. When he passed the Nelsons' house, just before turning into their driveway, he winced. He thought back over the events of the evening—the perfectly laid-out cat on the back porch and Rose's statement that she had left a message at the house. Had Sierra been right? Was Pogo's death related to Hayden, specifically Rose's search for Hayden?

Jason felt a little nauseated at the thought. The hands that poked his chest might have wrung Pogo's neck. He parked and went inside. Before going upstairs, Jason made a careful circuit of the house, checking every door and every window, clicking locks into place and tugging and pulling on knobs. He just felt better knowing the house was as carefully locked as possible.

At the top of the stairs, he heard low voices. He looked into the open door of the guest room and saw Nora sitting on Sierra's bed. His niece had the covers pulled up to her chin, a book open on her chest. Nora held Sierra's hand, and Jason heard her say, "I think you're right to try to get a good night's sleep. Things will probably look better in the morning. You're safe here, honey."

Then Nora bent down and kissed Sierra on the forehead. She reached out with her hand and smoothed the girl's hair down. Jason turned away.

What-ifs. What-ifs.

Chapter Twelve

When Jason woke up the next morning, he found Nora's side of the bed empty, the covers thrown back. He checked the clock. It was just past seven, early for Nora to be up and about, even if she did have to go into work at nine. In the hallway, Jason noticed that the door to the guest room—Sierra's room, he was starting to think of it—remained closed. He also caught a whiff of something cooking. Bacon. Eggs. His stomach grumbled.

As he approached the kitchen, the smell intensified. He heard the sizzle of the bacon and Nora's humming as she cooked, the scrape of a spatula against the bottom of a pan. He stopped in the doorway.

"What's the occasion?" he asked.

Nora concentrated on her work. "I told Sierra I'd make her breakfast this morning. Apparently she loves breakfast food. Bacon and eggs. I imagine she didn't get a lot of this growing up."

"Is there enough for everyone?"

Nora looked up and smiled. "Of course."

Jason had told Nora about his encounter with Rose in the park as well as his suspicions concerning the death of Pogo, but they had agreed to keep it from Sierra for the time being. They didn't think she needed anything else to worry about.

Jason took a seat at the kitchen table. Since they no longer received a morning paper, he picked up his iPad and found the news, skimming over the headlines.

"Are you going to go out looking again after you eat?" Nora asked.

"I guess so," he said. "I'll call in to work and take the morning off."

"You could take the whole day."

"I might."

"Do you want your eggs fried? That's what Sierra wants."

"Sure." Jason stared at Nora's back. She wore an old sweatshirt of his, one he had bought in college that was now full of holes. She cracked the eggs into the pan, where they hissed. "You know," he said . . . but then he didn't know what to say next.

Nora kept her eyes on the pan. "Come again?"

"I was just going to say . . . it's kind of nice having Sierra around. You know?"

"It is," Nora said. She looked over her shoulder and smiled. "Why don't you go wake her up?"

"Teenagers love being woken up."

Jason strolled through the house, glad to have a purpose. The sun came through the front windows, streaming rays that illuminated spinning dust motes. At the top of the stairs he tapped lightly on the door to Sierra's room. He waited, then knocked louder.

"Sierra?"

He checked the bathroom. Empty. He didn't want to try the door to Sierra's room. It felt like a violation of her privacy.

But then?

What else was he going to do?

The knob turned under his touch. When the door swung

open, he saw the empty bed. No computer. He turned and ran down the stairs.

"Nora?" he called.

She met him in the living room. "My keys are gone," she said. "And so is the car. She's gone, isn't she?"

"Where were the keys? How did she get the keys?"

"I left them by the phone. I always do."

Jason ran to the kitchen, then looked out the window and saw the empty spot in the driveway. He turned back to Nora, who had followed along behind him.

"She's gone," he said. "Absolutely. I'm calling the police."

"Should we?"

"She's gone. She's under eighteen. She either took our car—" Jason stopped himself. Was history simply repeating itself? Had Sierra wrapped their car around a tree somewhere?

"What else were you going to say?" Nora said. "She took our car or what?"

"She didn't take all of her stuff," Jason said. "Her clothes. Some of her books. They're still up in the room. I didn't see her computer, but I guess I'd expect her to take that."

"Are you saying she's just running an errand or something?"

"She's looking for her mom. She has to be."

"Probably." But Nora didn't seem at ease. She brought her hands together and rubbed the palms against each other. "But what if . . . You said Hayden is out with this criminal some-where. And that crazy woman killed the cat. What if . . . what if they came here and *took* Sierra?"

"Then why is the car gone?"

"I don't know," she said, her voice rising. "I don't understand any of this. I just know that if a child disappears, you call the authorities. You're right. She's probably looking for Hayden.

Even if she is, that could get her in trouble. Or something worse happened. She was taken or lured out of the house."

"What about foster care?" Jason asked. "What if she did take the car to go looking for Hayden? If the cops come . . . she could be looking at foster care, Nora. We'd have to tell them why she's here and what Hayden might be doing."

"I don't care," Nora said. "A child is missing, and we don't know where she is or who she is with. We have to call the police."

Jason dialed. Even though he hated the thought of dealing with the police, he knew she was right.

Chapter Thirteen

Colton arrived as the uniformed police officers left the house. Jason watched him speak to them for a few minutes, and their conversation ended with a laugh. Jason looked away.

"Colton's here," he said.

He and Nora had both already called in to work, using personal days in order to stay home. Jason wondered how many of those days they would need to take before all was said and done.

"Do you think we need a lawyer?" Nora asked.

"He's not really here as a lawyer. He's here because he knows everybody and everything in Ednaville. I figured he could help."

When Colton reached the door, Jason let him in, and Colton wore a somber look on his face. He clapped Jason on the shoulder. "How you hanging in there, buddy?"

"Not good." Jason introduced Colton to Nora.

She offered Colton something to drink, and he waved it off. He lowered himself onto the couch, exhaling a little air as he settled his body. He wore a tan summer-weight suit and no tie. When he sat down, his pants legs went up high enough to reveal the pale skin above his socks.

"Are you satisfied with what the police had to say?" he asked.

"I guess," Jason said.

"I thought there'd be more fuss," Nora said. "A missing girl."

"She's not missing," Jason said. He spoke more sharply than he intended, his voice almost like a whipcrack. "I'm sorry, but she's just looking for her mom."

"I'm going to get some coffee." She turned on her heel and left.

Jason turned to say something to her, but she was gone so fast he couldn't get the words out. He started to sit in a chair across the room, but before he could, Colton waved him over to the couch. "Come here," he said.

Jason sat on the couch.

"What are the police saying?" Colton asked.

"They're sending out her description. And a description of the car. We don't have a current photo of Sierra, so we couldn't help them there."

"If they need one, maybe they can go to Facebook or someplace like that," Colton said.

Jason nodded. "We told them about Hayden and Jesse Dean. And I had an encounter with Rose Holland at the park last night."

"Rose Holland? What about her?"

"She's looking for Hayden. Apparently, she and Jesse Dean are an item, even though he's married, and she isn't happy that Hayden might be spending time with her man. She looked like hell. You wouldn't believe it. Missing teeth. Dirty. She must be strung out or something."

"I'd heard that about her. It's weird."

"To make it weirder, Rose might have killed our neighbors' cat and left it on the back porch as a warning."

"Really? That's sick."

"Tell me about it. They're going to be on the lookout for all of them. They're even going to search up on the Bluff."

"You know why, don't you?" Colton asked.

"Sure. It's because of Hayden. Because of her problems."

"I'm sure you've noticed a lot of people don't even call it Thompson Bluff anymore. They all call it Heroin Hill now that the unseemly types have taken it over. Hell, when we were kids, it was a make-out spot. Maybe some kids drank or smoked a little weed. Now I wouldn't even let my kids go up there for a hike in the middle of the day. I hear all about the things that happen in those bathrooms."

"Everybody thinks their time was more innocent than the current time."

"Maybe. You guys don't have kids, so you don't think about these things as much."

Jason felt the harsh look he gave Colton. "What's that mean?"

"Easy, now." Colton leaned closer. "Anyway, I wanted to tell you something while Nora is out of the room."

"What?"

Colton looked toward the kitchen again, and Nora was coming back, carrying a mug of coffee. Colton straightened up, leaning away from Jason.

"You men love to conspire, don't you?" she asked.

"It's not that," Colton said.

"What were you going to tell me?" Jason asked.

"Well . . ." Colton appeared to be at a loss.

"If it's about Sierra or Hayden, we both want to know," Jason said. "Just tell us."

Colton looked back and forth between the two of them, then nodded to himself. "Okay. When you called me earlier, I couldn't get here right away. But I did do a little checking. I had my paralegal look into Sierra a bit." Colton swallowed. His eyes darted between the two of them again. "She's been in some trouble before. Not in Ednaville, but over in Redman County. Is that where the girl lives?"

"Yes." Jason felt a cool unease move through the center of his body. "She and Hayden live there now."

"What did she do?" Nora asked. She sounded skeptical, as though she didn't—and wouldn't—believe anything Colton said.

Colton shrugged in a "don't shoot the messenger" kind of way. "She got picked up for stealing a car."

"Jesus," Jason said.

"No," Nora said. "She's a good kid. She's smart."

"Smart kids steal cars. You kind of have to be smart to do it these days." Colton shifted around on the couch as he reached into his coat pocket and brought out a little notebook. He flipped it open and stared at the pages. "Here's the interesting thing. She was picked up with a girl from Ednaville. Name of Patricia Gibbon. Know her?"

"No," Jason said.

"Yes," Nora said. "Sierra mentioned her yesterday. We were just talking about school and friends, and Sierra said she had a friend here in Ednaville, a girl named Tricia. They met in grade school, but don't see much of each other anymore. I encouraged Sierra to get in touch with her. I thought she'd like to have some friends while she was here. Hell, I didn't know the girl was trouble."

"You couldn't have known," Jason said. "Don't worry about it."

"Of course," Colton said. "But you're right that this girl has issues. She was the one driving the car. Both girls went through a diversionary program. Their records will be expunged when they turn eighteen. Not a big deal in the broad picture, I guess. But I thought you all should know."

"Thanks," Jason said. "I think."

"I mentioned it to the police out there. This is another place they can look for Sierra. They can find this Gibbon hoodlum and ask her if she's seen your niece. If Sierra is off on some adventure, searching for her mom or whatever else, she might decide she needs a running buddy."

"Good point," Nora said.

Colton put the notebook away.

"What do we do now, Colton?" Jason asked. "What can we do?"

"Sit tight. Try to distract yourself, and let the police do their work. If this girl has a level head like you say, then she'll come back. Do you all have a good relationship with her?"

"I think we do," Nora said.

"Then it should work out in a positive way." He reached over and slapped Jason on the knee. "Hang in there." Colton stood up, and the three of them walked to the door together. "If I hear anything, I'll let you know."

"Thanks."

At the door, Colton turned back and asked, "Has someone told the girl's father what's going on?"

Jason and Nora looked at each other. "We don't know how to reach him," Jason said. "He's in Indiana."

"Well, at some point," he said. "A father has a right to know."

"He hasn't seen his daughter in two years," Nora said.

"He's still her father," Colton said. "He's the custodial parent if her mother doesn't . . . if Hayden isn't available."

When Colton was gone, Jason went upstairs to shower and dress. As he put his clothes on, Nora appeared in the bedroom doorway. "Are you going out looking now?" she asked.

"Yes. I think you should stay here in case she comes home. But keep the doors locked. Hayden has attracted quite a crowd of weirdos."

"That's fine. I can take care of myself. But stay in touch with me. Text or call. I don't have a car. And I want to know that you're doing okay."

"Of course." Jason pulled his shoes on, while Nora stood over him. "Is something else on your mind?" he asked.

"That Colton is an interesting guy, isn't he?" she said. "He seems full of information."

"He knows everybody in Ednaville." Jason stood up. "He's trying to help."

Nora seemed to be thinking it over, her finger tapping against the coffee mug in her hand. She said, "Just remember to stay in touch."

"I will. I'll have the phone on."

"Jason?" Nora said. "Do you think she's okay? Sierra?"

He really considered his answer before speaking. "I'd like to think so. I'd really like to think so."

Chapter Fourteen

Jason didn't have far to drive. He headed south, avoiding downtown by taking State Route 33, more commonly called "the Bypass." It brought him west, past open fields on one side and strip malls and car dealerships on the other. Then the road looped back to the east toward Ednaville again. While he drove, he called Regan on her cell phone. He thought about not calling her, of letting his attention and efforts remain fixed on his own family where they belonged. But he also worried about Regan. Hayden had mentioned her the night she dropped Sierra off, and with all the strangeness swirling around, he felt she needed a word of caution as well. So he called, and he told her about Sierra taking the car and leaving without telling them where she was going, and when he did, Regan gasped.

"Oh, God," she said. "That poor girl. She must be so worried about Hayden to do something like that."

"There's more," Jason said. "Guess where I'm headed? I'm going to Jesse Dean's house."

There was a long pause. "For God's sake, why?"

"Colton Rivers saw Jesse Dean and Hayden together last night at Center Park. We told the police, too, but I can't just sit around the house all day waiting for something to happen. I thought whoever lives in that house might be willing to talk to me. Do you know if Jesse Dean's mother is still alive?"

"I don't. Jason, I think you should just let the police handle this stuff. They know what they're doing."

Jason changed lanes, keeping the phone cradled between his ear and his shoulder. "I know. But you see . . ." Jason tried to gather his thoughts. Some things were coalescing in his brain. Fragments that had been loose and scattered were starting to join together. "I talked to you the other day about Logan, right? And now this stuff with Hayden and Sierra. Do you realize Sierra is almost the age we were the night we graduated from high school? The night Logan left?"

"You said she's seventeen. Yes, I thought of that."

"Well, let me ask you something, Regan. How many people am I just going to let walk out of my life without doing something about it?"

"It's not the same as—"

"It is," he said. "When Hayden came to our house two nights ago, I knew something was wrong. I could tell she might be in danger. Her voice wasn't right. The tone. I can read her. Even after all this time, I can read her like a book. Why didn't I insist on going with her? Why didn't I just follow her out the door and see what she was getting into?"

"You can't always be with everybody. You can't do that for kids or adults."

"I'm doing it this time."

He drove on while Regan was silent. He turned off the Bypass and onto Ridge Road, cutting east, heading toward the neighborhoods south of town. The houses grew smaller in size, the yards more cluttered with broken cars and paper and toys.

"Jason," Regan said finally, "just remember that guys like

Jesse Dean probably don't like it when people ask questions about them. I didn't even think he lived here anymore."

"But his family might. Somebody around here knows what he's up to. If I can find Hayden, then I can find Sierra. Or vice versa." He realized he sounded obstinate, a little like a stubborn child clinging to a fantastic notion for no better reason than that it brought him some comfort. "Do you ever think that if one of us had been able to talk to Logan that night on the Bluff, he may never have left? If we'd just been able to get through to him in some way? I want that chance with Sierra. And Hayden."

"Jason?" Regan said.

"What?"

"You say that about Logan, about trying to change his course. But you don't know if that . . . It probably wouldn't have . . . Look, just be careful. And don't spend too much time away from home. That girl's going to come back, or Hayden is, and they're both going to need you there. That's where you should be focusing your attention. Okay?"

"Okay. I just hope it's not too late. For them or for me."

The Pratt family lived on Washington Street. To get there from downtown, one literally crossed a set of railroad tracks and headed south. When Jason was a kid, the families there worked in factories—Henry Ball Bearings and Mission Electronics. As the years passed and the factories closed, they began taking jobs in places like Wal-Mart or McDonald's, if they found employment at all. The houses on Washington Street were boxy and small. They sat close together on playing-card-sized plots of land, and even late in what had been a rainy spring, the lawns were patchy and brown.

Jason pulled up in front of the Pratts' house, the address he found in the phone book. It looked no better or worse than the houses on either side of it, and as Jason approached the front porch, he saw that the railing was in need of a paint job as well. He stopped before he mounted the steps. There was one car in the driveway, a dented minivan parked above a large piece of cardboard, which was absorbing as much dripping oil as it could. He wondered if Hayden had been there recently, even though the listing in the phone book was for a Ruth Pratt, who Jason was pretty sure was Jesse Dean's mother. Would Jesse Dean have brought someone to the house if his mother still lived there? Would he hide or hold Hayden there if he had to? Could he do the same with Sierra if she fell into his hands?

Jason started up the steps, but before he reached the porch, the front door opened with a creaking of springs. A woman about his age stepped out, shielding her eyes against the sun. She was obviously not Jesse Dean's mother, and Jason looked her over, trying to determine if he knew her from growing up in Ednaville.

"Another cop?" she said.

Jason stopped halfway up the steps. "Excuse me?" Then the words registered in his head. "No, I'm not. Have they been here today?"

"Just a little bit ago. I figured you were a detective here for some follow-up."

The woman was thin and wore sweatpants and a tank top. Her hair was piled in loose curls on top of her head, and her feet were bare.

"I'm looking for Jesse Dean."

The woman snorted, like she'd just heard a slightly funny joke. "Do you think if Jesse Dean were here, *I'd* have to answer the cops' questions? He's not here. Who are you?"

"I knew him in high school."

"You and everyone else in this town."

"So he's not around?" Jason asked.

"No, he's not around. He doesn't live here anymore. Not really, anyway, even though I guess it's his house technically. I pay the bills."

"Are you Jesse Dean's sister?" Jason asked.

She snorted again. "Nice try. I'm his wife. I'm Mrs. Jesse Dean Pratt. Aren't I lucky? My name's Mandy Pratt. His mom gave us the house when she died, but Jesse Dean only lives here when he feels like it, which isn't very often. And you are?"

"My name is Jason Danvers. I live here in Ednaville, and I went to high school with Jesse Dean, although he was a couple of years older than me."

"He failed a couple of grades. I think he was the world's oldest tenth grader at one time."

The sun had risen higher, and Jason felt its warmth against the side of his face and neck as it climbed above the trees. Mandy shifted her weight. She placed one bare foot on top of the other and yet managed to remain still, holding her balance that way without wavering.

"The police probably asked you about my sister, Hayden, or maybe even my niece, Sierra."

Recognition spread across Mandy's face. She lifted her chin. "Ah, so that's why you're here. You're looking for your sister too."

"I'm sorry to bother you," Jason said. "But it's very important."

"Isn't everything important to somebody?"

"Have you seen my sister? Hayden? She was friends with Jesse Dean in high school, and someone, a mutual friend, saw them together at Center Park last night. By any chance did he mention her to you?"

Mandy's lips pressed together. "Do you think Jesse Dean tells me about his women?"

"It's not like that," Jason said. He thought of Rose, and her claim that Jesse Dean was "her man." He decided not to mention her. "Hayden dated one of Jesse Dean's friends in high school. She married him eventually. Derrick Borders? Do you know him?"

"Ugh," Mandy said. "I've met him a time or two. Not impressed."

"So you don't know anything about Hayden? Or Sierra?"

Mandy looked down at Jason. "I'll tell you what I told the police. I hadn't heard from Jesse Dean for maybe six months. Not unusual for him or for me. We're not always together. About a week ago he called and said he was going to be back in town. He does this from time to time. I know what it means. He wants to stay here, and he wants me to stay out of his hair."

"Does he make you leave?"

"Sometimes."

"Did he this time?"

"No. He showed up. We spent some time together as husbands and wives often do, and then he was gone. I haven't seen him since."

Jason felt deflated. He wasn't sure what he expected to find out at Jesse Dean's house. As he stood there on the steps, he felt the fruitlessness of the whole endeavor fall down upon him. What did he think he could discover that the police couldn't?

Jason reached into his pocket and brought out a business card. He leaned forward and handed it to Mandy. "My cell phone number is on there. If Jesse Dean comes back, or if you hear anything from him, can you let me know? Or just tell him to call. I think he'll remember me."

"He remembers everybody. That's one thing Jesse Dean does

well." Mandy studied the business card, flicking her thumb against the edge. "You work at America's Best? What do you do there?"

"I work in their marketing and advertising department."

"Fancy. I'm not from Ednaville, but it seems like everybody and their brother works for America's Best."

"It's a company town. Or it used to be."

"Yeah. Nobody's hiring now." Mandy slipped the card into her sweatpants pocket, and she studied Jason, her face inquisitive. "You say you knew Jesse Dean in high school?"

"Yes."

"What do you remember about him?" she asked.

Jason wasn't sure what to say. He tried to fix his mind on a single memory but couldn't. He just remembered that Jesse Dean was "trouble," as his mom would say. That he had a police record and other kids lived in a combination of fear and awe of him.

"I didn't know him well. We weren't friends."

"One thing," Mandy said. "Come on. Give me one memory of Jesse Dean."

"I have to go."

"Humor me," she said. "Look at this yard, at this street. I'm here all day watching *The View* and *Dr. Phil*."

"You have kids?" Jason asked.

She shook her head. "I can't. Jesse Dean has one that he claims, and probably more." She shrugged, trying to look casual and failing. "And I lost my job. Anyway, tell me one crystal clear memory of Jesse Dean."

Jason leaned back against the railing. He looked out over the sameness of the houses, the declining fortunes of the neighborhood that had produced Jesse Dean. Jason pictured Jesse Dean on the periphery of high school life, always smirking, always cool. Always somehow far away and yet still close enough to brush against the teenagers Jason knew. One night came back to Jason, one night that encapsulated his feelings about Jesse Dean's predatory viciousness—

"We were at a party once," Jason said. "It must have been junior year of high school. I was with my friends, and there were a lot of kids hanging out. It was one of those parties where the parents went out of town, and basically the whole school got invited. Like something from a movie, you know?"

Mandy nodded. "I remember those days."

"Jesse Dean made an appearance. It was always a big deal when he showed up at some party. It was like a celebrity was there, you know?"

"Please."

"No, really. Everyone knew him. Everybody was afraid of him, but they also wanted him to say hi to them or acknowledge that they existed somehow. Anyway, I don't know how it started."

"A fight?"

"Not even that really. Later on, people speculated that this kid had bumped into Jesse Dean when they were both at the beer keg. Maybe he spilled something on Jesse's clothes. I don't know. I'm not even sure if the kid knew what he did. He was a senior, a guy named Brad Barnes. He had just poured a beer for himself and went back to the party, minding his own business. But Jesse Dean walked over to Brad and tapped him on the shoulder. When Brad turned around, Jesse Dean said something. Then he punched the kid twice. Once in the stomach and once in the face. Hard punches. Brutal. The kid went down on the floor, and everyone was just standing around and looking. Watching."

Jason looked over at Mandy. She wasn't smiling, and without any inflection in her voice, she said, "That's my man."

"I watched the whole thing happen," Jason said. "It scared

the shit out of me. Not because of the violence, although that freaked me out. It was the *humiliation* of it all. It was like Jesse Dean wanted everyone to see what he could do. He wanted to send a message to every kid in that room."

"And the message was?" Mandy asked.

"Don't mess with me. Don't you dare ever cross me."

Mandy looked serious. "Do you understand what I'm trying to tell you here?"

"I think so. You're telling me to stay out of Jesse Dean's way."

"That's right," she said. "Do you work with anyone like that in the advertising department at America's Best?"

"No," he said.

She nodded as if confirming an important point. She seemed to be genuinely concerned for Jason. "He's bad news, friend," she said. "He doesn't care about anybody or anything. Keep that in mind when you poke around and ask questions about him."

Chapter Fifteen

Thirty minutes later, Jason saw Sierra outside a downtown store. She wore a red sweatshirt as she walked among the thin morning crowd, her hair pulled back in a long ponytail. Jason's hands shook as he guided the car closer to the curb. He hit the brakes when a pedestrian crossed ahead of him, the man shooting Jason a dirty look, and then he accelerated again, approaching Sierra. He rolled the passenger window down and slowed.

"Sierra?"

She kept walking. He honked the horn. Once and then again, longer and louder.

"Sierra?"

She stopped and turned. He saw her face.

It wasn't her.

"I'm sorry," Jason said. "I thought . . ."

The girl's lip curled, and she twirled away, her long hair flying. A couple of people looked at Jason as they watched the scene play out. If he wasn't careful, he was going to be the one getting arrested.

Nora called a few minutes later, and Jason answered with too much hope in his voice. She shut it down right away.

"No news here," she said. "What about you?"

"Nothing."

"Anything from Jesse Dean's house?"

"I met his wife. She hasn't seen him."

Jason flashed back to that high school party, the swiftness of Jesse Dean's justice. Had Hayden or Sierra run into something like that?

"Are you coming home now?" Nora asked.

"Soon. I'm going to check one other place first."

"Had the police been to Jesse Dean's house?" Nora asked.

"Yes, they had. Just before me. That's good news, isn't it?"

Nora sighed. "Maybe. But if you didn't learn anything there, that means the police probably didn't either."

Thompson Bluff sat three miles north of town. More than a century earlier, one of Ednaville's leading citizens, a man by the name of Charles Thompson, donated over one hundred acres of land to the county to be used as a nature preserve and park for its citizens. Over the years, picnic areas were added, as well as trails and a Frisbee golf course. When Jason was a child, nearly every church in town held their annual picnic at Thompson Bluff, and several times a year his science teachers dragged an entire class of children through the park's many winding trails, pointing out plants and birds and snakes to a group of kids who were only too happy to not be sitting in a classroom for a few hours. The park closed at eleven o'clock, but that didn't stop high school kids from going there after hours. There were plenty of places to pull a car over for a window-steaming make-out and groping session, and the picnic shelters and trails made convenient hideaways for drinking and smoking. The police mostly left the kids alone. An unspoken agreement seemed to exist among law enforcement in Ednaville: As long as no one acted too crazy, the police left everyone alone.

Jason and Nora had driven past the park many times. It was nearly impossible to avoid for anyone driving north out of Ednaville. The entrance to the park sat off Highway 27, the main road that led to and from Ednaville. Nora had mentioned on more than one occasion that they should go there and hike or picnic, and Jason always tried to put her off.

"It's not as nice as it once was," he told her.

And he was right. State funding for maintenance of the park had been steadily cut. As unemployment rose statewide, more people found themselves with little to do during the day but drink and get high, and like the teenagers of the past, they found a welcoming place for it. Jason didn't get the impression the park had become dangerous, just unpleasant, full of a different class of person than him. Colton was right when he said that more and more people called it "Heroin Hill," a reference to the drug and other activities both real and suspected that took place. The police saw that as a reason to look for Hayden there, so Jason decided to look there as well.

Jason hadn't been inside the park since their return from New York. To be more accurate, he hadn't been inside the park since the night of his high school graduation, the night Logan walked away. If asked, he couldn't have said why he'd never gone back, but as he drove down the highway and the entrance to the park came into view, he understood that going there alone, even approaching the park alone, would be a very different experience from going there with Nora. Before he even slowed the car and turned in at the gate, he felt a stab of nostalgia in the center of his chest, the twinge that reminded him of how much the place mattered, how large a role it had played in his past.

He followed the winding park road slowly. Listening. Absorbing. In so many ways, it looked exactly the same. Every curve in the road seemed familiar, and he guided the car effortlessly, as if a map had been imprinted in his brain and would never fade. But the closer he looked, the more he saw the cracks. Garbage overflowed and spilled on the ground. Picnic shelters were decorated with graffiti. Broken bottles and crushed cans littered the walking paths and trails. And he saw the people. Men sat in the shelters wearing dirty T-shirts and grimy jeans. The laces of their shoes or boots were undone and they smoked, one hand cupped in the other, looking at the ground where their ashes fell as if searching for answers. The women he saw smoked as well, their pale skin spilling out of ill-fitting clothes. He spotted a lot of tattoos, a lot of overweight and underweight people. The cars were dented and rusted, the tires mismatched, the taillights trailing wires. Jason went around again, making sure he hadn't missed anything, but he knew that Sierra, and even Hayden in her cleaned-up condition, would stand out in that environment. But as he made the second loop, the light filtering through the trees and dappling the road, he suspected there was nothing to be found on Heroin Hill. Nothing that related to Sierra or Hayden anyway.

He made a detour during the second loop. Instead of continuing all the way around, he turned on the far side of the park and took a side road that led down to the start of the Frisbee golf course. A smaller picnic shelter stood there, one where the disc golfers met before starting their rounds. When Jason pulled in, the lot was empty, the shelter no less degraded than the others. He remained in the car, taking in the surroundings. The trees were still filling out with leaves. The grass was the bright green of spring. In another week, seniors would be graduating from the local high schools. Would any of them come up there to celebrate? Was it even possible to believe that it had been twenty-seven years since his own graduation, since the night he last set foot in the park?

Jason leaned back in his seat. He rolled the windows down and let the breeze come into the car. Even with the changes, it was peaceful at the Bluff. He stared at the trees and let himself believe nothing had changed—not the park, not his life, not his sister's life. He wanted to think he could get out of the car and walk into the woods and follow the path he took that night with Regan, and somehow he would end up at that moment in time again, the moment when the two of them came so close to acting on the flirtation that consumed the second half of their senior year.

On graduation night, Logan interrupted all their forward momentum. A group of kids from their class, maybe thirty or forty, had gone up to the Bluff to drink and party. Jason couldn't say how he knew, but he knew it would be the night for him and Regan to finally get together, to finally *act*. He sought Regan out, making sure to find her in the crowd of drinking high school graduates as soon as he arrived, and the two of them walked off alone to talk. Almost right away, Regan told Jason that she had spoken to Logan earlier that evening, right after the ceremony at the high school.

"Logan says he wants to be with me," Regan said. They sat together, their bodies close. In the distance they heard the shouts and cries of their friends. "He says he and I should be together, that we should run off together."

"Is he drunk?" Jason asked.

"Probably." Regan paused. And then she said, "When I told him that you and I might . . . we might be about to get together, he got really pissed. He said he wants to talk to you. He needs to talk to you." She paused again. "I think you should go find him. He's here, somewhere. Probably with the other kids, drinking more. The two of you are such good friends. I'd hate to think I caused something."

"You didn't *cause* anything," Jason said. "He caused it."

"Jason," Regan said. "Just . . ."

"Just what?"

"Just remember the two of you are friends."

"I'm not the one who has trouble remembering that."

Jason didn't say more, but he knew exactly why Logan was doing what he was doing. As Jason went in search of his friend—his best friend—the anger in his chest grew, a slow-spreading stain on the inside of his skin. Logan took—and possessed—the best of everything. Clothes, cars, toys, girls. And Jason deferred and deferred and deferred. The two of them settled into natural roles over the years. Logan the brash one, Jason the quiet one. Logan the jokester, Jason the audience. Even when the jokes were directed at him, when Logan's little comments and digs turned away from other people and toward him, Jason laughed.

He stood up to Logan on a few occasions. When Jason did push back against his best friend, he saw another side of Logan, one that mostly remained hidden. That was the angry Logan, the one whose comments grew more biting and personal. In those moments, Logan took digs at Jason's family, at their small house, their rusting car. When Logan said those things, his eyes glazed a little and some of the light disappeared from them like the sun dipping quickly behind a cloud. And Jason always bent. He backed away and let Logan win.

That night, he was tired of it.

The fight, like most fights not in movies or on TV shows, didn't last long. It wasn't graceful or choreographed. The red tint in Logan's eyes told Jason that his friend had been drinking. A lot. But Logan struck with words first rather than fists. He told Jason that he could give Regan a better life because he had more money, and that Jason was doomed to a life of struggle because of his desire to major in art at college. Jason threw the first punch at that point. Jason had never been in a fight, not with Logan and not with anyone else. He'd never hit anyone. He swung wildly, adrenaline and emotion fueling his efforts. Logan swung back, screaming with every punch. Most missed their target, and the few that landed did little damage.

Until the last one Jason threw. His fist connected with the side of Logan's head, just above his left ear. Logan crumpled to the ground. He lifted his hands to his head, both protecting himself from further blows and trying to bring relief to the injury he had suffered. Jason saw that Logan was crying. It took a moment, and then Jason realized he was crying as well. The thought popped into his head as he stood there in the woods: *When was the last time you cried like this?*

He bent down to help Logan. But his friend sprang to his feet. "Don't touch me," he said.

"Logan."

"I'm gone," he said. "I'm done. I'm done with you. I'm done with all of it."

Jason never saw him again.

But Logan saw Regan after he left Jason. Logan found her

among the partyers and repeated his request—*demand?*—that she run off with him. He said he was leaving Ednaville and Ohio and everything he knew behind. Regan told Jason about this the next day, after people started to realize Logan was gone—and before the police came and started speaking with Jason about the events of that night.

The chime of his cell phone broke his reverie. It was Nora.

"Hey."

"Jason, the police are here at the house." She sounded breathless, frantic.

"Did they find them?"

"I think you need to get back here. Where are you?"

"I'm on my way."

He took one more quick look at the scenery before starting the car.

Chapter Sixteen

Jason parked behind the police cruiser in their driveway. When he reached the porch, Nora waited, holding the door open for him.

"What is it?" Jason asked as he went inside. Nora didn't answer. Jason turned right and entered the living room. He saw two men—one was middle-aged and wore a suit. The other was a young officer in a crisply pressed navy blue Ednaville police department uniform.

The man in the suit held out his hand to Jason and introduced himself as Detective Olsen. He wanted to ask Jason questions about their car.

"What's going on?" Jason asked. He looked back at Nora. "What happened to Sierra?"

"There's been an accident," she said.

"Is it Sierra?" Jason asked, turning back to the detective. He couldn't resist asking. He needed to know if Sierra was okay.

"Mr. Danvers, would your niece have any reason to be in Redman County?" Olsen asked.

"She lives there now. With her mother."

"I told them all of this," Nora said.

The detective, Olsen, was trim and of average height. He looked to be Jason's age as well, and he wore his hair closely cropped to his head. He used his index finger to push his rimless glasses back up his nose. The light blue tie that accented his tan suit and white shirt hung slightly askew. He was a far cry from the older, rumpled, and tired-looking man who questioned Jason after Logan couldn't be found. "But she's staying with you now? Temporarily? I learned that from Officer Van Poppel, who was here this morning."

"Yes, she's staying with us while her mother takes care of some personal matters. Can you just tell me what happened to Sierra?"

Olsen hesitated, moving his eyes back and forth from Jason to Nora. Then he said, "Your vehicle was involved in an accident a couple of hours ago. On Highway Thirty-eight. It clipped another car and kept going."

"Did someone get the license number?" Jason asked.

"The driver of the car that was hit."

"Did they see who was driving our car? Was it Sierra?"

"We don't know," Olsen said. "But she would have reason to go back to Redman County, right? She's looking for . . . ?"

"She's looking for her mother. My sister. Did you go and look at their house in Redman County? Maybe she went there."

"Of course," Olsen said. "There was no one home at the residence." He brought out a phone and tapped it a couple of times. "Four Eighteen Sweetgum Lane. Is that your sister's address?"

"I don't know her address. I hadn't seen her in five years."

Olsen looked up from the phone when that piece of news was delivered, his eyebrows lifting just a little. He said, "We did find some irregularities at the house."

"What irregularities?" Nora asked.

"One of the back windows was broken," Olsen said, reporting the news casually. "It appears as though someone broke the window with a rock and gained entry to the house." Olsen cocked his head, as though trying to anticipate Jason's reaction to his next statement. "We also found some bloodstains on the floor of the home. I'm guessing whoever broke the window cut themselves as they went inside the house, but we're not sure. It's possible we're dealing with a more serious injury. Or else something that resulted from a struggle."

Jason felt weak. He shifted over and let his body weight take him down into an overstuffed chair. He rubbed at his temple, then looked up at Nora, who wore a stricken look.

"Wouldn't Sierra have a key?" she asked.

"I don't want to assume anything at this point," Olsen said.

"And Hayden would have a key for sure," Jason said.

"I was just wondering if anything else has occurred to you since this morning," Olsen said. "I know I wasn't here when the report on your niece running off was initially filed, but maybe you've had time to think about some things. Where else she might go? Who she might be with?"

"Jesse Dean Pratt," he said. "That's all I know. Hayden was with him last night. She used to be friends with him. Find him and maybe you'll learn something."

"We're familiar with Mr. Pratt," Olsen said.

"And Sierra's friend," Jason said. "Patricia."

"We're trying to contact them as we speak. We're looking for both your sister and your niece, although since your niece is a minor, it's a more pressing matter." He turned to the officer who was with him. "Did you all look through the girl's room this morning?"

"I wasn't here," he said.

Olsen turned back to Jason and Nora. Before he could ask, Nora said, "Yes, help yourself. Look at whatever you need to look at."

"It won't take long," Olsen said.

"It's at the top of the stairs on the right," Nora said.

When the sound of them clomping up the stairs stopped,

Nora came over and sat in the chair next to Jason's. "Did you find anything out today?" she asked. "Anything?"

"No. Jesse Dean showed up about a week ago and then left again. His wife lives in the house. The police had already talked to her. I drove through the park. Thompson Bluff. Nothing there but broken beer bottles and shattered dreams."

Nora looked up at the ceiling. "I thought about going through her stuff, but it felt like a violation."

"But you're willing to let the police do it?"

"I've been sitting here all morning, waiting for news. At this point, I'm willing to allow just about anything."

They waited more long minutes. Finally Olsen called to them from the top of the stairs. "Mr. and Mrs. Danvers? Can you come up here for a moment?"

Jason and Nora stood and hustled up the stairs. Jason went first, and when he reached the top and turned into the guest room, he found Detective Olsen standing next to an open dresser drawer. The uniformed cop stood next to him, his thumbs hooked in his belt.

Jason came over and looked inside. Sierra's clothes had been moved aside. Beneath them, he saw a plastic sandwich bag containing what appeared to be a greenish brown clump. Even though it had been years since Jason had seen it, he knew it was pot.

"I'm assuming this doesn't belong to you?" Olsen asked.

"Would it help Sierra if I said it did?" Jason asked. He couldn't lie. He figured getting the truth out was the best thing for Sierra and Hayden. "It's not ours," he said. "I don't know where it came from."

Jason and Nora waited downstairs in the kitchen while the two officers finished looking through Sierra's room. Olsen told them that the drugs gave them the right to search the entire house, to turn the whole place upside down, but he wasn't going to do that since the pot appeared to belong to either Sierra or Hayden.

While they sat and waited, Nora and Jason said very little to each other. To Jason, the drugs felt like a violation. When he factored in the "borrowed" and apparently damaged car, it felt like he'd entered an absurd time warp, one in which he watched his niece transform into his troublemaking sister. He tried to wrap his mind around it all. The pieces didn't fit. How could Sierra be so levelheaded *and* involved with drugs? He understood taking the car. She wanted to find Hayden. But drugs? Unless—

"They probably don't belong to her," Nora said.

"Would I feel better if I knew they belonged to Hayden?" Jason ran his hands through his hair. "And someone broke into their house? The drugs are making it harder for me to be sympathetic."

Nora leaned in closer. "Was Hayden ever involved in anything like that? Those kinds of drugs?"

"She did a little bit of everything in high school. But alcohol was her drug of choice. She looked so cleaned up. . . ."

"There has to be an explanation," Nora said.

"I agree. And one of those two lunatics needs to come home and give it to us."

Nora reached out and squeezed his hand. "Think positive."

"I'm trying. Thanks."

The police finally came back downstairs. The uniformed officer carried the evidence out to the car in a plastic bag while Olsen stayed inside.

"We're considering everything right now," he said. "We have to make sure they're safe, that nothing happened *to* them. But if they aren't in danger, if they aren't up to something else, this isn't too deep for your niece or your sister yet," Olsen said. "But it could be headed that way."

David Bell

"We want to find them as much as you do," Jason said. "I suspect we want to find them even more than you do."

"Is there anything else you can think to tell us before we go?"

Jason paused, then said, "I went to Jesse Dean Pratt's house today, looking for . . . I don't know what I was looking for. I guess I was just hoping. I talked to his wife. I just wanted to tell you that. I figure you don't want a civilian mucking around in what you do."

"We don't. Do me a favor? Just stick close to home. You can do a lot more good here, for your sister and your niece. You know them, and they know you."

Jason lifted his head toward the ceiling. "Based on what you found upstairs, maybe I know a lot less than I thought."

Chapter Seventeen

Nora had gone up to the bedroom to try to read, and Jason sat in the living room staring at a Reds game on the TV. The players threw and hit the ball. They ran around. But the actions meant nothing to him in his distracted state of mind. If someone asked him the score, he couldn't have answered, even though it was in a box on the top of the screen. He didn't even notice who the Reds were playing. He thought of the police and the discovery in the drawer. The accident. The broken window in Redman County. Hayden gone. Sierra gone. Were they involved in something together? Why did Hayden really have to bring Sierra to the house? Were they both in the same trouble? And now was the trouble coming down on them?

When Regan called, he jumped again and scrambled to pick up his cell phone. Jason wanted it to be Sierra or Hayden on the line, someone bearing real news, but short of that, he was glad to talk to someone sympathetic.

"I'm just calling to see how you're doing," Regan said. "If anything new has happened."

Regan never called him at home, and Jason suspected Nora hadn't heard the phone ring. If she had, she would have come down the stairs to find out if there was news about Sierra. The

TV was playing loud enough and Nora was far enough away that the sound was masked.

"There's nothing new really," he said, his voice low. "We're just waiting."

"Is this okay? Can you talk now?"

"Sure. For a few minutes."

Then it seemed like Regan didn't know what to say. Jason assumed she wanted to talk, but she didn't, so he waited. On the screen, the manager from the opposing team argued a call. He screamed and pointed at an umpire who absorbed the barrage with a stoic resolve.

"I know I've been a little obstinate when you've tried to talk to me about Logan and the past."

"I noticed that."

"It's not that I don't care, or that I don't want to remember the past," Regan said. "I do. I care, and I want to remember most things." She paused, and it sounded as though she had taken a drink of something. Wine? "It's strange to live in Ednaville all this time. I don't really feel much nostalgia for the past. It's all around me, every day, so I guess I don't notice it as much. I feel it sometimes, like if I drive past the school or see someone we grew up with. But most of the time, it isn't really alive in a meaningful way. Does that make sense?"

"I think so."

"But when you and I reconnected and started talking a lot and seeing each other . . . I don't know. The past really did come alive, and I felt intense nostalgia as well as some loss to be quite honest."

"Loss?"

"Just the realization that a lot of water has gone under the bridge. You know?"

"I know."

"I think about everything that's happened since high school. College and then I got married and I had kids and, shit, I got divorced. I did all of those things. Jason, my kids are teenagers. Angela starts high school next year. That's crazy to have a child that old."

Jason's mind went to Sierra. He knew . . . kind of. At least for the last two days, he knew. And what did people say? To be a parent was to worry?

"I'm sorry," Regan said. "I bet you're thinking of Sierra."

"I went by the Bluff today," Jason said. "That's the first time I've been there since that night."

"Why did you go there?"

"Looking for Sierra. Or Hayden. Since Hayden's had some substance abuse problems in the past, and, you know, that place is so messed up—"

"It is."

"It was strange being there," Jason said. "I understand what you're saying. I felt the nostalgia too. Maybe I felt it even more because the place looked so different. I couldn't help but realize how much time had passed. I thought of Logan and that night."

"I want to apologize for something," Regan said.

"What?"

"The other day I said you hero-worshipped Logan, that you looked up to him too much. I realize that was a little bit of a cheap shot. You balanced him as well. That's a more accurate way to put it."

"No, you're right. I was always the runner-up to him. I followed along in his wake. He got everything he wanted."

"Not everything," Regan said quickly and with an edge to her voice.

"I said some awful things to him that night when we fought. I called him out for being spoiled, for thinking that all the best things should flow to him automatically. I told him he needed to let someone else have a turn in the sun."

"And what did he say to you?"

"He insulted my family. And me. My future as an artist."

"He always had a cutting tongue."

"Maybe he was smarter than I gave him credit for, at least about my career."

"Stop that."

"He told me I'd never understand the way the world works because I hadn't grown up with money. He said I just didn't get it."

"He was full of it."

"He was. But . . . I'm sure you saw through it sometimes. He was insecure. He was scared. He lived in his dad's shadow."

Jason remembered Logan's sixteenth birthday party, which was held at the country club. Logan's father had come late, and then after about thirty minutes was called to the phone. When he came back to the table, Mr. Shaw announced that he needed to head back to the office in order to deal with some crisis. Jason watched Logan's face. He shook his dad's hand and said good-bye as though it was no big deal, but Jason knew his dad's departure hurt him. When Jason asked Logan about it later, Logan just shrugged and said, "That's how the old man keeps the clothes on my back."

"I was angry with him graduation night," Jason said to Regan, "but I felt sorry for him a lot of times as well. He could seem so lost. His mother wasn't around because of the divorce. . . . That house must have been awfully lonely."

"I don't think you have anything to feel bad about," Regan

said. Her voice sounded tired. "He started the fight. He was a big boy."

"But that was the last conversation we had. Ever."

"Jason?"

Jason tensed a little. *Nora*. He put the phone down.

"What?" he said.

"Are you talking to someone?" Nora was calling from the top of the steps. "Is someone here?"

"Just a minute," he said into the phone.

"Is it news?" Nora asked.

"I'll be right there." Jason picked up the phone again and whispered, "I have to go. It's late."

"Is it Nora?" Regan asked.

"Yes."

"You're allowed to talk to an old friend," Regan said.

"I'll let you know if I hear anything else."

Jason ended the call, but he didn't head upstairs right away. He stared at the TV a few minutes longer, remembering the times he watched Reds games with his own father. He wouldn't have traded parents with Logan, not ever. But he certainly knew there were times when he would have gladly traded lives with him. House for house, bank account for bank account. Logan's life could look so enticing to anyone on the outside, but something that night twenty-seven years ago made him willing to throw it all away.

Jason turned the TV off and went upstairs. The bedroom was dark. Nora had already turned the lights out, and in the pale glow that leaked in from the street, he could see her shape beneath the covers. The ceiling fan overhead made a soft whirring noise, stirring the air. The windows were open and a light breeze moved the gauzy curtains. Jason didn't undress or get ready for bed. He sat in a chair across the room.

"Who was on the phone?" Nora asked.

"It was Regan. We talked about the past a little."

"The past? What about the past?"

"You don't mind that she called me?" Jason asked.

"Should I?"

"I don't think so," he said. "She's a friend. I'm just trying to be open about everything, the way the marriage counselor taught me."

"Me too. But you don't have to roll your eyes every time the marriage counselor comes up. It helped us."

"I know."

"I'm not arguing with you about Regan," Nora said.

"Thanks. Do you remember my friend Logan? The guy who left town on the night of graduation?"

The covers rustled. As his eyes adjusted to the dark, Jason could see Nora moving, turning over and sitting up with a pillow placed behind her back. "Of course I remember," she said. "Your best friend. What about him?"

"Colton's looking for him."

"Why?"

Jason explained about the will and Logan's dying father. He said, "Because we fought that night and had words, I've always felt a little responsible for him going away so suddenly."

"I remember. And I've told you that's you being unfair to yourself. You didn't make anyone go away. You didn't make Hayden or Sierra go away either."

"Just hear me out," he said. "I think all the time about the people who've gone away. My parents are gone. Your dad died last year."

He hesitated. He didn't know exactly where he was going with his thoughts.

"What?" Nora said, after a long pause.

"I guess I think that if all of them were here again, the ones who *can* be here. Logan, Hayden, Sierra. If they were all here, then . . . somehow things would feel complete in a way they haven't for a while. You and I are doing well, but there are so many other parts of my life that feel incomplete. My family. Friends."

"That's sweet, Jason," Nora said.

"Sweet but crazy?" Jason asked. "Naive?"

"Impossible maybe." Across the dark room he saw her yawn. "It's late and we've had a long day. Why don't you come to bed and sleep?"

Chapter Eighteen

The ringing phone brought Jason out of a deep sleep. He dreamed of a broken window, the glass shattered on the ground, blood smeared around the pane. He didn't reach for the phone, didn't realize what it was until Nora nudged him in the side.

"Can you get that?" she asked.

Then he came back to himself. He remembered everything. Hayden. Sierra. The missing car. The drugs. He picked the phone up and answered without looking at the caller ID.

"Hello?"

There was the briefest pause, the sound of breathing. And then a voice. "Uncle Jason?"

Jason snapped fully awake. The windows were still open, the room cool.

"Sierra?"

"I need you to come help me," she said. Her voice sounded breathy, frantic. Was she being hurt? Chased?

"Where are you? I'll come right away."

"I'm at that park . . . the one outside of town. Heroin Hill."

"I'm coming."

"Hurry," she said. "It's Mom."

"Hayden?"

"Her—" The phone faded, then came back. "—get here."

"I'm coming. I'm coming right now."

Jason bounded out of bed, grabbing clothes.

"Is she okay?" Nora asked.

"I don't know."

"I'm coming with you this time," she said. "You don't have a choice."

Jason didn't argue. He didn't want to. "I know. Let's get out of here."

It was ten after five when they turned into the park. The night was dark, the headlights providing the only illumination on the winding road. Nora called Sierra back while Jason drove.

"Where are you?" Nora asked. "We're here." She listened. "Walnut Grove shelter?" Nora said.

Jason nodded. He knew it was to the left, about halfway around the looping drive that circled the park. He went that way, driving as fast as he could and still feel safe. The woods were full of deer. They had a tendency to jump in front of vehicles. The past fall a man on a motorcycle was killed when he collided with one. But Jason couldn't help himself. He felt his foot getting heavier against the gas pedal, felt the car speeding up. Sierra was so close. She was right there.

And Hayden too? What did she try to say about her mom?

Had Jason been right there on top of both of them in the park earlier that day and missed them? He vowed not to miss again.

It took a few minutes for the shelter to come into sight. They hadn't seen any other cars, no other people in the predawn eerie quiet. The headlights caught the eyes of an animal along the tree line to the left. The orbs glowed red, but the animal—a rabbit?—turned and ran as the car came along.

Then he saw the two vehicles. At the picnic shelter parking lot, the headlights showed him their car, a black Honda Accord. The one Sierra took. As they approached, he saw the two-foot-long gash along the side as though it had scraped against something big. As the illumination of their headlights approached, the driver's-side door opened. Sierra stepped out. She looked thin and young and scared. The headlights made her appear ghostly, ethereal. Jason didn't recognize the car parked next to theirs, but he had a guess.

"There she is," Nora said.

Jason stopped behind the two cars. He didn't bother pulling into a spot. He jumped out, and Nora did the same.

"Are you okay?" Jason asked.

Sierra looked cold, even though the night wasn't. She wore a T-shirt and jeans. Her red Chuck Taylor sneakers provided the only color in the darkness. She just nodded in response to Jason's question, looking very much like a little child.

Nora came around and hugged Sierra. The girl didn't return the hug, but she didn't resist either. She let Nora fold her up in her arms. While Nora held her, she managed to take her own sweatshirt off and maneuver it over Sierra's shoulders, a series of gestures that struck Jason as particularly maternal.

"You said something about your mom when you called," Jason said. "Is this her car?"

Sierra nodded again.

It was a Toyota Corolla, about ten or twelve years old. It had dents in the front and the back, and the left rear tire, the one closest to Jason, looked underinflated. He couldn't have expected Hayden to drive a car nicer than that one. Not yet anyway.

"Is she here?" he asked. "Did you see her?"

Sierra shook her head. "Just the car. I came by here tonight, just about an hour ago, and I saw the car. It wasn't here before. I've been through the park about five times in the last day looking for her, and she wasn't here. And the car wasn't here either. But tonight it showed up."

"Why did you come back tonight?" Jason asked.

"I don't know. I've been driving around. I thought maybe if I came here at night, I'd have better luck. I've heard about this place, about the drugs and all of that. I thought if she were drinking or just hanging out with bad people, she might come here. I was desperate."

"You came here an hour ago?" Jason asked. "What took so long to call?"

"I looked around a little. I went down one of the trails."

"You shouldn't do that here," Nora said. "You don't know who could be in this place."

"I wanted to look. I didn't go far, and I couldn't see anything. I called her name. I thought if she was here and she heard my voice . . . but there was nothing. No response. I didn't see anybody. A couple of cars went by, but they didn't stop."

"Did you look in the car?" Jason asked.

Sierra had straightened up from the hug Nora gave her, but the two women still stood next to each other. Nora kept her arm over Sierra's shoulder, holding her tight, providing warmth and comfort.

Sierra shook her head. "The door's locked. All of them are locked." She paused. "Mom never locks the car. She always says that if someone wants to steal something, they can have it. It's an old car. It doesn't even have a decent stereo."

Jason's eyes wandered to the trunk. It was closed tight. He

thought of Hayden and her mysterious mission. Being seen with Jesse Dean. He turned and went to the passenger side of his car, opened the door, and reached in. He brought out a small flashlight, one he carried for emergencies and had never used. The few times in his life he had ever broken down, he had called someone for help. His dad. A friend. Later, he relied on Triple A.

As he approached Hayden's car again, he asked, "Did you see anything inside?"

"Too dark," Sierra said.

Nora must have been thinking along the same lines as Jason because she gave Sierra a gentle squeeze and said, "Why don't we sit in the car, honey? Where it's warmer?"

"No," Sierra said. "I want to see what's in the car."

Jason took the flashlight to the passenger side of Hayden's car, the side farthest away from Sierra and Nora. He really didn't want to shine the light inside. He worried about what might be in there. He hesitated. The night birds called in the trees, and up above, a bank of clouds slid past the half-moon. He turned the flashlight on and pressed it against the passenger's side window.

The car was messy. Jason expected that. He knew how Hayden kept a car in high school, and this one looked no different. Paper wrappers littered the floor on the passenger side. He flicked the light up and saw the keys dangling from the ignition.

"The keys are still in here," he said. "How is it locked?"

"They're not power locks," Sierra said. "You just push the button down and lift the handle. Mom couldn't afford anything else."

Jason continued to move the beam around. He saw nothing unusual, nothing besides the keys in the ignition. Someone didn't care if the car was found, or else had left in a hurry. He shifted the beam to the backseat, and as he did his anxiety increased. But again he saw nothing. More junk. More papers and empty cups

143

He wasn't even sure what he was looking for or what he thought he might find. Did he expect to see a note that said, "Here's where Hayden is and this is what she's involved in"?

Jason straightened up and turned to the trunk. He played the light across the metal surface. He saw a splatter of bird crap, a couple of scrapes and dings. But nothing else. He passed the beam along the ground around the car. Still nothing.

"Do you see anything?" Nora asked.

"No."

"I almost picked up a rock and smashed the window," Sierra said.

"Why?" Jason asked.

"I could get to the keys and see what's in the trunk."

"I think we should call the police," Jason said. "Let them handle all of this however they want."

"But what if . . . ?" Sierra said.

"What?"

"What if she's . . . in there. And she needs our help. Now."

"There's probably nothing in there," Nora said.

Jason leaned over and made a fist. He lightly rapped on the trunk lid, creating a metallic thump. He waited a few seconds and tried again.

"She could be hurt," Sierra said.

"I'm going to call," Nora said. She had already taken her phone out. "She's probably not here, but the police can arrive quickly. If they need to, they can get into the car."

While Nora dialed and spoke to a dispatcher, Jason moved back to the side windows of the car. He shone the light inside again, looking for anything he might have missed the first time. He heard Nora giving their location as well as the name of Detective Olsen.

She finally said to both of them, "They're on their way. Olsen's coming even though it's Saturday. Let's just sit tight."

Jason's light picked up a smear near the bottom of the back of the front passenger seat. He hadn't seen it before. It was small, only about the size of a half-dollar, and as he held the light on it, he almost convinced himself it was chocolate or shoe polish. Anything but what he feared it was. He wasn't going to say anything, but Sierra said, "What do you see?"

He didn't answer. He snapped the light off and stood up.

Sierra came around to his side of the car, her shoes scraping across the pavement. "Tell me," she said. "I'm not a kid. Just tell me."

"It's probably nothing."

"Show me."

She reached for the flashlight, and Jason pulled it away. He wanted to tell her she may not always act like a kid, but she still was. He wished she didn't have to know these things, even if it was she who took their car without permission.

She didn't need to know everything, did she?

But he knew the answer. Sierra did need to know. She'd find out in a few minutes when the police arrived.

He flicked the light back on and guided the beam to the spot on the upholstery.

"What is it?" Nora asked.

"I'm not sure," Jason said.

"Oh, bullshit," Sierra said. "Fuck. It's blood. It's my mother's fucking blood."

Chapter Nineteen

Detective Olsen and a crime scene technician arrived. They walked around Hayden's car, using flashlights, while a couple of uniformed officers took statements from Jason and his family. Olsen and the technician paid as much attention to the ground around the car as they did the trunk. Then the technician went into his unmarked vehicle and brought out a Slim Jim, which he took over to the driver's-side door of Hayden's car. He popped the lock and opened the door, reaching in for the trunk release latch.

"Jesus, they're going to open it," Sierra said.

"Do you want to go home?" Jason asked.

"No," Sierra said, her voice firm.

Jason felt relieved in a way. He wanted to stay as well. He wished he had picked up a rock and smashed the window. What if they'd waited too long? What if Hayden had suffocated in those moments while they called the police?

Nora tried to get Sierra to sit in the back of the car with her, to get out of the night air, as she put it, but Sierra refused. She kept her eyes glued to Hayden's car, her focus singular and intense.

The trunk opened, and Olsen leaned over, shining his flashlight inside.

"I'm going," Sierra said.

"No," Jason said. "Wait here."

"I'm not a baby," Sierra said. "That's my mother there."

But Nora continued to gently hold on to Sierra, and Jason placed his arm out in front of her, although she didn't make any real attempt to break away from them. She wanted to know, but she didn't want to see. Jason felt the same way. It was no real struggle for him to stay back.

Even though morning had almost fully broken, the police officers—including Olsen and the crime scene technician—had their flashlights out and were sweeping them around the inside of the trunk of Hayden's car. Olsen had pulled on rubber surgical gloves—they all wore them at that point—and occasionally he pointed to something inside the trunk that only the officers could see. But none of them reached in, and none of them touched anything.

As he watched, Jason felt hope creeping back into his body. Would they be so calm, so casual, if they were staring at the dead body of his sister? Then again, they were police officers, professionals who were trained to handle those kinds of moments. Maybe they simply treated the discovery of a dead body in the trunk of a car that way. Coldly detached, clinical. The same as dusting a door handle for a fingerprint.

Olsen straightened up and looked over at them. He pulled the surgical gloves off his hands and dropped them to the pavement. He said something to his colleagues, and received nods in response. Then he started back over toward Jason.

The day wasn't yet warm. The sun hadn't come anywhere close to rising all the way into the sky and burning off the night air. Despite that, Jason felt hot. His clothes felt confining and heavy, as though he were wearing a winter coat instead of a T-shirt and loose-fitting jeans.

"This is bad," Sierra said. "Look at the look on his face."

"He always looks like that," Nora said. "He's a cop. They try to be neutral and stoic."

Olsen reached them and said, "I was wondering if any of you would be able to identify personal items belonging to Hayden. There are some in the trunk."

"Is *she* in there?" Jason asked. "Is there a body?"

"Excuse me?" Olsen said. Then he seemed to understand. "No, there's no body in the trunk. But there are personal items. We want to see if they belong to Hayden, or if they indicate that someone else left things in the car. Would one of you be able to identify these items?"

A watery looseness passed through Jason's body. His joints slackened, and he felt his shoulders sag with relief. *Hayden wasn't in there. There was no body.* He flexed his hands, realizing how tense his body had been while they waited. Helpless.

Detective Olsen looked at Sierra, and Jason thought it might be too much for her. He spoke up and said, "I can do it."

"Will you really recognize her things?" Olsen asked. "You hadn't seen her in five years."

"I can do it," Sierra said. She looked at Nora and Jason. "Really. I know everything she owns."

"Are you sure?" Nora asked.

"I'm not identifying a body," Sierra said. She turned to Olsen. "Right? You're sure there's no body?"

"I'm sure," Olsen said.

"Let's go, then," Sierra said, stepping forward.

"Do you want me to go with you?" Nora asked.

"I'm fine," Sierra said. She didn't say anything else. She went with Olsen, and Jason heard him starting to give her instructions.

"You can't touch or remove anything. Nothing at all . . ."

Then they were out of earshot.

Jason and Nora stood next to each other, alone. Nora's hands kept moving. They worked against each other, rubbing and kneading. She didn't look at Jason. She kept her eyes forward on the activity around Hayden's car.

"Are you relieved?" Nora asked.

Jason thought he knew what she meant. "Yes."

Nora looked over at him. "I could tell by the look on your face you thought Hayden was going to be in that trunk. To be honest, I did too. I was standing there thinking I didn't know what we were going to do for Sierra if her mother was dead. I couldn't even imagine it."

"We're not out of the woods yet. We don't know where she is. And there's the blood in the car."

"I'm trying not to think about that," Nora said. "I'm just going to keep focusing on supporting Sierra and helping her."

"Makes sense," Jason said. "I'm not sure there's much else we can do."

Sierra stood with the police. She looked young and small next to them. Olsen pointed into the trunk, just as he had before, and Sierra nodded her head slowly, almost fearfully. Olsen pointed at a couple of other things, and every time, Sierra nodded in the same way. After a few minutes, Olsen pointed to one more thing, and Sierra shook her head back and forth. Olsen seemed to ask her if she was certain and she nodded her head again. Then they straightened up from the trunk, and Olsen stood facing Sierra. He seemed to be instructing her about something else. He talked, and she listened. Finally, he pointed toward Jason and Nora, and Sierra walked back over.

Chapter Twenty

"They want us to wait a little longer," Sierra said. "They have more questions."

"Are you okay?" Jason asked.

"Yes." She shivered a little. "I just want to go."

"What was in there?" Jason asked. "What did they show you?"

It took Sierra close to a minute to answer. She said, "Her shoes were in there. The shoes she was wearing when she dropped me off at your house. I think it's the only pair she brought with her."

She paused, and Jason asked, "Is that all?"

"Some clothes. They were hers. I think she brought them to change into while she was here or doing whatever she planned on doing. That seemed normal, I guess."

"Was that it?"

"That's all that belonged to her."

"You shook your head about something at the end," Jason said. "What was that?"

Sierra shivered again, but her voice sounded matter-of-fact. "There was a pair of gloves in there I'd never seen before. Black leather. And there were a couple more spots of blood."

No one said anything. Nora reached out and took Sierra's hand, but the girl barely registered the gesture.

Finally, Sierra said, "I'm sorry about taking it. I know I messed up."

"Taking what?" Jason asked.

"The car. I know I shouldn't have."

She and Nora leaned in closer to each other, huddling for warmth and comfort. Jason stepped forward and placed his hand on Sierra's shoulder. "It's fine," he said. "It's just a car."

When Jason was young, he found it easy to imagine that Hayden would die at an early age. She was simply too wild, too reckless, too much inclined to find trouble. In those days, he could imagine Hayden meeting her end in a car accident or from alcohol poisoning. She might drown or injure herself in some other way while intoxicated. Or she might try a new or exotic drug, something someone handed to her at a party, and overdose. But he never imagined her being murdered or injured by someone else's hand, even though she ran with a rough crowd. Hayden knew how to take care of herself. She was nobody's fool—and she knew how to read and manage people.

Jason understood that Sierra lived under that same cloud. When she cried after Colton came to the house, Jason knew exactly what the girl was feeling. It was a horrible thing for a teenager to have to live with—the looming threat of the end of someone she dearly loved. Jason had spent his teenage years with the same fears.

Jason laughed a little, and Nora looked at him.

"What's funny?" she asked.

"I said, 'It's just a car.' My dad said that once when Hayden scraped up one of our cars. He could be so calm in a crisis sometimes. 'It's just a car.'"

"I wanted to find Mom."

"We know," Nora said.

Sierra chewed on her fingernail. She seemed to be finished

with talking, but then she said, "It just felt like no one was interested in finding her. You wanted to keep waiting."

"We were just doing what your mom wanted us to do. She said give her forty-eight hours, and we were," Jason said. "There are no right or wrong answers in a situation like this. I guess we've never been in a situation quite like this."

"I wanted to find her so you could know she wasn't the same as she used to be," Sierra said.

"I understand why you did it," Jason said. "Believe me, I want her back, and I want to know that she isn't the same as she used to be. I think we all want that."

"And I guess I wanted you to know I wasn't just like her. I didn't just take the car for the hell of it. I'm not like her, but I love her."

"Of course. That makes sense."

"She said you wouldn't trust her. Or me, I guess. It didn't seem fair."

"We have things to talk about," Jason said. "The police went into your room. They found some weed."

"You let them go into my room?" Sierra asked.

"You don't have much choice when the police want to search something," Jason said. "Besides, we wanted to know where you were. We thought if they looked through your things, it might help us find you."

"That's true, honey," Nora said. "We didn't want to invade your privacy, but Jason thought—"

"I didn't *think* anything," he said. "It was the police."

"So I know what this is about, right?" Sierra said. "I guess it wouldn't do any good for me to say those drugs belonged to someone else. I know that's what every kid in the universe says when they get caught with something like that. They say, 'They belong to someone else.' But they do. I'm not involved with that stuff."

"Do they belong to your mom?" Jason asked.

"See?" Sierra said, although she seemed to be speaking to no one in particular. "You can't—won't—change your mind about Mom."

"You scared us, Sierra," Nora said. "That's all. We don't care about the car . . . or anything else. But we were worried about you. That's why Jason is asking about these things, even though it's probably better left for another time."

"It's a good thing you two didn't have kids," Sierra said. "You'd drive them nuts."

"Hey," Jason said. "You don't have to talk to us like that."

"Excuse me?" another voice said.

Jason stopped and turned. It was Detective Olsen. He approached them in the growing light. He either didn't notice the family squabble or chose to ignore it.

"I understand you've had a long night," he said. "Will you be home later?"

"Sure," Jason said.

"There's no reason for you to stay here now," he said. "I can come by and find you at the house later today. We're going to be working here for a while. We're processing the scene carefully. That's lab work, fingerprints and the blood. It could take a couple of days if they're backed up." He looked at Sierra again. "Did you go to your house recently? The house in Redman County you live in with your mom?"

"I did. Of course. I was looking for Mom. I thought she might be there."

"Did you break in?" Olsen asked.

"Break in? I have a key. Did someone break in?"

"They did. They smashed a window. Was it like that when you went there? I'm talking about the little window next to the back door."

"No," Sierra said. "I would have noticed that."

"When were you there last?"

"Yesterday. I was there for a couple of hours. I took a nap in my bed."

Olsen nodded. "I think you should go home. Wait for news there."

"What else is there to do here?" Jason asked.

Olsen pointed to the trees that surrounded them. "We have some searching to do," he said. "We'll probably have to call in some help from the county, maybe even the state. It's a Saturday, so it might be a little harder to round up the troops. But now that the sun's coming up, we intend to search through these woods for any other evidence we can find."

"Do you mean you're looking for Hayden?" Jason asked.

"We're trying to find out what happened to her," Olsen said. "If anything."

"But the blood," Jason said. "Doesn't that say something happened to her?"

"If it's hers," Olsen said. "We'll be checking on that as well. We're certainly worried about your sister's safety, given the blood. Maybe if we look around here a little more, we'll have a better grasp on things. If you hear from your sister, let me know immediately. Okay?"

"We will," Jason said.

He waited for Olsen to say something else, to tell him that the police felt confident that Hayden would quickly be found unharmed and returned to her life with her daughter. But Olsen didn't say anything like that. He turned on his heel and walked back to his work.

Chapter Twenty-one

Jason was hungry, and Nora offered to cook something for everyone. Sierra agreed, saying that she had barely eaten the past two days. She sat at the kitchen table while Nora brought out eggs and cracked them into a pan. Jason made coffee and toast and laid out dishes and silverware until the food was ready.

Sierra ate quickly, greedily. Jason expected her to pick, as he and Nora were, but Sierra dug in. In the streaming daylight of the kitchen, she looked unwashed, her hair greasy and matted. Had she been sleeping in the car rather than stopping in a hotel? She had the money Hayden had given her. Then he realized the fallacy of what he was thinking. Sierra wasn't old enough to rent a hotel room, at least not the kind of hotel room he would want his niece to be staying in. Maybe she was better off sleeping in the car, if that was what she did.

Sierra neared the end of her plate of food. Nora offered to make more, but Sierra shook her head. "No, thanks," she said. "This is good."

"You probably want a shower and nap," Nora said.

"I do." She took a bite of her second piece of toast. "And don't worry. I'm not going to run off again. I did that once. I know I fucked up—or messed up. Okay? I mean, I know I was wrong, and I'm sorry."

"It's okay," Jason and Nora said at the same time.

"I guess Mom and I have worn out our car privileges with you guys."

Jason couldn't help himself. He laughed at Sierra's comment. When he started laughing, Nora did as well. They all did. It felt good to have that release for a change.

"Remember, it's just a car," Jason said.

Sierra looked at him, smiling a little. "Thanks, Uncle Jason."

"You're welcome."

"You know," Sierra said, "I didn't find anything out there. Nothing except the car. I don't know what I thought I would discover. I thought it would be easy, looking for her. She's my mom after all. I guess I just didn't think she would be so far away I couldn't find her. Even when she was bad off, I knew how to reach her. I talked to her sometimes on the phone, if I was with Dad or Grandma. But now . . ."

Nora reached out and squeezed Sierra's hand. "We'll let the police do their work," she said. "That's about all we can do, honey."

Jason knew Nora was right. He didn't like it, but she was right. The three of them were completely powerless.

The house grew quiet after an hour or so. Nora and Sierra went upstairs to sleep, with Sierra once again promising that she wasn't going to "fly the coop." Jason promised himself he would stay vigilant. He listened for opening doors or windows, the sound of scurrying feet on the steps or the roof. He sat downstairs in the kitchen with his laptop, trying to catch up on work e-mails that had come through during the week, but he found his eyelids growing heavy, his chin dropping toward his chest. His phone jerked him awake, and he grabbed for it, expecting to be hearing from the police.

"Hey."

"Regan?"

"Did I wake you?" she asked.

"No. Kind of. It's been a long day already."

"Are you in the middle of something?"

"No," he said. "I can talk a little."

"I saw something on the news . . . and I was wondering if it was about Hayden."

"It's on the news? Already?"

"It's on a reporter's Twitter feed. They said there's some kind of search going on at the Bluff, but they didn't mention Hayden's name. I put two and two together. They found her car there?"

Jason rubbed at his weary eyes. He told Regan what happened—Sierra finding Hayden's car, the bloodstain, the opening of the trunk, and the items left behind. Regan didn't say anything while he related the tale, but she did gasp a little when he mentioned the blood.

"I'm sorry, Jason," she said. "Are you doing okay?"

"It's fine. I'm worried about Sierra more than anyone else. This is her mother we're talking about. Hayden wasn't perfect by any means, but she and Sierra mean a lot to each other. I worry about what might happen to her if . . . I shouldn't be thinking about that now. We don't know anything yet."

"Right," Regan said. "But I'm sorry. Really."

"Thanks."

There was a short pause. Jason wished there were something mundane to discuss—the weather, sports, local politics. But

159

nothing came to his mind. All he saw, all he thought about, was Hayden and Sierra.

"I heard from Colton Rivers today," Regan said.

"Really?"

"He came by my house this morning and asked me about Logan."

"Your house? Are you working from home today?"

"It's Saturday, Jason."

Jason paused. "It is Saturday, isn't it? Jesus. I forgot."

Regan said, "Your friend Colton asked me if I'd heard from Logan at all over the years, or if I knew his whereabouts."

"He's relentless," Jason said.

"He seems that way. I told him I hadn't heard anything either. He said they're going to hire an investigator to take a real look into finding him. Did you know they've tried that a couple of times before?"

"Colton told me."

"It sounds like they're getting serious now," Regan said.

"What do you remember about Logan and Hayden? Do you remember anything about them spending time together?"

"Not really. I know if we were all at your house, Hayden would act flirtatious with Logan. They acted that way with each other." Regan couldn't hide the disapproval or jealousy in her voice. "Every word they said to each other back then was laced with innuendo, but I never took it seriously. Did you? I thought it was just a game they were playing. It was a game Hayden played with everybody."

"You're right about that," Jason said.

"But she was dating Derrick back then, wasn't she? Wasn't she almost always dating Derrick, even when she was flirting with other guys?"

"Yes," Jason said. "I'm grasping, I guess. It's just that Colton saw her a couple of nights ago with Jesse Dean. And Jesse Dean and Derrick were friends. I know Hayden was here to try to make amends for something from the past. I don't know. . . . Could whatever Hayden was here for have to do with Logan?"

"How could that be?" Regan asked.

"What if Hayden and Logan weren't just friends?" Jason asked. "What if it went beyond a flirtation at some point?"

"We would have known," Regan said. "We were all so close back then. We knew almost everything about each other's lives. Could Logan have been mixed up with your sister and you not know about it?"

"I wonder how much I know about anybody. It's all strange."

"What is?"

"Her car was found up on the Bluff," Jason said. "What was she doing?"

"What if she isn't the one who put it up there?"

Chapter Twenty-two

Detective Olsen came by the house as the sun was going down. He didn't call first, and when he rang the doorbell, Jason and Nora and Sierra were all sitting in the living room, saying little to one another. Despite napping, everyone was still tired—emotionally more than anything else. No one mentioned Hayden's name, although, Jason suspected, they were all thinking about her. He knew he was.

When Jason looked outside and saw Olsen, he rushed to the door. Then he slowed down. He wondered why he was hurrying. What could the detective have to say that he would want to hear?

Olsen looked tired. His jacket was gone, and the cuffs of his pants as well as his shoes were covered with dirt. Jason held the door for him, his hand trembling. He tried to read Olsen's body for signs. Did he look like a man arriving with the worst news possible?

Everyone stood. Sierra had her thumbnail in her mouth again, and Jason wanted to rush across the room to her, to cover her ears, to cover and protect her completely so no bad news could reach her. But he couldn't. He was too far away. And the bad news was going to come whether he was sheltering her or not.

But Olsen said, pushing the glasses up on his nose, "There's nothing for me to report right now. We haven't found anything on the Bluff." He looked at all of them after he spoke these words, and he clearly intended for his look to be reassuring and comforting. But he just looked tired as well. He looked like *he* needed reassuring. "No sign of Hayden. No indication of where she might be. It's starting to get dark, so we had to stop." He quickly added, "Her car has been taken into custody. We'll process it further and hold on to it for now."

"Is that it, then?" Nora asked.

"For tonight. We plan on looking some more in the morning."

"On Sunday?" Sierra asked.

"No rest for the wicked," Olsen said. "We also have her description out to all of our units. We're casting a net." He cleared his throat. He looked at Jason and Nora and then at Sierra. He seemed to be considering if he wanted to say more in front of her. Jason nodded, trying to let Olsen know that he should go on, that there was nothing he needed to worry about hiding from Sierra. Jason didn't know if Olsen got the hint, or if he just decided to go on himself. "You know, there's a limit to what we can do or think here. We don't know if Hayden is in any danger. We don't know if she's been hurt."

"The blood——" Sierra said.

"I know," Olsen said. "But people get blood in their cars for a variety of reasons. She could have cut her hand. She could be menstruating."

"On the backseat?" Jason asked.

"I get it," Olsen said. "I know you're worried. We'll test it, don't worry. We'll see if we can get a match." He turned to Sierra. "You don't know your mother's blood type, do you?"

"A positive. We're both A positive."

Olsen looked impressed with Sierra's knowledge. "Okay, we'll check. But Hayden's an adult. If she left, if she abandoned her car, or if she's just spending time somewhere, those are all her choices. The only thing she's done wrong, in the eyes of the law, is leave her car overnight in a park. That's a twenty-five-dollar fine."

"You're saying the next move is up to her," Jason said.

"I'm saying we're going to look a little more tomorrow," Olsen said. "But we can't have a bunch of manpower searching for an adult who hasn't committed a crime and who hasn't given any indication she's in danger." He sighed and looked down at his dirty shoes. "It's been a long day, and I'm just trying to be forthright with all of you. There are limits to what we can accomplish."

None of them said anything, but Olsen's words hit Jason like a splash of cold water. What did he expect to happen if Hayden wasn't up there on the Bluff, alive or dead? Was Olsen going to devote his professional life to finding his sister? She had run off before and abandoned her responsibilities only to resurface at some later date, expecting that she could seamlessly return to whatever she had left behind. Was that what she was doing now? Was she having a last round of partying with Jesse Dean and company before coming back to pick her daughter up? Olsen was right. Blood showed up for a lot of reasons. Especially in the car of someone who had just fallen off the wagon . . .

Sierra sat down. She turned her face away from the three adults in the room. The only noise she made was a low sniffle. Nora walked over to her, and Jason took a step that way as well, the emotion Sierra displayed catching hold of him. He felt his eyes burn from tears, but when he moved, Olsen placed his hand gently on Jason's arm. When Jason looked at the detective, he motioned toward the door with his head, indicating he wanted to talk to Jason alone.

The two men stepped outside. The sky was turning red in the distance. The days were getting longer, and Jason knew they would, in just a few weeks, reach the longest of the year. Summer made him nostalgic—for childhood, for his teenage years with Regan and Logan, for a time when he didn't have to think about or deal with the things he was dealing with as an adult. He knew he couldn't and shouldn't remain untouched by such things. He had already lost both of his parents, after all, but he didn't like to think of Sierra getting hammered by those things when she was just seventeen. Instead of gearing up for a summer of friends, boys, swimming pools, and late nights, she was inside, absorbing the reality of her mother's disappearance. Jason wasn't sure which would be worse—the news that Hayden had met with foul play, or the news that she hadn't, leaving everything up in the air for who knew how much longer.

Olsen placed his hands in his pockets and leaned back against the porch railing. He let out a long, slow breath. A flock of birds passed overhead, a scattering of black dots against the darkening clouds. "I am sorry I don't have more information. But it's only been one day. Less than a day, really."

"I understand," Jason said.

"I wanted to talk to you a little more. This is about your niece."

"Okay. What about her?"

"We still have the matter of the car and the drugs. I didn't want to push her on it in there, but those things have to be addressed."

"Like I said, we don't want to press any charges about the car. It's fine."

"But she hit another car. It's been reported to the police. She has to face the music about that."

"You said no one in the other car was hurt, right?"

"That's right. But there's damage to the other vehicle. It's not a lot, but someone has to pay for it. Either your insurance will, or you will."

"We'll take care of it."

"Really?"

"We'll find a way."

"Okay," Olsen said. "What about the drugs? That's not something I can just make go away. That's possession by a minor."

"It's not hers. She's holding them for a friend."

"It's not really relevant," Olsen said. "Do you think she's holding them for her mother?"

"I don't know. I doubt it. Hayden never did a lot of drugs. Some, I know. Give me a chance to get the story out of Sierra. I don't want her to face some kind of legal issue that will follow her the rest of her life."

"She's a minor," Olsen said. "There are programs." Olsen cleared his throat. "I know she's already been in trouble before, over in Redman County. The stolen car. If she's starting down the road her mother went down, it might be good to get her help now."

"She's not on that road," Jason said. He wished his voice carried more conviction. He believed it, yes, but he also knew how empty promises and vows could sound when spoken with a great deal of force. "Can we just wait until we know more about Hayden? I appreciate the fact that you're trying to be sensitive. Can you just hold on to that for a little while longer?"

Olsen didn't give his word one way or the other. He moved his foot and kicked at a small pebble, sending it into the yard. "We're going to get in touch with Sierra's father."

"Why?"

"Why? Because he's her father." He took his glasses off and polished them with a tissue he drew from his pocket. "His child's mother is missing. The girl may be left here for a long time. We have to tell the other parent. He may want to come and be with his daughter, or he may want her to stay with him until this is resolved."

"Stay with him," Jason said, almost under his breath.

"He might," Olsen said. "I don't know what he's going to want to do. But he has to be informed about any situation involving his child. Don't you agree?"

"I guess."

"Is there something wrong with her father? Something we should know about?"

Jason didn't want Derrick out of Sierra's life. He wanted Sierra in *his*. The feeling had been slow to come over him, but he didn't want her to leave the house with someone else. He didn't want to think of her facing everything without his and Nora's help.

"He's always treated Sierra well," Jason said. "In some ways, I guess he's been more reliable than Hayden."

"But?" Olsen squinted as he asked the one-word question.

Jason paused. "He's had some trouble with the law. It's been a few years, but that's part of the record. He's been a troublemaker."

"Lots of people break the law and have children."

"Well, it's something to consider," Jason said, aware that he was trying hard to throw his ex-brother-in-law under the bus. "You should look into it."

"I will."

"Sierra hasn't seen him in a couple of years, and she's safe with us now."

"Maybe I'm just tired, Mr. Danvers, but if the matter of Sierra's custody went to court . . . let's just say the car accident and the drugs wouldn't be used to bolster *your* claim." Jason started to object, but Olsen said, "We'll notify the father. If he wants to come and see his daughter, he can. If he wants to ignore the problem and hope it goes away, he can do that as well. You all probably just want to do what's best for the girl right now. She's in the middle of a brutal time. Right?"

Jason nodded.

Olsen tried to smile. "Look, no one doubts you care about the kid. Keep her safe. But if the father decides he wants to play a role, she doesn't need to see a bunch of adults fighting over her. It's better if everybody joins hands, you know?"

"Sure."

"Good night," Olsen said.

"How early are you going to start looking tomorrow?" Jason asked.

"Early."

"Do you think you'll find anything up there? Anything that will tell us where Hayden is?"

Olsen considered the question, then said, "As long as we're looking, we're hoping."

Before going to bed, Jason stopped in Sierra's room. She had the light on, the door open. She sat up, her back propped against several pillows, and she held a history textbook. Despite the door standing open, Jason knocked anyway, and Sierra looked over. Her eyes looked tired, the lids heavy. Jason couldn't tell if the redness in her eyes came from crying or the accumulation of the emotion of the past couple of days. Nevertheless, when she saw Jason in the doorway, she tried to smile.

"I'm sorry to interrupt."

"That's okay," she said. "I'm not really reading. The words are just going past my eyes, and I'm turning the pages, but none of it is sinking in. I'll get through a few pages and then realize I didn't understand a thing I just read."

"I wanted to say good night and see if you needed anything."

"I'm okay. Aunt Nora has been checking on me every few minutes. I'm glad we heard from the police earlier. At least we know they're going to look more in the morning."

"It's something," Jason said. "You're right." Jason came in and sat on the bed. Sierra scooted over, her legs moving beneath the covers. She laid the book aside. Jason said, "I've been thinking about your mom a lot. Of course. And I realized something about her."

"What?" Sierra looked curious.

"I know I complain a lot, and have complained a lot, about her being untrustworthy. All those years she told us she'd quit drinking and then she'd start again. Or she'd be drinking on the side. Those things made her untrustworthy, right?"

"I guess so."

"That's different from being dishonest," Jason said. "I realize that, at least when it comes to a personal relationship, your mother is the most honest person I've ever known. The drinking could mess her up, and she'd lie about whether she was drinking or not. But she always told me what she was really thinking. And she always told me what I needed to hear, whether I wanted to hear it or not."

"That's true," Sierra said.

"I have a feeling that whatever she came back for was motivated by that. A desire for honesty. For telling the truth to someone or about someone. It might have gotten her in trouble, but—"

"That wouldn't stop her," Sierra said, finishing the thought.

"No, it wouldn't." The words Hayden spoke about Regan on the night she dropped Sierra off came back to him. Jason understood the real message his sister was delivering when she asked him about Regan—she was saying, *Are you happy, big brother? Are you really happy?*

Sierra was fingering the edge of her blanket, and her cuticles were chewed and raw. She needed peace and rest.

"Anyway," Jason said, "I wanted you to know that's the way I think about her. The other stuff . . . the problems she may have had, they're not important to me."

"Thanks," Sierra said. "I'll remember that too."

He reached out and clasped her hand. Sierra squeezed back, and then he left the room to try to sleep.

Chapter Twenty-three

Jason stepped out onto the porch the next morning, searching for the Sunday paper. He had slept off and on the previous night, finally waking around seven thirty. The rest of the house slept, even Sierra. She left her bedroom door open —for transparency's sake, Jason assumed—and when he walked by on his way downstairs, Jason heard her soft breathing. The history textbook lay on the floor next to the bed.

The morning was clear as he retrieved the newspaper, a late spring day full of promise. The sky looked like a clean slate, one that the events of the coming day could still be written across. The neighborhood was quiet, no human voices to be heard. A sprinkler up the block made a repetitious chittering noise, but nothing else stirred. He rolled the paper open, searching for any news about Hayden. A quick scan revealed nothing. He was turning to go inside when he saw someone walking toward the house.

He recognized the bulky, slow-moving figure. Jason wondered if Colton ever slept, or was he constantly on the move around the town, checking in with people, asking them questions, tending to their needs? Johnny-on-the-spot, Nora called him, even on a Sunday.

But Colton's face looked troubled as he came up the walk. His forehead was creased, the corners of his mouth turned down. Jason still held the open paper in his hands. He wanted to lift it up between his body and Colton's, use it as a screen of some kind. But Colton had already seen him, had already reached the bottom of the stairs that led to the porch. He stopped there, one foot on the bottom step. He rested his arm on the banister and huffed a little as though he had exerted himself hustling to Jason's house.

"What is it, Colton?" Jason asked.

Colton's face was red. He came the rest of the way. "Jason, you may want to sit down." He pointed to one of the chairs they kept on the porch.

"What?" Jason asked. "Tell me."

But he knew. He knew before Colton said the words, before he felt his body going backward and plopping into the chair as though someone had pushed him. He felt the words roll across him like the concussive wave from an explosion.

He knew.

"Are you sure, Colton?" he asked, even though Colton was always sure. He knew everything. He didn't speak without being certain.

"I'm sure," Colton said. He reached out and placed a heavy hand on Jason's shoulders. He even gave a squeeze, his attempt at comforting the bereaved. "The police will be contacting you soon. I only heard because I was up there." He paused before he said it again. "They found a body, Jason. They found a body up on Heroin Hill."

"What were *you* doing up there?" Jason asked.

It was the next question he thought to ask. What was Colton

174

doing hanging out at the Bluff? Why was he bringing Jason that piece of news instead of the police?

"I stopped by this morning to see how the search was going," he said. "My family was getting ready for church, so I went up there just to check things over. I'm nosy—you know that. I went by yesterday as well. The cops, they all know me."

Jason still held the newspaper. His grip tightened until the paper started to crumple in his hands. He looked down at the porch and saw ants running, the grain of the wood, and the cracks in the paint. Hayden was gone. He couldn't think of anything else. *His sister was gone.*

"Maybe I shouldn't have told you," Colton said. "I thought someone would have called by now. I thought you might need some help. This was almost thirty minutes ago."

"What happened to her?" Jason asked. "Was she . . . Did someone kill her?"

"I don't know," Colton said. "They hadn't even brought it— *her*— out yet. Her. I don't know what they're doing. It takes a while to gather all the evidence and everything. Secure the area. They have to be real meticulous with this stuff in case there's foul play."

Jason looked at the house. Through the screen door he saw the stairs that led up to Sierra's room. She slept, unaware of what she was about to learn.

"Are you sure, Colton?" Jason asked, and he realized he was repeating himself. He didn't know what else to do or say.

"I was there. I heard them talking. I heard them call the coroner."

Jason dropped the newspaper. He raised his hand to his mouth. He felt something stirring in his gut. Sickness. A tingling passed up the back of his neck and across his scalp. He imagined his face was bone white. Black dots danced across his vision.

Colton came closer and with a low grunt knelt down next to the chair Jason sat in. Again, Colton placed his hand on Jason's shoulder. Jason caught the sweetly clean scents of soap and shaving cream coming off Colton's body.

"Do you want me to get Nora for you?" he asked.

Jason uncovered his mouth. "No," he said. He took a few deep breaths, trying to restore his equilibrium. He squeezed his eyes shut, hoping to clear the spots. When he did, he saw Hayden. The little girl in the sandbox. Crying. In need of a helping hand. Hayden the wild child. Hayden making that toast for their parents and saying the exact right thing at the exact right moment. Hayden walking out the very door he sat next to for the last time. He let her go. He let her walk away.

Jason opened his eyes. "I should go up there to the Bluff," he said.

"No," Colton said. "You should stay here. With your family. They're going to need you. Very much."

"But Hayden's alone . . . just . . . tossed aside in the woods."

"You can't help them," Colton said. "Do you want me to go inside with you? Maybe you need some support."

Jason straightened up. He blinked his eyes a few times and cleared his throat. He tried to force the images of Hayden from his mind. He tried not to think of her body—rag doll limp, bloodied and bruised—lying in the woods.

"No," Jason said. "I need to do this. Colton, can you go back up there, back to the hill? Find out what's going on for me."

Colton hesitated just a moment before he said, "Okay. I will. Gloria drove the kids on to church without me. I'll get back to you as soon as I can."

But Jason wasn't really listening. He was looking inside the screen door again, trying his best to envision how he was going to do what he knew he had to do. He stood up. His legs felt jittery. When he stumbled, Colton reached out and steadied him.

"Are you sure you're okay?" Colton asked.

Jason didn't answer right away. The images flooded back in his mind. Hayden. A thousand moments rushed past his eyes. Hayden the child on her bike, Hayden the teenager at the beach, Hayden the mother who came to his house asking for help.

Hayden.

"My sister, Colton," he said. "My baby sister."

"I know. I'm sorry. She was really something."

Jason let Colton steady him for a few moments. When his uneasiness seemed to have passed, Jason nodded to Colton. "Thanks," he said. "I'm okay now."

"Are you sure?"

"I am. I'll be okay. This wasn't unexpected, right?"

"We don't ever expect these things," Colton said.

"Find out what you can," Jason said, looking at the house again. "I'll take care of things here."

Jason didn't go straight upstairs. He wandered out to the kitchen, not even conscious of his legs moving. Not even conscious of a purpose. He worried that Colton's arrival and their conversation on the porch had woken Nora and Sierra, but when he stopped and listened, he heard nothing from above.

In the kitchen, he stared at the walls. He thought of his mother and father. At least they were spared this news. They had lived in fear of the middle-of-the-night call for so long, and Jason saw them as the fortunate ones. They died before it came. He was the only one left, the one who would have to see to Hayden's burial and the tidying up of her affairs.

Her daughter.

He reached up and opened a cabinet. He brought down a bottle of bourbon, something called Rowan's Creek. A friend gave it to them after a trip to Kentucky. Jason occasionally sipped a glass in the evenings, but that morning he poured a shot and threw it back like a college kid. It was smooth, the oaky warmth spreading through his body as it reached his stomach. He didn't know what he thought it would do, but the act of downing the shot calmed him. He leaned against the counter and gave in, letting the sobs shudder through his body. For a moment, he felt out of control, his torso shaking as though it was being wracked by seizures. The shuddering slowed, but not the crying. He wiped at his eyes and nose with both of his hands and the back of his arm. He grabbed a napkin and used that to finish cleaning his face.

His mind turned to Nora and Sierra. What if they found him this way? He tried to gather himself by taking deep breaths. He needed to regain his composure so that he could go upstairs and tell them the news.

Then the phone rang. It was their landline, which they'd been planning to eliminate anyway. Only telemarketers seemed to call that number anymore, but the sound of the ringing jolted Jason. It could be the police. Olsen. It was probably Olsen. When he answered, there was no sound on the other end. For several seconds, nothing. Then rustling.

"Hello?" he said.

Someone made a noise on the other end. It sounded like laughing, or even perhaps crying. But no one said anything.

"Hello?" Jason said again.

Then the call ended. Whoever was there hung up. Jason held the phone in his hand, staring at it. Were they laughing or crying? Was it a wrong number?

He put the phone down slowly. Wondering. Could Olsen have tried to call and been interrupted? But the sound from the other end sounded lighter, higher. Like a woman's.

It couldn't be Hayden. She was gone.

"Who was it?"

Jason spun toward the voice. Nora and Sierra stood in the kitchen doorway, their faces expectant and fearful at the same time. Jason didn't know what to say, so he told the truth.

"No one," he said. "There was no one there."

"They just hung up?" Nora asked.

"No. They made a noise. Something. They might have been laughing."

Or crying. But he didn't say that out loud.

"Was it Mom?" Sierra asked. "Did it sound like her?"

Jason still didn't answer. He thought the same thing. Maybe it was Hayden. But why would she call and say nothing? He didn't even know if she had the number. And after what Colton told him just moments before . . .

"Jason? What is it?" Nora asked. She came into the room, moving toward him. "I can see that something else is going on. What is it? Why is the liquor out?"

Jason didn't look up at them. He could face Nora, but he couldn't face Sierra. He just couldn't. He was looking at the floor when he finally said, "They found a body up on the Bluff."

Sierra turned away. She shook her head over and over. Back and forth as she walked away. She didn't speak or make a noise, and Nora and Jason followed her. But Sierra stayed ahead of them until she reached the foyer, and then she turned around and looked at both of them.

"No," she said. "No. It can't be."

"The police will be by soon," Jason said. "They'll tell us more."

"How do you know that wasn't her on the phone?" Sierra asked. "How do you know?"

Jason didn't know what to say, so he simply repeated himself, and when the words came out of his mouth, he felt foolish. Incapable of handling the occasion that required him to be the adult, the strength for this young girl.

"They found a body up on the Bluff," he said.

"How do you know?" Sierra said again. Her voice rose as she repeated the line. Her voice grew louder, even as she collapsed to the floor. "How do you know? How do you know?"

Chapter Twenty-four

The three of them spent a long time crying. They sat huddled together on the floor of the foyer. Nora wrapped her arms around Sierra, and Jason held them both. They didn't move. Jason didn't try to stand up when his back started to hurt and his leg fell asleep. It felt good to be with them. Despite everything, it felt right to share his grief with these two people. If Hayden had died far away, if he hadn't seen her or Sierra again . . . would he have felt it as much? The fact that his sister and his niece had come back into his life, even for a handful of days, made the loss more profound. But it also allowed him to share the experience with Sierra. She wouldn't be sitting in some little house in Redman County, receiving the news alone.

Eventually they all got up and moved to seats in the living room. Nora grabbed tissues, and Jason brought the bottle of bourbon and three shot glasses from the kitchen. He poured them each a shot, even Sierra.

Nora objected, but Sierra said, "No, it's okay." She looked at both of them. "I hardly ever drink, even with my friends. But this seems appropriate somehow. Mom would think it's funny."

Jason took out his phone. "I'm going to call Detective Olsen," he said. "I want to know what the hell is going on."

He dialed and the call went to voice mail. He tried two more times with the same result, so he texted. It took a few minutes, but a text came back. *On my way to your house.*

"He's coming over," Jason said. "Olsen." He looked at Sierra. "You don't have to listen to this if you don't want. You can . . ."

"We can go somewhere, if you want to be away," Nora said. "Or you can be by yourself."

"No," Sierra said, sniffling. "I'm staying. I want to know everything I can know."

"There may not be much to say right now," Jason said. "They're at the very beginning of figuring this all out."

"I know," she said. "And I want to say something else, and you guys can think I'm crazy if you want. But if someone needs to go down to the police station or the morgue or whatever and identify her, I want to be the one to do it."

"No," Jason said. "I can."

"But I want to," Sierra said. "I don't want Mom to be . . . alone, I guess. That's the only word I can think of to describe it. Dying seems so lonely, and I don't want Mom to be like that. If someone is going to look at her and say, 'Yes, that's her,' then I want it to be me."

Jason started to object again, but Nora said, "That makes perfect sense. It may help you."

"And I know you might just be saying that now, Aunt Nora, you may just be placating me. But I mean it. I'm going to do it."

Jason tried not to let his imagination run wild and become consumed with speculation about what had happened to Hayden. There was the blood in the car, the shoes and keys left behind. He closed his eyes. He hoped she hadn't suffered, that whatever happened to her was fast and painless.

"Someone has to tell Dad," Sierra said. "Maybe I should call him."

182

"Do you have his number?" Jason asked.

"I have an old one. I don't know if it works. I've texted him there, and he doesn't write back."

"Maybe we should just talk to the police first," Nora said. "They'll know what to do about that stuff."

Sierra nodded. She was sitting back on the sofa, her feet tucked beneath her. She looked lost in thought. Composed but distant. She said, "Mom wanted to see my graduation from high school next year. That's all she talked about."

Jason knew what he was supposed to say to Sierra. He was supposed to reassure her, to tell her that Hayden would be able to see her daughter walk across the stage in a high school gymnasium and receive her diploma, that wherever Sierra went or whatever she did for the rest of her life, her mother would know and see. But Jason wasn't the kind of person who could say something like that, even when he needed to. And he wasn't even sure Sierra was the kind of kid who wanted to hear it.

So he kept his mouth shut as the moment passed.

When Sierra went upstairs to use the bathroom, Nora came over to Jason and sat next to him on the couch.

"Are you okay?" she asked.

"I'm all right."

"Can I do anything for you? Do you want to talk about this?"

"Not now. I feel like we have to make Sierra our focus. Don't we? I may have lost my sister, but she's lost her mother. Her only decent parent." Jason almost laughed. "Jesus. I almost said her only reliable parent. That's not exactly true. But I know Hayden always loved her. Sierra never had to doubt that."

"You're right," Nora said. "I wanted to talk to you about that too."

"About Hayden?"

"About Sierra. I want you to do something when that detective comes over."

"What?"

"You need to make it clear to him, in no uncertain terms, that Sierra is staying with us right now. She's welcome here."

"Of course. Why are you worried about this now?"

"I just don't want the police to think they have to . . . I don't know . . . take her off our hands. Like you said yesterday, she could end up in foster care. And we don't want that. We're family. She can stay with us as long as she wants."

"Of course," Jason said. "I'm with you on this."

"We have to steer her away from calling her dad. She's safest here."

Sierra came down the stairs. "What are you all talking about?" she asked as she entered the room.

"I was just checking on Uncle Jason," Nora said. "You've both had a shock."

Sierra slumped down on the couch. She let out a long breath. "What do people do in situations like this?" she asked. "Do they just sit around? Do we talk? Or eat?"

"Mostly you just wait," Jason said. "And time passes slowly."

Chapter Twenty-five

When Olsen showed up thirty minutes later, Jason was almost glad to see him. Even though Jason dreaded hearing the substance of what the detective was coming to say, he welcomed the chance to know something. Anything. He and Nora and Sierra had fallen into a glum silence, their conversation consisting mostly of small talk and mundane observations. It felt as though none of them dared bring up anything real—a memory, a theory about the crime—for fear of the flood of emotion it might unleash. They talked about anything but Hayden.

Olsen stepped into the living room, his face somber. He looked tired as well, and he hadn't shaved. He wore khaki pants and work boots, the better to trudge around in the woods and the dirt.

"I'm sorry it took me longer to get here than I said it would," he said.

"That's okay," Jason said.

"I just wanted to give you an update on where we stand in regards to the search for Hayden. Right now, we're suspending the search. Things haven't really changed as they relate to Hayden since last night, and—"

"What do you mean they haven't changed?" Nora asked.

Olsen looked momentarily confused. "Like I said last night, absent any clear evidence of a crime, or any witnesses who can report a crime, all we really have to go on is the blood in the car. We did get results from our test. It is Hayden's type. A positive. It's a very common blood type." His voice trailed off. He looked at the three faces arrayed around him. Jason couldn't tell if he understood what they were all thinking or not. "Of course that doesn't prove the blood is *hers*. Just that it's her type. It will take more time—"

"You found a body up there," Jason said, giving voice to their concerns. "We heard about that. You found a body this morning."

"Who told you that?" Olsen asked. "Is it on the news already?"

"Who cares?" Nora said. "You found a body, right? Hayden's?"

"We did find a body this morning on the Bluff. That's part of the reason we're suspending the search for Hayden. We have to process the area as a crime scene. And that's a big job with it being out in the woods and so much area to cover. But the body we found isn't Hayden's. I can assure you of that."

"How do you know?" Sierra asked.

Olsen paused, his lips pressed together. "We found a skeleton up on the Bluff," he said. "Scattered bones. From the looks of things, we'd say they've been there at least five years. Maybe a decade or more. Did someone tell you it was Hayden? If they did, I'm terribly sorry. We never thought that at all."

Jason felt lighter for a moment. Relief passed through him in a wave. He took a step back from Detective Olsen and sat in a chair, just as he did a few hours earlier when Colton arrived with his news. The problem hadn't been entirely solved. They still didn't know where Hayden was or what she was doing. But they knew one thing—the police hadn't found her body up on the Bluff.

"She's alive?" Sierra said. "Mom's alive?"

Olsen raised a cautionary finger. "I can't vouch for that. All I can tell you is that we haven't found anything in that park to tell us she isn't. We also haven't found anything to tell us she is. As far as any investigation into her whereabouts goes, there's nothing new to report. It's been long enough now that you could report her as a missing person, and if you'd like to do that, we can."

Jason looked over at Sierra. She leaned forward and placed her head between her legs, the same position someone adopts when an airplane is about to crash. She wasn't making any sound, but Jason saw her shoulders shaking as if she was crying. Nora went over and placed a hand on the girl's back.

"It's okay," she said simply. "It's good news."

Sierra nodded, indicating that she heard what Nora said. But she didn't raise her head or say anything.

Olsen turned to Jason and said, "Maybe I should let you all get your bearings again. I have some things to get back to up on the Bluff."

Relief didn't seem like the right emotion. Someone was dead. A body had been found. And Hayden was nowhere in sight. The last he knew, she was with Jesse Dean. And her car had been abandoned with the keys and her shoes and a couple of bloodstains inside. So, no, he didn't feel relief for very long. He felt what he frequently felt for Hayden—fear. Confusion. Anxiety.

"Do you mind walking to the door with me, Mr. Danvers?" Olsen asked.

Jason looked up at him. He nodded his head, then exerted what felt like a great deal of energy pushing himself out of the chair and up. He looked over at Sierra and Nora. Sierra hadn't moved. She still sat with her head between her legs. Her shoulders had stopped heaving, at least, but she didn't appear to be making any progress toward sitting up or changing her position. Jason walked over and placed his hand on her shoulder.

He started to say, "It's okay," but then thought better of it. It wasn't okay, not as far as he or anyone else knew. It was better than it had been. Maybe. But it wasn't okay. Nothing was.

Sierra still didn't move. She didn't acknowledge his touch in any way.

Jason lifted his hand and followed Olsen out to the front door. The two men stepped onto the porch together. The sun had moved high overhead and was bright, causing Jason to squint. Olsen reached into his shirt pocket and exchanged his regular glasses for a pair of sunglasses. Jason only saw his own image reflected back at him.

"I just want to say again how sorry I am about the mix-up."

"It's okay."

"Do you mind telling me how you found out that remains had been discovered up there at the Bluff?" Olsen asked.

Jason didn't want to get Colton in trouble. But Colton was a big boy—and why exactly had he come over and given Jason half-baked information?

"Colton Rivers," Jason said.

Olsen nodded as though he had suspected that very thing all along. "Are you friends with him?" he asked.

"We went to high school together," Jason said. "He and I were supposed to be doing a project together. I was going to design the poster for the summer festival. Hell, I haven't thought about work much lately. I've missed some time."

"I'm sure he meant well," Olsen said. "Do you want to file that missing persons report?"

"Does it matter?" Jason asked.

"If you file the report, she goes into the national database. It means law enforcement all over the country will have access to information about her. If she turns up in Little Rock, Arkansas, or Boise, Idaho, the police there will notify us. It's not a bad idea."

"I keep trying to convince myself she's in danger," Jason said. "The blood in the car and all that. But she's run off before. Disappeared for days or weeks at a time. I used to think she was like a cat. You know, you let the cat out of the house, and maybe it comes back at night and maybe it doesn't. Sometimes it comes back all scraped up like it's been in a fight. Or maybe it just doesn't come back at all. And no one ever knows why."

"Maybe that's an indelicate metaphor," Olsen said.

"Maybe."

"Well, if you want to file that report later today, let me know. We have officers in Indiana making contact with Hayden's ex-husband. I'm going to be occupied up on the Bluff for most of the day. We have to sort out that mess. A new mess."

"Thanks for coming by."

"Say," Olsen said, "when Colton was up there and we were securing the crime scene, he told one of the officers about someone he went to school with disappearing from the Bluff on the night of graduation. Do you remember anything about that?"

To that moment, Jason hadn't made any connection between the news of a body found on the Bluff and Logan. Why would he? But once the idea was raised, it started the wheels turning in Jason's head.

"Logan Shaw," Jason said. "He went to school with Colton and me."

"A friend of yours?" Olsen asked.

"Yes. A good friend. But Logan left town. He didn't disappear. Colton is involved with the family's estate planning. That's why he's bringing it up. He was talking to me about it the other day."

"So this guy, this Shaw, left town of his own accord?"

"Yes."

"So you're still in touch with him?"

"No. No one is."

"I see," Olsen said. "Thanks."

"You know . . ." Jason's words broke off. He wasn't sure how to proceed.

"What is it?" Olsen asked.

"I'm trying to figure out if this is relevant or not."

"You can tell me. I'll decide how relevant it is."

"You mentioned my friend Logan who left town way back when. As it turns out, Sierra told me that Hayden had mentioned Logan once many years ago. When Sierra asked about Logan again, maybe six months ago or so, Hayden acted angry that it had come up. It's not really like Hayden to be that short with people. She was—*is*—an open book."

"And that was all that was said about it?"

"Yeah. I'm just thinking about her car being found up there where Logan spent his last night. I don't know."

"You think your sister had something to do with this Logan disappearing?" Olsen asked.

Jason shook his head. "No. I guess I'm just speculating."

"I spend a lot of my time doing that." Olsen smiled. "Is there anything else?"

"The phone call."

"What?"

"Someone called here earlier. On the landline. They didn't say anything, but I couldn't tell if the person was laughing or crying or what. It sounded like a woman. Maybe it was a kid. I don't know."

"And you think this was your sister?"

"I thought it might be. But then why didn't she say anything?"

"Could have been a wrong number," Olsen said.

"Yeah."

"We can get into the phone records," Olsen said. "See if we can determine the source of the call."

"Sure." None of it made sense to Jason. He couldn't decide what was a rational concern and what was an irrational one. "Detective? Who do you think this is? The body you found in the woods?"

Olsen said, "That's what I'm going to try to find out. But a lot of things have been happening up there over the last ten or fifteen years. Drug deals. Robberies. Vagrants. It's pretty wide open right now."

"If this body has been there so long, how did you just stumble across it today?" Jason asked.

"Cadaver dog," Olsen said, smiling a little. He seemed pleased to brag about the police department's work. "We brought one in to look for Hayden. If you're looking for some good news, the dog didn't pick up the scent of decomposition in the trunk of your sister's car. It's not conclusive of course. There are a lot of factors. Time elapsed and things like that."

"But it's something," Jason said.

"If you're looking for the building block for hope, you could do a lot worse."

Chapter Twenty-six

Jason returned to work the next day. Nora took one more day off, agreeing to stay home with Sierra, to keep a close eye on her and try to distract her from thinking about Hayden. Jason felt conflicted. On the one hand, he worried that he should be staying home with Sierra as well, that it might take both of them to keep his niece distracted. On the other hand, he welcomed the chance to get away, to feel like some aspect of his life was returning to normal. When his mind started down the track that asked the question *What if Hayden never comes back?* he tried to turn his thoughts in another direction.

He spent that Monday playing catch-up. E-mails. Page after page of e-mails. He deleted most of them. He went to a couple of meetings. The people he worked with didn't know why he had been gone lately, and he didn't tell them. He let them think he'd been sick, laid low by a stomach virus or something. They didn't know much about his personal life or his family—or anything about Hayden and Sierra. He wanted it to stay that way. The little bit that ran in the paper used Hayden's married name--Borders—so people couldn't make the connection between them. The situation with Hayden had been years in the making. It felt like it might take years to unravel again.

He did make one phone call. He dialed Colton at his office.

Jason had tried Colton's cell phone twice the day before, hoping to understand how and why the miscommunication occurred about the body found on the Bluff. But Colton hadn't answered. When he called the law office and told the receptionist who he was, he expected to be put off again. Instead the call went through, and Jason found himself greeted by Colton's mellow voice.

"Hey, buddy."

Colton sounded relaxed, a man without a care in the world. And maybe he didn't have any. A wife, a couple of kids, plenty of money. A secure future. No disappearing siblings. No questions about what the future might bring. Colton was home. Always at home. All of these things irritated Jason. He wanted Colton to feel as uncertain as he did.

"I left you a couple of messages yesterday," Jason said.

"I know, I know. Crazy Sunday. Family stuff left and right."

"You said you would let me know what you found out up on the Bluff. I never heard from you. Instead Olsen told me it wasn't my sister's body up there at all. You turned our whole house upside down. Sierra thought her mother died."

Jason felt his voice starting to break as he spoke. The emotion came unexpectedly, and he cut off his words before he said or showed more.

"I know, I know," Colton said, his voice soothing and lawyerly. "That's all my fault. I can't apologize enough for that foul-up."

"Foul-up? It's more than that."

"I can only apologize, okay? Look, think about it from my point of view. I was up there, and I heard that they'd found a body. I figured it was Hayden, and I thought to myself that rather than you hearing the news in an impersonal manner from some cop, you'd rather hear it from a friend. That's why I came over, okay? I overstepped a little. You're right. Hell, I already got a visit this morning from Detective Olsen. He gave me a verbal spanking. I'm chastened. Really, I am."

Jason's temperature cooled. Venting at Colton brought some relief, and then hearing that Olsen had stepped in made him feel even better. At least someone in a position of authority was keeping Colton in line. Jason wasn't sure anybody could.

"What is your interest in all of this, Colton?"

"My interest? You know. You all are my friends, people I grew up with. This is my community. If things are going on, I want to know. I want to help if I can."

"Is this a campaign ad, Colton?"

There was a pause. "Now, that's a low blow, Jason. There's no call to say that to me."

Jason agreed. He didn't like the hurt-puppy routine Colton was pulling. It felt like something his mother would do when he talked back—act hurt instead of angry—and Jason never thought that was fair. But it was effective. He didn't know why he was taking shots at Colton. The guy had apologized. What else did Jason want?

"Okay, I'm sorry too. It's been a long few days."

"I know," Colton said. "I hear you. I can see it's been a terrible time for your family. But at least . . . Well, I don't want to say it's good news, but at least you didn't get the worst news about Hayden. Right?"

Jason tried to see it in a positive light. He'd been trying for twenty-four hours to get to that place. "Yeah."

"That's about all we can do," Colton said.

"Say, Colton, do you remember anything about Logan and Hayden in high school? I mean, did you ever suspect the two of them were a couple?"

"Hayden and Logan?" Colton said. "She was always with

Derrick—that's all I know for sure. She certainly liked other guys. We all knew that. You know, I was never really on the inside with that crowd. I wasn't really on the inside with any crowd. I might have been the last guy to know back then who was going with who." He paused. "What are you getting at? You think Hayden might know something about Logan?"

"I guess I'm just thinking of everything," he said. "Every angle."

"That's natural," Colton said. "Speaking of other angles . . . they found this body up on the Bluff. A skeleton."

"Right."

"Jason, have you thought about who that might be?"

Jason had thought about it plenty, turning it over in his mind like the churned earth of an excavated grave. "You mean Logan."

"I do."

"How could that be?" Jason asked.

"I don't know. I just don't. Well, I'm sure we'll be talking about this more. If you need anything else from me, just let me know. And if I hear anything, I'll give you a call."

"Right. Thanks."

"And don't worry about the poster."

"The what?"

"The poster for the summer festival. Don't worry about it."

It had slipped Jason's mind, the reason he ended up having lunch with Colton in the first place right before everything started to happen.

"I can get back to it soon."

"Like I said, don't worry. The committee found a company in town that can do it. You've got enough on your plate. Really."

After he hung up, Jason decided that Colton had never wanted him to do the poster in the first place. He just wanted an excuse to ask about Logan.

Chapter Twenty-seven

Jason left work just before seven o'clock. Only a few cars remained in the parking lot, and they likely belonged to members of the cleaning crew who came through the offices during the evening and overnight. On the factory side of the complex, which Jason couldn't see, the lot would be full. The factory workers went twenty-four hours a day manufacturing the cupcakes and pastries that were then shipped around the world.

Jason carried his keys in one hand and a satchel full of work in the other. A dented pickup truck sat two spaces down from his car, one of its taillights broken. Jason unlocked his doors with the remote and threw his bag in the backseat. As he closed the back and opened the front, the driver's side door of the pickup swung open. Jason barely glanced up. He slid into his seat, ducking his head a little, and pulled his door shut. Before he could lock the car—something he always did, even in Ednaville—someone pulled the passenger door open and came into the car with him.

Jason jumped. He turned his body a few degrees, so that he faced the passenger side of the car. The man wore a baseball cap, a flannel shirt, and a denim jacket. Jason saw his face in profile. It was unshaven, and the nose in its center stood out like a blade.

The thought crossed Jason's mind: *I'm being robbed. This is how it happens when someone gets robbed.*

Jason hadn't even buckled his seat belt yet. He grabbed for the door handle, hoping to push it open and get out. But the man reached a long arm across the cabin of the car and clamped down on Jason's wrist.

"Don't," the man said.

He didn't shout or yell. He didn't sound angry. He sounded certain, like all he needed to do was say one word and Jason would obey. And Jason did. His hand went slack, and the man's talonlike grip eased.

"You can have my wallet," Jason said.

The man let go of Jason's arm completely. "I don't want your wallet. Or your car."

Jason took in the face under the cap. There was something familiar about it. And then the man leaned back in the passenger seat, and he pushed the hat back on his head, revealing more. It had been nearly twenty-seven years, but Jason knew the face right away. Older. More wrinkled. A scar ran from the corner of the left eye out to his hairline. But he knew the face.

He was sitting in the car with Jesse Dean Pratt.

Jason's heart thumped. "Where's my sister?" he asked.

Jesse Dean acted like he hadn't heard. He wasn't even looking at Jason. He stared out the front windshield of the car as though he were contemplating the scenery. And there was nothing to see out there. Just parking lot and buildings. Few cars. And no people. Jason realized he was sitting on his phone. He had stuffed it in his back pants pocket before leaving the office.

"Where is she?" he asked again.

"Shut up," Jesse Dean said, looking over. He still didn't sound angry. By not raising his voice, he seemed more menacing to Jason, like the quiet before a bad storm.

Nobody said anything. Jesse Dean looked at Jason, studying him, then passed his eyes over the interior of the car. He shook his head. "I don't even think I remember you from school. Are you sure you went there with me?"

"I was a little behind you," Jason said, picking up the scent of cigarettes and a trace of alcohol, as though the liquid were leaking through Jesse Dean's pores.

The man made a noise low in his throat. It might have been a laugh. "I was behind everybody."

"You knew my sister, Hayden Danvers."

"I knew her," he said. "Sure. She told me she had a brother. I remember some skinny kid with preppy clothes. She'd point you out and say, 'That's my big brother,' and I'd think, *That little turd is related to Hayden?*" He shook his head. "You never can tell, though. I have a cousin who's a history professor at Ohio State. I bet you can't believe that, can you?"

"Sure."

"Sure you can't or sure you can?"

"I can believe it."

"I can too. Guy was always an asshole."

Jesse Dean's voice carried the country twang that a lot of the locals spoke with, and beneath that, his voice possessed the husky timbre of someone who had smoked for many years. Jason imagined that mornings for Jesse Dean consisted of a lot of coughing and throat clearing. Despite his calm demeanor, Jesse Dean gave off a sense of power. He looked like a man ready to fight, someone who didn't doubt his ability to prevail in a physical confrontation.

"What do you want?" Jason asked.

"What do I want? What do *you* want? You're the guy who showed up at my house, bothering my wife. For all I know, you're the one who sent the cops around. So let me ask you—what's your problem? You're wanting to know where Hayden is?"

"That's a start."

"I don't know where she is," Jesse Dean said. "Knowing her, she probably fell into a bottle somewhere."

"She was with you. Someone saw you together."

"A few days ago? Sure, I hung out with her a little bit. She came back into town and looked me up. We used to be friends, so we went out the one night. That's it. We had a good time, and then we moved on. Maybe she went back to that little house of hers in Redman County."

"You've been there?"

"I know things."

"Was Hayden drinking?" Jason asked.

Jason couldn't look at Jesse Dean after he asked that question. He wasn't sure he wanted to know the answer, but he couldn't stop himself from asking.

"Which do you care about more?" Jesse Dean asked. "Where she is, or if she was drinking?"

"You already said you don't know where she is," Jason said.

"Let's just say that some things about Hayden seemed different. She was older. Not quite as sexy as she used to be, but that happens with age. Her clothes were better. But she still knew how to have a good time. I'd say it's hardwired into her, like in her genes or something, but that must have skipped you."

"Did she say where she was going when she left?" Jason asked.

"Nope. And I don't care. You shouldn't either. You can go

back to your nice little life here and to your house with your wife and your niece—"

Jason looked up at the mention of Sierra.

"I know the girl's staying with you," Jesse Dean said. "Hayden told me." He scratched the stubble on his chin. "She told me she figures you and your wife think you'd be better parents for the girl anyway, seeing as how you have some money and jobs and stability and all that. Hayden . . . well, if she's here partying, she's probably not doing much to hold on to that job she has in the dentist's office in Redman County, is she?"

"Was Derrick with you? Have you seen him?"

"Derrick?" Jesse Dean scrunched his forehead as though he was trying to place the name and match it to a face. "He lives in Indiana. He's a Hoosier now."

"So you haven't seen him?"

"He's your brother-in-law. Ex, I guess."

Jason felt both physically and emotionally lower. He sank into the seat, his shoulders slumping as if under pressure. He said, "They found Hayden's car up at the Bluff. The keys were still in it, and there was some blood on the seat and in the trunk. We don't know where she is, and we're worried about her. She has a daughter. You have to understand that. Do you have any children?"

Jesse Dean considered Jason for a moment. Then he said, "I have a boy. He's up in Michigan with his mom."

"So you understand that it's important for Hayden to get back to her daughter. Her daughter needs her. Now, do you have any idea where she went? Or where she might be?"

Jesse Dean used his index finger to trace random patterns on the passenger-side window. Jason thought he wasn't going to say anything else or answer the question, but eventually he lowered his hand into his lap and said, "I have a theory about these things. They have a way of working themselves out."

"What does that mean?"

He started tracing on the window again. "It means you need to stay out of it. Just back away and remove yourself. None of this is a thing for you to be involved in."

"What do you mean by 'this'? Do you know where Hayden is?"

"Whatever Hayden is here for. Just . . . stay the fuck out of it." He spoke with more authority and emphasis than he had at any time since he'd climbed into the car. He punctuated his words with short karate-chop-type gestures. "Some things are beyond you, you know? Your sister travels in a different world from you. Working in a dentist office doesn't change that. Okay?"

"If she's in trouble, maybe I can help her. That's what I'm trying to say. How do I know she doesn't need something from me, and I don't even know where she is?"

"Just stay out of it, Professor. Swim in the shallow end of the pool, okay? And if the police come to my house again because they say you told them something about me . . . I'm giving you a freebie here because I don't think you know what you're doing. And because I'm friends with Hayden. But if there's another knock on my door like that, whether I'm home or not . . . I just can't let that stand."

Jesse Dean looked like a man struggling. His words as well as the look on his face told Jason he was trying to suppress some deeper impulse, one that would have likely resulted in the infliction of pain upon Jason. Jason felt sweat forming near his hairline. He was hot. He wanted to start the car, to at least get air circulating somehow. He felt like he was in a cage with Jesse Dean, but he didn't want the man to get out. When Jesse Dean grabbed the door handle and pulled, Jason reached over and placed his hand on Jesse Dean's left arm, an instinctual grab. He didn't want to hold on to the *man*. He wanted to hold on to the surest bet he had for finding Hayden.

Jesse Dean whipped around. He brought his right hand up and pressed its palm against Jason's throat, driving Jason's head back against the seat. Jesse Dean applied steady pressure. Jason felt his airway tightening, but he couldn't turn his head or slip free. Just as Jason felt the air completely shut off, Jesse Dean let go. He lowered his hand and pulled back. Jason's head slumped forward. He raised his own hand to his throat and placed it there, massaging the skin while the air came back with coughs and gasps.

"Don't do that," Jesse Dean said. "I told you. You're in over your head here. You're going to get fucked."

Jason's air came back. He cleared his throat several times.

"You're okay," Jesse Dean said, his voice still calm. "I didn't want to hurt you."

"That's reassuring," Jason said.

"I'm going now," Jesse Dean said. "Pretend you didn't see me if the police ask. I'm leaving Ednaville anyway." He reached for the door again but didn't push it open. "If Hayden doesn't come back . . . well, just remember that everyone makes their own choices in this life. Okay?"

When Jason spoke, his throat felt scratchy and raw. He believed he could feel the bruises forming. "Hayden's car? The Bluff? Do you know anything about that? They found a body up there, but it's not hers. It's a skeleton. They're going to stop looking for Hayden. Should they keep looking up there? Do you at least know that?"

"A skeleton?" Jesse Dean said. "I saw that on the news."

Jason waited for him to say more, but he pushed the door open and left, slamming it closed behind him. Jason looked up.

He saw someone in the cab of the truck next to Jesse Dean. The face looked over at Jason, laughing. It was Rose. Rose Holland. Before Jason could do or say anything else, Jesse Dean was in the pickup and driving away, the broken taillight looking back at Jason like a jagged smile.

Chapter Twenty-eight

When Jason arrived at home, he found Nora and Sierra watching a movie in the darkened living room, a bowl of popcorn and several empty Coke cans on the coffee table before them. They were sitting close to each other on the couch, their bodies supported by pillows brought down from the bedrooms. Jason didn't recognize the movie they were watching. On the screen, a man sat in a bar discussing his girlfriend with his best friend.

"You're trapped, man," the friend said. "You can't live with her, and you can't live without her."

Nora looked up without pausing the movie.

"We decided we needed a break," she said. "Something to take our mind off of everything."

"I don't want to interrupt."

"We've both seen this one before," Sierra said. "We're just getting to the good part." She didn't look back at the screen. She kept her eyes on Jason.

"Are you doing okay?" he asked.

"I'm fine," she said. She tried to put on a brave face, but Jason still saw the burden of Hayden's disappearance in her eyes. "Aunt Nora is a good playmate."

"Good." He didn't know what else he could say. "I'm heading upstairs to change."

"Hey," Nora said. "I wanted to show you some mail that came today."

"Do you want me to pause it?" Sierra asked.

"No. Not unless he gets to the train station. I want to see that part."

Nora followed Jason up the stairs. He started to undress, taking off his shirt and slipping out of his pants. Nora came into the room and closed the door behind her.

"What gives?" he asked. "You don't even look at the mail."

"What happened to your neck?" Nora asked.

"It's nothing."

"Nothing? Jesus." She stepped forward. "I didn't see this in the dark downstairs. It looks like someone tried to choke you."

"They did." He told her about Jesse Dean climbing into the car and his warning to back off. While he told the story, he found his hand reaching up and gently touching the irritated skin around his neck. He suspected it would hurt worse in the morning. "I think he knows something. First he denied that he knew where Hayden was, but then he started saying things that made me believe that wasn't true. I don't know. That's the sense I got from him."

"Are you going to tell Olsen?" Nora asked.

"Tell him what? They already know about Jesse Dean."

"He assaulted you."

"Sure. He also made it very clear to me that he knows where I live. And that he knows Sierra is staying here. He didn't phrase it as a threat, but it sure sounded like one."

"All the more reason to call the police."

"We'll see. The guy's always been a maniac."

"Sounds like it."

Jason looked at his throat in the mirror. He saw the angry red mark on his skin. "I think that's the first time I've ever talked to Jesse Dean. Maybe I said hi to him or something in school. He was always this mythological figure to me, larger than life. He seemed smarter than I expected."

"Most sociopaths are smart."

Jason turned away from the mirror. Nora was sitting on the bed wearing shorts and a Mets T-shirt and had her hair pulled back with a headband. She sat far enough back on the bed that her feet didn't reach the floor, and she swung them around in circles while they talked.

"You might be right," Jason said. "But there was something about him. It was as though he was telling me that I shouldn't assume things about him, that I shouldn't look for easy answers when it came to him. Or Hayden."

"And then he choked you?"

"I didn't say he was all soft diplomacy. Why are you up here anyway? Did something happen?"

Nora reached into her shorts pocket and brought out a slip of paper. She held it between her thumb and forefinger. "We got a call today."

"The police?"

"Derrick."

"Derrick? What did he want?"

"He wants to talk to you about Sierra. Apparently, I'm not good enough to hear whatever he has to say. He didn't say what exactly was on his mind. He was kind of evasive to be honest."

"What did he say to Sierra?" Jason asked.

"He said he didn't want to talk to her yet. I was relieved about that. We'd just come back from the video store, and she was making the popcorn when the call came. I took it in the other room. He did ask how she was doing, and I said she was hanging in there as best she could."

"Did he ask about Hayden?"

"Not really. He asked if there was any news, and I said there wasn't."

Jason came over and took the paper from her hand. He unfolded it and saw a phone number with an Indianapolis area code. "Did he sound . . . I don't know . . . unusual in any way?"

"He seemed pretty calm," Nora said. "Not that he and I have ever had much to say to each other."

"And you didn't tell Sierra he called?"

"No," she said. "I felt like a shit keeping a secret from her, but I figured it was best until we knew what he wanted. Why disrupt her mind even more? Do you think that was the right thing to do?"

"Yes, it was. I'll call him."

Through the closed bedroom door, they heard Sierra call for Nora. She stood up and opened the door. "Is it the train?"

"Yes."

"Be right there." Nora turned back to Jason and spoke in a low voice. "Find out what he wants. But don't take any shit from him, Jason. Don't let him convince you of anything."

"What would he convince me of?"

Nora pressed her lips together like she was holding something back. "I'm terrified he's going to say he wants to come and take Sierra away from here."

"I know," Jason said. "But if he wants to do that—"

"Talk him out of it. That's what you need to do. Talk him out of it. Man to man and all that shit. Just turn him in another direction."

"We don't even know what he wants, okay?"

Nora still looked upset. She pressed her lips together again and looked away from Jason.

"I hear what you're saying," he said. "I do. I'll do whatever I can. I will. I'm going to see what's on his mind."

"Fine," Nora said. "I just . . . This is important to me."

"I know." They stood awkwardly before each other. "Hey," Jason said. "At least I can't get choked through the phone."

Chapter Twenty-nine

Jason closed the door behind Nora. He placed the paper with the phone number on the nightstand. He tried to remember the last time he had spoken to Derrick. If he hadn't seen or spoken to Hayden in five years, it had to be longer than that for Derrick. Six? Seven? He and Derrick had always carried on a cautiously respectful relationship. Without saying it out loud, both men seemed to accept that they were vastly different from the other, and so they confined their talk and interactions to the most superficial topics. Sports. Weather. Jason realized something was about to change with his former brother-in-law. They were going to have to have a *real* conversation, either about Hayden or Sierra or both.

Derrick's voice had always sounded thin, like something in his lungs wasn't providing enough air to create full volume. And the voice fit the makeup of Derrick's body. He was a tall, reedy guy, and looking at Sierra, it was easy to see where she got her length and height.

"Derrick? It's Jason."

Jason didn't know how much time—if any—the two of them should spend on pleasant formalities. Should he be asking what Derrick was doing with his life? Did any of that matter in the midst of a crisis?

Derrick made the decision for them. He didn't waste any time in getting to the business at hand.

"Thanks for calling back," Derrick said. "I was hoping we could talk about Sierra."

"She's doing just fine, if you're calling to ask how she is."

"I talked to Nora about that already," Derrick said. "I know you two would take good care of her, but we have to make some decisions about her. About where she's going."

Derrick possessed a coldness. That was the only way Jason could think of it. *Coldness.* He always seemed to be holding something back and maintaining a distance from the people he interacted with. In that sense, he seemed like a good complement to Hayden, who laid everything bare for the world to see. But his manner made Jason uneasy as they talked about Sierra. Jason didn't want his niece's future to seem like a business transaction, something handled based on practicality and good sense.

"We don't mind having her here," Jason said. "She has schoolwork to do, and she's been trying to do some of that. We have an extra room for her."

"I know that. And I appreciate it. But it seems like maybe she should be with her father at a time like this. There's so much uncertainty about Hayden. There always has been, I guess, but now . . . Well, the police called and filled me in. They told me about the car. And the blood. I even had to prove my whereabouts to them. I guess if something happens to a wife, even an ex-wife, they look at the husband. I think they're backing off of me, at least for now."

"You know Hayden's all cleaned up," Jason said. "At least she was when she came to our house the other night. It seemed real, Derrick. But then——"

"Someone saw her with Jesse Dean."

"Yes. Are you in touch with him at all?"

"Jesse Dean and I aren't friends anymore. He's . . . he's always been a little too wild for me."

"Do you know why Hayden would be with him? She came here saying that she needed to make amends for something as part of her twelve-step program. Is there something that has to do with Jesse Dean that she would need to make amends for? Sierra says her mom was talking to Jesse Dean on the phone before she came here."

"Well, you know Hayden. If there's something bothering her, she's not just going to let it go. She's going to keep gnawing at it until *everybody* has to deal with it. She and Jesse Dean were friends of course. Sometimes they even spent time together without me. When I was at work and things like that, they'd hang out. I don't even want to think of what could have happened between the two of them."

"Are you saying there might have been something between them? Something sexual?"

"I'm not going to sit here and act like I don't know who Hayden was back then. So there's nothing she could do that would surprise me."

"Since you brought that up . . . do you know if there was ever anything between Hayden and Logan Shaw?"

There was a long pause. Jason feared he may have offended Derrick by bringing up something potentially unpleasant from the past. Maybe he was okay with speculating about Hayden and his good friend Jesse Dean. But Hayden and a guy like Logan? A rich guy? Was that too much?

"Derrick?" Jason thought he heard voices in the background, someone talking on Derrick's end of the phone. "Hello?"

"That's your friend, right?"

"Yes."

"I don't know. I never knew everything she did. I don't know anything now."

"You don't sound too worried about Hayden's safety. Are you? I mean, the blood in the trunk and the car just sitting up there on the Bluff with the keys in it. All of that."

Derrick sighed. "Let me tell you something you probably don't know. In fact, I'm sure you don't know about it, because I never told you, and I'm sure Hayden didn't either. She liked to act like she told everybody everything, but there were some things she wouldn't spill. And there were things she wouldn't tell *you* because she valued your opinion of her too much. She looked up to you. She always did."

"I know."

"One night when Sierra was about a year old. Maybe a little more. She was able to crawl by then and was even pulling herself up by the furniture and then falling down again. I came home from work. Do you know what Hayden was doing?"

"I don't know. Drinking, I guess."

"She was drinking all right. But she wasn't doing it in the house. She was gone. She went out drinking and left Sierra home alone. A one-year-old."

Jason felt heartsick hearing the story. He felt like someone had thumped him in the center of his chest. If Sierra seemed vulnerable as a teenager, then he couldn't bear to imagine her as a neglected child. . . .

"Did she come right back?" Jason asked.

"Two days," Derrick said. "Two days of partying. She told me she made sure she left close to the time I was getting home so the baby wouldn't be alone for very long. Can you believe that?"

Jason didn't try to answer right away, but he felt compelled to mount some defense of his sister, who had so frequently been indefensible. "She's changed, Derrick," he said. "I'd like to believe that."

He *wanted* to believe it. But he wasn't sure he could. How did he know that Hayden was a different person after all the broken promises? What made him think she meant it this time?

"I'm telling you this story not because I want to trash Hayden to her brother. I wouldn't do that. And I wouldn't trash her to Sierra either. She and I don't play those games."

"Then why are you telling me this?" Jason asked, although he could have guessed at the answer that came.

"She's left her child behind before," he said. "More than once."

"And you think this is just another one of those broken promises?"

"I haven't been the best father either. I know I haven't seen the girl in a while. You see, I want to come there and be with her and take her in. I want to play a more active role in things, the way a father should."

"Sure," Jason said.

"You don't sound like you believe me. You're probably lumping me in with Hayden, and that's okay."

"Derrick—"

"But I'm trying to get some things resolved in my life. Things have to be set up a little better. I'm starting a new job. I'm moving into a new place. It's tough starting over at our age, you know?"

"I know."

"Right. You've been laid off and had to move out of New York. You get it. Look, I'm hoping I'll have some things taken care of soon, and then . . . then things will just make more sense. I'm hoping Hayden does come back. I hope she sees her way through and puts Sierra first again."

"Are you supporting Sierra?" Jason asked.

"I am. Lately. Not that it's any of your business."

"What if Hayden doesn't come back?" Jason asked. "What if . . . You know awful things happen to people, especially up on that bluff. I'm sure you know they found a body up there when they were looking for Hayden. A skeleton. What if something similar happened to Hayden? What if her body is somewhere?"

Again, Derrick's end of the conversation seemed to have stopped. Jason listened for a moment and heard the sound of laughing, faint and distant, from downstairs. Sierra and Nora and their silly movie. He looked at the phone and saw the call was still active.

"I need to know . . . has Sierra said anything else about Hayden?" Derrick asked. "Anything besides hearing her talk to Jesse Dean?"

"I think she's as in the dark as we all are," Jason said.

"Good," Derrick said. "That's good. She doesn't need to be mixed up in this stuff."

"She's not."

"And you're really sure that's all she said?" Derrick asked.

"Yes. I'm sure. Are you sure? What exactly are we talking about here, Derrick?" Jason asked.

"Let's just keep her out of it, okay? We can all agree on that."

"Of course," Jason said, but Derrick had already hung up.

He went downstairs where Nora and Sierra were watching the end of their movie. When he came into the room and stood next to the couch, Nora looked up at him.

"So, how's it going?" she asked.

He knew that she wanted to know if Derrick was coming to get Sierra.

"I think everything seems fine," he said. "Just fine."

"Good," Nora said. She turned her attention back to the movie.

Chapter Thirty

"Are you at work?"

Jason was. He'd been there all morning, and when his office phone rang shortly before lunch, he picked it up without even wondering who might be on the other end. He recognized the voice right away.

"Regan?"

A long pause. "Yes, it's me."

"Of course I'm at work. Is something wrong?"

"Have you heard the news?" she asked.

"No. Did something happen?" Jason's heart dropped. What had he missed? "Is this about Hayden? Did they find her?"

"I wanted to try to catch you now. It's already been on the radio. That's where I heard it."

"Heard what?"

"That body they found up on the Bluff. Jason, it's Logan's body. They identified it this morning."

"Logan?"

Jason's mind couldn't catch up to the words he was hearing. Regan wasn't making any sense. Logan? His body on the Bluff? It couldn't be. Logan was gone. Long gone. But he wasn't dead. He wasn't a body. He wasn't a bunch of bones scattered in the woods, left there to be found by a cadaver dog years and years later.

"I have to go, Jason. I have work, and it's just too much right now."

"Regan? I think this is a mistake. You must have misunderstood what they said."

"It's not a mistake, Jason. I have to go."

She hung up.

Jason called Detective Olsen, who picked up after the first ring. Jason skipped the formalities and asked the question. "What is going on, Detective? I got a call from a high school friend."

"Are you at home or work?" Olsen asked.

"Work."

"I'll meet you there in about ten minutes. I'm in that area."

"My friend says this body or skeleton or whatever is Logan Shaw. Is it?"

"We should talk in person," Olsen said. "I know things are coming out on the news already."

"Is it Logan Shaw?" Jason asked.

There was a pause. Then Olsen said, "Yes, it is."

Jason met Olsen in front of his office building. The detective pulled up in a dark blue sedan, a Chevy Impala, and when he stepped out of the car, he wore a suit and sunglasses. He came toward Jason as the breeze picked up, blowing his tie askew. Jason met Olsen halfway and guided the detective toward a picnic table that sat in the grass under a shade tree. People ate their lunches out there and took their cigarette breaks. It would be a quiet place to talk.

"Tell me about this," Jason said as they sat. He felt hollow, like the husk of a person.

Jason positioned himself with his back against the table, and Olsen straddled the bench. "I wanted to see you so I could tell you in person about this," Olsen said. "Obviously, that didn't work out. But I'm sorry to report that the skeletal remains we found on Thompson Bluff are those of Logan Shaw. They were positively identified by the medical examiner's office."

"How?" Jason asked.

"How were they identified? We used dental records. You played a role in the whole thing. After you mentioned it to me, I looked into the case a little more. There isn't much on it since no one *really* considered Mr. Shaw a missing person, not after the first few days. But I did find some information in our old case files. I located Mr. Shaw's mother, and she gave me the right name. The dentist is retired but still has his records in storage. It was pretty easy from there."

"But Logan can't be dead," Jason said. "He left town. He went out west. He sent letters to his parents."

"I'm aware of all that," Olsen said. "As far as the medical examiner can tell, that body's been in the woods a long time. Maybe twenty-five years or so. Isn't that how long ago you graduated from high school?"

"Twenty-seven," Jason said.

"That's what I thought. And that's the last time anyone saw Mr. Shaw. It makes sense. He was on the Bluff that night, and he was never seen again."

"It doesn't make sense. The letters . . ."

"I haven't seen these letters. I understand they're in the possession of Mr. Shaw's father, and his health isn't that great. We'll get up there and take a look at them when we can, but chances

are those letters are a misunderstanding. Or an attempt by someone to cover something up."

"You mean to say that someone killed Logan? Is that what
you're saying?"

"Do you know of anyone who would want to?" Olsen asked.
"You and he were close friends, right? Wouldn't you know the
things that were going on in his life? Did anyone threaten him?
Was he having a fight with anybody?"

Jason couldn't answer. He tried to focus his mind. How long
had he known this news? Fifteen minutes? It hadn't sunk in. It
couldn't sink in.

But there was Olsen before him. So certain. So sure. They'd used
dental records. What else did Jason need to know? And as he sat
there, just a few feet away from the detective, he admitted to himself that it made sense in a way. Was it possible to believe that Logan
left all those years ago and never made contact with anyone again?
Jason assumed Logan would come back someday. When he and
Nora moved back to town after Jason lost his job, he felt defeated.
Wiped out. And his marriage needed serious attention. But when
adding up the pluses and minuses of taking that step backward to
Ednaville, Jason put the possibility of seeing Logan again into the
plus category. If he lived here long enough, and Logan's parents
aged and died, wouldn't he see his friend again then? At the very
least, wouldn't there be some occasion when he could see him again?

And, instead, he'd been lying in the woods all those years,
his body decaying back to dust while the rest of the world went
on with their lives.

It couldn't be.

"Would you like to talk another time?" Olsen asked. "I can
drive you home."

"He was my best friend. For years."

"I know."

Above their heads birds chirped. People came and went from the office, leaving or returning from lunch in small packs. Young secretaries. Older executives. It all went on and on.

"How did nobody find his body all those years?" Jason asked.

"It was in a remote area. Off the beaten path a little. Unless you were looking for something, as we were when your sister's car was found, you wouldn't see it. We only found it because of the dogs. And the search for your sister."

"Thanks, Hayden," Jason said.

"What's that?"

"Nothing. This wouldn't have happened if it weren't for Hayden showing up and getting into whatever clusterfuck she got herself into." Jason shook his head. He recognized that his anger toward Hayden was misdirected as he said, "She can't help but stir the pot wherever she goes. Disasters just seem to stream along behind her. I love her so much, but she really . . . sometimes she drives me to the brink."

"Do you think your sister being missing has something to do with Mr. Shaw's death?" Olsen asked.

"Do you?"

"I don't know anything right now."

"Neither do I." Jason looked down at his shaking hands. He brought them together, folded them one into the other in an effort at steadiness. "I was thinking about Hayden and Logan, ever since you mentioned that body being found up there. I tried to make a link between the two of them."

"And?"

"Nothing. Hayden was flirtatious with everyone. I don't know if she and Logan ever did anything or not. If Hayden were here, you could ask her. . . ."

"I'd very much like to ask her that," Olsen said.

Jason straightened up. Something clicked in his mind, something that seemed important. "How do you even know what killed him after all this time? I mean, how do you know he didn't just trip and fall? Or have an aneurysm in the woods? There'd be nothing left to examine."

"We know the cause of death," Olsen said.

"What is it?"

"Bones can tell a story," Olsen said. "Now, didn't you and Mr. Shaw have some kind of altercation that night?"

"Yeah, we did."

"What about?"

"A girl. We fought over a girl."

"You fought? With fists or just with words?"

Olsen's face and voice had taken on a slightly harder cast. To that point, the detective had seemed almost casual as they sat at the picnic table discussing the discovery of Jason's best friend's body. But Olsen suddenly seemed to be on the hunt for something, as though the entire conversation had been an elaborate warm-up for the questions he really wanted to ask.

"I talked about this with the police back then," Jason said. "They treated me like a suspect."

"*I* didn't say suspect."

"What are you doing to find Hayden?" Jason asked. "She's still missing."

"Have you heard anything from her?"

"No, I haven't. But maybe if you found Jesse Dean Pratt, you could figure it out. Maybe you could figure it all out."

"Have you seen him?" Olsen pointed at Jason's neck. "It looks like someone grabbed hold of you."

"I did see him. He's mad that I told the police about him. In fact, he threatened me. He said if I involved the police anymore . . ."

"We need to know everything that's happened," Olsen said. "We can protect you. And your family."

Jason sighed. "Okay."

Olsen took out a notebook and listened while Jason recounted his run-in with Jesse Dean. He asked Jason what kind of car Jesse Dean was driving and which direction he drove off in. Jason told the detective everything he could remember. When he was finished, Olsen closed the notebook and slipped it back into his coat pocket.

"Would you like me to drive you home?" Olsen asked. "Can I do anything else for you before I go?"

"Find my sister," Jason said. "Find out who killed Logan."

"We're working on it. The girl the two of you fought over back then? Who was she?"

"A friend of ours. Regan Maines. Now her name is Regan Kreider. She lives here in town. She's the one who called and told me you all had identified Logan's body this morning. She heard it on the news before I did. She wanted me to hear from a friendly voice, I guess."

"She lives here in Ednaville?"

"Yes."

"So you're still in touch?"

"We're friends," Jason said, his voice sharp.

Olsen nodded, apparently noting the hint of defensiveness that had crept into Jason's voice.

"Let me ask you something else," Olsen said. "You fought with Mr. Shaw that night, right?"

"Yes."

"And you say you fought over a girl. This Regan Kreider. So both of you wanted to date her? Is that it? You both had feelings for her?"

"We were all friends. Good friends. We became very close, the three of us, during our last couple of years of high school."

"Were either of you actually dating her?" Olsen asked.

"No." Then Jason hesitated. "Well, I know I wasn't. I guess I can't say for certain what anyone else was doing."

"So Ms. Maines and Mr. Shaw might have been an item?" Olsen asked.

"I doubt it. I don't know. I thought it was more likely she and I would have been. I thought we were closer back then. We seemed to have a real connection."

But Jason had to admit—at least to himself—that Regan had been evasive and guarded whenever Logan's name came up. If there was more to the story, she wasn't sharing it with him.

"So what precipitated this fight?" Olsen asked.

Jason looked at the bright blue sky. There were no clouds. Somewhere in the distance a plane sailed past, far overhead. Jason couldn't hear it. He just saw the faint silver streak against the sky, burnished by the sun.

"I told the police this back then. On that night, graduation night, we were all out at the Bluff. We'd been at one party. We were going to another later on. I was with Regan for a while, and then she and I split up. Apparently when we did, Logan found Regan and told her how he felt. She let him down. She said she was interested in me. He was drunk that night. He liked to drink, and when he drank, he could get mouthy. He came and found me and told me that I needed to stay away from Regan, that he wanted to be with her. We argued. We both said some things to each other."

"What did he say?" Olsen asked. "You said he could get mouthy. What kinds of things did he say?"

"Does it matter?"

"We can talk about it another time if you need to collect your thoughts." Olsen was saying the right things, but Jason could tell he didn't mean it. He showed no inclination to stand up or back off. "It's just that Mr. Shaw's death is going to be classified as a homicide, and anything we can learn about what we presume to be his last moments alive will help."

"You think you can solve it?"

"That's the idea," Olsen said. "So what happened that night?"

"I don't like to think about it."

"Because he was your friend? And you fought?"

"Yes. It was ugly." But Jason told the detective the whole story of the words and blows they exchanged. Even to his own ears, Jason's voice sounded distant and hollow. He didn't like the tone, but he felt powerless to change it. "In the end, he said that the sky was the limit for what he could do in life because his father had money, and that I was probably just going to end up working a middle-class job in Ednaville." Jason shrugged. "And here I am."

"There's nothing wrong with being middle-class in Ednaville," Olsen said. "Was that all he said?"

"It was enough."

"And what did you say to him?" Olsen asked.

Jason winced. He attacked Logan as hard as Logan attacked him. He fought dirty verbally. "I told him that at least my parents stayed together. That his father and mother hated each other so much his mother left and didn't give a shit about either one of them. We'd never talked about their divorce before. He always seemed a little ashamed of it, I guess. His mother left the house, and Jason was mostly raised by his dad. It was unusual. Most divorced kids stayed with their mothers."

"Why didn't he?"

"I don't know. I figured it was because the old man had so much money. He wouldn't lose if they fought about it in court."

"No way to know. Courts tend to favor the mother, that's true. Especially back then. So that set him off? The stuff about his parents?"

"I don't even remember who threw the first punch. I just know that all of a sudden we were swinging at each other. I'd never been in a fight before, and there I was fighting with my best friend. Over a girl. It seemed almost . . . surreal, I guess. I didn't feel any of the punches he landed. It must have been adrenaline. It was like I was outside of myself watching the fight happen."

"You say he punched you more than once. Did you hit him back?"

"Sure. I don't know how many times. At least a few."

"Body blows? Head blows?"

"I don't know. I was just swinging. I was mad." Jason looked down at his hands again. He had never made them into fists that way again. Never swung at anyone, had never been forced to. And that was the only way he would do it. If he were forced to. "Are you going to tell me how he died?"

"How did the fight end?" Olsen asked.

"I hit him. One good shot to the side of the head." A sadness crept over Jason just thinking of it. The feeling came back to him, a sense memory tingling in his hand. The rough thump of knuckle against skull. "I was crying. I know that. We both were. Like a couple of little kids. We were so worked up, so angry and distraught, we were both losing it. Logan was on the ground, and I was standing. He got up and walked away. He didn't even look back. He just walked away from me."

"And that was the last time you saw him?"

"Yes."

"And he was walking and moving fine? No injuries?"

"Not that I'm aware of."

"What did you do?"

"I went off walking by myself. I wanted to try to calm down. I'd been crying, so I sure as hell didn't want to run into other kids from school. I didn't want to be the guy who was found crying when he was eighteen years old because he got in a fight with his friend. I just walked around the park, back on one of the trails, trying to clear my head. I thought he and I would run into each other later and work it out. I knew we'd said some things, some awful things, but I didn't think we'd have that between us. We'd been friends for too long."

"But he was gone?" Olsen asked.

"Yes, he was gone. I didn't see him the rest of the night. His dad called our house the next day. He asked me if I knew where Logan was. I told him I didn't know. His dad never showed any emotion. He was stoic and distant. But I could tell by the tone in the old man's voice that he was actually worried. It unnerved me when I heard that. I thought something might really be wrong, and the next thing I knew, the police were at my door asking me questions. That's how the whole thing started with me and the police. But what could I tell them? All I knew was that Logan was gone."

Chapter Thirty-one

"What about Regan Kreider?" Olsen asked. "You must have talked to her about Logan back then?"

"Yes, I did."

"And what did she have to say about him? Did she see him after you did?"

"She did. He went back to her after our fight. He told her that he was done with the whole town and that he wanted to run away. He said he wanted Regan to go with him. See, that's the thing about Logan. He was always talking about running away. He always said he wanted to go out west and start a new life where nobody knew him."

"Why did he want to do that?"

"Doesn't every kid want to do that?"

"Sure," Olsen said. "Few actually do it."

"I assumed Logan did. Regan said she wasn't going anywhere except to college, which she did. After she told Logan that, he left. He seemed upset and angry, but he left."

"Did she know the two of you had fought?"

"Yes. I think she tried to calm him down."

"So she didn't notice any injuries? Bloody nose? Swollen eye?"

"You'd have to ask her. I don't think she ever mentioned it to me, but I'm not sure I ever asked. Don't you have old reports about all of this?"

"Some. The detective who investigated originally died about ten years ago. There's not much to go on." He stretched his back a little. "You probably have to get back to work."

Jason looked up at the building. The light hit the front, reflecting off the windows. He squinted. "I don't even know if I'm going back in today. I've missed so much time lately."

"You've had a lot going on," Olsen said. "I'm sure they understand. If you'd like, I can contact your HR department and inform them of the events involving your sister and your niece."

"No, thanks. It's fine."

"If you'll indulge me a few minutes longer, then . . . What did you do after Logan was gone and after you were questioned by the police?"

"I didn't want to stay here. The college I was going to—Ohio University—had a summer program, something where you could arrive early and take a couple of classes. I asked my parents, and I went off to that." Jason shook his head. "I just didn't like the idea of being around here and being forced to remember everything that happened with Logan. It felt like a page had been turned. He left, so I needed to leave too."

"And the girl?"

"Regan? What about her?"

"What happened with the two of you?" Olsen asked.

"That moment was gone. It just dried up and blew away. The spell was broken."

"And you didn't worry about Mr. Shaw?" Olsen asked.

"He started writing to his dad. It all fit. And I figured he'd come back in six months or a year. I kept expecting him to show up in my dorm someday, a big grin on his face. Or I'd come home for

Christmas, and he'd just be here full of stories about whatever bullshit he was doing out west. Working on a ranch or living in L.A. I still thought that day would come even once I moved back here."

Olsen nodded. He seemed to be finished with Jason. "I'll probably be talking to Ms. Kreider about this as well."

"It's Mrs. Kreider technically," Jason said. "She's divorced, but she kept her husband's name. She has kids."

"Got it." Olsen stood up. He arched his back again as though it had grown stiff sitting on the bench. "If you think of anything else, let me know."

"I will."

"You'll be around, won't you?"

"Where would I go?" Jason asked. "I'm not leaving, I can't leave, until I know what's going on with Hayden. And now this."

"We'll be in touch, then."

"What about Jesse Dean Pratt?" Jason asked. "He was with Hayden, and now Hayden is missing. If Hayden was here because of something to do with Logan, then doesn't it stand to reason that Jesse Dean might know about all of it?"

"We're looking for him," Olsen said. "At this point, everything is on the table." He pointed to Jason's neck. "Would you like me to take a report about that? We could add it to the list for Mr. Pratt."

"No, I don't want you worrying about me. I told my coworkers I was mugged. It's been getting me a lot of sympathy and questions I don't want. I just want you to find out what's really going on with everything else."

"If you see him again—"

"I'll call an expert. Don't worry. I like being able to breathe."

Chapter Thirty-two

After Olsen left, Jason remained at the picnic table. He stared down at his hands. They dangled loosely, his elbows resting on his knees. The hands felt numb, seemingly disconnected from the rest of his body.

Logan was dead. Not Hayden. No one knew where Hayden was. But they knew about Logan. Finally. He was dead. He had been dead for all those years.

What the hell had happened to Logan after he left Jason?

An awful realization crept over him, aided by some of Detective Olsen's words: *And he was walking and moving fine? No injuries?*

How did Jason know what injuries Logan had? A healthy young guy ends up dead on the night of his high school graduation. What could have happened after he and Jason parted ways? Had Jason hit him hard enough to cause an injury that led to his death?

Olsen *knew* how Logan died. The detective said he knew the cause of death, but he didn't share it with Jason. *Bones can tell a story,* he had said. It meant that whatever they thought killed Logan was obvious from an examination of his skeleton. Did that mean a beating? A crack in the skull or other bones?

That last punch came back to him again. Knuckle against skull. Bone against bone.

"Jesus," Jason said. "Jesus Christ."

He lowered his head into his hands. He ran his fingers through his hair, pulling at the roots until his scalp burned.

He spoke through gritted teeth. "Oh, Jesus. God. What did I do?"

He leaned forward, placing his head between his knees.

He stayed like that for a few minutes, his eyes closed. His teeth remained clenched so tight his jaws started to ache. He felt the pain around his ears and into the back of his skull.

For the second time he found himself a suspect in the disappearance of Logan Shaw. For the first time he wondered if he might very well be guilty.

At Farmers' Bank and Credit, the assistant branch manager told Jason that Regan wasn't in. He seemed reluctant to give Jason any additional information. Just getting him to admit that Regan wasn't in the branch took some doing.

"Is she out for the day or is she off at a meeting or something?" Jason asked.

"I can't say," he said. "Is this business or personal? If it's work related, maybe I can help you."

Jason stood on the springy carpet while the hushed work of the bank went on around them. Phones lightly trilled and keyboards clacked. Jason swore he could hear the paper money rustling. He wanted to jump onto a desk and yell just to do something to break the intense calm.

The man was staring at Jason's neck. He had pulled on a sweatshirt, hoping it would hide some of the marks, but the man still stared.

"I got mugged," Jason said.

"Oh," the man said, suitably horrified. "How awful."

"I've tried calling Regan's phone, and she isn't answering," Jason said. "That's why I came by here. I thought maybe she was in a meeting."

"If she were in a meeting, you wouldn't be able to talk to her either," the man said.

The man was clean-cut, his clothes sharply pressed and starched. His voice remained level as he spoke.

Jason started to turn away, but he stopped himself. He couldn't just walk out without learning more, without taking one more chance.

"Look," Jason said, "she and I, we're old friends. We received some bad news about another friend of ours today. Is that why she left? Did something seem to happen?"

The man studied Jason, his face still revealing nothing. Jason assumed his efforts at making a human connection had failed as well, but the cast of the man's face shifted beneath the bright fluorescent lights. Something softened. He blinked a few times and lowered his voice.

"I don't know why she left," he said. "But she got a call from someone, and then she came and told me she had to go tend to a personal matter. Normally she tells me what these things are about. We're a friendly group here. But she didn't offer anything up this time. She just said she wouldn't be back today. I figured maybe one of her kids was sick, but that's the kind of thing she would have told me before. That's pretty common for a working mother."

"It is. And you don't know who this call was from?"

"No," the man said. "But . . ." He jerked his head and started toward an office. Jason followed. When they went inside, the man closed the door behind them. It was a small space, and the desk looked amazingly uncluttered. Only a computer and a neat stack of business cards sat on the smooth and dust-free surface. Jason wondered how anyone worked in such cleanliness.

"What is it?" Jason asked.

"I don't want to start any weird rumors about Regan." The man ran his hand through his short hair, and Jason saw that he didn't wear a wedding ring. "But she's been getting a lot of calls at work this week. Calls that seemed more personal than anything else."

"And you don't know who they're from."

The man shook his head. "I only say that because Regan is so professional, so focused when she's here. Her kids, her babysitters, they almost never call and bother her. Her ex-husband, Tim, he comes by from time to time."

"Still?"

"I'm sure he has to talk about the kids. When she's in this building, it's all about work. But this past week, she stepped out of more than one meeting to take another call. She seemed distracted, a little distant."

"I see," Jason said, noting the use of the word "distant." Were the man's concerns about Regan's behavior extending beyond work?

"Have *you* noticed anything about her?" the man asked. "I mean, you said you're friends with Regan. I've seen you here before."

"We grew up together. And, no, I haven't noticed anything too unusual. Like I said, this friend of ours . . ."

"I'm sorry about that," the man said. "I'm assuming. I mean . . . does it have anything to do with the body they found on Heroin Hill?"

"Yes," Jason said. "That's our friend. He died the night we graduated from high school apparently."

The man bit down on his upper lip and made a low grunt of sympathy, a sound that said, *That's tough*.

"Thanks," Jason said. "I suspect that's what she's upset about. A lot of memories have been coming up." He thought of his own fragmented memories and possible culpability, a sensation that manifested itself as a needlelike jab in his chest. Jason reached out and shook the man's hand. "I'll let you get back to work."

"One more thing," the man said as he let go of Jason's hand. "Again, I don't want to sound indelicate."

"What is it?"

"Yesterday, Regan left with a man. Now, I try very hard not to judge people. I try to—because I deal with all walks of life in here—I try to see everyone as worthy of my respect. Do you understand?"

"Of course," Jason said.

"But some people just seem beyond that consideration. When I was leaving here yesterday, I saw Regan in the parking lot, and she was talking to a man who just didn't seem to fit the kind of person Regan is."

"What did this man look like?"

"He wore a ball cap and a flannel shirt, work boots. But it's not his clothes that bothered me. It was something about the way he looked at me as I walked to my car. The expression on his face carried a warning, and I could see from the man's eyes that he meant it. He seemed to want me to challenge him in some way, and I have no doubt he would have welcomed the chance to show me what he could do if it came to a physical altercation."

"Did he have a scar here?" Jason asked, touching the skin around his eye.

The man looked at Jason's neck again. "Yes. You know him?"

"He's another old friend from school. You say Regan left with him?"

"She got into his truck and they drove off together."

"Did she say anything to you?"

"She waved. She didn't look happy to be going with the man, but she didn't seem to be in a lot of distress either. Believe me, if she were crying or something, if she'd signaled me that there was trouble, I would have called the police."

"She didn't say anything?" Jason asked.

"No." A sheepish look spread across the man's face. He blushed a little as well. "I admit I thought about the whole scene during the evening. I couldn't stop. I didn't want to call Regan and seem to be checking up on her, so I did something else."

"What?"

"I came back," the man said. "Around eight thirty or so I drove back here to the branch. Regan's car was gone by then, so I assumed she was okay. I know it's not conclusive, but it made me feel better. And then she was back at work this morning as though everything was normal."

"Until she got that call," Jason said.

"Exactly."

"Thanks again," Jason said.

"So you and Regan are old friends," the man said.

"Yes," Jason said. "Just friends. Always have been."

The man looked relieved, and Jason took comfort in knowing that at least one person's mind had been eased about something.

Chapter Thirty-three

Jason called Regan a few more times as he drove to her house.

Her house. Jason had never been there. Regan had told him the address and described the home she shared with her two children—and used to share with her ex-husband—but Jason had never set foot there. He respected the boundaries of her family life, just as Regan respected the boundaries of his marriage.

But it felt like all bets were off. He needed to talk to Regan more than ever, to ask her if there was anything else she remembered from that night Logan disappeared—*died*—and also to ask her about what he just learned at the bank: Why was she going somewhere with Jesse Dean Pratt?

As he drove to Regan's house, his phone rang. It was Nora. He had to answer. In the midst of everything else, he hadn't checked in on Sierra.

"Hello?"

"Jason? Are you still at work?"

"Not exactly."

"It sounds like you're in the car."

"I am. I have to take care of something."

"Jason." He heard the sympathy in Nora's voice. She'd heard already. "Have you spoken to Detective Olsen? He was looking for you."

"Yes, he came by the office."

Jason made a couple of quick turns and headed south on the Bypass toward the older subdivision where Regan lived.

"I'm sorry, Jason. I know that news is shocking. I can't imagine."

"Is Sierra okay?"

"Yes, she's fine. We're both fine. This news threw both of us for a loop. She's in the shower now. We were thinking of watching another movie or something. I don't know. I'm trying to keep her distracted."

"She'll be fine. She likes spending time with you. I can tell."

"That's nice of you to say. But I'm worried about you. Do you want to come home and talk about this?"

"I'll be home . . . shortly. I have to talk to Regan about Logan."

"Okay, well, remember that we'd like to see you here. It's a little unnerving to know that Hayden is missing and your friend is dead. And that guy you ran into yesterday tried to hurt you. We're here at the house, trying to keep our sanity."

Jason turned down Regan's street. "Keep the doors locked. And don't open them for anybody who shows up unless it's a cop."

"Is that supposed to reassure me?"

Jason began reading the house numbers on the mailboxes. He saw Regan's ahead on the left.

"No," he said, "it's not. But the police said they'd keep an eye on us. Call me if there are any problems."

No one answered the bell when Jason rang it. He tried again and then stepped back from the front door. He looked up at the two story brick house and saw that most of the blinds were closed and no lights burned. No one moved a curtain aside to see who was out on the stoop. Jason gave the knob a gentle turn, but felt the resistance right away. The door was locked.

He started to walk back to the car, the phone still in his hand. He considered calling Regan again, but what was the point? Wherever she was and whatever she was doing, she couldn't or wouldn't answer the phone. Her situation might be serious enough to warrant calling the police, and for a moment, that thought flickered through Jason's mind. But, again, what would he tell Detective Olsen? That his friend from high school was seen with Jesse Dean Pratt. Talking to him. Driving away with him. For all Jason knew, Regan was involved with something he couldn't comprehend—and bringing the police into it might make more trouble for Regan, the kind she didn't need or want right then.

A noise from the back of the house interrupted Jason's thoughts. It sounded like a raised voice, a shout. His body tensed. He waited for the sound to come again, and when it didn't, he wondered if he had imagined it or mistaken the sound of something else for the sound of a human voice. But before his feet moved again, he heard another, similar shout. The voice might have belonged to a child. Or to a woman.

Jason looked down the driveway to where it bent around the side of the house. He saw nothing. A few trees around the perimeter of Regan's property, and beyond that, a jungle gym in the neighbor's yard, one of those plastic monstrosities that seemed to dominate the suburban landscape. He started back that way, the phone still clutched in his hand. As he moved down the drive, his body close to the side of the house, another voice reached him. This one was masculine, deeper, and definitely adult. Jason recognized something in the tenor of that adult voice. It didn't indicate fear or danger. Instead, the voice sounded celebratory, almost joyous. When he reached the back, Jason saw the source of the noise. A man about his age, somewhat burly and wearing a red Windbreaker, threw a football to a boy who looked to be about twelve. They punctuated each throw and catch with one of the shouts.

The man stood with his back to Jason. As he caught the thrown ball, the boy pointed in Jason's direction, and the man turned around. He raised his eyebrows in greeting.

"Hello."

Jason felt stuck for an answer. He looked from the man to the boy and then back before saying, "I was looking for Regan."

A hint of suspicion spread across the man's face. "She's not home. Can I tell her who came by?"

"I'm Jason Danvers. I'm an old friend from high school."

Jason could tell the man recognized his name. Why wouldn't he? Jason was one of Regan's oldest friends. She had to have mentioned him from time to time over the years.

"I'm Tim," the man said, but he didn't offer a hand to shake. He held the football as though it were a precious object. "I'm Regan's husband. Ex-husband, I guess. I'm spending time with Chad while she's out."

"I'm sorry to interrupt your game."

Jason looked past Tim to the boy. He carried his resemblance to his mother around the eyes and in the color of his hair. He didn't appear impatient. He stood with his hands on his hips, squinting against the daylight.

Tim lowered his voice. "I'd give you some kind of hint about when she'll be back or how you can reach her, but I don't know those things. I guess you don't either."

"No," Jason said. "We didn't have plans. I just needed to ask her about something." Jason paused. "You know, she got some bad news about another old friend of ours this week."

"I know." Tim sounded more sympathetic. "That knocked her off the beam a little. She and I have spent some time talking through it." He studied Jason's face. "I guess it did the same to you. I'm sorry."

"Thanks."

"I'm sorry I can't be more help either," Tim said. He took a quick glance down to the end of the yard where his son still stood. "But Regan and I . . . Things are a little tentative between us."

"Tentative?"

"You're married, right?"

"Yes."

"Then you understand. It's complicated."

"Sure. I guess I'll see her somewhere."

"You know she's always been skittish about the past," Tim said.

Skittish? Jason didn't know and couldn't guess what Tim meant.

He explained without prompting. "Whenever the subject of the past came up, high school and old friends, Regan seemed guarded. She had a wall up about that. I'm from out of town. I didn't grow up here, and I never pressed hard, but I suspected something must have gone wrong when you all were in high school. I guess that's all being made clear this week with them finding the body of your friend."

"It was a shock to all of us," Jason said.

Tim shrugged. "I guess maybe I'll find out about it someday. I may have to read it in the papers, but I'll find out something." He held the ball up in the air between them. "Would you like to throw it around with us a little? Maybe Regan will come home in that time."

Jason took in the scene. The smell of the perfectly cropped green grass, the bright sun. The boy and the father working up a little sweat with a wholesome game of catch. Making memories, as Jason's mother would say. What could be more perfect and inviting? What could be more normal?

But Jason knew he couldn't stay.

"Sorry," he said. "I have somewhere else I have to go."

Tim patted the ball twice, then turned and threw a tight spiral to his son while Jason walked back down the driveway to his car.

Chapter Thirty-four

Logan's father lived in the same house Logan grew up in, the same house Jason spent so much time in when they were kids and teenagers. It sat in an upscale subdivision on the east side of Ednaville, about half a mile from the town's older and more exclusive country club, Indian Lake. Logan's father brought the boys to the country club for dinner several times a month—awkward meals during which the old man rarely spoke—and they made liberal use of the pool during the summer. Jason knew even as a kid that he'd never get inside the country club any other way unless he went to work there—busing tables in the restaurant or hauling some doctor's clubs around the golf course.

When Jason was young, the house looked massive. Every time he went to see Logan, the same thought cycled through his mind: *They're rich. This is what it means to be rich.* As an adult, driving past the entrance to Forest Glen subdivision, Jason was struck by how much smaller everything seemed. The houses remained beautiful, the yards perfectly manicured, but they had nothing on the mini-mansions being built in other subdivisions around Ednaville, the places that housed executives from America's Best and other companies. By current standards, Mr Shaw appeared to be a man of modest means. And Jason knew what the old man would say if someone questioned him about it. He'd heard Logan's father make similar comments during those long awkward dinners at Indian Lake. "A house is a house. It's better to have just enough than too much."

Mr. Shaw lived in a ranch that sprawled in both directions away from the double front doors. Jason remembered that the main floor felt formal and unused, the furniture sparkling new and unblemished. He and Logan spent their time in the large finished basement, where the Shaws had a TV, a bar, a pool table, and a stocked refrigerator. The main floor, including the kitchen, was just a place to pass through. Logan claimed that, except for the occasional fried egg or pancakes on the weekends, his father never ate at home.

Jason parked in front. The sun was still bright in the late afternoon, but Jason could see that the lights along the driveway and on either side of the front door burned as though they were always lit. There were no other cars present, which wasn't a complete surprise. Jason knew Mr. Shaw—Peter—wasn't well and probably didn't drive anymore. As he approached the front door, Jason wondered what level of care the man needed at that point in his illness, and if professional nurses or health aides tended to him around the clock.

Jason received his answer shortly after he rang the bell. An African-American woman in a light blue smock and white pants and shoes opened the door. She was about sixty, and the hair she wore pulled back on her head showed streaks of gray. Jason experienced a moment of recognition.

"Hello?" she said.

"Pauline?" Jason said. The name popped into his head as his mouth formed the word. "Are you Pauline?"

"I am. It's good to see you again, stranger."

"Do you remember me? I'm Jason Danvers."

"Of course I do. You haven't changed that much."

"Wow. You still work here."

"I still do."

Pauline smiled at Jason, but she didn't step aside or offer to let him in the door. She stood with her arm blocking the way as though he were an annoying salesman. He hadn't seen Pauline since before Logan went away. *Was killed,* he reminded himself. But during those years when he was a regular visitor to the Shaw house, Pauline worked as their housekeeper. Jason didn't see her every time he went to the Shaws' house—she seemed to be on duty during the day—but she was in the home quite a lot, a quiet presence in the background. Dusting shelves, folding laundry, directing a plumber to a leaky sink. She occasionally cooked for the boys, although she always made a point of telling them that cooking wasn't part of her job, and she seemed to dote on an unappreciative Logan. Jason assumed, as only a clueless teenager could, that Pauline's entire life was dedicated to the Shaws, and he was surprised once when Logan informed him that Pauline had three children of her own.

"I'm sorry I didn't call first," Logan said.

"That's okay. The door is always open for an old friend."

Pauline didn't seem to catch the irony of her statement. The door was open, but not enough to let the old friend inside.

"I guess the police have been by here," Jason said.

"They left a couple of hours ago. Mr. Shaw is resting."

"I'm sorry about the news."

"Thank you," Pauline said. "I'm sorry for you too. It must have been a shock after all these years."

"It was."

Pauline cocked her head. "Were you just coming to express your condolences to Mr. Shaw?"

Jason sensed the possibility of an opening. Without that, he really wasn't sure what he was doing out there. "Yes, that's it," he said. "Is he seeing people right now?"

"He's tired." Pauline lowered her arm from the door and moved it to rest on her right hip. "He's not well, you know. I'm not even sure he understands what the police were telling him."

"Is he frail? Mentally?"

Jason felt like an idiot saying it that way. Why did they all have to tap-dance around these problems? Why couldn't Jason just ask what he wanted to ask: *Does the old man still have any marbles rolling around in his brainbox?*

"It's hard to tell," Pauline said. "He has a neurological disorder called progressive supranuclear palsy. It affects the frontal lobe, kind of like Parkinson's, and he has trouble speaking. It's hard to tell what he's able to comprehend sometimes." She leaned forward. "Although I suspect he catches a lot more than he lets on. He's like that, you know. Sneaky."

"Most men are, right?"

Pauline smirked, but her look told Jason she wasn't going to be easily swayed by his attempt to make a joke. She was too smart for that. Working for Peter Shaw all those years guaranteed she wouldn't be a pushover.

Jason tried a different tactic.

"I guess when I heard the news, I just wanted to be out here. You know, to be someplace that I associate with Logan. I thought maybe Mr. Shaw would feel the same way."

"You've met the man, right?"

"Yes."

"And you thought he'd want to share his feelings with someone else?"

All Pauline needed to do was say "checkmate" and Jason's
defeat would be complete. He had nothing else to fall back on
but the truth.

"Look, I'm just trying to make sense of all of this," he said. "I
don't understand how Logan could be gone for so long, and we
all thought he was alive, and we find out today that he was dead.
It's not sinking in for me. And I know Mr. Shaw might have
some insights about it. I've heard he got letters from Logan."

Pauline raised her eyebrows at the mention of the letters. "He
did get letters."

"Can I just come in and try to talk to him?" Jason asked.

Pauline dropped the hand off her hip and took a step back.
"You can come in and wait here. I'll have to see if Mr. Shaw is
even awake."

Jason waited in the foyer. Even though everything looked and
smelled clean and shiny, Jason could tell that the decor—the
wallpaper, the sconces and lamps—hadn't been changed since
the last time he'd been in the house. He chalked it up to the lack
of a woman's touch. Mr. Shaw could easily find someone to keep
everything clean and repaired, but was he likely to call a
decorator and insist on an update to his house's style?

Only one photo sat on top of the credenza, and it hadn't been
there all those years ago when Jason last visited. It was Logan's
senior portrait. Jason wanted to pick it up but didn't. He stared
into the smiling, somewhat cocky face of his oldest friend, who
wore a striped tie and a blue jacket. He was tanned from the
summer, his cheek dimpled. He looked like someone who had

everything he wanted, and it seemed absurd to think he would run away never to return.

"You can come back, Jason," Pauline said. She noticed that Jason was staring at the photo. "Would you like a minute?"

"When did this get put out?" Jason asked. "I don't remember seeing it before."

"Mr. Shaw asked me to frame it and put it there after . . . about a month after you all graduated."

"It looks good in this spot," Jason said.

"I've never seen Mr. Shaw take a moment to notice it," Pauline said. "He always came in through the garage."

Jason followed Pauline down a hallway toward a back bedroom. The house was silent. Hushed. Their feet made no noise as they moved across the plush carpet, and the slightly sour odor of disinfectant tickled Jason's nose. Pauline stopped outside the door to a bedroom, and she turned back to Jason and said, "He has trouble speaking. His voice is a whisper if it's anything. And sometimes he doesn't talk at all."

"Okay."

"I think he can talk all the time. He just doesn't feel like it on some days. He uses the disease as an excuse."

She stepped across the threshold, and Jason followed. Peter Shaw sat in a wheelchair in the center of the room. A hospital bed stood off to the side, and a large, flat-screen TV played with the volume down. Jason felt pity at the sight of the man. He would have recognized the face and head anywhere. They looked the same. Somewhat drawn and more wrinkled, but basically the same. Peter Shaw had never really looked young, but it was his body that gave Jason pause. The man Jason remembered, the man Jason feared and respected, used to be thick through the upper body and shoulders. He walked with an assertive gait, chest out, as though he were always about to barrel through an obstacle. The version of Peter Shaw that sat before him in the wheelchair was withered, as though strong winds had been battering him, chipping away at the substance of his body. He must have weighed fifty pounds less than he did the last time Jason saw him. His clothes hung on him like loose, draped fabric, and Jason could tell by the way the man's knees rested together in the wheelchair that he had little control over his legs.

Pauline stood next to the wheelchair and spoke, the volume of her voice raised just a bit. "Mr. Shaw? Do you remember Jason Danvers?"

The man turned his head slowly. He wore the slightly stunned look of the fading elderly, one that said any interaction or response required a great deal of effort. He glanced at Pauline but didn't speak.

"Jason Danvers?" Pauline said. "Logan's best friend from growing up?"

Mr. Shaw still made no response. He turned away from Pauline and focused on the TV screen. A cable news show played, and the host was gesturing toward the camera, a large pen held in his hand like an extra finger.

Pauline turned to Jason. "Here, take a seat." She pulled a chair away from the wall and placed it near the wheelchair. "I'll be back in a little bit, Mr. Shaw," Pauline said. "The nurse will be here in an hour, and then I'm going home." Again, the man made no response. As Pauline passed Jason on her way out of the room, she said, "That might be all you get."

"Thank you," Jason said.

When she was gone, he sat down. Mr. Shaw may have been

disabled and fading, but he looked clean. His face was shaved, his remaining wisps of hair combed into place. He wore a yellow button-down shirt and pressed slacks. The only apparent concession to his illness was the navy blue house slippers he wore on his feet. The room felt sterilized and cold, like a hospital or nursing home, and the tools and implements of sickness were all around. Bottles of pills, a large plastic water bottle with a long straw, boxes of tissues, and two bouquets of flowers and some greeting cards.

The man acted like Jason wasn't there. The TV played with closed-captioning on, and Jason wondered if Pauline arranged for that so she wouldn't have to hear the news show's bickering and haranguing.

"Mr. Shaw? Do you remember me?"

The man turned his head in Jason's direction. He seemed to be seeing him for the first time since Jason entered the room. "Yes," he said.

The feeble sound surprised Jason. Peter Shaw had possessed a booming voice years ago. He spoke so infrequently that when he did, the sound often made Jason jump. But the noise that came out of the man's mouth in that little room barely qualified as a whisper. It sounded more like a gasp, a labored exhalation. The only thing pleasing about it to Jason was that the man admitted he remembered him.

"I'm sorry about Logan," Jason said.

At the sound of those words, the old man turned his head away. Jason saw tears beginning to fill Mr. Shaw's eyes and wanted to look away, toward the television or the wall or anyplace else. He asked himself why he had come—to inflict additional pain on a sick and lonely old man?

Mr. Shaw said something else in that faint whisper. Jason

didn't understand. He leaned forward and said, "I'm sorry. I didn't hear you."

The old man repeated it, and this time Jason understood.

"Not true," he said.

"Not true?" Jason asked. "You mean . . ." He thought he understood. "Are you saying it's not true that Logan is dead?"

Mr. Shaw moved his head up and down.

Before he could stop himself, Jason said, "But the police—" Then he cut his own words off. Why argue?

But Mr. Shaw repeated his statement, his voice growing a little stronger. "Not true," he said. "Logan isn't gone."

Jason remembered what Pauline said. There was no way to tell what the old man understood and what he didn't, that he might be sneaky, pretending to be confused when he really wasn't. But what would he gain by pretending to Jason that he didn't comprehend that the body found in the woods belonged to his son? That dental records proved that Logan likely died on the night of his high school graduation? Mr. Shaw's behavior seemed more like willful denial than dementia, so Jason decided to move in a different direction.

"I heard that Logan has been sending you letters and cards over the years," Jason said. He spoke of Logan in the present tense. *Has* instead of *had*. That wasn't simply for Mr. Shaw's benefit. Jason wasn't sure he could speak about Logan in the past tense yet. He didn't know if he ever could. "I was wondering if I could see those letters. Do you have them handy?"

Mr. Shaw shook his head. "No," he whispered.

"No, I can't see them? Or no, there aren't any letters in the first place?" Jason asked.

"No," Mr. Shaw said. "No means no."

"I was hoping if I saw the letters, I might understand where

Logan's been all these years," he said. "I thought you wanted your lawyer, Colton Rivers, to find him so he could make sure he gets what's coming to him in the will."

Mr. Shaw shook his head. He tried to say something else, but the words didn't seem to come. He waved his right hand around in the air as though punctuating the words that refused to form. Jason even leaned closer, but no sound emerged. A stream of spittle crept out of the corner of Mr. Shaw's mouth. Jason leaned over, grabbed a tissue, and dabbed the mess away.

"Did Logan's mom get letters from him?" Jason asked.

Something, likely the mention of Logan's mother, snapped the man's posture into a more rigid position. He suddenly possessed an energy and strength that he hadn't displayed during the rest of Jason's visit.

He shook his head. "No."

"She didn't?"

"Not important," the old man said.

"Are you saying Mrs. Shaw isn't important?"

Whatever will had infused the man's spine with iron for those few moments drained out of him just as quickly. He slumped lower in the wheelchair, and his head sat heavier on his shoulders. His eyes grew unfocused in such a way that Jason thought he was on the verge of falling asleep.

"So he didn't send any letters to his mother?" Jason asked, unable to let the matter go.

Mr. Shaw turned to Jason, his eyes a little less glassy. "No letters for her," he said.

But the old man looked spent. Jason could only imagine the morning and afternoon he had been through. The police showed up and informed him that his son was really dead. Then Jason, someone he hadn't seen in twenty-seven years, showed up and started asking more questions. Jason felt ashamed of himself for pushing the old man at all, even as he realized he wouldn't have been able to stop himself. He needed to know something. Anything.

"Did the police ask to see those letters?" Jason asked.

"She left," Mr. Shaw said.

"Who did? Who left?"

The old man struggled to make sounds again. He shook his head.

"Mrs. Shaw?" Jason asked. "Logan's mother? She left?"

"Yes."

"She left before Logan did," Jason said. "Long before."

The old man remained silent.

"Did the police see those letters that Logan sent?" Jason asked.

"Never cared," Mr. Shaw said.

"What's that?"

"Never cared," he whispered. His voice seemed to be fading. Jason leaned in. "His mother. Never cared."

"I'm sorry," Jason said. "I didn't really know her that well. She wasn't around much."

"Never."

Pauline appeared in the doorway. Jason felt like he'd been caught doing something wrong, pushing the old man too hard and bringing up unpleasant memories of the past. Jason knew a little about aging parents—and he understood that the past might be all the old man had to remember.

"Maybe Mr. Shaw needs to get some rest," Pauline said.

"Of course." Jason stood up. He reached out to shake Mr. Shaw's hand and felt the man's papery skin. Mr. Shaw's grip still retained some strength, a surprising amount. "Thank you," Jason said. "I'm sorry if I kept you too long."

Mr. Shaw held on to Jason's hand a beat longer than would have been normal. They locked eyes.

"Never cared," the old man said again.

And then Pauline was there, gently guiding Jason out of the room.

Chapter Thirty-five

Pauline walked with Jason out to the front of the house. When they reached the foyer, she tapped Jason on the arm and pointed toward the kitchen. Jason didn't ask any questions. He followed her, and Pauline said, "Just sit tight here a second."

He still didn't ask any questions. He looked around the room. It was immaculately clean and out-of-date like the rest of the house. A gold fleur-de-lis pattern covered the wallpaper, and in the corner sat a shelving unit covered with decorative plates that Jason felt certain Mr. Shaw hadn't chosen. The appliances did look new. They were all stainless steel and gleaming in the late afternoon sunshine. Jason imagined that Pauline spent a good deal of her time polishing them, whether they ever became dirty or not.

It took a good twenty minutes for Pauline to return to the kitchen, and Jason had waited so long he worried that she'd forgotten he was still in the house. She breezed back into the room, wiping her hands with a paper towel, and apologized for the delay.

"He needed to be put in bed and changed," she said. "He naps a lot."

"I see."

"He's not incontinent, you know," she said as though she wanted to defend Mr. Shaw. "He knows he has to go. He just can't walk to the bathroom. That's why he has to wear diapers." She seemed to be waiting for some response, and when Jason didn't say anything, she added, "He has a catheter as well. It makes him prone to infections."

"I'm sorry if I kept him awake or disturbed him," Jason said. "He seems to not understand what happened to Logan. Or is he . . . being stubborn?"

"Who knows?" Pauline said. "He never thought that boy was dead. Never."

"I have to admit I didn't think he was dead either," Jason said. "Maybe I'm a bigger fool. I don't have old age or an illness as an excuse."

"You have the same excuse as him," she said. "You loved Logan. You didn't want to believe he was gone."

"You sound like you thought he was dead all along."

Pauline threw her paper towel away and then came over and sat across from Jason. She folded her hands and rested them on the table. "I'm not really paid to have an opinion around here," she said. "Unless it's a question about getting a stain out of the carpet or who to call if the gutter falls down. You know what I'm saying?"

"You were expected to be seen and not heard?"

"Mmm-hmm. But just because I didn't express my opinions doesn't mean I didn't have them." Her eyes narrowed, as though she were sifting through distant memories. "I didn't really know what to think when Logan didn't come home that night. He'd just graduated from high school. I know some kids take trips when that happens. Not my kids, but kids like Logan do. They go to Florida or Myrtle Beach or wherever. And he was always talking about leaving town and living somewhere else. I think he used to say that just to irritate his father. The man may not say much, but he does love his son. He wanted him here, in Ednaville. He's been alone a long time."

"So you thought Logan just ran off?"

"I did. For a time, I figured he was out of town somewhere, living the high life. He'd come back someday when he ran out of money or got tired of fending for himself. It would be like the Bible. You know, the Prodigal Son? His father would welcome him back with open arms."

"And kill the fatted calf?"

"Exactly. You paid attention in Sunday school, didn't you?"

"Rarely, but I remember that one. I've had experience with someone coming back home after a long absence."

"I see. Well, then Logan never showed up. Never called. Nothing. I know they sent an investigator out there a couple of times. Hell, once Mr. Shaw even got on a plane and flew out there to follow up on some lead. It ended up being nothing. If you ask me, that was just someone stealing money right out of Mr. Shaw's pockets. At some point, I think something broke inside of him. Maybe it just hurt him too much to get his hopes up all those times and have them dashed. He stopped mentioning Logan at all. But I knew they weren't ever going to find that boy."

"How did you know that?" Jason asked. "You said, for a time you thought he'd come back. What changed?"

Pauline stood up. She walked over to a built-in desk. She upended a penholder that sat on its neatly organized top and a small, silver key fell out. She fitted the key into a lock in the desk drawer, slid it open, and brought out a small bundle of what appeared to be letters. She came back to the table and dropped them in front of Jason.

"Are these what you came to see?" she asked.

The bundle contained six or seven envelopes, which were tattered as though they'd been ripped open quickly. Everything was held tightly in place by a rubber band.

"These are the cards from Logan?" Jason asked.

"Not all of them. The police took most, but I held a few back. I couldn't stand the thought of Mr. Shaw losing everything he thought came from his son."

"You're not worried about getting into trouble?"

"Please."

"I'm the one who told Detective Olsen about them."

"I don't think they really care too much what I do. I think they're more interested in playing Sherlock Holmes with their dead body in the woods, you know? So I thought I'd let you see them."

"Thank you."

"You grew up with Logan. You went to school with him a long time, right?"

"You know that."

"Well, I'll let you look those over. I have some laundry to put in. When I come back, I want you to let me know if you see anything strange in there."

She stood up and left the room. Jason didn't care. He'd been fighting the urge to rip the rubber band off ever since she'd dropped the letters in front of him.

The cards were not arranged chronologically. The first one he picked up was from 1995, according to the postmark, nine years after they graduated from high school. The card came from Salt Lake City, Utah. The postage stamp showed an image of Mount Rushmore. Jason noticed right away that the address—Peter Shaw's address—had been generated by a computer. Someone entered it and printed a label, then affixed it to the front of the envelope. There was no return address.

Jason removed the birthday card for Mr. Shaw. The front showed a forest scene with an embossed caption that said, "For a special father." Jason opened it up and inside there was some syrupy verse, no doubt written by a starving poet trying to make a little money on the side. At the bottom Logan's name was signed. Jason stared at the signature for a long moment. Who printed an address label on a computer when sending their father a birthday card? And on what planet would Logan even get his father a sappy card?

Jason flipped through the others, checking postmarks and dates. The postmarks came from various places in the country. Arizona and New Mexico, with one from Denver and a couple during 1999 from Chicago. The cards arrived for the same occasions—Mr. Shaw's birthday and Father's Day, which both fell during the summer. Jason noticed there were none for Christmas or Easter. There were never personal messages or greetings in the cards. Just Logan's name, and Jason almost immediately realized what Pauline was talking about. A couple of the cards had handwritten addresses, which only raised Jason's suspicions.

He studied the writing, trying to remember clearly what Logan's looked like. He felt confident it didn't look like the signature before him. In grade school, they had had a particularly uptight teacher who liked to criticize the way Logan made the "L" in his name. No matter how much she rode him, Logan never could—or never tried— to make it the way it looked on the chart above the chalkboard. His "L" was always tilted almost to the point that it was horizontal. The writing in the cards seemed familiar, though, almost feminine. The person had tried to copy Logan's tilted and horizontal "L" but didn't get it exactly right.

Jason thought: *Chicago, 1999.*

He'd seen that "L" before. The other times it had much more flourish to it. The person copying Logan's handwriting had tried to tone it down but couldn't quite. Not completely.

By the time Pauline came back into the kitchen, Jason was looking through the cards again. She sat down across from Jason. "Well?"

"I wish I'd seen all of them," he said.

"If wishes were horses . . . I can't promise you that Mr. Shaw doesn't have a stash of them somewhere else. But he's a neat and orderly man. He tends to keep his things organized."

"Why are they just sitting in the kitchen like this? Doesn't he have a study?"

"All I know is I've come into the kitchen a couple of times over the years—I'm talking twice maybe—and I've found him sitting at that desk over there looking at these cards." She tapped the stack again. "When I came in and saw him doing that, he hurried and put them away, almost like he was embarrassed."

"He probably was if they made him feel emotional."

"Exactly."

"And you asked me about school because you figured I saw Logan's handwriting a lot when we were growing up."

"I'm guessing you've seen a lot of his tests and quizzes and papers and other things. You'd know his handwriting pretty well. Even after all these years." Pauline wore a satisfied smile on her face. She had proved her point. "So what do you think now that you've seen these cards?" she asked.

"It's not Logan's handwriting," Jason said. "It's similar, but I don't think it's his."

"Are you sure?" Pauline asked, taking on the role of detective. Jason wondered if everybody he met wanted to question him about something. "Hasn't it been a long time since you've seen his writing? And do boys really notice such things?"

"I'm sure," Jason said. "Jesus, we were best friends. We studied together. I know. And I'm guessing you're positive it's not Logan's writing either, or you wouldn't be asking me. It seems a little too feminine."

"I didn't think it was his, but I wanted a second opinion."

"I have a more important question—why doesn't Mr. Shaw know that it isn't Logan's writing? Or does he know it isn't?"

Pauline took her time answering. She seemed to be giving the question a good going-over in her mind before she spoke. "I've wondered about that. It's not something that can be attributed to his illness, because these letters started arriving a long time ago. And, like I said, he never acted like he thought Logan was dead. He had the chance to file a missing persons report many times over the years, and he didn't. When the police came, he insisted that Logan was still alive. That's why he hired the investigators eventually, to prove them wrong." Pauline stopped speaking and held up her index finger. She tilted her head toward the other side of the house, the side where Mr. Shaw's bedroom was, and listened. She shook her head. "I have to listen carefully. Sometimes he tries to get up. I forgot to bring the monitor out here with me."

"So he just chose not to believe that Logan was dead. He chose not to recognize that this wasn't his son's handwriting."

"Denial is a strong force," Pauline said, as though she knew from experience.

"Could he just not recognize Logan's handwriting?" Jason asked. "He was a pretty detached father when I used to come around here."

"I know he seemed that way. But he cared about Logan a

great deal. A great deal. He always got the boy the right birthday presents. He always knew the things he was interested in. He got him to the doctor's and the dentist like clockwork. He could have handed that stuff off to a nanny or a new wife, but he didn't. I think he just didn't want to or couldn't accept that the boy was really dead. He couldn't get it into his head. Logan was all he had left."

"What about that?" Jason asked.

"About what?"

"Logan's mother."

Pauline made a snorting noise. "What about her?"

"You don't like her?"

"I have to admit, I don't really know her. I started working here not long before they got divorced. But she never seemed that interested in the boy. When she came around here, and that wasn't much, she had her nose in the air. She didn't have much time for me, of course. But to not be totally involved with your boy? What's going on there?"

"Did she ever see these cards?"

"I don't know. For all I know, she's been getting Mother's Day cards the whole time."

"But she'd see that the handwriting wasn't Logan's. She'd have to. A mother wouldn't be that far out to lunch."

"Maybe she knows. Maybe she doesn't."

"And why didn't she file a missing persons report?" Jason asked. "I would guess any relative could. Maybe anybody can. But certainly his mother could do it. If Mr. Shaw was in denial, then wouldn't Mrs. Shaw be able to file a report and get the police asking questions?"

"If you're looking to me to explain all of these things, then you've come to the wrong place."

Jason placed his finger on the stack of cards. "Can I take these?"

"No, sir. I couldn't bear to take them away from that man, even if they are fake. He might ask to see them someday, and if I couldn't produce them, it would break his heart."

"That's fine." Jason stood up. "Thanks for your help."

Pauline didn't stand. She looked up at Jason. "You know, the former Mrs. Shaw still lives about an hour from here, over in Barker County. She's remarried. Her name is Mrs. Tyndal now."

"Elaine, right?"

"That's right. You could go ask her yourself."

"Thanks."

"Is there any chance you recognize that handwriting?" Pauline asked.

"Why do you ask that?"

"You had a strange look on your face, like you knew something but didn't want to say. Are you going to let me in on the secret?"

"I have to ask someone else about it first," he said. "The way things are going, maybe we'll all know a lot about it soon."

Chapter Thirty-six

When Jason stepped outside the Shaw house, it was getting close to five o'clock, and he needed to head home. But when he saw the car parked behind his, he knew he wouldn't be able to go right away.

Regan leaned against the driver's side of her car, and she straightened up when she saw him. They walked toward each other, stopping when they were just a few feet apart.

"Are you okay?" Jason asked.

"Why wouldn't I be?"

"Because I've been trying to call you all day, and you haven't answered. And at work they told me you went off with Jesse Dean last night."

"Who told you that?" She sounded only mildly agitated. "Oh, wait. Never mind. I know who." She crossed her arms and looked down. "I didn't go off with him. He . . . wanted to talk to me about something."

"Why didn't you call the police? He might know where Hayden is."

"He says he doesn't know where Hayden is. That's about all I could get out of him."

"Oh, you asked him. And since he's such an honest guy, he told you the truth. What did he want with you?"

"He wanted to talk about everything that's going on," she said. "He's . . . I don't want to say he's scared. That's not right. He's agitated that people are hounding him. He mentioned you."

Jason pointed to his neck. "Who is hounding who? And why did he want to talk to *you* about it? Are you his confidante? Jesus, Regan. The guy's dangerous."

"It's not so simple."

"You need to tell the police—" Jason stopped. He looked Regan in the eye. "Is there something about him? I mean, were you friends in high school and I didn't know? Were you and he . . . ?"

"No, Jason. Jesus. We didn't fuck. Then or now."

"Then I don't get it. What's the connection between the two of you?"

"There's no connection, Jason." She looked away, and her hands moved before she spoke. "He knows I'm friends with you. He wanted me to tell you to stay away from him."

"Is that why you're here? To deliver Jesse Dean's threat?"

"I thought you might be at the Shaws'. I tried your house."

"Did you talk to Nora?"

"No," she said. "I looked for your car. I tried your office too. Then I thought that on a day like this, with the news about Logan, you might come out here and try to talk to his father. You mentioned visiting him the other day. I wanted to see how you were doing. I know the news is terrible, and it's going to land on you like a ton of bricks."

"You too," Jason said. "You sounded upset this morning."

"I was. I am."

"None of it makes any sense to me. All these years I thought

Logan was alive. Was I just a dumbass? A dreamer? Am I so naive that I couldn't accept the truth?"

"He was your friend. It's tough to accept."

"You know what I just found out? I found out that Logan's
dad had those cards, and they're clearly not written by Logan.
And despite that, the old man never accepted that Logan was
dead. Am I no different than him? Am I as clueless as that old
man in there, thinking Logan couldn't die?"

"Don't beat yourself up over it. There was no proof he was
dead."

"You don't seem surprised that the letters weren't written by
Logan?" he asked.

Regan hesitated. "He's dead. He couldn't have written the letters."

"Do you know who did write them?"

"How would I?"

"Have you seen them?"

"No, I haven't. I don't know anything about them except that
they were sent to Logan's dad." She studied Jason. "Did you
learn something about them? Is that why you're here?"

"I just saw them."

"And?"

"I think it's Hayden's handwriting. Hayden sent those cards
to Mr. Shaw."

Regan seemed to be processing the information, but she
didn't look surprised. She raised her hand to her jacket and
touched the zipper. "I thought the cards all came from out west."

"Mostly. Hayden was gone all the time. She ran around a lot.
I didn't always know where she was or what she was doing. Hell,
she could have written the cards here and given them to someone

who was going out west. And a couple of them came from Chicago in 1999. Do you know where Hayden was in 1999?"

"Chicago?"

"She got arrested there for public drunkenness. In the summer of 1999."

"And now you're wondering why she did it?"

"Yes, I am," Jason said. "Whatever she knows about the cards must be related to why she came back here."

"You're assuming things."

Jason paced in between the two cars. He brought his hand up and rubbed at his forehead, working on the tension that grew there. He turned back to Regan. "Are you going to call the police on Jesse Dean?"

"He didn't do anything to me." Her voice was calm, firm. She stood there, watching Jason pace. She moved her head in time to his movements, like she was following a tennis match.

"Regan?" he said.

"What is it?"

"The police wouldn't tell me how Logan died," he said.

"They said it was a homicide."

"Right. But they wouldn't say how. Or what caused it."

"How could they know after twenty-seven years? There must just be bones, I guess. What else could be there?"

Jason stopped moving. He leaned against the back of his car. "The detective said something. He said bones can tell a story. He knows how Logan died, but he didn't want to tell me." Jason looked down at his hands. He closed them into fists and then opened them again. "They don't tell a suspect how a victim died. They keep things from him so they can trip him up later."

"What are you saying?"

"I'm a suspect again," Jason said. "They're going to keep

asking me questions about that night. What if I hit him hard enough to break his skull and they can see that?"

"What if he was drunk, and he tripped and fell? That could happen too, you know. Just tell them the truth. That's all you have to do."

"I *wanted* to hurt Logan that night. I wanted to punch him in the face. Hard. I wanted to draw blood. I tried to do that. Draw blood. I hit him, though. I really did. What if I did something to him in that fight? What if I hit him so hard that he walked away from me and then eventually just collapsed and died? That happens, you know. People have car accidents and hit their heads, and then hours later they die. What if that is what happened to Logan? I'd be responsible. I'd have killed him."

"You can't jump to that conclusion. The police are being cautious."

"What if Hayden saw Logan? What if Hayden knew how he died, and she was covering for me? Wouldn't that be a switch? My crazy sister covering my ass for something awful I did?"

"I think you just need to go home," Regan said. "You've had a long day. You've had a lot to process. The police are going to come to all of us again eventually." Something passed across Regan's body as she said that, something like a shiver, as though she was recalling or anticipating something unpleasant. "Just . . . tell the truth."

"You saw Logan that night, after we fought. Was he . . . Did he seem hurt?"

"No. He seemed . . . agitated. But not hurt. It was dark, of course, but I don't think you bloodied him or anything. He was fine. Jason, all of this speculation isn't productive. I think you need to just head home."

Regan came over to Jason and placed her hand on his arm.

She applied some pressure, trying to nudge him off the back of the car and toward the driver's-side door.

Jason took a couple of steps toward his car, then stopped. He looked back at Regan.

"We came close back then, you and I," he said.

"Close?"

"To trying it as a couple."

Regan nodded. "Sure." She smiled. "We were good friends. That doesn't always work the other way."

"I probably would have driven you nuts," Jason said. "And I wouldn't have met Nora. You know, we've had our problems, but I think we're doing better. We're getting closer as time moves on."

"That's good, Jason. Take it from me, divorce is no fun."

"I saw your husband at your house. Tim. He seemed like a good guy. He was playing ball with your son."

"He is a good guy," Regan said. "And a good father."

She turned and got into her car.

Chapter Thirty-seven

When Jason came in the front door, he saw Sierra sitting on the couch watching TV. And she wasn't alone. Another girl about the same age sat next to her, holding a phone in both hands, her thumbs dancing across the tiny keypad with machinelike precision.

"Hello," Jason said. "Where's Nora?"

"She's upstairs," Sierra said. "This is my friend Tricia. I mentioned her before, remember? We've known each other since I was a kid."

Tricia finished with her phone and laid it aside on the couch. "Hi," she said, looking up.

She didn't look to Jason like someone who would be friends with Sierra. She wore thick eyeliner and torn jeans, and a leather, stud-encrusted bracelet circled her left wrist. She was thin and pale and sat with her feet propped up on the coffee table. She looked like the resident of the house, and Sierra comported herself more like a guest.

"Are you watching a movie?" Jason asked. He didn't know what else to say.

"TV," Tricia said. "Thanks for letting me hang out here."

"You're welcome," Jason said, even though he played no role

in having the girl in his house. If it were up to him, he felt certain he would have closed the door in Tricia's face. Sierra had enough to deal with. She didn't need her wild friend coming around. "I'm going to talk to Nora," he said.

"Hey," Tricia said. "I'm sorry about your friend."

"Yeah, Uncle Jason, we heard the news. I'm sorry. That's the guy Mom was talking about, right?"

"Right."

He turned and went up the steps. Nora lay in bed, reading. She wore her hair pulled back and slipped her glasses off the bridge of her nose when Jason walked into the room. She sat up, sweeping her legs off the bed.

"There you are," she said.

"What's going on down there?" Jason asked.

"What do you mean?"

"Who's that girl? I'm assuming that's *the* Tricia. Car-stealing, pot-smoking Tricia."

"Relax," Nora said. "Sierra is getting cabin fever, I can tell. She doesn't want to be cooped up with fortysomethings all day. Tricia called, and I told Sierra to invite her over. They're just hanging out. I said they couldn't leave the house."

"That's never stopped them before apparently. Tricia will probably take Sierra out later and they'll knock over a convenience store."

"It's okay, Jason. Sierra needs friends and distractions." She patted the bed. "So do you. Come on. Sit here."

Jason did as she asked. He sat next to her and leaned in as Nora placed her arm around his shoulder. "I heard," she said. "It's all over the news here. I'm sorry."

Jason closed his eyes and leaned in close to Nora. He let his head rest against her body and inhaled the scent of the soap she used, something mildly sweet like vanilla. He kept his eyes closed, being still like that and trying not to think.

"Do you want to talk?" Nora asked. "Do you want a drink or something to eat? I'm afraid I'm just not sure what to do for you or what you need right now."

"This is good," he said.

They stayed in that position for a few more minutes, and then Jason straightened up. He opened his eyes and the light from the lamp on the bedside table seemed brighter than ever.

"I feel like I should be crying for Logan," he said, "but I can't. It just doesn't seem real."

"Did Detective Olsen say anything else? Do they know what happened to Logan?"

"They're not saying."

Jason stood up and went into the bathroom. He turned on the tap and splashed cold water on his face. When he looked up, he saw a tired, middle-aged man, someone who seemed to be bearing a burden. He dried off with a towel, and the softness of the material against his face felt good.

Nora came to the doorway. "I know this has always plagued you, Logan leaving like that. And I know you've always blamed yourself a little. I wish I could say or do something to make it easier for you."

"I know. And I appreciate it. I really do." He hung the towel across the rack while Nora remained behind him in the doorway.

"I guess maybe someday I'd like to understand all of this," she said.

"That makes two of us."

Jason moved past her into the bedroom and started taking off his clothes. He stripped down to his boxers and T-shirt.

"We can just go to sleep or read," Nora said, "if that's what you want. I need to get ready for bed and I'd like to finish my book."

"I'm sorry," Jason said. "I'm not sure what I'd say if I did feel like talking. You know? Are you doing okay?"

"I'm fine."

"Anything new here besides the car thief showing up?"

"Not really."

Jason could tell there was something beneath her words. "What?" he asked.

"We shouldn't get into it."

"Is something wrong?"

"No," she said. "Look, I wasn't going to say anything, but Sheila called today. They still want us to come to New York, and I know that's not possible now. But she said there might be a job opening for me, a better job with the library."

"Oh."

"It's a bad time, so we can talk about it later. I shouldn't have mentioned it."

"I asked," Jason said.

"Well, okay. Another time, then. And, look, I'll do whatever you want. Ednaville has its charms. The pace of life here has been good for us in a lot of ways. We've grown closer. Things are better. Maybe we shouldn't mess with it." Nora remained in the bathroom doorway and she said, "I guess we'll have a funeral to go to."

Her statement stumped Jason. He hadn't even thought of it. If Logan was dead, and they had something to bury—bones or whatever remained—then there would have to be a funeral at some point. Except . . .

"His old man is in denial," Jason said. "That's one of the places I went today. He doesn't believe Logan is dead. He may not be well in the head. He's definitely sick physically, but he can't seem to accept that his son is gone. So I don't know what that means for a funeral."

"He can't let go?" Nora asked.

"Can't or won't."

"That's always a danger," Nora said. "Hanging on to things for too long."

A half an hour later, Sierra came to their bedroom. She knocked lightly on the open door, then stepped in. Jason and Nora were both in bed, books in hand. Jason was struggling against sleep and getting close to losing the battle.

"What's up?" Nora asked.

Sierra came over and sat on the edge of the bed on Nora's side. "Tricia asked me to go back to her house and spend the night," she said.

"Really?" Nora said.

"I know you want me to stay close, but Tricia is pretty persistent. Besides, I kind of feel bad about her."

"Why?"

"Well, we were really good friends when we were younger. We spent all of our time together for a couple of years. Then we drifted apart as we got older." She lowered her voice. "You can tell why that happened. We don't really have that much in common." She shrugged. "But I guess I realize how nice it is to have friends. Friends of any kind. Tricia is pretty loyal. Anyway, it's just to her house for the night. I'll be back in the morning."

Friends who lost touch. Friends who drifted away. Jason knew all about that. He couldn't help but think of Regan and Logan. For a brief, intense period of time they were everything in his life, more important than his family in some ways.

"You're right about that," Jason said.

"About what?" Sierra asked.

"Friends. And how important they are. Especially at your age. It's good that you value them."

"It is," Nora said. "But you can't go anywhere tonight."

"I can't?"

"No. There's too much going on, and with your mom missing—"

"She's not missing. She's gone," Sierra said. "Off on a bender with that Jesse Lee Twat guy."

"Jesse Dean Pratt," Jason said. "And you shouldn't say that about your mom."

"We don't know where she is," Nora said. "But we're responsible for you, and we want you close until we know more."

Sierra uttered the most theatrical sigh and paired it with a world-class eyeroll. She suddenly looked so much younger, so much more immature than at any time since she'd walked through their door.

"Tricia said you'd act this way. She said she knew you two would be too uptight to go along. You judge her because of the way she looks, don't you?"

"And her police record," Jason said.

"You don't know anything about that," Sierra said. "I was there too. Am I a criminal?"

Nora sat up and took her reading glasses off. "I know you're getting a raw deal here, but it's the only one we can offer right now. If you want to have Tricia back to the house tomorrow, you can."

"Forget it," Sierra said, and she left the room.

Nora turned to Jason. "You need to go downstairs and tell Tricia it's time to go."

"Why do I have to be the bad cop?"

"You're a man. She might be more inclined to listen to you."

"Really?"

"You think that girl has a father in her life?" Nora asked. "She'll listen to a male authority figure."

"Doesn't this make you glad we don't have kids?"

Nora sent a half-serious glare in his direction.

"Okay," he said. "I'm going."

He pulled on a pair of pants and walked downstairs. When he entered the living room, Sierra looked away, but Tricia met his gaze. She stood up and grabbed her purse, a saggy canvas bag with long straps.

"I was just going," she said.

"Thanks for coming by," Jason said. "If you want to come back—"

"I get it," she said. "It's cool." She passed Jason on her way to the front door. "I should go back to my trailer park and make friends there."

"No one said anything like that," he said.

"You don't have to." Tricia pulled the front door open and looked back at Jason. "The truth is, you're smart to keep her here. Very smart."

Then she was gone like a puff of smoke. Behind Jason, Sierra stormed up the stairs. Her bedroom door slammed.

Chapter Thirty-eight

When Jason woke up the next morning, he saw that Nora was already awake and out of bed. Jason stepped out into the hallway and saw Sierra's bedroom door closed. He eased over and leaned his head against the door, listening for any sign of his niece. He heard nothing and went downstairs, where he found Nora sipping orange juice in the kitchen.

"Have you seen the kid?" he asked. "Is she here?"

"I assume she's in her room."

"But you haven't seen her?"

"I'm trying not to crowd her. I know she ran off once, but I'm trying to trust her. I believe her when she says—"

But Jason was already on his way up the stairs. He stopped outside Sierra's room again and he knocked. He waited, hearing nothing, and then he knocked again.

"What?" Sierra said from the other side of the door. Her voice was muffled and scratchy, but he couldn't mistake the irritation.

"I'm just . . . Are you okay?"

He heard shuffling and then Sierra pulled the door open. Her face was puffy from sleep, her hair a tangled mess. She wore a T-shirt and gym shorts and she squinted at Jason like she didn't recognize him.

"What's wrong?" she asked. "Is it Mom?"

"No," Jason said. He felt like an idiot for startling the girl, for not trusting her as much as Nora seemed to. Or if Nora was uncertain about the trust, at least she didn't let it dictate her actions. "I'm sorry. I thought . . ."

Sierra's shoulders sagged. "You were just checking up on me. Jesus."

She closed the door in Jason's face. He really couldn't blame her.

"I think one of us should stay home again today," Nora said.

They sat across from each other at the kitchen table. Jason had brewed coffee and he was drinking from a mug with a big smiley face on it.

"I can call in," Jason said. "I probably have more time saved up."

"Are you sure?"

"It's fine. You've missed a lot of work too."

The word "work" brought their conversation to a halt. Jason hadn't thought of the talk from the night before, but it was there with them all of a sudden. Nora had a potential job offer back in the city.

"I know we need to talk about New York," Jason said. "I was hoping things would be more settled here soon."

"You mean that we'd know where Hayden is."

"Yes."

"I agree that we should wait. I said that last night. Then again . . ."

"What if she never comes back?"

"What if we never know?"

"Let's give it a couple of days," Jason said. "We can wait a couple of days to make bigger decisions."

With Nora gone, Jason tried to occupy himself around the house. He used his laptop to catch up on some things from work. He tidied up the kitchen, putting clean dishes away and dirty ones into the dishwasher. While he did these things, he paused from time to time to see if he could hear any sounds from upstairs that would tell him Sierra had woken up. He heard nothing. For all he knew, she was awake but choosing to sit in her room rather than come downstairs and join him. He tried to remind himself not to be hurt by the teen's moodiness but felt a little stung anyway. He thought of all the times he had snapped at his parents or stormed away from them or shut them out of his life. Had they developed a thick parental skin, or did they also carry silent hurts inflicted by their children around with them?

At midmorning the front doorbell rang. Jason's hopes and fears rose with every bell—phone or door—that might be bringing news of Hayden or Logan or anything else. He walked to the door feeling a mixture of dread and excitement, and when he looked out through the small window, he saw a man standing with his back to the front door. He was taller than Jason, and his once dark hair was more than half gray. Jason saw something familiar in the way the man stood, his rail-thin build and long, loose arms. He wore a light jacket and he stood with his hands resting on his waist, the jacket pushed back. As Jason stared, the man turned around and saw Jason staring at him. He waved. It was Derrick, Sierra's father.

It took Jason a moment to act. He froze, staring back, not

even waving. Derrick smiled without showing his teeth, and he held the smile for a long awkward moment. And then when Jason didn't move to open the door, his former brother-in-law's smile sank. Jason knew he was being rude, so he recovered himself and undid the lock. He pulled the door open and felt the morning air hit him.

"I'm sorry I didn't call first," Derrick said. "To be honest, I figured you'd be at work."

"I'm working at home."

Jason still stood in the doorway, his body filling the frame so that Derrick couldn't enter. If Derrick thought he and Nora would be at work, what did he intend to do at the house? Was he hoping to come by and find Sierra alone?

Derrick looked older. In addition to the graying hair, his face showed more lines, especially around his eyes and mouth. But he maintained his long and skinny frame. His lantern jaw looked like it could break rocks, a contrast to the soft pitch of his voice.

"I wanted to see Sierra," he said. "Is she here? She must be."

"She's asleep."

Derrick checked his watch. "A little late."

Jason wanted to ask how Derrick would know what was late for his daughter when he hadn't seen her in almost two years, but he didn't. He pulled the door shut behind him and stepped out on the porch. Derrick moved back, giving Jason room.

"You're not even going to let me in?"

"It's not that."

"Jason, I want to be honest with you. I don't want to beat around the bush here. I think Sierra needs to come and stay with me until we know what's going on with Hayden."

"I thought you said you were okay with her staying here."

"I did say that. But I thought about it a little after our phone call." Derrick resumed his pose with his hands resting on his waist. Jason noticed that his belt looked worn. "I just think she should be with me. With Hayden missing . . . and now I've heard all about this Logan thing."

"What does that have to do with it?" Jason asked.

"It just got me thinking. Life is short. Very short. Shorter for some than others obviously. Sierra is that age, about the same age as Logan when he died. If Sierra ever found herself in a tough spot like that, I'd want to be there to help her."

"She's already been in some trouble."

"You mean the car thing? I know. That's what we can't have, can we?"

"No, we agree on that. I guess it would be pointless to ask if Hayden would have any reason to cover for Logan. Or Jesse Dean."

"Why are you bringing that up again?"

Jason started to tell Derrick about the letters, but then decided it wouldn't be productive. If Derrick knew something, he wasn't sharing. And if he didn't know, why give him the chance to possibly tell Jesse Dean what Jason knew?

"Nothing. I guess it's in the past."

Derrick stood with his feet close together. He looked like a man about to make a giant leap. "I know you don't think much of me, you and Nora. Hell, your family never really thought much of me. Not your parents and not you."

"Derrick—"

"No, no. It's fine. No bullshit, remember?"

Jason felt chastened. His parents hadn't liked Derrick, but in retrospect it seemed less about him and more about Hayden. How could they put any faith in a guy who wanted to be with Hayden? Who acted so wholly devoted to such a wayward, unpredictable soul? And they all knew the crowd Derrick ran with.

"You know," Derrick said, shifting his weight a little, "I had to ask myself sometimes why Hayden gave me the time of day. She could have had any guy she wanted. You know that, right?"

Jason felt strange contemplating such facts with Derrick just as he had with Colton, but he nodded in agreement.

"I spent so much time thinking about that when we were young. Why is Hayden with me? What if she decides to dump me? She did that more than a few times. Threw me over. But when you have a kid, it's different." He looked at Jason, a sly smile turning up the corner of his mouth. "You wouldn't know this, of course, but when you have a kid, you stop thinking about yourself all the time. You start thinking about the future more."

"Is this why you and Hayden have been so responsible over the years?"

Derrick started nodding. "Sure," he said. "That's an easy shot. You might as well take it. Like I told you on the phone, things are different for me now. This Hayden thing, it woke me up. I'm a father, and I need to act like it."

"Are you just going to take Sierra back to Indiana?"

"I have to. That's where my job is."

"Can you do that? I mean . . . she's supposed to be with Hayden, and Hayden lives here in Ohio."

"I thought you might say that," Derrick said. "Sierra's a pretty smart kid, isn't she?"

"Of course."

"Mature?"

"Sure. What are you driving at?"

"I don't know where she got it from. Not from me, that's for sure. But don't you think she knows herself pretty well?"

"She's seventeen. There's a limit to what she knows."

"All I'm saying is, I'm prepared to let Sierra decide where she wants to stay or who she wants to go with." He pointed behind Jason. "Don't you think we could just open that door and call up to her and find out what *she* wants to do? I mean if we really do care about the girl at all?"

Jason felt outmaneuvered. He couldn't very well stand in the doorway of his own home and deny his former brother-in-law access to his daughter. Derrick was correct——Jason never much cared for him. But Jason had always admitted—and remembered again—that Derrick had been at least a decent father. He'd been the more reliable of the two of them, Derrick and Hayden, and despite his absence from Sierra's life for the past couple of years, he appeared to have achieved a measure of stability.

Jason turned around and opened the front door. Derrick remained on the porch behind him, so Jason turned back and said, "Come on in."

Derrick followed as Jason held the door, and when the two men entered the foyer, a voice called from the top of the stairs.

"Uncle Jason?"

"Yeah?"

"Is someone here? Is that . . . ?"

Sierra took two steps down the stairs, ducking her head so she could see the man behind Jason. When she did, her mouth opened wide, and in that moment, she looked very much like a surprised little girl, which Jason knew she was. A little girl surprised by her father.

"I thought I heard you," she said.

She came down the stairs quickly, and Jason stepped out of the way as Derrick opened his arms and embraced his daughter. He raised her off the floor about a foot, Sierra lifting her legs and squealing as Derrick held her. Then her feet were back down on the ground. Jason watched Sierra lean in and place her head against her father's chest, and as she did, she reached up and wiped a tear from her eye. He wasn't sure, but it looked like Derrick wiped at his eyes as well.

Jason didn't know what to do. He took a couple of steps toward the kitchen. "Would you like some coffee, Derrick?" he asked.

"Are you okay, honey?" Derrick asked.

"I'm fine."

"I heard about Mom. I'm sorry."

Jason walked out to the kitchen. He brewed a new pot of coffee and checked the refrigerator and the pantry for food to serve. He found some cheese and set it on a plate with some crackers and a knife. He was still setting that up and waiting for the coffee to finish when Derrick and Sierra came into the kitchen.

"There's coffee," Jason said.

"I'll have some. Thanks," Derrick said.

"Me too," Sierra said.

Sierra stood close to her dad while Jason poured the coffee into mugs. They each took one, and Jason invited them to sit at the table. When everyone was seated, Sierra sliced the cheese and started eating. Jason just waited. He wasn't going to introduce the topic. Derrick seemed to pick up on this and gave Jason an irritated look. He probably wished Jason would leave the room so he could speak to his daughter in private, but Jason stayed rooted to his seat. If they were going to talk about Sierra's future, they were going to do it with him involved in the conversation.

Sierra looked at both of the adults at the table. "What?" she said. "Is something happening?" She leaned over toward Derrick. "Do you know something about Mom?"

"No, I don't." Derrick reached out and took her hand in his. "Honey, I came here to ask you something."

"What?"

Derrick looked at Jason again. Jason thought he saw some doubt on Derrick's face, as though he wasn't certain his attempt to get Sierra to go with him was going to work. But he forged ahead.

"I talked to Jason on the phone the other night."

"You did?" Sierra turned her head to Jason and then back to her father. "I didn't know you called."

"I asked him not to bother you. I wanted to talk to Jason first. You see, we have to figure out what's going to happen next with you. And with all of us. I know you like staying here with Jason and Nora, but it's not a permanent solution. You know that, right?"

"I guess so. I'm waiting for Mom to come back." She looked at both of them again. "I know that might make me sound like a little baby, but that's what I'm hoping for."

"We know," Derrick said. "And I suspect she'll be back soon. I do."

"You don't know that," Sierra said, her voice soft.

"I'm hopeful," Derrick said. "But in the meantime, I think you and I should be spending more time together. And I'm here because I want you to come live with me. Just until Mom gets back and everything returns to normal again."

"It's up to you," Jason said. "We're not trying to get you to do anything you don't want to do."

The words sounded hollow and forced to Jason. He knew he didn't mean them. Of course he wanted Sierra to stay in their house. The closeness and attachment he felt for her made him afraid. He couldn't imagine it if she went away, and he knew it would be even tougher for Nora.

"I like the idea of staying here because this is where Mom was last seen. If she comes back, she's going to come back here and not to Indiana." Sierra lowered her voice. She sounded small and young. "Besides, you haven't been around. I never know if I'm going to see you. It's been such a long time and . . . I just don't know who to trust anymore."

The knot in Jason's insides untwisted a little.

"Everything you say is true," Derrick said. "But if she returns, I'll bring you right over here to see her. Remember, she and I have a custody arrangement. We can't break that. I know I haven't been holding up my end lately, and Mom has been good about it. She hasn't pressed it. She could, you know. She could make trouble for me, and she hasn't. And if I kept you in Indiana when you were supposed to see Mom, then I'd be breaking the law. We've both let you down a lot. We can't change the past. I wish I could sometimes."

"But if she does come back—"

Derrick looked at Jason. "I'm sure Jason and Nora would let you know as soon as something changed."

Sierra looked over at Jason, her face full of hope.

"Of course we would," Jason said. "You know that."

"There's school," Sierra said.

"It's summer. By the time summer's over, Mom will be back. She will. I'm . . . confident. And then you can get back to living with her." Derrick leaned in closer. "But I do hope that once you are back with Mom and back in school, you'll come see me more. Some time at Christmas. More time in the summer. Indiana's nice. Maybe you'll go to college over there."

"Do you want to take a couple of days to think about this?" Jason asked. "It's a big decision."

Derrick couldn't contain the exasperated sigh that slipped

out of his mouth. He looked at Jason before leaning back in the chair. "Of course," he said. "It's just . . . I started a new job. And I don't have a lot of time off."

"I heard you got a new job," Sierra said. "That's amazing."

"I know. A sales job. It's kind of like my old one. It took me long enough, but I landed on my feet, kiddo."

A look of pride crossed Sierra's face. Jason saw the mist in her eyes, which practically glistened as she looked at her father. The tight parent-child connection between the two of them glowed like a laser light.

"Do you have room for me?" she asked. "Are you living in a house or an apartment?"

"I have two bedrooms. You can fix your room up any way you like."

Jason knew the battle was lost even before Sierra turned to him, her eyes no longer glowing with parental love but instead dimmed by a sense of pity. She was about to let her aunt and uncle down.

"You don't mind, do you, Uncle Jason?"

What could he say? Could he deny Sierra the chance to be with her father?

"Whatever you want to do," he said, nearly choking on the words. "Whatever is going to work best."

"It might be perfect," she said. "If Mom comes back—when Mom comes back—I'll be staying with her, and that's not far away from you and Aunt Nora."

"No, it's not."

"I used to ask Mom if we could come and see you guys. I really did. I can see all of you more than before."

"Great," Jason said. He didn't try to force a smile. If he did, he thought his face might crack.

"Do you have a lot of stuff to pack?" Derrick asked.

"I didn't bring much. Most of my stuff is at the house." She frowned. "That house. What's going to happen to it? I know Mom paid the next month's rent early before we came here. After that . . ."

"We don't need to worry about that," Derrick said. "But if you need stuff from there, we can drive over. It's Redman County, right?" Derrick checked his watch. "That adds a couple of hours to our day."

"Have you been there, Derrick?" Jason asked.

"Where?"

"To Hayden's house in Redman County."

"I've never been there. Why?"

"Just wondering."

Sierra stared at him, her forehead wrinkled.

"I haven't seen it either," Jason said. "Maybe someday."

"I'll get my stuff from upstairs. It's just one bag." Sierra popped up, and on her way to the bedroom she bent down and hugged Derrick around the neck. "Thanks, Dad. What a great surprise to see you here today."

Chapter Thirty-nine

Nora bustled and rushed through the door, dropping her bag as soon as she crossed the threshold. She came into the living room where Jason was sitting, working on his laptop. He looked up. Nora wore a concerned, expectant look on her face. He knew what she was going to ask.

"Is she still here? Did they leave?"

"About thirty minutes ago."

Nora stood in the center of the room, her hand raised to her mouth. She turned a little bit, almost as though she was going to spin around in a circle. She stopped the movement and said, "Jesus. Shit. Why didn't you tell me sooner?"

"I did. I called three times. You were in a meeting."

She nodded her head and slumped onto the couch, still wearing her jacket. "I know. I'm sorry. I know. Shit. Shit." She didn't look at Jason. She stared off into the distance, her eyes half-closed. "I can't believe this."

"We can't stop her from going with her father. He has rights."

"I feel like a sentimental fool. I got attached to this girl we really don't know during the week and a half she stayed here, and I shouldn't be letting it get to me that she's gone."

"There's nothing wrong with that."

"I should be glad she's gone. We can get back to our normal life, right? We don't have to worry about her taking the car or running off with that friend of hers who's a convict. We can just . . . be ourselves."

"I feel the same way you do about her. I know I was reluctant to get mixed up in anything with Hayden, but I liked having Sierra around. She's a good kid. A great kid. She's our niece."

"We can just be ourselves now and keep working on us. We need that. It's good." Nora moved around on the couch and slipped her jacket off, dumping it on the floor. She never did anything like that. She was never messy. "I thought this is the way to have a kid, you know? Just have her plopped in your lap when she's kind of grown-up, and you can talk to her and influence her life but you don't have to worry about all that little-kid stuff like diapers and chicken pox and getting hit by cars. God, I think I sound like a fool. Even to my own ears, I sound like a fool."

"She's not gone forever," Jason said. "She's still our niece. She'll still be . . ."

"What?"

"I was going to say around."

"But you can't," Nora said. "You can't because you don't know where she'll be. Just like Hayden. We don't know."

"I couldn't stop him. He's her father. And she wanted to go. You should have seen how happy she was to see—"

"I know. I get it. I just don't want to hear about it."

Jason closed his laptop and set it aside. The house and the neighborhood seemed suddenly and completely silent, as though they were experiencing not just the absence of noise but its removal, its subtraction, like the darkness in a room when a light goes out unexpectedly.

"Is it okay for her to be with Derrick?" Nora asked.

"He's her—"

"I know that part. He's her father. I get it. But he's friends with that Jesse Dean guy. Did you ask him about all that?"

"He said he doesn't know what Jesse Dean is doing these days. And he said on the phone the other night that the police in Indianapolis came and questioned him about Hayden. I guess it all was kosher."

Nora shuffled around. She picked up her coat and stood. On her way to the stairs she stopped and looked back at Jason.

"Do you ever wish we had children? Really wish it?"

"Sometimes. When Sierra was here, it was easy to see what our life might have been like."

"Here I am worrying about whether I should take a job opportunity in New York, and if we should maybe move back there, and I wonder if I'm just focused on all the wrong things."

"What do you mean?" Jason asked.

She sighed. "I'm starting to like it here. With Sierra and Hayden back . . . it felt like home. It felt like we were connected. Our lives here felt the fullest they ever felt."

Jason agreed, but he didn't know if it would ever be that way again.

Chapter Forty

Jason sat in a reception area at the police station. It was pleasant enough. Early in the morning, the room smelled clean and freshly scrubbed. Coffee brewed somewhere, its aroma drifting out to where Jason waited with an elderly woman who kept reaching up and patting her bouffant hairdo into place. Jason didn't bother picking up a magazine or checking anything on his phone. He was full of a nervous energy, one that kept him from concentrating.

Jason wasn't sure how long he waited. Olsen came out eventually, wearing a tie and a crisply pressed white shirt. He nodded formally to Jason, as though the two of them had just agreed to something meaningful and profound, and then he led Jason back to a small cubicle cluttered with loose papers and pictures of Olsen with his children. Jason took it all in while Olsen shuffled some of the work to the side, clearing a space on the desktop.

"How have you been doing?" Olsen asked.

"Fine," Jason said. "Okay, I guess."

"Did you have something on your mind?" Olsen asked.

"A couple of things. I went out to see Mr. Shaw, Logan's father."

"To express your sympathies," Olsen said.

"To do that, yes. But also to ask some questions."

The detective's eyebrows rose. "Questions?"

"Do you remember I told you that Logan had been sending cards and notes to his father over the years? Father's Day cards, birthday cards?"

"I recall that."

"And you took them from the house?" Jason asked.

"Of course. In fact, I'm heading back out to the Shaw house again this morning. I'm hoping that Mr. Shaw will be more communicative in the early part of the day."

"Have you looked at the cards? Ask the housekeeper, Pauline, about them when you're out there."

"And? I'm assuming there's an 'and.'"

"And it's not Logan's handwriting. It's not the 'L' he used to make in school."

"Obviously. He was dead all these years."

"Right. But what's interesting is who the handwriting belongs to."

Jason stopped himself. If he went forward, he was selling his sister out, implicating her in something illegal. Obstruction. Conspiracy. Possibly murder. But if he didn't tell the police everything he knew, they might never find her. If Hayden was involved with a crime, one related to Logan's death, then the police should have that information. The better to locate her.

"Are you going to tell me?" Olsen asked. "Or do I have to guess?"

Jason loosened his lips. "It's my sister's handwriting. Hayden. *She* wrote the cards. Hayden *Lynn* Danvers. She used to practice her signature in her room when she was a kid. Maybe she thought she was going to be a movie star. I don't know. But I've seen that 'L' many, many times. It's not exactly like my sister's, but it's close.

She can't hide herself. She wrote the cards and mailed them when she was out west traveling. Or she got someone to mail them somehow. We didn't always know where she was or who she was with."

Olsen may have tried, but he couldn't hide the interest that passed across his face. He couldn't play the cool, disinterested public servant when presented with something choice.

"You're sure it's Hayden's handwriting?" he asked.

"Would you know your own sibling's handwriting?"

"I'm an only child, but I see your point." Olsen nodded, still absorbing the news. "Thanks for bringing this to my attention. I'll look into it."

Jason leaned forward. "See, the two things are probably related. Hayden and Logan. If you find Hayden, then maybe we find out what happened to Logan."

"Thanks for piecing that together for me," Olsen said.

"I want my sister found."

"I was being sarcastic," Olsen said. "I could piece that together on my own. But I'll check out the handwriting on those letters today. Was there something else you wanted to tell me?"

"Right. Okay." Jason didn't even know if he wanted to bring up the next thing. He didn't know what Olsen could do for him. "Maybe I'm just looking for you to set my mind at ease about something that happened yesterday."

"I'll ease your mind if I can. The police are good at that."

"My brother-in-law came to Ednaville yesterday. Ex-brother-in-law. Sierra's father. He came to the house, and he asked to take Sierra with him. I guess he thinks she should be with him now until Hayden resurfaces."

"He is her father."

"He is."

"What did the girl think of this? Did she offer an opinion?"

"She wanted to go," Jason said. "We put the question to her, and she said she wanted . . ." Jason felt the emotion rise unexpectedly and catch in his chest. He cleared his throat. "She said she wanted to go with Derrick, to stay with him this summer or until all of this blows over."

Against all logical hope, Jason wished that the detective didn't notice the emotion in his voice. But how could he not? He was a detective. He noticed just about everything, especially the emotions of a man in the midst of a criminal investigation.

"Are you worried for the girl's safety?" Olsen asked.

"No. I don't think so. She seemed happy to see him."

"He's not abusive in any way, is he?"

"No."

"Do they have a custody arrangement?"

"It sounds like they do. I don't think Derrick has been utilizing it or supporting Sierra."

"Then you probably did the right thing letting her go with him. She might benefit from being with her father at a time like this."

"Right."

"Which is not to say you weren't doing a good job with her, you and your wife."

"Thanks."

Olsen glanced away. He seemed to take a quick look at the photos of his own family that adorned his cubicle. He looked back at Jason and said, "So your sister wrote those letters to Mr. Shaw?"

"It looks that way."

"Was your sister up on the Bluff that night with you and your friends?" Olsen asked.

Jason paused and thought about it. He could see so many

aspects of that night vividly, more vividly even than recent events in his life. But it didn't mean he knew every single thing that happened.

"I don't know," he said. "She might have been. I don't remember seeing her."

"Did she know about the fight between you and Mr. Shaw?" Olsen asked.

"Everybody did. Once the police started questioning me, everybody found out. A lot of people heard about it that night. You know how it is with kids and fights. A fight happens and then everybody starts talking about it."

"So your sister may very well have been up there on the Bluff, and she may very well have known about the fight you had with Mr. Shaw."

Jason started to say something, but the detective kept talking.

"If this is your sister sending these letters, then that implies that she's covering for somebody, right? I mean, why else do it? Unless she herself was responsible for Mr. Shaw's death way back when. Is that possible?"

"I doubt it."

"What kind of relationship did she and Mr. Shaw have? Were they friendly? Or more? You brought this up the other day. You said they were flirtatious or something like that. Now that you've had time to think about it, do you have any other sense of their relationship?"

"No, I don't. Hayden wouldn't hurt someone."

"But she had a drinking problem. Some people drink and get violent."

"Hayden didn't."

"Not ever?"

"No. She was careless. Reckless even. But not violent."

"She's back in town now. She needs to make amends for something from her past. She's seen with Jesse Dean Pratt. She leaves her daughter behind and hasn't made any contact with her. Or with you. And now these letters are in her handwriting, at least as far as you can tell. And you seem pretty certain."

"I'm the one who fought with Logan that night," Jason said. "If anyone hurt him, it was me."

"You've been thinking about that fight more?"

"Of course."

"Is there anything else you need to tell me, then? Anything else you remember?"

"I just remember that I hit him. I knocked him down." Jason shook his head. "I don't know what happened after he left me."

Olsen's face looked inscrutable, a blank mask. "Thanks, Mr. Danvers."

"Can you tell me . . . is there anything new? Any news about Hayden?"

"As soon as there is, I'll let you know."

Chapter Forty-one

Jason waited again in Colton's office. He walked over there after leaving the police station. He didn't bother to call first. He didn't want Colton to duck him. He had no reason to think the lawyer was intentionally avoiding him, but Jason hadn't heard anything from him for a couple of days.

The waiting room in Colton's office suite was well-appointed. A middle-aged receptionist handled the phones, and magazines about financial planning and retirement were fanned out across a coffee table in an order too casual to be anything but staged. Jason couldn't think of any subject more boring than those. He crossed his legs and jiggled his foot in the air. After ten minutes, the receptionist's phone buzzed. She listened for a moment, said, "Yes, sir," and then stood up and led Jason through a wooden door and down a long hallway to Colton's office, where the lawyer stood in the doorway, a smile on his face, when Jason arrived.

"Come in, bud," he said.

Jason did, and Colton closed the door behind them. Colton lumbered to the other side of his desk and clicked a few things on his computer before turning away and looking at Jason. Colton wore a white shirt and a red tie, the knot pushing against his neck and creating a bulge of cleanly shaven skin.

David Bell

"How've you been?" he asked in his best sincere voice. "Heck of a few days for news, isn't it? I'm deeply sorry to hear about Logan. I know you two were close. I know it must be tough."

"Thank you," Jason said.

"It's a real gut punch," Colton said.

"I went out there the day I heard the news."

"To the Bluff?"

"To the Shaws' house."

"Oh." Colton perked up a little. "What were you doing out there?"

"I know I should have been going to offer sympathy or whatever to the old man, but I had my own agenda. I wanted to see those cards that the old man got from Logan. Have you ever seen them?"

Colton shook his head. He wore a cautious look on his face. "No, I haven't."

"I talked to Pauline, the housekeeper."

"What did *she* say?"

"Nothing. You don't sound like you like her."

"She's fine," Colton said, although he clearly thought she wasn't. "Mr. Shaw would never let anyone remove her from her position in the household. It's confidential, obviously, but he's made provisions for her in his will. She'll be well taken care of." Colton drummed his fingers on the desktop. "What about the letters?" he asked. "You saw them?"

"Pauline showed some of them to me, the ones the police hadn't taken."

"And?"

"Obviously they weren't written by Logan."

"I could figure that out," Colton said. "Do you know who did write them?"

304

"Hayden."

Colton mostly maintained his poker face. His eyes shifted just a bit, a quick glance away and then back to Jason. "Hayden," he said, almost under his breath. "That is a surprise." The phone trilled on Colton's desk. He looked irritated as he picked it up and said, "Yes." He listened for a moment, then sighed. "Ten minutes." He hung up. "Sorry," he said. "I have a meeting at city hall. So, Hayden sent those cards. It makes sense in some ways. She was kind of a rolling stone, and I've heard that those cards came from all over the country."

"Exactly."

"But the question would be why she'd do it. Who would she be helping?"

"What about Mrs. Shaw?" Jason asked.

"What about her?"

"Pauline didn't seem to be a fan of hers."

"No one in the Shaw house was a real big fan of hers," Colton said. "Even Logan. Right?"

"He didn't talk about her much. I figured it was because of the divorce. He ended up with his dad, so there must have been a reason for that."

Colton didn't say anything, but Jason saw the knowing look that washed across his face. There was something else there, something Colton knew about Mrs. Shaw.

"What is it?" Jason asked.

Colton opened his mouth and just as quickly closed it. He pressed his lips tight. But Jason suspected that Colton really did want to spill whatever he knew. The man was a lawyer. If he wanted to hold his cards close, he could. Colton didn't seem to want to.

"What?" Jason asked. "What's the deal?"

Colton cleared his throat. "Well, Mr. Shaw is a decent man. Very decent. He likes to take care of people. He doesn't like attention." Colton pointed at Jason. "That's why he still lives in the same house. He could afford more and bigger, but he just doesn't feel that he needs it."

"What are you driving at?" Jason asked. "Is there something about Mrs. Shaw?"

"Mrs. Shaw had some problems when Logan was growing up. A drinking problem. Some emotional instability as well."

"She was sick."

"You know better than I do about the effect these things can have on families," Colton said. "Hayden's been a parent all this time, and a pretty good one to hear you tell it."

Jason remembered Derrick's story about Sierra being left alone while a baby. He shivered a little. "Mostly."

"The kid turned out okay, right?" Colton asked.

"She did."

"How is she, by the way?"

Jason swallowed. "She's spending some time with her dad."

"Derrick's in town?"

"He came to get her. You know, until Hayden . . . until we know more about Hayden's situation."

Colton gave Jason a sincere look. He seemed to recognize and understand Jason's attachment to and concern for his niece. "Anyway," he said, "Mrs. Shaw. She struggled with these things. Not a good recipe when you have a little one, especially not a boy like Logan who could be . . . high-spirited, I guess is the term. Smart-mouthed. Rambunctious. 'Challenging,' I think is the word the parenting books would use now."

The phone rang again. Colton picked it up and snapped one word. "Wait." He hung up, shaking his head. "People don't even know how to tell time." He tugged at his earlobe. "There's no way to sugarcoat it. When Logan was about ten, not long before Mr. and Mrs. Shaw divorced, Mrs. Shaw shoved Logan down a flight of stairs at their house. The stairs into the basement out there."

Jason's hands were gripping the armrests of his chair tighter than he realized, but he couldn't seem to let go. He looked down and saw the veins standing out on the back of his hand, rising from the pressure he exerted.

"Are you okay?" Colton asked.

"No."

"Shocked?"

Jason's mouth felt dry. "Yes, I am. He never said anything about it."

"He loved his mother, Logan did. I'm sure of it. But the old man wanted to keep her away from Logan as much as possible. That's the arrangement they made. She was allowed supervised visits with him. Eventually, she saw Logan a little more. But always in the Shaws' house and always with someone around, usually Mr. Shaw. Sometimes Pauline, I would gather. Mrs. Shaw remarried, as you know. She has stepchildren. To be honest, I don't know how she's doing. I guess she's living a normal life now. But she wasn't allowed to have a normal relationship with Logan when he was growing up. That's why you really didn't see her, even if you spent a lot of time out at the house."

Jason loosened his grip on the chair. His knuckles hurt, and he flexed his hands, trying to get them to feel normal again. He wasn't sure they would.

Colton stood up. "Look, I have to run to city hall. Thanks for coming by."

"Thank you."

"People surprise us, don't they?" Colton said, as he slipped into a sport coat. "I know I threw you for a loop with that news. I was surprised to hear about Hayden and those letters. Do you want to sit here for a minute and regroup?"

"I'm okay."

Jason stood and walked to the door, where Colton rested his hand on the knob. Colton didn't open the door yet. He held his hand out, stopping Jason.

"All that stuff I told you about Mrs. Shaw? It's been hush-hush for years, of course. Only the family knew. I probably shouldn't have told you, but with everything going on here, I thought you should know. Maybe you can understand Logan a little better. Maybe you can understand the whole situation a little better."

Jason nodded, but he wasn't sure he ever would.

Chapter Forty two

The brightness of the day hurt Jason's eyes. He drove home with his sunglasses on and the visor tilted down, but the midday sun still poked at him, dug at him until he felt a headache developing. Colton's bombshell reverberated in his mind. Logan's mother had pushed her son down a flight of stairs. She was so abusive she wasn't allowed to see him. And Jason had never known this about his very best friend. It was a secret shame Logan carried with him all his life, something he shoved away and wouldn't or couldn't share.

Jason had to ask himself: What else didn't he know about Logan? What else lay buried beneath the surface of his friend's life?

Nora was scheduled to work until the late evening. When Jason went inside their house, he again noticed the quiet. It hit him in the face like a blast of heat from the oven. No one was home. With Sierra gone, everything felt more empty.

He dialed Regan's number. He didn't expect her to answer, but she did. She sounded energetic, almost cheery.

"What do you know about Logan's mother?"

"His mother?" she said, her voice flattening. "She wasn't around much."

"I know that. But did you have a sense of her? As a person?"

"Why are you asking me this?"

"I'm just curious. You mentioned her the other day. You said you liked her."

"I did."

"You said she talked to you from time to time about your career and your plans. Was that it?"

"Why are you asking me this again?"

Jason told her. He told her that Mrs. Shaw had shoved Logan down the stairs when he was just a little boy, that she was forced to keep her distance from her son. After he finished speaking, he listened to her breathing on the other end of the line. It took Regan a long time to speak.

"Did you know that when we were kids?" she asked.

"Never. Did you?"

"No. Logan wouldn't tell me something like that."

"Why not?" Jason asked. "He had a thing for you. And, as you so accurately pointed out, you were a girl. I thought maybe he'd feel more comfortable telling you than me. I never knew."

"I—" She stopped herself.

"What? You what?"

"I don't believe it. I don't see how that nice woman could have done that."

"Nice woman? She sounds like a monster. You're a mother. Would you ever do that to a child? To any child?"

"Of course not. You don't have to be a parent to know that. I'm just wondering why Colton is telling this to you now."

"I went to talk to him about everything that's been going on, and the conversation got around to Mrs. Shaw."

"That poor woman," Regan said. "She just found out her son is dead. She always seemed so alone. You know how you get a sense of that from some adults, even when you're a kid? I got that sense from her. She seemed very alone."

"She deserved it."

"I don't know, Jason," Regan said.

"Don't know what?"

"How she could have done that. That sweet lady."

"People manage to keep parts of themselves hidden."

A sound came over the line like Regan had placed her hand over the mouth of the phone. He heard muffled voices.

A man's voice?

"Regan?" he asked. "Are you there?"

"I have to go, Jason."

"Are you at work?"

"No. Not yet."

"Where are you?"

"Bye, Jason."

Jason expected Nora home after nine. Just after eight, a knocking came from the back of the house. Jason sat up straight on the couch, where he was trying to distract himself with a Reds game. They were playing in New York against the Mets, but nothing looked the way Jason remembered it. When he lived in the city, the Mets played at Shea, and so the sparkly new stadium reminded Jason of how far removed from that world he really was.

He muted the sound and walked through the house. The skin at the base of his neck felt pinched and tight. He pictured Rose Holland leaving poor little Pogo out there. And then an image of Jesse Dean slipped into his head—the feel of his hand against Jason's throat, the sound of the threats.

Should he call the police just because someone knocked?

Jason almost wished it were Jesse Dean, that some news about Hayden would be delivered to his house, regardless of the messenger.

Jason pulled the back door open. Tricia stood there in her all-black clothes, a cigarette between two fingers of her left hand, her right arm across her chest. She looked like she practiced the pose in front of a mirror.

"Hey, man," she said.

"What do you want?" Jason asked. "And why are you at the back door?"

"Whoa," she said. "Mr. Hostility. Careful or you'll stroke out one of these days."

"Sierra isn't here. She left with her dad."

"I know that." Tricia took a drag and let out a long plume of smoke. She was polite enough to mostly send it away from Jason's face. "She texted me and told me."

"When did she text you?" Jason asked.

"Yesterday. Day before. I don't know."

"Is that all she said?"

"Dude, can I come in the house? I want to talk to you."

Jason examined the girl. Her eyes, inside the circle of heavy eyeliner, looked sincere, almost pleading. He pointed to the cigarette. "Put that out."

Tricia leaned over and rubbed it against the side of the house, then tossed the butt into the yard. "Cool?" she said.

Jason stepped back and let her enter the kitchen. Tricia moved along the counters, stopping to pick up a couple of objects as she walked by. A piece of fruit, a bag of coffee. She seemed in no hurry.

"Do you want something to drink?" Jason asked, trying to be polite.

"What kind of beer do you have?"

"I'm not giving you beer. You're seventeen."

"Jesus. Uptight much."

"What do you want, Tricia?"

The girl turned around and leaned back against the counter. She was rail thin and pale under the overhead lights. Jason wondered if she ever ate or if she just smoked instead.

"I know you're looking for Jesse Dean."

"How do you know that?"

"I know things. You think he killed your friend."

"Did Sierra tell you that?" Jason asked.

Tricia's foot bounced against the floor, the sole of her shoe making a squeaking noise against the tile. Her knee went up and down. She said, "Look, let me tell you something. I know Jesse Dean. I've partied with him. The guy's an asshole. That's why I'm here, okay? He fucked me over. He wanted me to do something for him, and then when I did it—or I tried to do it—he didn't live up to his end of the bargain. You see? He screwed me over, so I'm here to give you the lowdown. You can do whatever you want with it."

"What are you talking about? What did he want you to do for him?"

"It's your fault," Tricia said. "You stopped me. You and your wife."

Jason couldn't make sense of what she was saying, but the girl didn't offer anything else right away. It slowly came together for Jason while Tricia continued to pump her leg.

"Sierra? He wanted something from Sierra?"

"Not something. *Her*. He wanted her. I was supposed to bring her to him the other night, but you stopped me."

Chapter Forty-three

Jason raised his hands to his head and ran his fingers through his hair. He resisted the urge to grab hold and pull the roots right out of his scalp.

"What did he want Sierra for?" he asked.

"I don't know," Tricia said. "Look, the guy approached me, okay? He knew Sierra and I were friends."

"How did he know that?"

"I don't know, but he did. He tracked me down. He came to my house. I live with my mom and her boyfriend. They don't exactly care who my gentlemen callers are. But Jesse Dean showed up, and he tells me he'd like to party with me, so I did a little bit."

"You went out with a strange guy?" Jason asked. He dropped his hands from his head and started pacing.

"He said he wanted to talk about my friend Sierra. Shit, I hadn't seen her in a while, you know? But Jesse Dean said he knew Sierra, that he was an old family friend. And then he told me that he and I could party together. I know what that means. It's like a code."

"Sex?"

"Maybe sex. But drugs, man. He had some pot and some meth. I don't use it that much, the meth, but I'm not going to turn it down if it's free. Mom and her boyfriend were all over the house, playing kissy-face. I wanted to get out."

"Did you give Sierra the weed that was upstairs?"

"I had to. My mom's boyfriend steals mine. I figured you'd have a cow about that, but Sierra was just holding it for me. I lost all that stuff to the cops when they came here and searched. That's why Jesse Dean's offer was so appealing to me."

"Where's Sierra? Is she in danger?"

"Listen. So the dude takes me out and we get high and everything, and once we're good and high, he says that he needs to see my friend Sierra. He told me that he's friends with Sierra's mom. Your sister. He didn't say what he wanted from Sierra, but I got the feeling it had something to do with her mom. I'm not sure. He mentioned her a few times."

"How long ago was this?"

"A few days. Right before I came here that night." Her foot stopped pumping. "Jesse Dean said if I could bring Sierra to him, then he would give me some more meth and weed. In fact, he said he'd give it to me either way, as long as I tried. That's when I came over here to hang with Sierra."

"Didn't it occur to you that you were putting Sierra in danger? The guy's a criminal. He's doing drugs."

"He knew her mom. He said something to me, something that made me think he'd been hanging out with her recently. I don't know. Trust me, it seemed safe."

"Are you crazy?" Jason asked. "You should have called the police. Or told an adult."

"Listen. I can take care of myself. I'm not a child. I don't call an adult whenever there's trouble of some kind. But when I came over here that night, you all wouldn't let Sierra out of the house. I was going to take her to Jesse Dean right then."

"Did you tell Sierra?"

"No. I told her I had some friends we could hang with. I figured you'd told her how dangerous Jesse Dean is, so if I mentioned his name, she'd freak out. She didn't really want to go anywhere. She's not much of a partyer." Tricia crinkled her nose a little when she said that. "She would have gone, though. But you all blocked it. You wouldn't let your precious little niece out of the house. So I went back to Jesse Dean and told him I tried and struck out. And then guess what he does?"

"Did he hurt you?"

"The asshole doesn't give me the stuff. He said he'd give it to me either way, but he didn't. He said I failed, and he told me to get lost. That's why I'm here now. I figure if he can't play straight with me, then I'm not going to play straight with him. I'm going to rat him out to you. He can live with the consequences."

Jason realized his hands were trembling slightly. He felt like he had little control over them. He stepped forward and pulled out one of the chairs and sat at the table. "Sierra's dad showed up the next day, the day after you were here. He's friends with Jesse Dean."

"I didn't see Sierra's dad. I don't know what he has to do with it."

"And you never found out why Jesse Dean wanted Sierra?"

"He just acted like he wanted to talk to her," she said. "You know, Jesse Dean didn't really give off the creepy sex vibe to me. He's a creep, but not that way. He didn't give me that look that creepy guys give. I can feel when that's happening." She shivered. "He wanted something else from Sierra. I promise."

Jason stared at the tabletop. He felt the weight of his actions pressing on his shoulders. He let Sierra go with Derrick. He handed her over. Derrick had to be working with Jesse Dean. Why else would he show up the day after Tricia had been sent to get Sierra? Derrick was Jesse Dean's backup plan when Tricia couldn't get Sierra out of the house.

"You keep acting like you knew how to find Jesse Dean. You said you went and saw him. Is this at his house?"

"No. He said his wife is staying there. No partying with her around."

"Then where is he?"

"I don't know where he is now. I met him in town once, and then the other time he took me to his little getaway."

"Where was this?" Jason asked.

Tricia didn't answer. She started pumping her foot again.

Jason stood up, pushing the chair back. "Where is he?"

"Do you know where Barnes Hollow is?" she asked.

"No. I've heard of it, but I don't know where it is."

"South of town."

"I know it's south of town, but I don't know where exactly."

Tricia shook her head. "Typical. You haven't even bothered to get out of town."

"Where is it?"

"It's about ten miles south of here. You take County Road Three Hundred. People hunt there in the fall. They have cabins and things. People, kids mostly, go out there and party other times of year. It's a lot of rednecks to be perfectly honest. That's where Jesse Dean was hanging out. I assume he owns the place he was staying in."

Jason walked across the room. "I'm calling the police."

"Then I'm out of here."

"You have to tell them what you know."

"No, I don't." Tricia started for the back door, moving quickly. Jason moved faster and intercepted her. He reached out and grabbed her arm. "Ow."

Jason felt his fingers dig into the soft flesh of the girl's biceps. She looked up at him, her face a mixture of surprise and pain. But he didn't let go.

"You have to," he said. "Sierra could be hurt."

"Get off of me."

She squirmed, twisting her body to try to break Jason's grip, but he didn't let go.

"The police won't bother you," he said. "Just tell them how to get there."

"Fuck you."

Tricia delivered a solid kick to Jason's shin. He jumped back but still held on. The pain shot up his leg, and he recognized the absurdity of his physical struggle with a seventeen-year-old girl. But he wouldn't let go.

"Then tell me where it is," he said. "Just tell me."

"I don't know the street names back in the Hollow," she said, her squirming easing.

"Then show me. Just show me."

"No."

Jason loosened his grip but didn't let go. He felt sweat forming on his forehead. His clothes felt tight and bunched.

"What do you want? Money? Is that it?"

Tricia looked at him, her eyes wide but the anger there easing. "I don't want anything."

"Fifty bucks," Jason said. "A hundred bucks. Is that what you want?"

"Let go."

He did. He released the girl and straightened up. She rubbed her arm with her opposite hand and pulled her shirt down and back into place. But she didn't make a move for the door. She studied Jason, her mouth a thin line.

"A hundred dollars," Jason said. "Cash. And I won't back out like Jesse Dean. Here." He reached around and brought out his wallet. "Here's fifty to start. I'll give you the other fifty when we get there. Okay?"

Tricia stared at the two twenties and a ten as if they were magic. It took her a long moment to make a move for them, but she reached out and grabbed the bills from Jason's hand.

"You ready to get the other fifty?" he asked.

Tricia tucked the bills into her pants pocket. "How do you know I just won't run as soon as we walk out the door? How do you know I won't fuck you over?"

Jason leaned closer to the girl. "Because despite all evidence to the contrary, I think you're worried about Sierra too. I don't think you came here to screw Jesse Dean over. I think you came here to try to help Sierra. Right?"

Tricia didn't answer.

"And because you want that other fifty dollars so you can buy more meth or pot or whatever it is that floats your boat. Right?"

"No cops," she said. "I can't get busted again."

"I'll call the cops after you show me. You can leave then if you want. Okay?"

"Can I smoke in the car?"

"Roll the window down."

"Fine," she said. "Let's go. This conversation is getting really boring."

Chapter Forty-four

They drove south into the darkening night. Jason gripped the wheel with both hands, his shoulders hunched slightly forward. He left the radio off and listened instead to the steady thump of the tires against the road. Tricia sat next to him in the dark, remaining silent for most of the trip. She didn't speak until Jason started asking her questions.

"Aren't you going to smoke?"

She shook her head. She sat low in her seat, her arms folded across her chest. After she shook her head, she lifted her hand and used one fingernail to dig at another on the opposite hand. She looked tiny and shrunken, so small and defenseless it might have made sense to have her ride in the back, like a child.

"Did you really just come to the house because you're pissed at Jesse Dean?" Jason asked.

She shrugged, then shifted her weight. "I like Sierra. She's the kind of friend my mom wishes I had more of. Smart, you know. A good kid."

"I know," Jason said.

He tried to think ahead to the cabin in the woods, the place where Sierra might be with Derrick and Jesse Dean. He couldn't imagine what he would do when he arrived there, except hope that he found Sierra and brought her home. It was possible she was gone, and also possible that if she was there, she might not want to go anywhere with him. She might be perfectly content to stay with her father and Jesse Dean.

The tops of the trees grew over the road, making a canopy that blocked out the stars. They passed few cars going the other way. Once, a rabbit or a raccoon showed up in the cone of the headlights, its eyes a quick flash of red in the dark.

"Your turn's coming up," Tricia said.

"Where?"

The girl leaned forward, straining against the seat belt. She squinted.

"There," she said, pointing.

Jason slowed, his foot shifting from the gas to the brake. As he flipped the turn signal on, he saw the weathered, wooden sign. BARNES HOLLOW. The sign looked somewhat familiar to him. He'd passed it a time or two as a kid or a teenager but never understood what went on there. His father didn't hunt. His friends partied at the Bluff if they partied anywhere. Barnes Hollow might as well have been in another state.

A narrow road cut through the trees. Jason slowed and turned on the brights. His tires crunched over the gravel, and the car jounced on the uneven ground. They hit a pothole, one Jason didn't see coming, and the bump almost knocked his head against the roof.

"Jesus," he said, slowing down more. He didn't need a flat or a busted axle in the middle of the woods with Jesse Dean waiting nearby.

"The road sucks," Tricia said. "It's not big-city living."

"Roads suck worse than this in most big cities."

They approached a fork. Jason saw it coming and said, "Which way?"

Tricia hesitated. "Left, I think."

"You think?"

"I was high."

Jason went to the left. The tree cover started to thin. On the right, back from the road, Jason saw a cabin. It sat dark and apparently empty. Then farther on he saw another cabin and another on the opposite side of the road.

"Are we getting close?" Jason asked.

"Couple more turns."

"How far in are we going?"

"Deeper." Tricia pointed again. "There's the next turn. Right."

Jason took it, and then just a few hundred yards farther on, they came to another fork. Tricia pointed to the left, and they turned that way.

"Slow down a little more," she said. "We're getting close."

The car eased almost to a crawl.

"Turn the lights off," Tricia said.

Jason started to object, but then he followed her instructions. When he flipped them off, the only glow came from the dashboard, a neon green wash across their faces. Outside it looked like they'd driven into a cave or fallen off the edge of the world.

"Pull over here," Tricia said.

Jason guided the car into the grass and weeds on the side of the road. When they were stopped, he turned the car off, dropping them into greater darkness.

For a quiet moment, they sat. The engine ticked as it cooled, and Jason left the keys in the ignition. Tricia shifted in the seat next to him.

"What are we doing?" Jason asked.

"It's over there," she said. "To the left side of the road. I'm waiting for my eyes to adjust."

Jason followed the line of Tricia's gaze into the gloomy night. At first, he saw nothing, just a black, inky veil, not even the outline of trees. But the longer he stared, the more the night assembled itself into coherent parts. Tricia's eyes were ahead of his.

"There it is," she said. "I see it."

"I don't."

"Back from the road over there." She pointed. "Can you see it yet? It's set back against those trees."

Jason continued to stare, and then he saw the outline of a small cabin resolving in the night. "Ah. Got it."

"They don't have any lights showing," Tricia said.

"No one's there?"

"They could have the curtains pulled. If they're getting high, they might be passed out. Or sleeping it off."

"Sierra wouldn't do that, would she?"

"Get high? Not by choice."

"Okay, I'm going over there. What are you going to do?"

"I ain't walking back to town, chief."

Jason hadn't considered that. He knew Tricia didn't want to stay if the police were involved, but he hadn't thought of how she'd get back.

"Shit," he said. He worked around, turning his body so he could reach into the pocket of his pants. He drew out his phone. "I want to call the police, but if no one's in there . . ."

"That's the risk you take, unless you want to go take a peek. I'll wait here if you do that, but you might get caught. From the looks of things, you aren't exactly the type to put up a good fight against a guy like Jesse Dean."

Jason lifted his hand to his neck and lightly touched the fading bruises there. "Right."

"We had a deal. No cops for me."

"I know how much you care about honoring deals," he said. "Okay, I'll call the police now. Worst-case scenario, they come out and look around this place, see if they can figure out what Jesse Dean is up to. Right? You can wait in the car."

"Wait? Out here?"

"Sure. What other choice is there?"

"Let me take the car and get out. I don't want to be here when the cops show up."

"Are you for real?"

"I'll leave it at your house. When the cops get here, they'll give you a ride back home."

Jason didn't feel like arguing. "Fine. Take the car."

"Cool. In the interest of full disclosure, my license was suspended."

"But you drove to our house the other night."

"I said suspended. I still know how to drive."

"I'll pretend I didn't hear that." He lifted the phone and started dialing.

"Hey," Tricia said. "Wait until I'm gone."

She grabbed his arm and pulled, but it didn't matter.

Jason didn't have a signal. "Shit," he said. "No service."

"That happens out in the sticks."

"Try yours."

"No way. Then they'll know who's calling."

"Just try it."

Tricia pulled her phone out and tapped it. "Nothing," she said. "Why don't you drive back to the main road and call? You can wait there for the police."

Jason looked over at the little cabin. Sierra might be right inside there. With Jesse Dean. He couldn't leave.

"No way," he said. "I'm waiting here. You take the car and call when you get a signal. Tell them where to go."

"Are you sure?"

"I'm sure." Jason studied her face. "That also means I'm trusting you to do the right thing. Can you handle it?"

"I could just lie to you, you know? I could just lie and take the car and be gone. You'd be out here with your dick in your hand."

"You won't do that, will you?"

Tricia held his gaze, then looked away. "I won't. Fuck. You seem so sincere. And you care about Sierra and all that. I can't help myself. You almost make me wish I had a dad."

"I'm going to get out now. Hurry up, but don't make too much noise."

"I know the drill."

Jason reached over and squeezed her hand. "Thanks."

"Wait a minute," she said.

"What?"

"Fifty bucks, chief. Remember?"

Jason took out his wallet and handed her three twenties. "That's sixty. You owe me ten."

"I'll make change the next time I see you."

"If you do this right, consider it a tip," he said, opening the door and stepping out into the night.

Chapter Forty-five

Jason listened to Tricia drive away. She kept the headlights off a long time, and it was only when she went around a bend in the road that Jason caught a brief glimpse of red flaring in the distance. He checked the glowing dials of his watch. Nine o'clock. The air carried some humidity, a sneak preview of the heavier and thicker days and nights to come. He looked around at the blackness. He wasn't sure he'd ever been so alone in his life. Above, the thin clouds slipped across the moon and stars like wisps of smoke. The sky looked almost unreal, like a special effect.

Jason walked up the road a little way until he came even with the cabin. Crickets and other insects called from the grass and trees. The sound of his shoes against the gravel blended in with the noises of the night. He stopped and stood with his hands in his pockets, his heart beating faster, the hairs on the back of his neck rising. No one knew where he was except Tricia. Not Nora. Not Regan. He turned to the left and looked back down the road in the direction Tricia had driven off. He wondered if he should just leave. He could meet the police—*if* she had called them—and let them lead the way in.

But he couldn't turn his back. He couldn't will his body to

walk down that road and away from the cabin if Sierra might be inside. He'd already made the mistake of handing her over to Derrick—and the parade of faces of people he'd walked away from or let slip out of his life seemed to grow longer by the moment. Logan, Hayden, Regan . . . even Nora. Jason felt the frustration ride up his spine, a rigid, aching tension. He gritted his teeth and kicked at the loose pebbles at his feet.

"Hurry," he said, though no one could hear him, certainly not Tricia, the seventeen-year-old delinquent he had pinned his hopes to. But it made him feel better to say the word. It brought a release, so he said it again and again like a child scared of the dark. "Hurry. Hurry. Hurry."

He stopped saying it only when the door of the cabin opened, and he saw a young girl backlit from the inside.

He froze and studied her, trying to see who it was.

And then the girl was running. Toward him and away from the cabin.

Jason ran across the road and called out.

"Sierra!"

They reached each other in the dark. Sierra's hair hung loose and ragged, her eyes bulged wide with fear. Jason took hold of her hands and pulled her close.

"Uncle Jason. You have to go in there."

"What's happening? Are you hurt?"

"I'm fine. I ran away."

"Who's inside the cabin?"

"My dad's in trouble in there. He's fighting with that guy Jesse Dean. He's going to hurt my dad. You have to stop him. I got away when they grabbed each other, but I should go back."

"No," Jason said. "Go down this road." He pointed in the dark. "A right, a left, and then a right. Keep going. You'll come out on County Road Three Hundred. Tricia just went that way."

"Tricia?"

"She brought me here. She's getting the police."

"Will you help Dad?"

The girl's eyes were pleading in the dark. He saw the fear there, as well as the hope. Was he supposed to turn away again and save himself?

"If you go, I'll help your dad," he said. "Go and don't look back."

"Promise?"

"I promise. Wait for the police. Now, go."

Sierra started down the road, picking her way over the gravel in the darkness. Jason waited until she left his sight, and then he turned and headed for the cabin.

Chapter Forty-six

Jason's shoes brushed across the medium-high grass as he approached the cabin. The door Sierra came through remained ajar, a shaft of light spilling onto the ground. Through the opening, he saw a wooden table, rustic looking, with two chairs standing nearby and another chair tipped over on the floor. A figure quickly passed across the open door, a blurred motion. Jason couldn't tell if it was Derrick or Jesse Dean or anyone he knew. Then raised voices reached him. A couple of shouts, one in anger and one apparently in pain. Then the angry shouts grew louder.

Jason pressed himself flat against the exterior wall of the cabin. It was made out of rough, weathered boards, and pieces of it grabbed at his clothes. He slid along to the edge of the door, listening. Something thumped inside, then thumped again.

"Derrick?"

The noises stopped, but no one said anything.

"Derrick? It's Jason."

Muffled voices came from inside the cabin. Jason couldn't make out what was being said.

"Derrick?"

"What the fuck, Jason? Get out of here."

"Sierra's okay," Jason said. "She ran off. She wanted me to see how you were."

"Go," Derrick said. "You don't have anything to do with this."

"I'm coming in," Jason said. "I'm alone. But the police are on their way."

More muffled voices and cursing. Then a familiar voice said, "Jason? Get in here. We need you."

Jason moved quickly, stepping into the open doorway. He blinked in the harsh light. It took his eyes a moment to adjust, and then he saw everything.

He saw Derrick standing over Jesse Dean, who lay motionless on the floor. And crouched next to Jesse Dean, reaching for his neck and then his wrist as though feeling for a pulse, was a woman he recognized all too well. She made a hurry-up gesture toward him with her free hand.

"Get in here, Jason," she said. "We need you."

It was Hayden.

"What the hell is going on, Hayden?"

Jason stepped inside.

Hayden kept making the hurry-up gesture with her hand. Jason crossed the wooden plank floor until he was next to her—and standing over Jesse Dean. Jesse Dean's eyes were closed, his neck bent at an awkward angle. The side of his head that faced Jason showed a long gash, one that ran from just under his hairline and down the length of his cheek to his chin. He didn't move and didn't appear to be breathing.

Jason looked at Derrick, who had backed away. He stood against the far wall of the cabin, his eyes fixed on Jesse Dean as well. He held a thick, gold-plated object in his hand, and it took Jason a moment to realize it was an andiron from the fireplace.

"I don't think he's breathing, Jason," Hayden said. "Can you check?"

Jason bent down, but he kept his eyes on Derrick. A large abrasion showed on Derrick's cheek, and his shirt was ripped. One of his shoes was off and lying against the wall near where Derrick stood.

"What happened here, Hayden?" Jason asked.

"Just check him. Please. We can explain later."

Jason wasn't sure he knew what to do. He hadn't taken a first aid class since high school. And something about touching Jesse Dean's body felt odd. He remembered Jesse Dean's grip against his own neck, the power and the threat carried by those hands that lay stretched out at his side, open and useless.

Jason pressed his fingers against Jesse Dean's neck. The skin was warm and sweaty. His fingers slipped against the perspiration. Jesse Dean's skin didn't seem dead. It lacked the rubbery, clammy feel of his parents' flesh when he touched them in their caskets. He pressed his fingers against the skin again and felt nothing. He moved his fingers a little. He kept searching, hoping that he'd find a spot that indicated some life still flowed through the man's body.

"Is there a pulse, Jason?" Derrick asked.

"Let me check his wrist."

Jason moved down a little, and Hayden scuttled out of the way. He picked up Jesse Dean's hand and felt around. The skin seemed cooler but still sweaty. Jason moved around, placing his fingers all over the man's thick wrist.

Nearly under her breath, Hayden said, "Nothing there, right?"

"Let me try this."

"Quit it, Jason," Hayden said. "He's dead. There's nothing there, right?"

Jason looked up at Derrick, whose eyes were still wide and frightened.

"I don't feel anything," Jason said. "I'm not getting a pulse."

"He's dead," Hayden said. "I told you. He's dead."

Jason nodded. "I think you're right."

Jason stared at Derrick, who shut his eyes tight and leaned back against the wall. He slowly slid down, his knees rising until his butt hit the floor, and then he tipped over to the side in a fetal position. He raised one hand and pounded the floor just once and then stopped.

"My God," he said. "My God."

Hayden and Jason stood up. Hayden took a step toward her ex-husband.

"Derrick," she said, "it's not your fault."

"I killed him."

"You were protecting Sierra. And me."

"My God."

"Derrick," Jason said, "if it was self-defense, you'll be okay. Jesse Dean is a criminal. The police know that. They're on their way, and you can tell them exactly what happened."

Derrick opened his eyes wide. He pushed himself up so that he sat with his back against the wall, his legs straight out in front of him. "The police?" he asked.

"Yes. I called them. Well, Tricia, Sierra's friend, went to get them. I thought Sierra was in here with Jesse Dean, and I wanted to get help."

Derrick stood up. He let the andiron go, and it thudded against the floor. His chest started to heave as he breathed more heavily. A flush rose in his cheeks.

"What is it?" Jason asked.

"Derrick?" Hayden said. "Jason's right. It was self-defense."

334

"Get out, Hayden," Derrick said.

"Derrick—"

"Where's Sierra?" he asked.

"She left," Jason said. "I sent her back to the main road. She's running away to find Tricia. If the police are coming, they'll pass her on the way in. She'll be fine."

"Get out, Hayden," Derrick said again.

"It's self-defense."

"They'll find out everything," he said. "All of it." He sounded calmer as he repeated himself. "All of it."

"All of what?" Jason asked.

"Get out, Hayden. Go find Sierra. Make sure she's okay. That's your job now, making sure Sierra's okay."

"Derrick —"

"Get out," he said, his voice rising temporarily and then calming again. "Get out. I want to talk to Jason. Alone. Man-to-man. I want to be here with Jason."

Jason turned to Hayden. "Do it. Go. Make sure Sierra's okay."

Hayden leaned in close to her brother. "He has a gun."

Jason tried not to show any reaction to what she said, although he wasn't sure he succeeded. Her words only added to the fear slowly growing inside of his chest, the knot that bundled together and swelled with each breath he took.

"We'll be okay," he said, hoping his voice sounded as calm as he wanted it to. He reached out and gently nudged his sister toward the door. "Just go find Sierra. Follow the road back to the right."

Hayden looked at Jason as though she wanted to say something else, but Jason shook his head.

"Just go," he said.

Hayden looked at both of them, and then she left the cabin.

Chapter Forty-seven

"Close the door," Derrick said to Jason when Hayden was gone.

"Derrick, we can still just walk away from this—"

"Close the door," he said again.

When he spoke, he shifted his hand, which had been stuffed into his jacket pocket. Jason looked down and saw that Derrick had eased something out of the pocket a few inches, the butt of a black handgun. Jason nodded, the gesture meant to show his former brother-in-law that he understood who controlled the situation.

"Close the door," Derrick said one more time. "I don't want Hayden or Sierra to hear any of this."

"They're gone."

"Just close it."

Jason backed up the few steps, Derrick watching him all the way. He reached out and gave the door a gentle nudge. It swung shut, the latch clicking.

"Okay?" Jason asked.

Derrick seemed to relax a little, but his eyes still looked wide and red. He kept one hand—his right—tucked into the jacket pocket. The other hung at his side, and he clenched it into a fist and unclenched it as he stood there.

"How long before the police get here?" he asked.

"I'm not sure. I don't even know if the girl notified them. She took my car. She could be on her way to Florida for all I know."

"But if she did tell them? If she made the call right away?"

"Ten minutes, I guess. Maybe less. We're pretty isolated. Our phones weren't working."

"I know. That's why Jesse Dean brought us here."

"What is this all about, Derrick? Why was Hayden here? And Sierra? What did Jesse Dean want with them?"

Derrick reached up with his free hand and rubbed his eyes. Then he brushed his hand across the top of his head, letting out a long sigh as he did so. "I'm tired," he said. "I've been up for two days."

"You came out here after you left our house?"

"I did. I needed to bring Sierra to Jesse Dean. That's the only thing I could do. He wouldn't rest until he saw her in the flesh." His composure cracked even more. His chin quivered.

"You brought your daughter to Jesse Dean?"

"I didn't have any choice. I thought if I brought Sierra out here, then maybe Jesse Dean would let both of them go, Sierra and Hayden. I thought maybe he'd be done with them."

"What did he want them for? What does Sierra have to do with it?"

"Can't you guess what this is all about?" Derrick started to pace, side to side in front of the wall, one hand still in his coat pocket. "Don't you know?"

"It's about Logan?"

"Yes."

"Jesse Dean killed him, right?"

"Mostly. I mean, yes, Jesse Dean killed him. But he didn't do it alone. Do you know who helped him kill Logan and bury his body in the woods?"

"You?"

"Yes, yes. Me." He continued the pacing. He still wore only one shoe, so he moved with an awkward shifting gait. *Step-clomp. Step-clomp.* Again he raised his hand and ran it through his hair. "I helped him kill your buddy Logan. Pretty boy, rich boy Logan. And we buried him in the woods on graduation night. Hell of a present when you get right down to it."

Jason swallowed. "Why did you kill Logan?"

Derrick stopped pacing. "You always thought we were trash, didn't you? Troublemakers. Hillbillies."

Jason couldn't—wouldn't—deny it. He had always looked down on Jesse Dean as well as Derrick.

"You lumped me in with Jesse Dean," Derrick said. "Your family did. I wasn't good enough for Hayden, even when she was drinking a fifth of vodka mixed with grape juice before school every day. Even that didn't make her fit for me."

"That was a long time ago," Jason said. "Things change. Lord knows you were better for Sierra a lot of the time. Better than Hayden."

"A long time ago?" Derrick said. "Nothing is a long time ago in this life. Doesn't it feel like just yesterday we were all up on that bluff on the night of graduation? Tell me, how long ago does that seem?"

"Sometimes it feels like five minutes," Jason said. "Other times like it was another life."

Jason saw beads of sweat popping out on Derrick's forehead, and in the enclosed space of the cabin, he smelled body odor, some combination of anger and fear leaking out of his ex-brother-in-law's body. Jason looked down where Jesse Dean lay. His pants were stained around the crotch, a physiological release of urine at the moment of death. It added to the pungent mixture of smells brewing in the heat of the room.

"Did Hayden know you killed Logan?" Jason asked.

"She knew enough."

"And she wrote those cards to Logan's dad to cover for you?"

Surprise showed on Derrick's face. "How did you ever see those? Did you go out to pretty boy's house or something?"

"I did. I saw Hayden's handwriting."

"That was her idea. Her and Jesse Dean's. They had a lot of ideas together, I guess. I was opposed to it. I thought it would just call more attention to the fact that Logan was gone. I thought his parents would take one look at those cards and say, 'That wasn't written by my son.' Hayden thought she was so clever, and so did Jesse Dean. I guess they were right, weren't they? Everybody believed he was still alive all those years until they dug him up on the Bluff. Hayden and Jesse Dean. They made quite a team."

"Why did you kill Logan, Derrick? Was Hayden cheating on you with him? Is that it? Was it jealousy?"

Derrick was shaking his head. "Your sister's a whore, and Jesse Dean and I are trash who settle our problems by killing somebody. Is that it?"

"What was it, then? Why did you do it?"

"What makes you think we had a choice?"

"Why wouldn't you have had a choice?"

Derrick froze. He raised his hand, the index finger extended.

"What?" Jason asked.

"Shh." His hand remained in the air, and he tilted his head. "Did you hear that?"

"What?"

"Listen."

Jason turned his head toward the front of the cabin. He heard nothing at first; then something emerged from the quiet night. A soft rushing. It sounded like—

"It's a car," Derrick said. "Shit. The police."

"It might be Tricia."

"It's the police." He started pacing again. "I killed Jesse Dean. I killed Logan. That's all they're going to hear."

"Tell them the truth. You were protecting your family."

"They don't care about that. Not with a guy like me. Look at you. You can't help but think I'm a killer."

"Sierra and Hayden will back you up."

"I got arrested again. Almost two years ago. Assault. That's why I had to get a new job. I punched my boss."

"It's okay."

"That's why I didn't see Sierra. If they know about this—"

Derrick stopped pacing. He pulled the gun out of his jacket pocket and turned it toward Jason.

Everything in Jason's body went cold. Something unclenched in the center of his body, and he thought his bowels might release right then and right there.

"Derrick—"

"Get out."

Jason started backing away.

"Faster. Get out."

"Don't fight with the police, Derrick. Drop the gun. They'll kill you if they see you with that."

"Get out. Go. If Sierra's out there, take her away from here. I still care about her, even if people have always disrespected me. That doesn't change things with her and me. Tell her that."

"What would change that? Killing Jesse Dean?"

"Go."

Jason stopped at the door. His shaking hand rested on the knob.

"Come out, Derrick."

Derrick shook his head. He pointed the gun at Jason's torso. "Last chance," he said. "Go."

Jason didn't hesitate. He fumbled the door open and stepped out into the night.

Chapter Forty-eight

Jason didn't run. His eyes had adjusted to the light inside the cabin, and stepping out into the night again left him blinded. He moved toward the road, and as he did, he saw two small circles of light, and then behind the circles of light the looming figures of two men.

"Get on the ground!"

Jason froze.

"Get on the ground, sir!"

He raised his hands, surrendering. The two figures reached him. He saw the uniforms, the flash of the badges in the reflected glow of the flashlights. As they came closer, Jason heard leather creak and equipment rattle.

Police.

The police had arrived. Tricia had done her job.

Jason fell to his knees. One of the officers came up to his right side and took his arm. Not so gently, he forced Jason to the ground, his chin and the side of his face thudding into the grass. The officer placed his knee against Jason's back, while the other officer stood nearby.

"Are you armed, sir?"

Jason tried to answer, but the officer with his knee in his

back was already running his hand over Jason's body, patting his back, his legs, the insides of his thighs, and then rolling him a little to get at his front pockets.

"No," Jason said. He smelled the rich earth, which was practically inside his nostrils.

"Is there anyone else inside?" the standing officer asked.

"My brother-in-law."

"Is he alone?"

"Yes."

"Is he armed?"

"He has a gun. Please be careful. He's upset."

"Is anyone hurt in there?"

The officer rolled Jason onto his back. Saliva caught in Jason's throat, and he tried to swallow to work it free so he could speak.

"Is anyone hurt?" the officer asked.

"One man," Jason said, his words choked. "I'm pretty sure he's dead. My brother-in-law beat him. Killed him."

The standing officer spoke into his lapel microphone. He requested backup as well as an ambulance. He referred to a possible hostage situation.

"Is my niece okay?" Jason asked. "My niece and sister ran away from here."

"Sir, for your own safety and for ours we're going to place you in handcuffs."

"Are they okay?"

"We're dealing with the situation in the cabin right now."

The officer pushed Jason over onto his side and took hold of his hands.

"Please," Jason said. "Are they okay?'

"Just let us take care of this, sir."

The officer drew his gun and stepped toward the cabin.

"Be careful," Jason said, although he doubted they heard him. Jason buried his head against the ground.

"Suspect with a gun in the building."

Jason closed his eyes. His body went limp as another officer placed handcuffs around his wrists.

"Get him out of here."

He was pulled to his feet, and he went along without even thinking. One officer held his arm and moved him back toward the road, while the other officers, including the one who had been standing over him, moved closer to the cabin. When they reached a police cruiser, Jason was placed in the back. Before he closed the door, the officer removed the handcuffs.

"Just sit tight," he said.

Jason didn't know what else he could do except worry about his family.

Chapter Forty-nine

More officers arrived, as well as an ambulance, and for the longest time Jason felt as though he'd been abandoned in the back of the police car. Close to twenty minutes passed and then thirty while police and paramedics came and went from the cabin. Their movements and gestures lacked any real sense of urgency, which confirmed what Jason already suspected. Jesse Dean was dead, killed by Derrick. And Derrick was inside the cabin with the police . . . confessing? Resisting? Had he been hurt or even killed by the officers who saw him with a gun?

Jason couldn't open the car door once it was locked, and the air in the cruiser grew musty and close. He started sweating while he waited, and as the minutes ticked by, he worked hard to convince himself that Sierra and Hayden were okay, that they had managed to get down the road and were found by the police. What else could have happened to them once they left the cabin? *Jesse Dean was dead*. For all Jason knew, Sierra and Hayden were very close at that moment, safe in one of the other police cars that lined the small road in the middle of the woods.

Jason began replaying his final conversation with Derrick inside the cabin. He admitted that he and Jesse Dean killed Logan on graduation night. He knew that Hayden covered for them. But he didn't know *why* any of it had happened.

He looked out the window of the cruiser, where a light rain had started to fall, spitting against the glass and partially obscuring his view of the comings and goings around him. He wondered if he'd ever know.

Eventually a figure appeared outside the window of the cruiser and pulled the door open, letting in a welcome rush of fresh air. The man bent down, and Jason saw a familiar face.

"Hello, Mr. Danvers," Detective Olsen said. "Are you doing okay in here?"

"I'm hot. And I want to know if my family is okay."

"They're doing just fine. We've been talking with both your niece and your sister to get their versions of events. We have to get yours as well."

"But they're okay?"

"They're okay." Olsen reached up and wiped some rain off his forehead. "Understandably they're shocked by the turn of events here. Your brother-in-law is in some trouble."

"Is he okay? I was worried because he had . . ."

"He's lucky. The responding officers showed a lot of restraint when they went into that cabin. He had a gun. Things don't always end well when someone has a gun out."

"But he's okay?"

"He's settled down now," Olsen said. "He's telling us a lot. It's going to be a long night of talking to him. And then . . . well, we'll just see where things go from here."

"Is he going to be charged with something?" Jason asked.

"Something. But let's worry about that later. Would you like to stand up and get out of that car? We can talk out here. It's raining a little, but you're probably tired of sitting."

Jason left the vehicle. It felt good to move and stretch his legs. The night air had cooled, and the drops of rain that pinged against his head and shoulders were much more of a relief than an annoyance. He leaned back against the car with Detective Olsen facing him.

"Can you tell me what happened in there?" Olsen asked.

Jason did. As he spoke, he remembered certain details more vividly than others—especially the smell of fear coming off Derrick and the wild, haunted look in his eyes. Jason left nothing out, even going so far as to include Derrick's comments about Jason's judgment of him. He felt like that part of the story needed to be shared.

"So your brother-in-law admitted being involved in the killing of Logan Shaw?"

"Yes. He said he and Jesse Dean killed him and buried him on graduation night."

"And he didn't say why?"

"No. The police arrived. That's when he sent me away."

"And you didn't see the fight between the two men?"

"No. Jesse Dean was dead when I arrived. Like I said, the first thing I did was help Hayden check his pulse."

Olsen absorbed the story without showing any emotion. There was a pause while he reached into his pocket and brought out a small notebook. He flipped it open and looked it over. He didn't say anything.

"Detective?"

"Yes?"

"I realize my wife doesn't know where I am. And I can't call her because my phone doesn't work out here. She's going to worry, and I don't want that. Is there a way you could reach her and tell her what's going on?"

"Sure. We'll be done here pretty soon." Olsen stepped away and summoned a uniformed officer. He had Jason give the man in uniform the pertinent information—Nora's name and address—and instructed him to take care of the notification.

As the officer turned away, Jason said, "And can you make sure to tell her that Sierra and Hayden are okay as well?"

"He will," Olsen said.

When the officer was gone, Olsen flipped the notebook shut and tucked it back into his pocket. The rain had picked up a little, and Jason squinted as a couple of drops hit him in the eye and face.

"Your sister has already given a partial statement tonight," Olsen said. "We still have more to talk to her about. Understandably, she's worried about her daughter right now. We're aware of that."

"Thanks."

"What I'm saying is . . . she still has more to account for. And it's possible you will as well."

He turned and walked off toward the cabin.

Chapter Fifty

Jason walked along the line of cars. He counted six police cruisers as well as two ambulances and two unmarked sedans. No one paid much attention to him as he made his way down the row. He looked inside every car he passed until he reached the ambulance. Hayden leaned against the side of the large vehicle, wrapped in a blanket. She smoked a cigarette, but when she saw Jason, she dropped it on the ground and came toward him.

"Jason, my God."

They hugged and held on to each other tight. He held her a long time, her body pressed against his, listening to her sniffling. He was prepared to hold Hayden as long as she needed it, but she gently slipped free from his grip and took both of his hands in hers and looked up.

"Are you okay?" she asked.

"I was going to ask you that. And Sierra? Where is she?"

Hayden nodded toward the ambulance. "They're checking her out in there. Just routine. They have to do it, I guess. They did it to me first."

"Does she know they're going to arrest Derrick?"

Hayden nodded and turned her eyes down to the ground. "They told us. That crazy kid, she didn't run out to the road like you told her to. She was coming back to help you and me—that's when I ran into her out here. I grabbed her and said, 'Let's go,' and we ran away. We came across the police on the way out. And Tricia was still there, too, down at the end of the road. She waited until the police came and made sure they knew where to go."

"What happened to you, Hayden? What were you doing out here?"

"Jesus, I wish I had another cigarette. One of the cops gave me that last one."

"Did you know they killed Logan? Is that why you came back to town?"

"Oh, big brother, there's so much to tell. So much you don't know."

"I'm listening. You've been out here with these guys for over a week, haven't you?"

Hayden looked up, anger in her eyes. "I didn't *choose* to stay out here with them, with Jesse Dean."

"They held you somehow?"

She crossed her arms across her chest. "It wasn't that rigid or restrictive. I wasn't a hostage or anything. But I sure wasn't free to just walk out the door. I didn't care about that so much, but I knew you and Sierra would be worried. I was still in town when I texted her that time. I was just seeing that things weren't going the way I wanted them to go with Jesse Dean. I probably scared her more than anything, but I knew she'd be worried."

"She was a little freaked out by that text."

"I figured, but I had to say something. Then Jesse Dean took my phone away. I snuck it back from him once, but there was no service out here. He took me with him to the little grocery store up the road, and I called you. Do you remember that?"

"I do."

"He got the phone back and that was that. I was talking to Jesse Dean most of the time and it was usually pretty calm. 'Negotiating' is maybe the right word for it."

"Negotiating what?"

"I was trying to get them to tell the truth and come clean. About Logan. About all of it. If they'd listened to me . . . if they'd gone along with me . . ." She raised her arms and gestured toward the police cars and the ambulance. Her gesture encompassed the dead body in the cabin as well as her ex-husband in custody. "None of this," she said. "None of this."

"You've known all these years that they killed Logan?"

"I used to think I just suspected that they did it," she said. "That was the lie I told myself." She contemplated those words for a few moments, and then she said, "I knew. I was a fool, and I guess I always knew."

"Were you with them when they killed Logan?"

"No. I wasn't on the Bluff that night. Don't you remember? I was grounded. Mom and Dad wouldn't let me out on your graduation night because they'd caught me—"

"Taking the money from Mom's wallet." Jason remembered it all. Their mother had been so angry she cursed at Hayden and grounded her for two weeks. It was one of the rare times that grounding Hayden worked, probably because she'd been so shocked at their mom's display of anger. "That was right before graduation."

"They let me go to the ceremony, so I could see you get your diploma. But they dragged me home afterwards. They said I couldn't go to any parties. Jesus, Mom was furious. And all over twenty bucks."

"So you weren't there."

"I wasn't. I didn't find out that Logan was gone until his dad

353

called our house the next day looking for him. That's when you found out too, right?"

"Right."

"I didn't see Derrick for another five days because I was grounded. Mom wouldn't let me talk to him on the phone. Nothing. It would have been longer, but he showed up at our house one night. Late, after everybody was asleep. He came by and threw little pebbles at my window. Then he climbed up the downspout and came in."

"And nobody heard him?"

"Hell, no. We always did that. We had it down to a science. But this time Derrick wasn't looking for what he was normally looking for. He just laid in bed next to me, cuddled up like a little boy, and let me stroke his hair. He acted like he wanted to talk, but really he just laid there. I could tell something was wrong. I thought maybe his parents had a fight. He got that way sometimes when his parents fought. I asked him if that's what was going on, and he said no. Shit, I'd been locked up in the house so long I wished he had wanted sex, but that didn't happen. And then I started to wonder . . ."

"Wonder what?"

Hayden shook her head. "I asked him about partying on graduation night, and he got real quiet. He just said it was a bust, that nothing happened. You know how strange that would be for Derrick or Jesse Dean. And then I mentioned all the stuff that had been happening in our house, the stuff that had to do with Logan being gone. The police coming over and pushing you so hard. How upset Mom and Dad were that their son was getting dragged into the middle of a police investigation just as he was supposed to be going off to college. I tried to talk about that. I thought he'd be interested. He knew Logan a little. And he knew you pretty well. But when I brought it up, he just shut the whole conversation down. He said he knew that Logan had run away, and they were making a big fuss over some spoiled rich kid who was having a temper tantrum. To be honest, I kind of thought the same thing."

"A lot of us did."

"He was very sympathetic to you."

"Really?"

"He said that they were treating you like a criminal because Logan was rich, and that it just went to show that the police would push anybody around when they think a rich kid got hurt."

"I was Logan's friend. And we had a fight that night. It wasn't out of the blue for them to question me."

"I know. But then Derrick said the most interesting thing of all. At least it's interesting looking back now. He said that if someone did do something to Logan, if they really hurt him or killed him, then Logan definitely deserved it."

"He didn't explain any more?"

"I asked him, and he wouldn't say. I thought it was just his typical anger at a rich kid."

"But?"

She turned away and looked toward the end of the ambulance where Sierra was being treated. She listened to the muffled voices for a second and then turned back. "I'm worried about my baby."

"I know. Do you want to go check on her?"

"I've been smothering her ever since I got out of there," she said. "I hadn't seen her in days. I hate that. And now . . . who knows what's going to happen to Derrick . . . ?"

"He's with the police now. They're questioning him. He's lucky they didn't shoot him."

Hayden sniffled, reaching up and wiping at her nose and eyes with the backs of her hands. Jason stepped forward and put his arm around her.

"Thanks," she said.

"Let's talk about this another time."

"It's okay. There isn't that much more that I know anyway. What I know is that about six months after graduation night, Jesse Dean came to me. He came alone. Derrick didn't know about it. We hung out on our own sometimes, but he seemed to be up to something. He had a fifth of Wild Turkey with him, and he started getting me to drink it. He drank it too, don't worry. We both threw back our fair share."

The rain had mostly stopped, and the clouds overhead were parting again, revealing a crisply defined half-moon.

"What did he want?" Jason asked.

"He said he wanted me to do a favor for him and for Derrick. He emphasized that *Derrick* would really benefit from the favor. He implied that if I wanted to be able to keep dating Derrick, I needed to make this thing happen."

"He wanted you to write those cards and send them to Logan's dad."

Hayden looked up, the surprise on her face almost comical. "How do you know that?"

"I saw them. I thought I recognized your handwriting. And a couple came from Chicago in 1999. Remember that?"

"Shit. Of course." Hayden looked down. She shuffled her feet. "I know I committed a crime. Covering up a murder or conspiracy." She shook her head. "When Jesse Dean asked me to do that, I knew they'd probably killed Logan. But I went along with it."

"Why did you?"

"Why did I, Jason? I can hear the judgment in your voice.

You're thinking that poor dumb Hayden couldn't say no to any guy and couldn't avoid trouble if her life depended on it. Is that what you're thinking? Is it?"

Jason didn't answer.

"You're right, of course. That's true. I was a dumbass who couldn't say no to a man. I was a drunk and a mess. Those aren't excuses, but there they are." She spread her hands apart. "I was worried about Derrick, okay? I loved him. And I was afraid of saying no to Jesse Dean." She laughed a little, a bitter sound. "Jesse Dean even let me pick out the Father's Day cards. It was like he was saying I was the little woman, the secretary or something, who was going to do the big man's bidding. And I did. I bought the cards and wrote them. I tried to copy Logan's handwriting out of one of your old yearbooks. When I ran off out west, I mailed them, and I sent more from Chicago. Later on, Jesse Dean knew some guy out west who mailed them for him. I wrote the cards because he wanted the handwriting to match every time. I never thought that stupid plan would work. What parent wouldn't know their kid's handwriting? I mean, dads can be pretty clueless, but a mother? Wouldn't a mother know her child's handwriting?"

"Logan's mother had some issues, apparently."

"I guess so. I'd never win mother-of-the-year. I took some years off being a mother, so maybe I'm no one to talk. Look at tonight. I got my daughter dragged out into the middle of this. But I'd always know my kid. Always. Her handwriting. Her smell. Her voice." Hayden started crying again. "That girl's mine. I'd never forget anything about her."

Chapter Fifty-one

Doors slammed on one of the police cruisers. It started up and drove off slowly, its headlights making a cone of brightness through the trees and the gloom. After it was gone, Jason turned his attention back to Hayden.

"Colton Rivers saw you with Jesse Dean. Downtown in Center Park. This was right after you came back and left Sierra at our house."

"Jesse Dean wanted to cruise, just like in high school. He said we were having our own little reunion."

"That's a small reunion."

"Derrick was there too. We were good friends the way you and Logan and Regan were."

"Derrick was there?"

And then he remembered what Colton had told him about that night at Center Park. There was someone in the backseat, someone Colton couldn't see.

"Wait a minute. Derrick was already in town back then?" he asked.

"I met him and Jesse Dean here. I needed to talk to both of them. I came to town to tell them that I knew they'd killed Logan on graduation night. When we were younger, and I was so messed up and irresponsible, I told myself I didn't want to know about all the stuff they'd done. But I couldn't stay quiet forever. I told them I didn't really care why they did it, but they had dragged me into the middle of it, and I wasn't going to be quiet about it anymore. If they wanted, they could step forward and admit what happened. Otherwise, I was going to tell. I didn't even know who I was going to tell. Logan's family. Maybe the police. I certainly didn't know how that would go. But I was going to admit what I knew."

"What made you think those guys would listen to you?"

"I've got a little news flash for you, big brother. Your little sister thinks that people can change and grow. She thinks that if you present someone with an opportunity to be a different person, a better person, they'll take it. It happened to me when I cleaned up, so I assumed they might be open to it as well. Hell, years had gone by. I thought maybe everyone would welcome the chance to make things right. And, short of that, I had to be the kind of person, the kind of mother, I wanted to be for my daughter. I had to do, or try to do, the right thing. I had to try. I couldn't live with myself if I didn't."

"But a guy like Jesse Dean? Jesus, Hayden."

"I was going to come forward no matter what. I cared about those guys. I married Derrick. I wanted to give them the chance. I didn't want to blindside them."

"Do you know how insane that sounds? How did you think you would stop Jesse Dean from coming after you or Sierra? Obviously, it didn't work."

"Didn't work? That would be the understatement of the century. The whole thing blew up in my face. Not only did Jesse Dean refuse to come forward—he threatened me. He said he'd kill me if I tried to do It. Derrick helped with that a little. He stood up for me. He said there wouldn't be any killing."

"Was he here the whole time? The police talked to him in Indianapolis."

"He went back and forth. When Jesse Dean calmed down a little and was keeping me out here, Derrick went home to Indiana."

"He left you with Jesse Dean?"

"I told him to. He really did get a new job and a new start there. I wasn't alone. Jesse Dean had that awful Rose Holland with him some of the time." Hayden shuddered. "Talk about how the mighty have fallen."

"She killed our neighbors' cat because she wanted to send a message to you."

"Figures. She's disgusting. But Derrick was going to come back eventually, when he could, but then Jesse Dean made things even worse."

"What did he do?"

Hayden looked toward the back of the ambulance again. She motioned with her hand in the opposite direction, and she and Jason moved away from the vehicle where it was certain Sierra couldn't hear them.

"Jesse Dean got it into his mind that I had told other people what I knew. First, he asked me about you. He thought I'd spilled this whole story to you, and if something happened to me, you'd go to the cops. I guess maybe he had a little talk with you about that."

"He did. He was very convincing."

"Well, guess who he was worried about next?"

"He sent Tricia to try to get Sierra away from us."

"I know."

"He offered her drugs if she got Sierra out of the house. We said no."

"Thank you. That was smart."

"But then Derrick showed up. We couldn't say no then."

"That was Jesse Dean again. He wouldn't stop talking about Sierra. And let me tell you, that was the worst part of the whole thing for me. I wanted her to be as far away from here as possible. I left her with you because I wanted her to be with family, you know, if something happened to me. And I knew you'd both protect her. But Jesse Dean wouldn't let it go. I think he might have even gone and looked for Sierra at my house. He left me alone a couple of times. He tied me up good. See?"

She held up her arm, and Jason saw a raw bruise that encircled her wrist.

"I thought you weren't a hostage," he said. "Don't try to sugarcoat what these guys did to you. And Sierra. And how did blood get in your car?"

"That was my fault."

"Your fault?"

"I tried to get away from Jesse Dean, and I smacked my nose against the doorframe of the car. Really. It was klutzy, but it just bled. He took my shoes then. He locked the keys in the car, so it would look like I'd run off or something. I don't know what he was thinking."

Jason looked down and noticed for the first time that his sister wore no shoes. "Jesus, Hayden."

"I was worried about Sierra more than myself."

"Sierra spent some time in your house. Jesse Dean must have just missed her. Somebody broke in the back window."

"Jesse Dean had my house keys, but he must have wanted to

make it look like a random burglary or something." She sniffed. "Eventually, Jesse Dean called Derrick and told him to get Sierra and bring her out here."

"Why did Derrick do that, for Christ's sake?"

"Because of me. Derrick was worried that Jesse Dean would hurt *me* if he didn't. And Derrick is as dumb as I am. He thought he could calm Jesse Dean down. He thought if he brought Sierra out here and let him see that she didn't know anything, then Jesse Dean would let her go. I guess Derrick thought he could get us all out of it. I wouldn't have brought Sierra out here. I was willing to trade my life for hers."

"And that's when Derrick killed him?"

"Jesse Dean didn't calm down. He didn't act reasonable. He threatened all of us. Sierra was there. I made sure to get between her and Jesse Dean in case he tried something crazy. Eventually Derrick made a move to get us all out of there. I could tell he was working up to something. He had a look on his face. I tried to tell him not to. I gave him a look that said not to do it."

"Why?"

"I don't know. I was hoping there was another way to end it all. I thought maybe someone would come out here and help. And, look, someone did. If he'd only waited a few more minutes."

"What did he do?"

"He grabbed ahold of that andiron. The thing from the fireplace. He thought Jesse Dean didn't see him, and he went for him." Hayden looked away from Jason as her body shivered. "I've never seen a fight like that. It was like two animals. Jesse Dean was pummeling Derrick, but then Derrick managed to get one good swing in, and that killed Jesse Dean. Split his face open like that."

Jason knew they were both seeing the disturbing visual, the

ugly sight of Jesse Dean's dead body they had left behind in the cabin. He suspected they'd both be seeing it for a long time.

"Are you okay?" Jason asked. "Really okay?"

Hayden arched her back. She stretched like someone who had been sitting still for a long time. She seemed to be trying to release a lot of tension from her body. "You know me, big brother. I always land on my feet. I can't worry about myself too much. I have to worry about Sierra now."

"I'm sorry."

"What did Derrick say to you after I left the cabin?"

Jason felt his skin flush in the dark. He was embarrassed just thinking about it, embarrassed that he ever drove Derrick to feel the way he did.

"He told me the truth," Jason said. "That I always thought he was trash."

"He was sensitive about that. Especially with our family. He didn't want Sierra growing up thinking her dad wasn't good enough for the family."

"I did the same thing to you," Jason said. "I asked Derrick why he and Jesse Dean killed Logan. I assumed it was about you, that you and Logan . . . that you two were fucking or something and that's why they killed him."

He turned his eyes to Hayden. She was watching her brother, but she didn't show any hurt or disappointment. In a way, Jason wished she would. He felt he deserved it, and somehow her lack of a response made him feel worse.

"I'm sorry," he said.

"Logan and I just played games with each other. We weren't going to do anything. Do you want to know why?" she asked, raising her eyebrows. "Because he wasn't interested in me. I wasn't good enough for him. I never would have been."

Jason paused a moment, then said, "Derrick said something about Sierra before I left. He said that he still cared about her . . . Wait. Also that nothing had changed between them. What was he talking about?"

Hayden looked at the ground. Her shoulders rose and fell as she heaved a big sigh. "I came clean with Derrick about something else when we were out in that cabin, something having to do with Sierra."

"What about her?"

"It's not about her so much. It's about me . . . and Jesse Dean and Derrick. I wasn't going to tell either one of them about it, but then I thought it might help protect Sierra. I don't think it did because it just drove Derrick further over the edge."

Jason's mind spun with possibilities. "Something you thought would protect Sierra from Jesse Dean?" Then the pieces fell into place in Jason's head. "Are you serious, Hayden?"

She nodded. "I told them both that there's at least a decent chance Jesse Dean is Sierra's biological father. I was out of control back then, and we were all friends. And a few times Jesse Dean and I . . . Derrick suspected. He suspected, and he didn't say anything about it. One of the times with Jesse Dean happened around when I got pregnant with Sierra."

"That doesn't prove anything, I guess."

"No. But Derrick and I tried to have another baby later on. We really tried, and it never worked. I wonder if he couldn't. You see, that's why I thought Jesse Dean could be reasoned with. I thought if he knew that Sierra might be his . . . well, I thought he wouldn't hurt her. And I thought he might want to come clean on everything to set the record straight after all these years. Maybe he'd have something to look forward to. I didn't tell Sierra."

"Tell me what, Mom?"

They both turned in the direction of the voice.

Sierra stood by the side of the ambulance. She looked uncertain, slightly unsteady, but she smiled when she saw her mother and uncle.

"Nothing, baby," Hayden said, and she went to her daughter. "Nothing at all."

Chapter Fifty-two

"You can let go, Mom. I'm fine. Really."

Hayden stepped back and cupped Sierra's face in her hands. She studied her daughter intently. "Are you sure?"

"They said I'm fine. Nothing happened to me. Nobody hurt me."

"I'm still worried."

"You were the one who was out here in the woods for more than a week."

"I'm good," Hayden said. "Don't worry about me, okay?"

Sierra looked past her mother and made eye contact with Jason. She smiled when she saw her uncle, then slipped past her mom and came over to give Jason a hug.

"It's good to see you again," Jason said.

He held his niece for a long time. It seemed as though she might be ready to let go, but Jason held tight to her a little longer. The length of the hug and his desire to extend it surprised Jason, but it felt right.

When he finally did let go, Jason asked, "Are you sure you're okay?"

"I'm fine."

"I'm sorry . . . about everything you've been through."

"Have you seen my dad?" she asked.

"He's with the police still," Jason said. "He could be there a while."

Sierra nodded. She folded her arms across her chest and looked to her mother, who came over and placed an arm around her daughter's shoulders.

"You should go home," Jason said.

"Home?" Hayden laughed. "All the way to Redman County? I don't even know where my car is."

"The police have it," Jason said. "Sierra's the one who found it up on the Bluff."

"I know," Hayden said. "She told me."

"Come back to our house," Jason said. "You're both welcome there. You can spend the night and get the car back from the police tomorrow." Jason looked around. "I don't even know where *my* car is."

"The police said they'd take us where we needed to go," Hayden said.

"Uncle Jason?"

"Yeah?"

Sierra seemed to be choosing her words carefully. She didn't speak right away, and then she looked over at her mother. Hayden nodded, as though the two of them had discussed what Sierra wanted to say. She turned back to Jason.

"It's not your fault I left with my dad," she said. "I wanted to go. I was kind of pissed at you, to be honest. I didn't like the way you seemed to be looking at Mom, like you didn't trust her. And like you didn't really trust me either."

"I shouldn't have—"

"I just want to say . . . when we were in that cabin . . . I knew you were going to come. I told my dad that I wasn't worried about being there because I knew somehow you'd make it out here and find us."

Hayden pulled Sierra closer to her. Jason looked away, his eyes turning up to the stars, which swam a little in his vision. One of them blinked on and off, a distant satellite tracking through the night.

"Thanks," he said. "I just wanted to make sure both of you were all right."

"We are," Hayden said. "Or we will be. Right, kiddo?"

"Right, Mom. Of course."

As the police cruiser neared town, Jason checked his phone. He had service again, and he called Nora to let them know the three of them were on their way to the house.

"Thank God," Nora said. "The police called me and told me you were all out in the middle of the woods somewhere."

"Everybody's okay. Well, the three of us are okay. Derrick's in some trouble, but I can explain it all when we get there."

"Okay," she said. "I'm glad you're safe."

"I know. We'll see you soon."

"Jason?"

"Yes?"

"Are you really okay?" she asked.

"I am. I promise."

He put the phone away. As they approached the house, Jason saw a familiar sight parked on the street. "My car," he said.

When they climbed out of the cruiser, Jason walked around to the front of his car where he saw a note tucked under the windshield. He read it to himself, the writing an erratic scrawl.

"Hey Chief—I did what I said I'd do and brought the car back too. Now leave me alone."

Jason smiled. He folded the note and tucked it in his pants pocket. Sierra and Hayden stood on the sidewalk with him, and they all looked up as Nora opened the front door. Jason wanted to go to his wife, but he stopped himself. There was more he had to find out from Hayden.

"Sierra?" Jason said. "Do you mind going on in for a second? We'll be right there."

"Sure," she said.

He watched Sierra go up the steps and get folded into Nora's arms. Nora held her niece for a long time, then looked down to the sidewalk where Jason and Hayden were standing.

"We're okay," Jason said to her. "Just give us a minute, okay?"

"Okay." Nora waved, her face showing concern. But she guided Sierra into the house and closed the door.

Jason turned to his sister. "You know I have one more question I didn't get the chance to ask you, right?" Jason said.

"I figured as much."

"I told myself I wasn't going to ask tonight. Hell, I tried to tell myself I never needed to know, but that isn't going to work for me. Not after all this, not after enough people risked something to help me and you and Sierra out."

"I get it."

"Why, Hayden? Why did Jesse Dean and Derrick kill Logan that night?"

Hayden leaned against the car. She lifted her shoulders, a halfhearted shrug. "I don't know for sure."

"Hayden."

"I asked. Believe me, I asked. And like I said, I don't know.

But I can tell you the one thing I know for sure. When we were in that cabin, I heard one name mentioned more than any other."

Jason didn't have to ask. He knew, and he said the name out loud.

"Regan."

Hayden nodded. "I know she's involved. That's why I said it was good you reconnected with her, that you were being a friend to her. If she was mixed up in Logan's death, she'd need the support."

"Thanks," Jason said.

He went up the stairs and into the house. Nora and Sierra sat close to each other on the couch, and when he came in, Nora stood up and embraced him. "Are you okay? Jesus. Sierra just started to tell me what happened."

"I'm fine. We're all fine." He held his wife for a long moment and then stepped back, looking into her eyes. "I have to go take care of one more thing."

"What?"

"I have to see Regan," he said. "I have to know some final answers."

"Can't the police do that stuff?" Nora asked. "Is it safe?"

"After twenty-seven years," he said, "I need to do it myself." He turned and started out of the house. "I'll be in touch, I promise."

Chapter Fifty-three

Jason pulled into Regan's driveway just after midnight. A single light burned in the front window, illuminating the closed sheer curtains. When Jason stepped out of the car and started up the driveway, he heard a neighbor's dog bark, a sharp, staccato call in the night. Then someone hushed the dog through an open window, and the night grew silent again.

He tapped on the front door. The lighted curtain moved, her familiar face pressing against the window. Jason waved, and when he did, he saw the hesitation in Regan's movement. She remained frozen behind the pane of glass for a moment, as though contemplating whether she wanted to let him in. Then she let the curtain fall, obscuring her face, and the locks untumbled behind the door. Regan revealed herself, still dressed from work apparently, and stepped back, letting Jason come inside. She didn't say anything by way of a greeting. She pointed toward a sitting area off the foyer, a small room with bookshelves, a desk, and two comfortable chairs. Jason went in. Between the two chairs sat an end table, and on the table an open bottle of wine and a half-full glass.

"Would you like one?" Regan asked.

"Do you have any whiskey?"

"Sure."

Regan stepped away. Jason settled into one of the chairs, the one closest to the door. He looked around the room, taking in the books and the neatness of the desk. Regan came back with a short glass half-filled with amber liquid. In her other hand she carried a bottle of bourbon and another small glass.

"I didn't know if you wanted ice."

"This is fine," he said.

She put the extra glass down on the table and poured a shot. "I'm switching now," she said. "Wine before liquor, never sicker? Did we have a saying for that in high school?"

"We didn't drink wine in high school."

"Right." She sat down and sipped from the glass. "Something's happening, isn't it?"

"A lot of somethings."

"I had a feeling. I don't know why. I couldn't sleep. The kids are at Tim's house. I just got back from dropping them off, so it doesn't matter if I want to sit up and sip some wine or liquor with an old friend."

"Jesse Dean is dead. And Derrick is in custody. He's facing a lot of heat."

The hand holding Regan's glass started to tremble. Her knuckles turned white as she tightened her grip. "You're not beating around the bush with the bad news," she said, her voice closer to a whisper.

Jason swallowed the bourbon, felt its pleasant burn down his throat. "I decided to be direct. Does it bother you that Jesse Dean is dead and Derrick's in jail?"

Regan's eyes slid toward Jason. "Shouldn't it? Should I not be bothered if someone died or got in trouble?"

"Jesse Dean was a common criminal. Derrick is my brother-in-law, ex-brother-in-law, and the . . . the father of my niece. But you barely knew them. People die every day, don't they?" Jason waited for a response and didn't get one. He finished the liquor in his glass and reached out and poured more. He held the bottle up toward Regan, but she shook her head. "Why do you care about these two unless you have some special connection with them? You were just talking to Jesse Dean. They were talking about you out at that cabin in the woods where they were holding Hayden."

As Jason spoke, Regan lowered her head, staring into her own glass, but at the mention of Hayden's name, she perked up. "Is Hayden okay?"

"She is. She's at my house with Sierra and Nora. But she said those guys talked about you a lot. And it was Hayden who was covering for them all those years after they killed Logan. Yes, I know they killed Logan. And Hayden knows. What I don't know is why, and I have a feeling you do." He paused a moment, preparing himself. A thought raced through his mind: *Do I really want to know?* "What happened that night, Regan? Why did Jesse Dean and Derrick kill Logan on the Bluff?"

Regan finished what was in her glass, and she reached out and poured another, the tip of the bottle clinking against the glass. She swallowed that one and sat quiet for a moment.

"You know, right?" Jason asked. "You can tell me finally?"

"I can," she said. "After Logan fought with you over me, he came back. He found me again in the woods. I'd wandered down the trail a little bit, just clearing my head. I was worried about you and about him. And, to be perfectly honest, I was feeling a little . . . I don't know, nostalgic, I guess. I started thinking about graduating from high school and the changes that were coming whether I was ready for them or not. You were going away. I was going to school right here. It just seemed like . . . a door was closing on a lot of things. And after I turned Logan down, and he went to find you, it seemed like that door might stay shut forever."

Regan picked up her glass again, but there was nothing in it to drink. She tilted it and examined the drop that remained in the bottom before she drank it away.

"Logan was upset. I could tell he was angry, and it looked like he'd been crying. He had a little scrape on his forehead as well. Do you remember it that way?"

"I know he was upset."

Jason remembered the final punch. He held his glass in two hands and looked down at his knuckles.

"When he found me, he asked me the same thing he had asked me before. He said he wanted to be with me and would I run off with him. I told him that my answer hadn't changed in the thirty minutes since he had last talked to me. I guess I was a little flip. I could be that way when I was a teenager." She almost smiled. She uncrossed her legs and scooted forward in her chair. She reached for the bourbon bottle and unscrewed the cap. "If I have another one of these, I may have to use a sick day at work."

"I'm sorry," Jason said.

"For what?"

"That you have to tell me whatever it is you're about to tell me."

"I've wanted to tell you for years," she said. "You deserve to know. And I deserve to get to tell you." She poured the drink and recapped the bottle. "There was something different about Logan when he came back that night. He was crying, yes, but he also seemed angry. Silly me, I thought I could calm him down. I thought that I could just talk to a guy like that, reasonably, and things would be okay. We were friends after all, right? He'd listen to me. He'd see me as a human being." Regan's voice rose as she spoke, and she seemed to make an effort to control her tone. "I'm sorry," she said.

"It's okay."

"I sat down with him," she said. "There was a log there, and we sat. And I took his hand. And I told him he needed to relax." She swallowed. "He tried to kiss me. It was awkward. He leaned in and came right at my mouth, and I pulled away and put my hand up. He didn't come in gently or romantically. It was aggressive, almost like he wanted to bite me or something. I pushed him back, and he came at me again. He grabbed my arm." She pointed to her wrist. "Here. I'd never been afraid of Logan. I'd never really been afraid of any guy. But I was afraid that night. Really afraid. He seemed like he was possessed."

As Regan told the story, she stopped looking at Jason. She stared into the room, at a fixed point somewhere in the air. But Jason knew she was seeing the events of that night playing out in her mind's eye.

"It's been so long, and things happened so fast, it's hard to say exactly how it all unfolded. What I do know is that I ended up on the ground. He wrestled me off the log, and I was on my back. I felt the rocks and twigs and things pressing against my skin through my shirt. I remember that clearly, how freaking uncomfortable it was on the ground. And when he got on top of me, it hurt even more because his weight pressed me into the dirt with more force."

An icy, churning sickness welled up inside Jason. Against his will, he pictured the scene. He also thought of all the women he knew——Hayden, Sierra, Nora. He took a drink, but the burning was no longer pleasant. He gagged and had to swallow back hard.

"I felt my clothes tear. I felt his hands moving below my waist. I tried to fight him off, but he was a strong fucker. I just couldn't stop him. My underwear tore, and his hands went down there."

"Did you scream?"

"I don't know. I don't know if I could. Have you ever had one of those dreams where you're terrified, just terrified about whatever is happening, but when you open your mouth to make a noise, nothing comes out? That's what it felt like to me. I couldn't make a sound. Or, if I did, I didn't know I was making it."

"I'm sorry."

"His finger. I was a virgin then, as you could probably guess. I'd never really been with a guy in a real way. His finger. It hurt. I remember that." She sighed and looked at Jason. "And then suddenly the weight was off of me. Whatever Logan was doing or trying to do stopped, and his body was off of mine. I thought he'd just fallen or lost his balance. I thought he was going to get right back on before I could scramble away." She paused. "But then I saw that someone else was by us. Derrick had ahold of Logan and wrestled him off of me. And Jesse Dean was standing right there watching."

Chapter Fifty-four

"I remember the look on Jesse Dean's face," Regan said. "He looked almost pleased, like he was happy to be there, watching this happen."

"Happy to be watching you or watching Logan?"

"I don't know. Both. He just seemed to have a look on his face that said this was exactly where he wanted to be." She ran her hands up and down her upper arms as though she was cold. "I rolled away. Derrick had Logan on the ground and held on to him. While that was happening, I . . . pulled my clothes back on and buckled my pants. When I got home that night, I found the blood. It was kind of a mess. But I didn't notice it then, I don't think. I was so relieved and scared at the same time."

"I would guess so."

"Eventually Logan was standing up. I thought Jesse Dean was going to jump all over him, but he didn't. They just stood there staring at each other. That was the scariest part of the whole thing for me, that long moment when the three of them faced off that way. Do you know why?" She sighed again. "I really thought they were in it together, that Derrick and Jesse Dean were going to join with Logan and finish what he started. I was going to run, just get out of there. That's when Logan started mouthing off to Jesse Dean."

"What did he say?"

"Again, I don't remember all of it. Logan told them to leave him alone. And I know Derrick said something like, 'You can't get it on your own, so you have to force a girl this way.' Jesse Dean didn't say much. He was quiet while Derrick and Logan argued with each other. But I do remember the last thing Logan said to Jesse Dean. He said something about Jesse Dean failing two grades and how pathetic it was that he was always hanging around where the high school kids were. He made fun of the trashy little house that Jesse Dean lived in. He was lashing out, being nasty and cutting."

"He could be that way. I've seen it."

"It happened so fast, Jason. I wasn't even sure what was going on. I thought they were just wrestling. It almost seemed playful. They were both on top of Logan. Jesse Dean raised his fist three times and brought it down three times. Just like that. Bam bam bam. Three fast, hard punches. Then Derrick was pushing Jesse Dean back, away from Logan. And Jesse Dean kept trying to get at him."

Jason could imagine it. He remembered the quick, savage beating he had seen Jesse Dean give Brad Barnes at that party all those years ago and all over some minor slight—a jostled beer, a bumped arm. What would he do if a rich kid insulted him over his lack of brains and station in the world?

"Jesse Dean killed him," Jason said. "Just like that."

"Derrick eventually got Jesse Dean away, and it was Derrick who bent over the body, over Logan, and checked him out. He was dead. Derrick figured it out right away."

"They were defending you. They should have called the police."

The look Regan gave to Jason told him all about the foolishness of his statement. "People like Jesse Dean don't call the police apparently. Believe me, I suggested that right away. Derrick might have suggested it too, although not as forcefully as I did. Jesse Dean had already been arrested twice, he said. He was on probation. He asked me a question that night, one I'll never forget. He said, 'Who do you think they're going to believe? Me, a guy with a record, or some rich kid with a rich father?' I understood what he meant. I believed it. They were defending me. They saved me from God knows what else. But how would the whole situation have looked? Jesse Dean killed Logan. Mostly Jesse Dean, but Derrick was there. The whole town thought of Jesse Dean as a thug, a criminal. We all did."

"You're right."

Regan looked at that distant spot in the room again. "And I would have had to tell the police about it. Maybe I would have had to go to court and testify. I don't—" She kept looking at that distant spot, but her words felt more intensely directed at Jason. "It was embarrassing. I know I shouldn't have been embarrassed. I know it wasn't my fault. But still . . . and, to be honest, I thought about you. I thought about the fact that you would hear what happened to me, what you might think about me."

"You shouldn't—"

"I did, though. I'm not telling you this to make you feel bad. I'm just telling you everything that went through my mind that night. And why things ended up happening the way they did."

"Why *did* things happen the way they did?"

"What do you mean?"

"What happened to Logan that night that he acted that way? He seemed . . . like he'd reached some breaking point. He acted like he wanted to throw everything away."

"He had that streak in him. He always talked about leaving."

"But that night? So suddenly and so crazily? Why did it happen then?"

"I don't know."

Jason became aware of the muscles in his legs and back. They had been clenched, and he'd barely moved for several minutes. He didn't want to stretch or stand up. He feared he'd break the spell they were under, the one that allowed the truth of that night to finally come out.

Regan said, "So they buried him out there. Jesse Dean and Derrick. I was in a fog while it happened. I just sat there in the woods, alone, while they went off and did what they had to do. And when they came back, Jesse Dean stood over me. He told me that they weren't going to tell anyone what happened if I didn't. And if I did say anything . . ."

"Did he threaten you?"

"He didn't. Not exactly. He said that if I told, he'd claim I asked them to kill Logan. Even then, sitting there in the middle of the woods, I knew that wasn't a real threat. If the police wouldn't listen to them about what they did to Logan, why would they listen to them about anything else, right? I could have told the truth, and the police would have believed me. I had bloody underwear to show them. No, Jesse Dean didn't have to threaten me. I wanted it to go away, to stay buried out there. I told the truth to the police when I told them that Logan said he wanted to run away. That's not a lie. He always did say that. It's funny the little things I remember from that night."

"What do you mean?"

"I dropped my purse. In the middle of Logan's . . . attack and the aftermath, I left my purse lying up there. Jesse Dean saw it and gave it to me. I'll never forget that. Jesse Dean Pratt had just killed a guy, but he took the time to hand me my purse. My sunglasses weren't there. I never got them back. For all I know they're still up in the woods on the Bluff. Anyway, I don't know when Hayden got involved. I heard there were letters and cards sent to Mr. Shaw, but I didn't know who was writing them. I figured Jesse Dean was behind it somehow."

Jason stood up. His body felt like a coiled spring, and he finally needed to stand and walk around the room a little bit. He heard the cap on the bourbon bottle being unscrewed, the sloshing of liquid into a glass. He'd never seen Logan clearly. Logan had always stood above him, loomed over him really, and Jason managed always to make excuses for his callous and snobby behavior. Not only had Jason not seen Logan clearly, but he simply hadn't known him. Jason had spent the past twenty-seven years carrying around the memory of someone who never really existed. That memory was as dead as the body buried out in the woods.

Jason turned around. "I think you have a problem."

"What?"

"The police know that Hayden was involved."

"So?"

"Even if she doesn't know why they killed Logan, she knows that they did it. And she wrote those letters. She heard them discussing you out at the cabin. Do you see? The police are going to come and talk to you. They're going to want to know about your involvement, and you're going to have to tell them."

"I don't care if they know at this point. I guess my kids will find out. I always thought I'd tell them when they were old enough. They might as well understand the ways of the world."

"But the police could still think *you* were involved. They could say you were involved, that you covered up a crime."

Regan closed her eyes. She looked like she was praying, her head slightly bowed. "What you're saying is that I could get into trouble because there isn't anyone to corroborate my story. Jesse Dean and Logan are all dead. Derrick is in enough trouble himself."

"Right. And those guys . . . they may be miscreants, but their families . . . Everybody is going to think they're guilty. That's what the police will conclude based on their records and reputations." Jason sighed. "Sierra is going to hear these things about her dad."

Regan opened her eyes after a moment and said, "What if I were to tell you that there is someone who can corroborate my story? Someone I told all about this right after it happened?"

Chapter Fifty-five

Jason woke in a chair. His neck hurt from the way his head hung while he slept, and his brain hurt from the whiskey. Someone—Regan—had draped a blanket over him, and when he sat up, it fell down his body and pooled at his feet.

"Shit."

He checked his phone. Two missed calls and texts from Nora. He called her immediately. "I'm sorry," he said. "I should have called sooner, but I fell asleep."

"It's okay." Nora didn't sound convinced, but she was trying to be agreeable. "Hayden explained some things to me last night. She said she thought you might be out for a while."

"I have one more stop to make this morning, and then it's home."

"Okay." She paused. "I hope this is the end of all of this. It should be, shouldn't it?"

"I think so."

"You know the police are looking for *you*. Detective Olsen already called here once."

"I know. I'll get back to him in a little bit."

"He said he was coming over to talk with Hayden and Sierra. I got the feeling Hayden might be in some kind of trouble. I'm sure they'll be happy to see you when you get back. Especially Sierra. She's worried about her dad."

"Is she okay?"

"She's okay. I think she had a long night, but Hayden was with her the whole time. She's a good mother."

"She is. I know. I'm just trying to find out some last pieces of information."

"Should I tell the police where you are or what you're doing?"

Jason stood, trying to work the kinks out of his body. "No," he said. "They'll know soon enough."

"I like living here," Nora said. "But I like it because you're here. I don't want to lose that."

"I'll be careful. I promise."

On the way, after he and Regan had mostly been riding in silence, Jason felt compelled to say something to her he'd been meaning to say since the night before.

"I'm sorry about what happened to you. With Logan."

"It's okay."

"I've been talking to you about him a lot over the past couple of weeks. Ever since Colton came to me and brought him up again. I didn't know that every time I mentioned his name, I was dredging up some awful memory."

She reached out and patted his hand. "You didn't know." She stared out the window as he drove. "It made me angry sometimes. I blamed you, and you didn't know. It's why I said you needed to stop idolizing Logan. He wasn't who you thought he was. He wasn't who any of us thought he was."

"You just knew sooner than most."

A sign on the side of the road told them they had crossed into Barker County.

They entered a middle-class neighborhood. The houses were postwar construction, mostly ranches with neatly manicured lawns. They passed by two joggers, a healthy, smiling couple who waved without missing a step. Regan's phone told them where to go in search of the address they found in the phone book.

"It's up there on the right."

They eased to a stop in front of the house. It was yellow brick with a large picture window across the front. Brightly colored perennials filled several planters on the porch.

"It's a nice house," Regan said.

"Not as nice as she could have been living in."

"Should we have called her first?" Regan asked.

"This is fine."

"Should we have called the police?"

"I've thought about that the whole way. I don't think so. She's old. Let's make sure she still remembers what we need her to remember. And let's make sure she's willing to repeat the story to Olsen. If she is, she can really help Derrick. And everybody."

"Wouldn't Olsen have already been here? When they found Logan's body?"

"I'm sure he was," Jason said. "But if she hears from you, that might make her more willing to talk now. Right?"

Regan nodded and opened her door. Jason came around the front of the car, anticipation building in his chest. He took a deep breath, and when he came beside Regan, the two of them walked up to the house together.

Chapter Fifty-six

The woman who opened the door wore her gray hair in a short, sensible fashion. She was thin and wore a plain white button-down shirt and large glasses. She looked at the two faces before her, moving her head a little from side to side as she studied them. It didn't take her long to smile when the recognition passed through her brain.

"Oh," she said. "Well."

"Mrs. Shaw?" Regan said. "I mean, Mrs. Tyndal? Do you remember us?"

"Of course I do. Of course." She blinked her eyes. "This is a surprise. But not really surprising, I guess. It's always good to see old friends."

Jason stared at the woman. He hadn't seen her in . . . he couldn't even guess how long. He saw the familiar face from his childhood beneath the wrinkles and the years. He held few memories of her. More than anything else, he remembered this woman as a series of impressions, most of them taken in at a distance. He saw her at a few of the baseball games he and Logan played at the Little League park in town. He saw her driving away from the Shaw house, waving as she went up the street. And he remembered seeing her at their high school graduation, standing near the back of the crowded gymnasium with a man by her side who must have been her new husband. He tried to reconcile her kindly appearance with the monstrous story Colton shared. Had this woman thrown her young son down a flight of stairs in a drunken rage?

"We're sorry we didn't call," Regan said. "But we needed to talk to you."

The woman turned her gaze on Jason. She continued to smile, but it appeared to be coming with more of an effort. "Jason," she said, but she didn't say anything else. And Jason didn't know what to say in response. He averted his eyes, looking to his left and off at the house next door, another ranch with another nice yard. "Well," she said. "Come in. Please."

They entered the living room. A thick carpet covered the floor, muffling their steps and giving everything a hush. The room was spotless, the walls white. Mrs. Tyndal pointed to the sofa, and he and Regan sat side by side while Mrs. Tyndal brushed at her short hair with her hand and settled into an over-stuffed chair. She crossed her legs and placed her hands in her lap. Before she could say anything, an elderly man appeared in the doorway that led to the kitchen. He wore long shorts and a polo shirt and carried a newspaper. He took in the scene without speaking.

"Andrew?" Mrs. Tyndal said. "These are friends of mine from Ednaville."

He looked in their direction but still didn't speak.

"They're friends of Logan. My son, Logan? Remember?"

The man nodded slowly and then turned and walked back into the kitchen. Mrs. Tyndal kept a smile plastered to her face when she turned back to Regan and Jason. "Andrew is a lit-tle . . . slower these days. He forgets some things."

"That's okay," Regan said.

"Yes," Mrs. Tyndal said. "Forgetting has its benefits." She looked over at Jason. "You know, Jason, I read about your parents' deaths in the newspaper. I meant to send you a card each time, but I didn't know where you were living. Apparently, you've been back here in Ohio for a while."

"About five years."

"Home is a draw, isn't it?"

"To some extent, yes." Jason cleared his throat. "I was going to tell you how sorry I am about Logan, but I guess it wasn't a surprise to you that he was dead."

Mrs. Tyndal rubbed at a thick, arthritic knuckle. "I should tell you how sorry I am for you. The two of you were close, and I know you went through some difficult times when Logan . . . when everyone was wondering where he was. Believe me, I'm sorry about that."

"And I'm sorry too," Regan said. "For that."

"It's okay," Jason said. "I think I understand why things happened the way they did. At least from Regan's point of view."

"But now you want to know my side of things," Mrs. Tyndal said. "You want to know why a mother would find out that her son had been killed and not do anything about it? Is that right?"

"Yes," Jason said.

"It's no surprise that I've asked myself that question on more than one occasion over the years. More than one." She looked over at Regan. "But it's not really my decision to tell that story now. I can only tell it if it's okay with Regan. And since you're here together, I suspect it is."

"It is," Regan said. "I already told him most of it. We just need you to confirm it. And, if that's okay with you, confirm it with the police. They're going to need to know that I told you these things back then, right after Logan died. They're going to need someone to verify my story. Jason's brother-in-law, Derrick, is in some trouble. It would help to have someone to back up the story I have to tell."

Mrs. Tyndal nodded her head slowly. As Jason watched her, he could imagine that in her mind she was traveling back all those years to a moment just a few days after their high school graduation, a day when Regan came to her apartment in Ednaville and told her a story about her son—

"The police had already been to see me," Mrs. Tyndal said. "When Logan didn't come home after graduation, they came and asked questions. His father called as well. He was angry, of course. Suspicious. He assumed I had Logan at my apartment, hiding him out or something. I told them all the truth at that time—I had no idea where Logan was or where he had gone."

"That was the truth," Regan said. "Until I came to see you."

"When you knocked on my door, I knew you were going to tell me something about Logan. I wasn't sure I wanted to know. Either you were going to tell me what happened to him, which I probably didn't want to hear. Or you were going to tell me something he'd done. I thought that might even be worse."

"Did you expect her to tell you he was dead?" Jason asked.

"No." She lifted her hand and placed it against her chest. "I wasn't ready for that." She looked over at Regan. "You saw me that day. I was devastated."

"You were."

"I wanted to crawl in the floor and never come out. That was my child, my only child. And he was gone." She was still looking at Regan. Intently. "You're a mother. You know."

"I can't imagine," Regan said.

"But when Regan told me the how and the why of all of it, I

understood a lot more. At first, I didn't want to believe it. I didn't want to hear those stories about my son, and I wanted to accuse you of lying. But I couldn't hide from what I really knew. I realized how something like that could happen."

"Why did you agree to keep quiet about it?" Jason asked. "I guess that's the thing I don't really get. And I'm not sure Regan has helped me understand either. Your son was killed. He was doing something awful, something terrible, but that doesn't mean a mother would think he deserved to be killed. Does it?"

"Not deserved," Mrs. Tyndal said. "I certainly wouldn't say he *deserved* to be killed. But I could understand how it happened. Those young men were protecting Regan."

"Okay, but wouldn't you want the truth to come out about all of it? Wouldn't you want the world to know that Logan wasn't alive? That he hadn't just run off somewhere? People were going to think he was living the high life somewhere. . . . That's what I thought. I thought he'd turned his back on everything."

"You mean he turned his back on everyone?" Mrs. Tyndal asked.

Jason didn't answer right away. Regan turned her head a little and gave Jason an encouraging look.

"Yes, everyone," Jason said.

"I had to think about two things," Mrs. Tyndal said. "I had to think about this young woman's feelings. And she had made it very clear to me she really didn't want the whole story coming out. Regan, you had only come to my apartment that day because you said you couldn't imagine me not knowing the truth."

"I thought about my own mother," Regan said. "I'd want her to know. And you were always so nice to me growing up. Looking back, I realize I was taking a huge risk. I didn't know that you wouldn't want to go to the police and have the whole story come out, which was exactly what I didn't want to happen. I was so dumb back then. So naive and just . . ."

"You weren't dumb," Mrs. Tyndal said. "You were distraught. In shock."

"Yes," Regan said. "I thought you'd understand. You were the only adult I thought I could turn to."

"I understood that. The other thing I had to think about was my son. His memory. Would I want the world to think that my son was a monster? Someone who had attacked a young woman in such an awful way? That's all they'd remember. That's all his father would have to face over the years. I thought about it a lot when Regan was sitting in my apartment, and I decided it was better off for everyone involved if we just pretended Logan was gone. That he ran away. I would live with my private grief. I was okay with that. I'd carried things inside before. And carried them alone. Things about Logan."

"Things about Logan?" Jason asked. "What things?"

So much had fallen away over the past twenty-four hours that he didn't think it was possible for anything else to be revealed. But there he was on the brink of learning something else, and his stomach rose and fell with the anticipation, like someone who had just ridden a roller coaster to the top of a tall hill and was about to plunge down to an uncertain destination.

"You've been talking to that lawyer, haven't you?" Mrs. Tyndal asked.

"Colton?"

"Yes. Him."

"We all went to school together. He's trying to find Logan."

"His family, him and his father before him, have always been shills for my ex-husband. Whatever they do, the motivation is to make my ex-husband look good. And to line their own pockets, of course."

Her vitriol surprised Jason a little, although Colton had certainly irritated him on more than one occasion. "I think that's an accurate assessment of his character."

"And he probably told you something about me. Something about me and a staircase."

"He did."

"And he said that I shoved Logan down the stairs while I was drunk?"

Jason didn't want to answer. He really didn't need to. The answer to all of the questions was hanging in the air between them.

But Jason felt the anger rising inside his chest again, the rage at the injustice of his friend being an abused child.

"He told me that," Jason said. "Yes."

"But that's not really true," Mrs. Tyndal said.

"What's not true?" Jason asked.

"It was Logan," Mrs. Tyndal said. "Logan pushed *me* down the stairs that day."

Chapter Fifty-seven

Jason looked over at Regan. She stared straight ahead, her lips slightly parted.

"I don't understand," Regan said. She went from looking at Mrs. Tyndal to looking at Jason, her neck rotating to the left in an almost mechanical fashion. "Jason, you told me that *she* shoved Logan down the stairs."

"Colton told me that, and I told you. He said that's why she wasn't around Logan as much when we were growing up. Basically he implied that Mrs. Tyndal wasn't allowed to see Logan, that they were afraid she would harm him."

Regan turned back to the woman before them. "That's not true, is it?"

Mrs. Tyndal spoke without any real trace of emotion. She seemed resigned, accepting. "It's not true at all." She raised her hand quickly. "Well, let me say, I did drink too much back then. I admit that. I was a lonely housewife. I found different ways to get through my days. But I never harmed my child. Never. Not in that way. I harmed him in other ways, mostly by letting his father have such an influence over his life. I know that now. But I never laid a hand on him."

"What happened?" Jason asked, his voice low even to his

own ears, his eyes staring at the pristine carpet. When the woman started to speak, Jason forced himself to look up and meet her eye.

"The boy had a temper," Mrs. Tyndal said. "Temper tantrums, we called them back then. I guess today he'd be at a shrink and taking a lot of medication, but we didn't do those things back then. Especially not if your father was a prominent businessman who didn't want people to talk. But it could be bad with Logan. I was with him all the time. I had to discipline him. His father would come home and take his side. Indulge him. That made it tough to parent, as you can imagine."

"Sure," Regan said.

"I remember what it was," Mrs. Tyndal said. She pointed at Jason. "You boys, you used to play with these things. These giant monsters . . . they used to shoot things at each other. What were they?"

Jason knew. "Shogun Warriors."

"Yes, that's it. No computers back then. Not many video games."

"No."

"I guess one thing about video games, there wasn't a mess to clean up. Logan never cleaned up his messes. He left it there, and Pauline took care of it for him most of the time. I didn't want my boy to grow up like that, thinking that someone else would always clean up for him. I didn't come from money. I didn't understand it. I just wanted Logan to be"—her voice caught a little—"normal, like everyone else. Like the kids you were both turning out to be."

She hesitated a moment. Jason felt embarrassed for her. His own face flushed. They'd shown up unannounced and opened a quarter of a century of old wounds for her.

"Well, I told him to clean up his mess that day. Like I had

done many other days. This was after school, maybe just before dinnertime. His father was coming home, and I admit, I'd been drinking. I wasn't drunk, but that sounds like hairsplitting, doesn't it? That's when I knew I had a problem of my own, when I used to make that fine distinction over and over again. *I'm drinking, but I'm not drunk.* Not a way for a mother to be."

The television started playing loud in the other room. A sitcom from the sound of it. People laughed uproariously, an odd counterpoint to the conversation they were involved in.

"Are we disturbing your husband?" Regan asked.

"No," Mrs. Tyndal said. "He knows all of this. Or he knew it at one time. I'm afraid he and I are in the middle of a long good-bye."

"I'm sorry," Regan said.

"It's what we do as we get older." She adjusted herself in her chair, then said, "I told Logan to clean up that day, and he wouldn't do it. He just wouldn't. Like an idiot I tried the oldest trick in the mother's playbook. I told him to wait until his father got home. Even as I said it, I knew it wouldn't work. It sounded like an empty threat as it left my mouth. His father . . . he wasn't going to do anything. We all knew it. Most of all, Logan knew it." Her mouth drew into a tight line as though she were biting back on decades-old anger. "He laughed at me, Logan did. He just laughed at me, a cutting, mocking laugh." She shook her head. "I got angry. Angrier than I should have. I should have walked away, or sent him to his room. Something. I wish I'd done something different. But isn't that the story of so many things? We wish we'd done something different?"

"Amen," Regan said.

"I went for him," Mrs. Tyndal said. "I tried to grab his arm. I missed first, and then I got ahold of him. A good tight grip. I realized I was squeezing too tight, that I was going to leave a bruise, so I let go. And when I did . . . we were right at the top of those stairs in the center of the house. You remember them?"

Jason nodded. "I do."

"Logan put both of his hands on me, right around my waist. He was a strong kid, always was. Feisty. And the alcohol made me a little unsteady on my feet. That contributed to the whole thing. But he pushed, and down I went. I fell backwards, and my feet swung up in the air above my head. I went down those stairs like someone doing a couple of reverse somersaults. Until I hit the wall at the bottom."

A rushing sound filled Jason's ears. He tried to pinpoint the source by cocking his head and listening to see if it was an airplane passing above the house. But it wasn't. The sound came from inside of him, and it was coupled with the sense that he was being overwhelmed.

"I'm sorry," Regan said. She seemed on the brink of letting her emotions spill out. "Were you hurt?"

"In the end, I had a concussion," she said. "Self-diagnosed."

"What did you do?" Jason asked, the noise in his ears still there but lessening.

Mrs. Tyndal hesitated, a smile on her face that was more sad than anything else. "I called the police. I didn't know what else to do. I was dizzy and a little shaky. So I called the police. Then I called Peter. Mr. Shaw. When he found out I'd called the police, he flipped."

"What was Logan's reaction after you went down the stairs?" Regan asked.

Mrs. Tyndal's eyes grew distant behind the big glasses. The television continued to play from the other room, an announcer's voice asking the viewers if they wanted to save money on their car insurance. "When I figured out what had happened, when I first gathered my bearings and looked back up to the top of the stairs, Logan was up there on the top step looking down at me. He had a look on his face that I didn't understand. There was some fear there. I could see that. But it was . . . How do I want to say this? A happy fear?"

"Gleeful," Regan said.

"Yes. I guess so."

"Like he was afraid of what he had done, but at the same time, he'd enjoyed doing it."

"Yes, I think you're right." Mrs. Tyndal scooted forward in her chair and held her hand out toward Regan like she wanted to pat her on the leg and offer comfort. But it was too far for her to reach. "I forgot that you've seen that very same look."

"What happened with the police?" Jason asked.

"Peter Shaw couldn't have the police coming to his house," Mrs. Tyndal said. "And he certainly couldn't have the police coming to his house because of something that his ten-year-old son had done, something that if everyone found out . . . well, you can imagine the way people would talk. We couldn't have that. Not in Ednaville. Not about his son. Peter arrived at just about the same time as the police. And the police had to be told something. It was a different time, over thirty years ago. A man with Peter's influence could make the police go away, and he did. I know he told them some story out of my earshot, something about me."

"He said you were drunk," Jason said.

Mrs. Tyndal nodded. "I have a feeling he showed them the bruise on the boy's arm. It all added up."

"And after that, you got divorced?" Regan asked.

"We were going to get divorced anyway. That was coming.

The only question was how much time I was going to be allowed
to spend with my son. Peter was determined to see that I only
spent a limited amount of time with him. I wanted to see Logan
get into therapy and find some help. He clearly had some problems. Anger management. Narcissism. I've read the books over
the years. I know some of the terms. But Peter didn't want any
of that. He said Logan would be better if I was out of the picture.
He said *I* was the bad influence. Me and my drinking."

"He needed the discipline," Regan said.

"He needed something." Mrs. Tyndal held her hands in the
air, turning them palms up. "It wasn't going to be me giving it
to him on a daily basis. I was shaken after that incident with the
stairs. Not scared, really, but shaken. To my core. I didn't know
how responsible I was for what happened that day, but I knew
some of it belonged to me. I stopped drinking after that, after I
moved out. *I* went to therapy. I got better." She shifted in the
seat again. "But Logan didn't. I saw him as much as I could. I
loved him. But I could tell he wasn't getting the help he needed.
He was becoming more and more . . . I don't know. . . ."

"Reckless?" Jason said.

"That," Mrs. Tyndal said. "Reckless and self-centered. A
dangerous combination." She focused her look on Regan. "When
you came to me and told me what happened on that graduation
night, it was a confirmation of everything that I feared about
Logan. I didn't think he was going to have a good end."

"And you respected my wish not to tell anyone," Regan said.
"To not get those boys into trouble for what they'd done."

"It wouldn't have mattered, would it? It wasn't going to bring
Logan back. And those boys were protecting you." She swallowed
and licked her lips. "I grieved for him, my boy. For many years, I
grieved. Alone, mostly."

"I don't understand something," Jason said.

They both turned to look at him. He moved his body so he was sitting up straighter. "I don't have children, so maybe I don't understand. But I'm wondering how a mother could let the men who killed her son go. How were you okay knowing that nothing was going to be done to those two?"

Mrs. Tyndal stared at Jason as she formulated her answer. He'd never seen it before, but the resemblance to Logan was there. The brightness of the eyes, the toughness, the intelligence. Logan inherited it from his mother and not his father.

"It was my fault," she said. "None of this would have happened if I had fought harder for Logan's well-being when he shoved me down those stairs. I enabled him as much as his father, so I felt I bore a share of the responsibility for what happened to Regan that night. I wasn't in a position to ask for anything else."

Chapter Fifty-eight

"Are you willing to tell all of this to the police?" Jason asked. "You're the only person who can corroborate Regan's and Derrick's stories about our graduation night."

Mrs. Tyndal didn't hesitate. She turned to Regan. "I'm willing to do it if it's okay with you."

"It's okay with me," Regan said. "That's why we came here."

"That's what I was wondering," Mrs. Tyndal said. "What does it matter if everyone knows the story now? After all, you're asking me to tell the world that my son was a . . . that he sexually assaulted a woman."

"I just don't think those guys, especially Derrick, should have the world think they did things they didn't do," Jason said. "It doesn't seem right for their families. For their children. It all started because they were protecting you."

"No, it doesn't seem right," Regan said. "We've all been keeping these things to ourselves for decades. Maybe it's time we just got it all out."

Mrs. Tyndal's husband came back to the doorway, still holding the newspaper. He didn't say anything, but he stood there staring at Mrs. Tyndal.

"Are you hungry, Andrew?" she asked.

"Yes," he said.

"I'll be out there in a minute. Why don't you sit at the table?"

He turned and left, the newspaper rattling as he walked away.

"I'm sorry," Mrs. Tyndal said, turning back. "I have to feed him. He does better with a routine."

"We're sorry," Regan said. "We've taken too much of your time."

"It's okay. It's just that duty calls here." She scooted forward in her chair and with a little bit of effort pushed herself to her feet. She wobbled once she was standing, and both Jason and Regan reached out to steady her. But she waved them away. "I've got it," she said. "It's just old age." She tugged her shirt back into place, smoothing the material. "Have you seen my ex-husband lately?"

"I saw him," Jason said.

"I hear it's bad," she said.

"It is."

"He has enough money to have round-the-clock care," she said, a trace of bitterness creeping into her voice. "Andrew and I are pretty much on our own. He has children, but they don't live around here." She reached out and patted Regan on the arm. "It's good that the two of you have each other."

Regan took a half a step back. A flush rose on her cheeks, and she said, "No—" but then cut her words off. She just smiled instead, a look that seemed forced.

"I'm married," Jason said. "To someone else."

"Oh." Mrs. Tyndal raised her hand to her hair. "I just thought . . ."

"No, not us," Regan said.

"Well," Mrs. Tyndal said. "I know you two were always good friends." Something clattered in the kitchen, the sound of a dish hitting the floor. Mrs. Tyndal didn't flinch. "I think I need to excuse myself."

"Thank you," Regan said. "For then. And for now."

The two women hugged and held each other a long time before Jason and Regan stepped outside and walked back to the car.

They drove back to Ednaville, mostly in silence. Jason didn't know what else to say, so he talked about the case, the thing that had come to dominate their lives.

"If she tells the police, then that will help Derrick's situation some and explain the circumstances of Logan's death. At least they won't think Derrick killed Logan. He covered up but didn't kill him. He still could find himself in a mess of trouble."

"Yes."

"The police will know what Logan did, but I don't know if it will all become public. Maybe his dad will never know. Or understand."

"I guess not. Maybe the whole thing will be a closed case."

"Of course, Hayden . . ."

"It's been a lot of years, Jason. Maybe they'll cut her a break. I don't know."

"I guess Mr. Shaw had his hopes raised," Jason said. "He might have had them raised no matter what—he's been in such denial. Besides, you know what I say about Hayden."

"What?"

"She always lands on her feet."

His comment felt hollow. He thought about that cabin in the woods and Hayden's escape. She never would have made it out of there if it wasn't for someone helping her. Derrick was there to save her. She had Sierra to live for. Hayden needed those things. *We all need them,* he thought, as they pulled up to Regan's house.

A car sat at the end of the driveway, a red Prius. The blinds were open along the front of the house.

"Company?" Jason asked.

"That's Tim's car."

"Is he dropping off the kids?"

"Yes," she said after a pause.

"There's something else?"

Regan turned away from the house and back to Jason. Her hands were folded in her lap.

"He and I . . . we've been talking about trying again. For the kids. For stability."

"Oh. That's great. Isn't it? Are you happy about it?"

"I am. I know you've been through something somewhat similar. Tim and I have known each other a long time. Since just after college. And the kids . . . they need two parents."

"Does Tim know about . . . about Logan and all of that?"

"No," she said quickly. "Sometimes it's nice to be with someone who doesn't know absolutely everything about me."

The front door opened and her children stepped out. They didn't cross the lawn, but they waved at the car, and Regan waved back.

"Okay," Jason said. "Well. I don't know what else to say, then. Except I guess I'll be seeing you around town."

"Yeah, I guess so." She smiled. "We can still get coffee from time to time. It's not like we won't have things to talk about."

"Do you ever wonder . . . do you ever wonder what would have happened if we had dated back then? If we'd actually tried to be a couple?"

Regan considered this for a moment. Really considered it. "I remember all those days we walked home from school together. Something could have happened then, couldn't it?" Then she said, "It's so hard to comprehend really. Despite everything, I'm not sure I'd change the way things went. My children, my job." She laughed a little. "We might have ended up hating each other. You know how that goes when friends try to date."

"Right. My life has turned out pretty well, too. All things considered. I need to remember that."

"Sure." She opened the door, but before she went to rejoin her family, she leaned back into the car. "Thanks for everything, Jason."

"I'm not sure I did anything. Not really."

"You're my friend," she said. "And I'm sorry if I was so hard on you about Logan, saying all the time that you idolized him too much. It's not a bad thing to hold on to memories of people from the past, people we care about. It can really help sometimes."

She closed the door and went to her family.

Jason drove through the streets he'd driven through so many times. The town looked cleaner somehow in the bright, early summer sun. Freshly scrubbed. He saw the old, familiar place with new eyes. It felt more like home than at any time since they'd moved back. Maybe because he knew more, maybe because he saw it for what it really was. Not a nostalgic time capsule and not the solution to all his problems. It was just a town he knew well, and he wanted to stay there with Nora.

And, he thought, Hayden and Sierra were in that life as well.

He pulled into his driveway and sat, staring at the house. The door swung open. Sierra emerged onto the porch with Hayden behind her. Jason felt his heart lift just seeing them. He smiled through the windshield.

As he came up the walk, Sierra reached out for him, hugging him. He held his niece tight.

"Where's Nora?" he asked, letting Sierra go.

With that, Nora stepped out onto the porch, and the two of them hugged.

"Well, well," she said. "Look who's here. Did you get everything taken care of?"

"I did," he said. "At last. And it's really good to be home."

Acknowledgments

Thanks to the Office of Sponsored Programs at Western Kentucky University for a grant that helped with the writing of this novel. Thanks also to my friends and colleagues in the English Department at WKU, especially Rob Hale, Tom Hunley, David LeNoir, Mary Ellen Miller, and Dale Rigby.

Thanks to all my friends and family. Special thanks to Kristie Lowry for both her help and her humor.

Thanks to everyone at NAL for your support. And a big thanks to Loren Jaggers and Heather Connor for getting the word out.

My editor, Danielle Perez, is amazing. Thanks for your patience, wisdom, and wit.

My agent, Laney Katz Becker, is a dynamo. Thanks for your tireless work, high expectations, and vast knowledge. And thanks to everyone at Lippincott Massie McQuilkin Literary Agents.

Thanks to the readers, bloggers, booksellers, and librarians who keep books and stories alive.

And thanks, as always, to Molly McCaffrey for everything else.

THE FORGOTTEN GIRL

David Bell

QUESTIONS
FOR DISCUSSION

1. Jason and Hayden have a strained relationship, primarily due to Hayden's struggles with addiction. Do you understand Jason's reluctance to let Hayden back into his life? Would you let her back in?

2. Jason seems to realize that it was difficult for Hayden to grow up in his shadow. Do you think it's challenging for younger siblings to establish their own identities as they grow up? Also, is there more pressure on an older sibling to set the tone in a family?

3. Sierra seems to be a bright, successful teenager despite the difficulties her parents have been through. Are you surprised by the bond between Sierra and her parents?

4. Jason and Regan were close friends—and almost dated—in high school and have recently reconnected. Do you understand the friendship they share even after all those years of not being

in touch? Do you think Nora should be concerned about the time Jason spends with Regan? How would you feel if your spouse were Jason?

5. Jason and Nora made the choice not to have children, but when Sierra enters their lives, they find themselves reexamining that decision. Do you think Jason and Nora regret not having children? Can having their niece in their lives serve as some kind of a replacement?

6. Jason seems to be having something of a midlife crisis due to losing his job in New York and moving back to his hometown in Ohio. Is it unusual for someone at Jason's stage of life to be reevaluating this way? Do you think he's happy with the choices he's made?

7. Regan tells Jason that he "hero-worshipped" Logan and didn't see him clearly. What kind of person do you think Logan was? Is Regan correct when she says that Jason didn't see him clearly? What do you think is the cause of some of Logan's behavior?

8. Were you surprised to find out what really happened on graduation night? Are you surprised that Regan was willing to keep it a secret for so many years?

9. Logan's mother knew the truth about her son—both the act of violence he committed against her as well as what he did on

graduation night. Was she right to keep those things secret for so many years? Do you think she could have—or should have—done something to help her son, or were the cards too stacked against her because of the influence and power of Logan's father?

10. Mr. Shaw seems like something of a distant and distracted father. Do you blame him for Logan's behavior? Do you think he really loved his son?

11. Jesse Dean was responsible for Logan's death on graduation night, and then Derrick was responsible for Jesse Dean's death in the cabin. Do you blame these men for the acts of violence they committed? Were there extenuating circumstances in one or both of the cases? How do you view the men differently? Would you want to see them prosecuted for the things they did?

12. When Jason returns home at the end of the book, he seems genuinely happy to see his family, including Hayden and Sierra. Do you think he has a new appreciation for his life, one he didn't have when the book started? Do you think he and Nora have found a way to be happy in Ohio?

13. Sierra turns out very different from her parents. And despite being siblings, Jason and Hayden take divergent paths in life. Do you attribute these differences to nature over nurture? Do you know people who turned out significantly different from other people in the same household?

Chapter One

When I saw the girl in the grocery store, my heart stopped.

I turned the corner into the dairy aisle, carrying my basket with just a few purchases inside. Cereal. Crackers. Spaghetti. Beer. I lived alone and rarely cooked. I almost ran into the girl. I stopped and saw her in profile, her hand raised to her mouth while she studied products through the glass door of the dairy cooler.

I felt like I was seeing a ghost.

She looked just like my college girlfriend, Marissa Minor, the only woman I ever really loved. Probably the only woman who ever really loved me.

The girl didn't see me right away. She continued to study the items in the dairy cooler, slowly walking away from me, her hand still raised to her mouth as though that helped her think.

That was the gesture that really got me. It made my insides go cold. Not with fear, but with shock. With feelings I hadn't experienced in years.

Marissa used to do that very same thing. When she thought, she'd place her right hand on her lips, sometimes pinching them between her index finger and thumb. Marissa's lips were always bright red—without lipstick—and full, and the gesture, that lip-twisting, thoughtful gesture, drove me wild with love and, yes, desire.

419

I was eighteen when I met Marissa. Desire was always close at hand.

But it wasn't just the gesture this girl shared with Marissa. Her hair, thick and deep orange, matched Marissa's exactly, down to the length, which fell just below her shoulders. From the side, the girl's nose came to a slightly rounded point, one that Marissa said looked like a lightbulb. Both the girl and Marissa had long, slender bodies. This girl, the one in the store, looked shorter than Marissa by a few inches, and she wore tight jeans and knee-high boots, clothes that weren't in style when I attended college.

But other than that, they were twins. They really were.

And as the girl walked away, turning the corner at the end of the aisle and leaving my sight, I remained rooted to my spot, my silly little grocery basket dangling from my right hand. The lights above were bright, painfully so, and other shoppers came past with their carts and their kids and their lives. It was close to dinnertime, and people had places to go. Families to feed.

I stood there.

I felt tears rising in my eyes, my vision starting to blur.

She looked so much like Marissa. So much.

And Marissa had been dead for just over twenty years.

I snapped out of it.

I reached up with my free hand and wiped away the tears.

No one seemed to notice that I was having an emotional moment in the middle of the grocery store, in the dairy aisle. To anyone passing by, I looked like a normal guy. Forty years old. Clean-cut. Professional. I had my problems. I was divorced. My ex-wife didn't let me see her son from a previous relationship as much as I wanted.

He wasn't my kid, but we'd grown close. My job didn't pay enough, but who ever felt like they were paid enough?

Like I said, I looked like a regular guy.

I needed to talk to that girl. I started down the aisle, my basket swinging at my side. I figured she had to be a relative of Marissa's, right? A cousin or something. I turned the corner in the direction she had gone, dodging between my fellow shoppers.

I looked up the next aisle and didn't see her. Then I went to the next one, the last aisle in the store. At first, I didn't see her there either. It was crowded, and a family of four—two parents, two kids—blocked my view. One of the kids screamed because her mom wouldn't buy her the ice cream she wanted.

But then they moved, and I saw the girl. She was halfway up, opening another one of the cooler doors, but not removing anything. She lifted her hand to her mouth again. That gesture. She looked just like Marissa.

I felt the tears again and fought back against them.

I walked up to her. She looked so small. And young. I guessed she was about twenty, probably a student at my alma mater, Eastland University. I felt ridiculous, but I had to ask. I wiped at my eyes again and cleared my throat.

"Excuse me," I said.

She whipped her head around in my direction. She seemed startled that anyone spoke to her.

"I'm sorry," I said.

But I really wasn't. I finally saw her head-on, and the illusion that she looked like Marissa wasn't shattered. Her forehead was a little wider than Marissa's. And her chin came to a sharper point. But the spray of freckles, the color and shape of her eyes . . . all of it.

If I believed in ghosts . . .

Ghosts from a happier time in my past . . .

"I'm sorry," I said again.

The girl just looked at me. Her eyes moved across my body, sizing me up. Taking me in. She looked guarded.

"What is it?" she asked.

"I was wondering if you were related to the Minor family," I said. "They lived in Hanford, Ohio. It's been about twenty years since I've seen them. I know it's a long shot—"

The girl had been carrying a box of cereal and a carton of organic milk. When I said the name "Minor," she let the milk and the cereal go, and they both fell to the floor at my feet. The milk was in a cardboard carton, but the force of it hitting the ground caused a split. Milk started leaking out onto the dirty floor, flowing toward my shoes.

"Careful," I said.

But the girl took off. She made an abrupt turn on her heel and started walking away briskly, her boots clacking against the linoleum. She didn't look back. When she reached the far end of the aisle, the end that was closest to the cash registers, she started running.

I took one step in that direction, lifting my hand. I wanted to say something. Apologize. Call her back. Let her know that I hadn't meant any harm.

But she was gone. Just like Marissa, she was gone.

The family of four, the one with the child screaming for ice cream, came abreast of me. Their child appeared to have calmed down. She clutched a carton of Rocky Road, the tears on her face drying. The father pointed to the mess on the floor, the leaking milk and the cereal.

"Something wrong with her?" he asked.

My hands were shaking. I felt off-balance. Above my head, the cloying Muzak continued to play, indifferent to my little drama with the girl who looked so much like Marissa.

"I have no idea," I said. "I don't even know who she was."

Chapter Two

I thought about Marissa a lot that evening.

It's safe to say I was feeling sorry for myself. Indulging in nostalgia and self-pity at the same time.

I drank beer on the couch in my apartment while a basketball game I didn't care about played on the TV. A pile of work waited in my briefcase, but I ignored it. I ate some cheese and crackers but gave up on my plan to cook the spaghetti I had bought at the store. My only company was Riley, my aged mutt, whom I had rescued from the local Humane Society shortly after my divorce. By the Humane Society's estimates, Riley was at least twelve, maybe older. He didn't like to do much. As I sat on the couch brooding, he sat at my feet, hoping for cracker crumbs.

Marissa and I had met during our freshman year at Eastland. We fell in love right away. She got me like no one ever had. And no one has since. I didn't even have to say anything to her, and she understood me. How many people meet someone like that in their lives? I did. And then it was all taken away in a house fire when we were juniors in college.

That was why seeing the girl in the grocery store shook me to the core. I'd managed to go on with my life. I'd managed to tell myself I'd gotten over Marissa and her loss.

But I hadn't.

That was why I sat on my couch drinking beer that night. I never drank very much, never more than one in a day, if that. But when I came home from the grocery store, I threw back three and then four and opened a fifth, wondering who that girl was. And why she had acted so spooked when I spoke to her.

I fell asleep on the couch, the TV still playing, the open but unfinished fifth beer on the coffee table before me. My neck felt like hell from sleeping at an odd angle, and a trail of drool ran down my chin.

Something pounded against my apartment door.

Someone was there, beating on the door. Each heavy knock caused a miniature earthquake in my skull. I winced. A hangover at my age. Pathetic. I vowed to never have more than one beer again. I vowed to stop thinking about Marissa.

I'd do anything if the person outside my apartment would stop hammering on the door. But they didn't.

I looked at the clock. Six fifty-three a.m.

I normally woke up around eight. Made it to the office by nine. I felt like shit. I needed a shower. Coffee. Food. I stood up, feeling a little wobbly. I looked down at Riley. He hadn't barked despite the pounding on the door. He never barked.

"Nothing?" I said to him. "Not even a growl?"

His tail thumped against the floor. He yawned.

"One of these days, I'm really going to need your help," I said. "I hope you're ready."

Riley walked off toward the kitchen, which meant he was hungry.

I still wore the pants and collared shirt from the previous

day's work at the Housing Authority. My tie and my shoes were off, and I needed to pee. But whoever was outside the door really wanted to talk to me. They pounded again, shaking my brain.

"Stop," I said. "Jesus."

I thought about calling the apartment complex's security guard and asking him to come by to see who was making the racket. It wasn't the knock of a friend or someone selling something. But my desire to make them stop overwhelmed any fears I had about who was out there. I stumbled to the door and looked through the peephole.

It took a moment for the scene outside to make sense to me, but when it did, my heart started racing.

I understood why the knock was so heavy.

Through the peephole I saw two uniformed police officers and a detective I already knew.

"Mr. Hansen?" the detective said. "Nick Hansen? We know you're in there. Open up."

"Shit," I said.

A rough morning just became rougher.

The morning sun nearly killed me.

It poured in when I opened the door, its rays penetrating my eyeballs like knitting needles. I took a step back, feeling like a man under siege.

"Can we come in?" the detective said.

I didn't have to answer. He was already stepping across the threshold with the two uniformed officers right behind him.

"You can do anything if it means you'll stop knocking," I said.

Detective Reece stood about five nine, a few inches shorter

than me, but he was powerfully and compactly built. I suspected he had wrestled in high school. Or maybe played nose tackle at a small college. He looked like that kind of guy. He didn't offer to shake my hand, but I'd shaken it before, the last time he and I had encountered each other. He had nearly crushed my fingers.

Reece saw the beer cans on the coffee table, and his eyebrows went up. He was probably a few years younger than me, and his hair was thinning. He wore it cropped close to his head, and his suit coat looked too small for him.

"It's recycling day," I said.

"Think green, right?"

"Exactly," I said.

He pointed at Riley. "Does the dog bite?"

"Only his food," I said, trying to sound light.

But Reece wasn't smiling. He looked around the room, taking it all in. The TV still played with the sound down. It showed highlights of a hockey game. There were dirty dishes in the sink, discarded gym clothes on the floor. I needed to pick up, and I would have, if only I'd known the police were going to drop by.

"Have you seen your ex-wife lately?" Reece asked.

"Not in six weeks," I said. "Not since . . . that night we met."

"The night of the late unpleasantness," Reece said.

"I wasn't stalking her."

"She said you were."

"I was trying to see Andrew," I said. "I told you that then."

"Her son from a previous relationship," Reece said. He stopped looking around and turned to face me. The two uniformed officers stayed near the front door. They acted like they didn't hear anything we said. "Not your son."

"Gina and I were married five years. I got to know Andrew

well. We became close, and I just want to see him from time to time. It's not unusual. I just wanted to see the kid."

"But she didn't want you there, and you showed up anyway."

"Is that what this is about?" I asked. "Did Gina decide to press charges? That was six weeks ago. I thought it was over."

Reece gestured toward my cluttered dining room table. "Why don't we sit down and talk, Mr. Hansen?" He waited for me to move. "Please?"

He acted like it was his apartment, and I was the guest. He'd reversed everything and taken over my turf. I couldn't say anything to stop him, so I sat down. Reece took the seat across from me, and he reached out with his hand and brushed some old crumbs off the table and onto the floor. Then he took out his phone and started scrolling through it. I waited. For all I knew, he was checking his Twitter feed or looking up movie times.

"Can I ask—"

"Where were you last night, Mr. Hansen?" Reece asked.

I looked over at the beer cans on the coffee table, the deep indentation in the couch where I'd slept without a pillow or a blanket.

"I was here," I said.

"All night?"

"All night."

"Were you alone?"

"Yes. I usually am these days. Riley was here."

"What time did you get home from work?" Reece asked.

"About six fifteen."

Reece nodded. He looked down at his phone, tapped it a few times, and then looked back up at me. "I'm going to show you a photograph of someone. I want you to tell me if you know this person, and if you do know them, I want you to tell me where you know them from."

"Okay."

He turned the phone around so that I could see the photo. I should have guessed who it was going to be before he even handed it to me.

It was a photo of the girl from the grocery store.

Chapter Three

It looked like a driver's license photo. Not many people look good in those, but the girl from the store did. Her hair was piled on top of her head, and she wore a friendly smile, a far cry from the look of fear she flashed at me when I had spoken to her the previous evening.

"Do you know her?" Reece asked.

I cleared my throat. A little of the emotion from the grocery store welled up in me again.

"I think I know what this is about," I said.

"You do?"

"Yes," I said. "After what happened with Gina, and then the way this girl acted in the grocery store when I spoke to her, you're over here thinking I'm some kind of serious creep. Someone who is stalking strangers now and not just my ex-wife."

"What happened in the grocery store?" Reece asked.

"If you just let me apologize to her, I will," I said. "I'll call her or write a note—"

"The grocery store. What happened?"

I took a deep breath. I told him I saw the girl in the store and she reminded me very much of someone I once knew. When I told Detective Reece that she reminded me of my college girlfriend, his eyebrows rose again, even higher than when he'd seen the beer cans. I said I had just wanted to talk to the girl, to ask if she might be related to Marissa's family, but when I had approached her she took off, dropping her groceries on the floor at my feet.

Reece took this all in, and when I was finished, he asked, "Did she say anything to you?"

"She said, 'What is it?'"

"That's it?"

"That's it. She acted like I was Attila the Hun. She ran off. Maybe she's had a bad experience with a man before and is skittish out in public. I don't know."

"Who did you think this girl was related to? Your ex-girlfriend?"

"My girlfriend from college. I guess technically she was my ex-girlfriend. She broke up with me right before . . ." I couldn't bring myself to say it. I held the image of the girl in my mind, and I could see Marissa's face there as well, the two of them as vivid as anything. A piercing stab of nostalgia traversed my chest, hitting every major organ and even some minor ones. I felt like I couldn't breathe.

"Before what?" Reece asked.

"Before she died," I said. "She died in a house fire one night when we were twenty. Right here near Eastland's campus. She and her three roommates were killed. But right before the fire, a couple of days before, I guess, she broke up with me."

"She broke your heart," Reece said. It wasn't a question. He must have read something on my face or in my voice. I knew I couldn't hide my feelings for Marissa, then or any other time.

"She did," I said. "Completely."

"And what was her family's name?" Reece asked. "The ex-girlfriend, or girlfriend. Whoever she was. What was her family's name, and where did they live?"

"Her name was Marissa Minor. Her family lived in Hanford, Ohio. It's about an hour from here."

"I know it." Reece wrote something down in a little notebook he had pulled from his jacket pocket. His fingers were stubby, the nails bitten. "And you thought maybe this girl in the grocery store was related to your ex-girlfriend, and so you wanted to talk to her. Instead, you spooked her."

"It all sounds far-fetched and ridiculous, I know. At least, you're making it sound that way."

"I'm not making it sound any way. It sounds the way it sounds."

"Look, Detective, I have to get to work. I had a shitty, embarrassing night last night. And I'm sorry if I bothered that girl in the store. If you just give me her name or something, I'll apologize. I know you've checked my record. You did six weeks ago. And you know I've never been arrested and never hurt anybody. I'd just like to make this go away, if I can."

"And you think an apology will make it go away?" Reece asked.

"It seems like the gentlemanly thing to do," I said. "I apologized to Gina when she called you."

Reece put away his notebook. He looked around the apartment again, his eyes passing over the clutter, the beer cans, even the impassive officers who still stood by the door. One of their radios crackled, but the officer ignored it. He pressed a button, silencing the sound.

"You can't apologize to this girl," Reece said. "This girl from the grocery store."

"What do you want me to do, then?" I asked. "You can't

charge me with anything. It's not a crime to talk to someone in a store."

"You can't apologize to her because she's dead. She was found dead in a motel out on Highway Six sometime last night."

I studied Reece's face after he had delivered those words. I looked for some sign that he was joking, that he was trying to scare me by saying something so patently ridiculous and absurd. But he wasn't joking. The news hit me like a blast of cold air. My body tensed, locked up. I felt a pain at the base of my skull and realized I was clenching my teeth as tight as I could.

That girl, that beautiful young girl, couldn't just be gone, the sudden extinguishing of a light.

"What happened to her?" I asked. The question sounded dumb to my own ears, insufficient to the gravity of the situation. But there was nothing else I wanted to know. *What happened?*

Reece continued to study me, as though I were a specimen in his lab. He reached up and rubbed his chin, his thumb and forefinger easing over the freshly shaved skin. He seemed to have decided something.

"She was murdered," he said. "Most likely strangled, although we'll wait to hear from the medical examiner's office for the official word."

Then I felt cold inside, as though the bitter wind that had first buffeted me had been internalized. I shivered, my torso shaking involuntarily.

"Murdered?" I said, sounding dumb again.

Reece nodded. "Are you sure you don't know this girl? I mean, outside of chatting her up in the grocery store."

"I don't know her," I said. "I never saw her before yesterday. Never." But then some things started to come together in my mind. I was telling the truth—I had never seen the girl before.

And when I had spoken to her, I hadn't said my name or identified myself in any way. So if I didn't know who she was, how had the police ended up at my apartment—

"You didn't know her," Reece said. "But she seemed to know you."

"What do you mean?" I asked. "Why are you here?"

"This young woman you talked to in the grocery store, we examined her body when we found her. In her pocket she had a slip of paper with your name and address written on it."

Photo by Victoria Taylor

David Bell is a bestselling and award-winning author whose work has been translated into six languages. He's currently an associate professor of English at Western Kentucky University in Bowling Green, Kentucky. He received an MA in creative writing from Miami University in Oxford, Ohio, and a PhD in American literature and creative writing from the University of Cincinnati. His previous novels are *Cemetery Girl*, *The Hiding Place*, and *Never Come Back*.

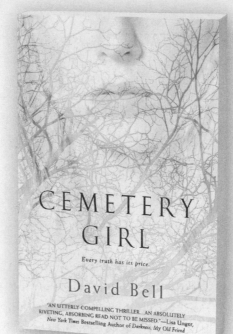